SHIRAZ MUKHERJEE

TIGER IN YOU

NIYOGI BOOKS

Published by

NIYOGI BOOKS

D-78, Okhla Industrial Area, Phase-I
New Delhi-110 020, INDIA
Tel: 91-11-26816301, 49327000
Fax: 91-11-26810483, 26813830
email: niyogibooks@gmail.com
website: www.niyogibooksindia.com

Editor: Jayalakshmi Sengupta
Cover Design: Misha Oberoi

ISBN: 978-93-85285-12-7
Year of Publication: 2017

Printed at: Niyogi Offset Pvt. Ltd., New Delhi, India

Dedicated to the tiger within us

Our noblest hopes grow teeth and pursue us like tigers

John Gardner

1 The Five Friends

A perfect picture—five friends with animated faces, all suspended in mid-air—some stretched, some with their legs stuck to their bellies with hands reaching for the sky—and the image of a roaring Royal Bengal tiger in the background.

Mrs Mukherjee, standing in the middle of the auditorium, had saved this image in her mind. This single image could have been the pictorial epithet for the youth of this generation. It had it all—a mood of celebration, an underlining festivity intrinsic to the salad days, coloured with the carefree disdain of youth.

Rahul, the fittest of them all with clenched fists and an excited face, was soaring over the rest, hanging in the air.

Rahul was a champion. The best in everything. There was tremendous self-pride and a look of achievement on his countenance. A fearless belief in being able to get away breaking the rules, and a sort of revelry radiated in everything that Rahul did. He not only had the passion but also the alacrity to turn every rudimentary routine action into a supreme physical exploit.

Simply pressing the buttons on the remote control to turn on the television, for instance, was a lacklustre affair for Rahul. Instead, an epic leap over the sofa, then a cartwheel, followed by a one-eighty-degree split on the ground, culminating with his fingers stabbing on the remote felt like a satisfying creative feat. With the channel of his choice coming alive, he would then do a backward flip to restore him back into the sofa where he would then rest contented. Life had to be made innovative.

Imran on the other hand was podgy. The slightest activity involving the body was a struggle for him; even turning over in his sleep was a tedious job. He was in the middle of the group, holding a colour-palette, with evident pain on his face as he laboured to take his feet off the ground.

They say painting and drawing come naturally to artists. Requesting live models to be painted came even more naturally to Imran. Imran is known to have requested, virtually unknown people he encountered on the streets, for five minutes of their time, *to do something interesting*. Innocent pedestrians sometimes acquiesced. But what Imran promised to be interesting turned out to be dreary, more often, than not—like being made to sit at the bus stop, looking at the buses hurtle past, or even absurd, for that matter—when asked to repeat an act like popping a panipuri into the mouth while in mid-air, for it to be captured on canvas. Imran was in love with realism and would admonish the models if they even dared to defy.

Keya was the romantic one. She held a gas balloon in one hand and a piccolo in the other hand, only appearing to be playing it, while struggling to stay close to Rahul. She had weaved her way through the throng of students to participate in the epic soar only after she spotted Rahul amidst them.

That was her pastime. Keya always wanted to hang out with Rahul. There had been other boys she was interested in during her first year of college, but all of them had gradually disappeared from her radar. Only Rahul had loomed large for the past couple of years.

Jassi, the Sikh boy, could not have been really interested in the jump, but had nevertheless participated to express his solidarity with the group.

Jassi had the talent of creating rhythm out of anything. A miniature congo hung around his neck, like a signature. Plates, saucepans, garbage bins, and even heads of friends doubled up as things that could be struck innovatively, to create musical beats of varying notes that reverberated in the classrooms and corridors, in-between lectures, and sometimes even during them.

For Hazel everything in life was dead serious. So what if it was a casual leap? Her feminine figure, sandwiched between Keya and Jassi, was poised in the rigid attention-position, as if she was inspecting a guard of honour. This collective leap had thus been sanctified.

Hazel had learnt playing the piano, sitting on her father's lap, an organ player in the church, from the time she was barely three years old. She was now the keyboardist in the group. She was an English girl who had come to study music in India on a student exchange program. She had a diploma in music from the Trinity College of Music, London, which was quite an impressive qualification to have.

Playing the keyboards had its limitations. It was not like Jassi who could roll his drumsticks (and sometimes even himself) in the air during an interlude, or like Rahul, who literally played with the guitar, at times—performing various gymnastics with his fingers, such as plucking, strumming, hitting or bending the strings, as he wished, with sporadic epileptic fits of madness striking him when he took on the guitar, solo. He could get the crowd on their feet, and the applause could get deafening. Rahul had thus acquired colossal popularity among the students—amongst both who loved his music and who could not care less—all unanimously appreciated his acrobatics on stage during a performance. None of those funny innovative creative tricks could be performed with a keyboard, unfortunately.

Haze, what her friends in England called her, had brooded over this misfortune ever since adolescence, but then, one day, she discovered her own gymnastic talent.

Once during a concert, a song request in the form of a paper plane had floated in beautifully, over the heads of the roaring crowd and landed in front of her keyboard. Keeping the keyboard on a preset track, Hazel had walked ahead to pick up the paper missile—a simple act that changed her life.

The chit of paper had flown past under the "whoosh" of the fans placed in the wings. She had had to sprint across the stage to grab the chit that got stuck below the stands of Jassi's drum pedals, only to unwrap and then get entangled again. By the time she had managed to extricate the paper it was torn in places. She could barely read the words of the song: *Sweet Ch … d of M … e.*

Rahul had finished playing the guitar solo by then, and the rhythm had changed, which was a cue for Hazel. But she had no time to resume her position behind the keyboard. She had rushed to her keyboard, standing with her back to the audience, holding a few chords at first. This was easier said than done as all the keys had been reversed, and she had to do the impossible—play it all from a mirror position. Her sharp mind and the years of training in classical music had come to her rescue, that day.

She had continued playing in this unconventional position, which was no mean feat, by any standards.

It had taken the audience a while to grasp what she was doing, but when they finally realised, they erupted into a thunderous applause. Hazel's day had been made. Finally, she had succeeded in pulling off a stunt as a keyboardist.

As the principal of the college, Mrs Mukherjee had seen these friends sail through the three undergrad years. She had also taken personal interest in this group as she, indeed, had a *personal* interest—Keya was her daughter.

In the auditorium, Mrs Mukherjee tried her best to be heard, but her voice was drowned under the collective roar of the students. She had no other option but to scream. Normally, for a college principal to be screaming at students was an everyday affair in most colleges, but Mrs Mukherjee handled her students like uncut diamonds, wrapped in cotton wool. Her occasional scream was, therefore, always justified.

Once the five landed on the ground, Mrs Mukherjee's voice acquired the lovely timber of personal care, something that made her so popular among her students.

"Remember, I have personally promised your parents that you shall follow the careers of their choice, and this is just a weeklong excursion that you guys are going for ... no unnecessary roaming around in areas that are not safe, and you will come back in time as promised."

"Ma'am, we shall remain true to our word, but please try and get us a sponsor, so that we can pursue music in the future ..." Rahul pleaded.

Mrs Mukherjee looked away. She could not promise something that she was not confident of delivering. As the college principal, she had seen their ardour for music as a career of their choice. But what could music offer in today's world, where only the fittest rat had a chance to survive?

Yet, she had done what was within her realm. She had let the gang participate in several inter-college festivals. As a group they had won many medals and trophies in musical competitions, and Rahul had even been approached for autographs, on some occasions—something that miffed Keya at times.

She had, for instance, noticed this particular girl cozying up to Rahul, on two different occasions. When the same girl appeared a third time, it had made Keya rather uncomfortable. They had finished a concert and was walking off the stage, the applause had not even died, when Keya spotted her approaching Rahul with an excited face. She had taken out a mobile, perhaps, to take his number, and started chatting up with Rahul.

"Excuse me … Oh! Hi, how are you? Isn't that a third time you are taking his autograph?" Keya had barged in.

"Must be for someone else? Why don't you bring your friends and family over to the Andheri Sports Complex, Friday night? Rahul would love to meet all his fans, personally." Keya had cut her short.

As a child, Keya was quite adept at snatching away candies from her little brother. Here too, she swept Rahul away and left the girl standing with a face of a child who had lost her candy.

After that famous leap, embedded in Mr Mukherjee's mind for posterity, the friends surrounded Mrs Mukherjee and thanked her for her cooperation. If it was not for her, they could not have won this tour.

The year 2011 was the International Year of Forests. She had got a corporate body, with enough interest in the working of the college, to sponsor an educational excursion to the Sunderbans, and these five youngsters had won the contest, hands down.

It had taken a while, for the five, to take it all in. Were they actually heading for the Sunderbans? The realisation of having won a lifetime's opportunity to see a Royal Bengal tiger, right in its den, if they were lucky, had not quite sunk in.

2 Prof. Bhaduri

Prof. Bhaduri came into the hall in a wheelchair that evening, helped by two women. He was not feeling too well after the last round of chemotherapy, but this was an important occasion, and he would not give it a miss. An errand boy followed him, holding his trustworthy crutch.

The spectators had started clapping at the image of a slain tiger with a hunter resting his left leg on its body, holding a gun, which came up on the giant screen, right then. The wheelchair rolled up to the dais easily on the wooden ramp that went up to the stage.

It was believed in social circles that the professor had been mauled by a Royal Bengal tiger, one night, during his tenure as a forest officer in the Sunderbans. But the whisper mongers, who went around in the corridors of the Zoological Survey of Mumbai, made it known that Prof. Bhaduri had, in fact, not hurt his leg in that encounter at all. Apparently, insurgents from across the border had attacked him in the jungle.

Prof. Bhaduri had got wind of the rampant flesh trade involving minors across the porous borders with Bangladesh, and had waged war on it. His efforts had made the pimps scatter, and the flesh trade had taken a beating in the area. However, since the local politicians were involved in the dastardly malaise, that news was given a quiet burial.

One night, when Prof. Bhaduri was on one of his rounds on the river on a bhotbhoti, (a boat with an engine, making a bhot-bhot sound), some local goons attacked the boat. He was saved by the timely intervention of his guards who loved him. One guard was killed in the process, and the professor's leg was broken.

The local mafia, in tandem with the politicians, promptly cooked up a story about a man-eating tiger prowling the area and how it had attacked Prof. Bhaduri. A male tiger was subsequently shot dead by the merciless criminals, and that news got widely publicised—making a hero of the man who shot the tiger.

A picture of the man—with a gun resting on his left leg, which was placed over the body of the dead tiger—would haunt Prof. Bhaduri for the rest of his life. He could not dispute the picture and come out with the real story—the local goons had threatened to harm his family, otherwise. The criminal activities in the area had roots as deep as its mangrove trees, with people in the power corridors deeply entwined in the rotting system.

The authorities looked at Prof. Bhaduri's case with some pity, which resulted in a four-figure pension after a "voluntary" retirement. Prof. Bhaduri's story of valour and courage became folklore in the area, but the killing of the tigers continued, and mindless prostitution of the minors thrived.

Prof. Bhaduri lost all hope. The man had incredible knowledge about the Sunderbans and had indeed come face-to-face with the tiger many times during his service period.

The severely damaged leg had given him a permanent limp, and he had decided to migrate to Mumbai with his family. His M.Phil. degree in environmental science helped him get a decent job in the college, but he had to forgo the pension. The professor had reconciled himself to his fate and tried forgetting the entire incident. And now, nearly seven years later, he had somewhat settled down and accepted the machinations of his destiny.

With his more-than-decent oratory skills and a zest for life, he continued to live a normal life. But in recent times, he had been diagnosed with colon cancer, and even though his spirit was robust his health was getting frailer by the day.

As Prof. Bhaduri was wheeled onto the stage a girl took away his walking stick and helped him climb the few stairs that took him straight to the microphone. College students were giving finishing touches to the fabulous collage of the Royal Bengal tiger that snarled out of the wall behind Prof. Bhaduri.

"Dear Students, it is my great pleasure to announce that like each year, this year too, there are five students from our college who shall be going on an educational excursion. This year's tour will be the Sunderbans, to learn about the flora and the fauna of that area. But before they embark on this expedition it is imperative that they get some knowledge about the area and other information that should be necessary during their trip."

An attendant at the side of the stage held a the remote control in his hand, and the slides kept changing as Prof. Bhaduri spoke. He looked back, fleetingly, at the picture on the wall—the one with the man with the gun—and exhaled heavily. It was a breath of helplessness.

"The Sunderbans in West Bengal is the estuarine segment of the Ganges as well as Brahmaputra river systems. This littoral forest is the only ecological habitat of the tiger of its kind, not only in India, but also in the world, except for Bangladesh.

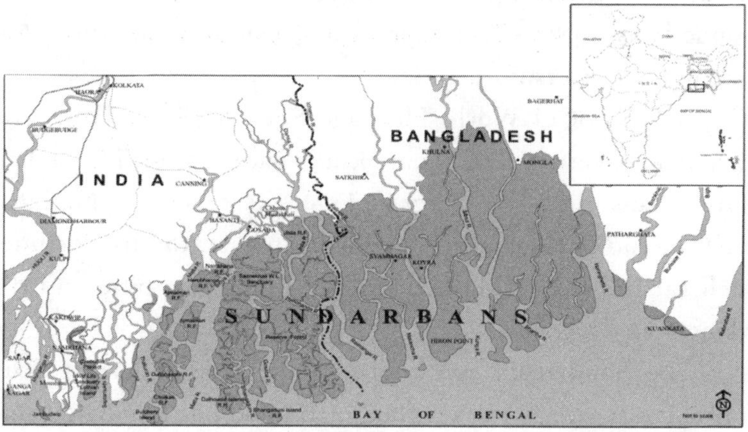

Source: http://assets.wwfindia.org/img/original/sundarban_map.jpg

"The mangrove trees here are adapted to grow in salt water, but they require regular flushing with fresh water. They will die if immersed in salt water, all the time." The professor was reading from the paper given to him.

"In the Sunderbans, which is hidden away from the bustle of the city, you experience a harmonious equilibrium of peace and beauty. It is also an area of considerable border skirmishes and other complications as Bangladesh shares her borders with India.

"I am sure that you all have lots of queries. You can fire them one by one, and I shall try my level best to answer them."

"Sir, what is so special about the Sunderbans, and why are we sending the students there, this year?" A student from the audience asked.

"The Sunderbans is the world's largest estuarine forest. It is stitched together by hundreds of creeks and tributaries. It is one of the most attractive and alluring places on earth—a truly undiscovered paradise. It is here that the land meets the sea at the southern tip of West Bengal, and here lies the Indian Sunderbans—a stretch of impenetrable mangrove forest of great size and bio-diversity.

"A UNESCO World Heritage Site, the Sunderbans is a vast area, covering 4264 square km in India alone. The Indian Sunderbans form the largest Tiger Reserve and National Park in India. A paradise for birdwatchers, the list includes such rarities as the Masked finfoot, Mangrove pitta and the Mangrove whistler.

"The Sunderbans are a part of the world's largest delta formed by the mighty rivers Ganges, Brahmaputra, and Meghna. This area is a must visit for students who love nature."

An impish boy from the back of the auditorium raised his hand and was given the chance to ask his question.

"Sir, we have all heard of the Royal Bengal tiger ... have you seen it with your own eyes? What is it like? Are they man-eaters?"

Prof. Bhaduri coughed a few times into the microphone as though this was the question that he dreaded to answer.

"Royal Bengal tigers are the biggest cats in the world. Unlike lions that live in a pride, the Royal Bengal tiger is a solitary creature. It lives alone, hunts alone and dies alone. Yes, I have had the pleasure of encountering one many a times, and finally had the grave misfortune of encountering one right inside its den." Prof. Bhaduri pointed at his left leg as he spoke his lines.

"You see, the Royal Bengal tiger is a supreme animal. Because of their intimate association with the estuarine environment, the uniqueness of the habitat is said to have contributed to certain behavioural trends, characteristic of Sundarban tigers only. It is considered that man-eating propensity of tigers in this area is hereditarily acquired over generations, in the process of consumption of saline water.

"Their kidneys and livers are affected with constant contact with saline water and that is why they are so aggressive. The English colonialists gave Royal Bengal tiger its name. Unfortunately, they loved a Royal Bengal 'hide' on their wall as much, and therefore, the first steps toward extinction were set by the very name-givers themselves."

Keya had been listening intently to all this. She remembered the issue of poaching. It had emerged as a very major threat to the tiger.

"Sir, have any significant steps been taken to stop poaching?" She asked.

Prof. Bhaduri thought for a moment and again coughed into the microphone a few times, then looked back at the piece of paper before answering.

"Protection against poaching and theft of forest produce has been ensured through intensive patrolling by staff in motorboats and launches. The offices and camps are located at strategic points to keep a watch over the area. There exists an effective communication network for protection. Furthermore, the staff is well armed."

Keya stood up suddenly, out of excitement and startled the student beside her.

"Sir, what about the locals in the area? What can you tell us about the tribals who live there? Are they threatened by the tigers? I have seen several documentaries which show the tigers of the Sunderbans as habitual man-eaters. Do they like human meat?"

Prof. Bhaduri became interested in the conversation as this was a little different from the rudimentary information that he was asked to simply read out. His voice expressed his deep interest in the subject.

"My friend, the tigers of the Sunderbans are NOT habitual man-eaters. No animal anywhere in the universe wants to ever harm humans on purpose. That is a universal law. Whatever led you to believe that is simply rubbish."

He realised that he was getting too animated and took a breath to calm down.

"There are many reasons why they attack humans. One of the main being the loss of their habitat and increasing human encroachment. As a result, they often attack the honey collectors who venture into their territory."

An errand boy serving water dropped a glass somewhere, and this led to a minor commotion among the listeners. Prof. Bhaduri took this as a signal and remembered that he had to keep to the script. He looked back at the paper.

"My advice to all of you is to enjoy the surroundings, but be careful not to venture out in the dark, and also be careful about the crocodiles in the water and the snakes on land. The mobiles will hardly work there due to signal problems so you have to make do with whatever little modes of communication present. I suggest, since you have the advantage of technology, please keep your phones charged at all times. You can only do that in the evenings at one of the shops that offer electricity from the generators. There is no electricity in general in the area."

There was another question from a young boy.

"Sir, the area doesn't have electricity; there are tigers and snakes on land and crocodiles in water. And one can't even charge mobile handsets easily. Isn't it too dangerous to visit?"

Prof. Bhaduri looked out of the window for a moment, and then the words flew out in a torrent.

"There is a little more in the world to explore than the manicured faces at nightclubs, or the sights from your car rear-view mirror. You must have heard the saying that India lives in its villages. The land is so enticing that I am sure you shall find things more important than talking on the phone."

It became very obvious that Prof. Bhaduri not only had in-depth knowledge of the Sunderbans, but was also immensely attached to the place. After a few more questions, the professor got off the stage. A stranger behind a pillar gave him a nod and disappeared in to the crowd that was filing out of the auditorium.

3
Kolkata

The monsoons were still teasing the city, and the tar between the tram tracks on Howrah Bridge was softening and melting. The Duronto Express pulled into a rather subdued Howrah Station, at 7:30 pm. This train had lived up to its reputation for punctuality as well as comfort.

A Bengali gentleman sitting next to Rahul, on the train, smiled when he saw the five friends staring at the commotion outside on the platform.

"Look outside and you will notice that the arrival of the long distance train seems to ignite a sudden feeling of haste into everybody."

Rahul momentarily turned to smile at him, acknowledging his comment. Looking at the crowd he now noticed an unmistakable hurry amongst even those who had nothing to do with the incoming train. The decibel level of conversations had also automatically escalated.

"But, my friends, you will notice, there is a fresh breath in the air, over the Hooghly these days."

Now all turned to hear him intently. He obviously belonged to Kolkata and seemed to know a great deal about the city. The man, thrilled to get such coveted attention, cleared his throat and continued.

"Look out and you will see poriborton … change. The red brigade that had ruled over the state for the last thirty-four-odd years has finally given way. The opposition, Trinamul Congress, has stormed in with a resounding victory in the assembly elections that was, till a few years ago, considered unthinkable in the State. Look, even the Howrah Station is decorated with green flags in anticipation, and every bystander, every commuter, and even the coolies have a sheen of green reflecting on their bare skins. They are waiting to usher in the long-awaited change," the man added, almost sentimentally.

Imran noticed that the coolies indeed were wearing green. That would have made Karl Marx turn in his grave.

"And now it looks like the gods have decided to celebrate too," the man added joyfully peeping out of the train window.

As if on cue, a thunderous clap in the heavens above, welcomed the incoming train, applauding the arrival of the youngsters.

Keya's mother called to enquire whether the train had reached on time, but it was impossible to hear anything, due to the commotion around her. Keya said she would call later and switched off her phone.

Platform number 22, where the Duronto Express arrives, is completely open on one side, aiding sufficient ventilation. A strong gust of wind blew in eddies of paper and dust into the platform. A middle-aged man, pre-empting the rains, casually unfurled the plastic sheet covering a magazine stand on the platform, and draped his head and shoulders with it almost as if he owned it.

"Poriborton, dada, poriborton!" He grinned.

Numerous expletives escaped the lips of the furious young shopkeeper, shaking in spasms of anger and frothing in the mouth as he chided the old man.

"Kolkata! So what if the colour had changed. It would take years for its character to change!" Said a young man sitting at the adjacent shop sipping tea, casually picking up the thread of a debate. Anything for a good adda.

"Ei dekho brishti! Here come the rains. Divine tears of joy, bujhhechho tumi? Do you understand?" claimed another. "The gods have been sulking, looking at the three decades of gradual degeneration of a state, which had contributed so much with blood and intellect to the Indian Freedom Struggle. The rains are meant to wash away our troubles and usher in better days. Hope springs eternal!"

Another was quick to refute: "Tumi ki bhabo? What do you think? All this mess will be cleared by chanting 'poriborton'? Gopal Krishna Gokhale had remarked that what Bengal thinks today, India thinks tomorrow. And then what happened? The capital of British India shifted to New Delhi; Mahatma Gandhi assumed control of the National Movement; and Bombay supplanted Calcutta as the financial hub of modern India." The man was showing off his knowledge in history.

Truly so. In later decades, Bengal and Bengalis collected a long series of laments, both in political and economic terms. They fell further behind other parts of the country. Once a hub of real talent, it gradually became a dead state.

"The misrule of the communist party of India for over three decades, has sapped the state of all her intellectual wealth. Look at the mass exodus of talent to other cities and countries." The man spat out the words, sounding disgusted with the information he offered.

He quietened only when the rains became heavier and drowned his voice. The city reeled under the burst of thunder, and the downpour inundated the buildings and the iconic metallic structure of the bridge. The rain could also be heard on the station roof, making a rhythmic pitter-patter sound that Jassi did not miss. He peeped through the iron bars of his window to absorb it.

It was quite interesting to notice how innovatively people found sheds and corners to use as covers, to stay dry when the heavens opened up. Obvious places like tea stalls and telephone booths with awnings, suddenly, became desperately overcrowded as young and old elbowed and jostled each other, to make space for themselves. Others entered unoccupied taxis, and some even sneaked into shops to find dry areas.

The rains had coincided with the announcement that Duronto Express was entering the platform. Coolies streamed their way to the train even before it had come to a complete halt. Soon no one could move in the isle of the compartment, which got submerged in the cacophony of abuses and vulgar oaths heard in a variety of languages. Everybody wanted to get out of the compartment first, but the five friends were sober enough to wait, till all the commotion and excitement calmed down.

Soon they were standing below the clock tower, on the platform. Rahul always assumed additional responsibilities due to his physical prowess, and his friends, only too happy to comply, waved away coolies with their hands.

"You can carry all the big bags till the exit, and then we shall all help you to load the stuff into the taxi," Jassi said.

Keya stood her ground, for a while, looking around the station as if she was trying to spot someone in the crowd. Slouched under her rucksack Hazel moved slowly, envying Rahul who had his guitar slung over his shoulder. While other musical instruments like the piccolo or even the congo could be a part of a luggage, Hazel and Jassi could never imagine lugging their keyboard and drum set around on holidays.

A woman came running from the far end of the platform and bulldozed into Hazel almost knocking her down. The sight of a beautiful foreigner trying to regain her footing in a crowded Howrah Station, drew many stares.

Rahul had a good mind to stop the running woman, to extract an apology from her, when they heard a whistle, loud and clear. For a whistle to be heard amidst the hustle and bustle of Howrah Station would have required an instrument of astronomical size, so when it was found that the sound emanated from the lips of a twenty-year-old boy, everybody was stunned.

He was like any another twenty-year old from the neighbourhood. He was perched atop a tall pile of parcels, in his Bermudas, holding his index finger and his thumb, curved and joined in a semicircle, into his mouth. Whistling aloud at Howrah Station, made him nothing less than an alien in a civilised society. What came out from his mouth in the form of sound waves was a stinging shrill like a referee's whistle.

Keya froze for a moment. Then she swiftly loosened her grip on her luggage—it appeared that this was what she was waiting for—joined her index finger to her thumb to form a similar semicircle, which she then inserted in her mouth and echoed the whistle, creating three short and shrill bursts in metronomic perfection.

What followed, on platform number 22, was nothing short of a sleekly scripted climax, straight out of a movie. Keya let her bag slip from her hand, which twirled on the platform coming to rest on the oval shaped metal begging bowl of a cripple. The beggar would have never dreamt of getting such a big haul in his begging career.

Keya then started running down the platform. The boy atop the pile of parcels leaped into the air and landed beautifully on the platform floor and started running towards Keya. The two met in the middle of the platform and paused. A rhythmic exercise with their hands and fingers followed, each touching the other for a fleeting second and then pausing again before the next move. Everybody on the platform thought this was a film shoot and watched in awed silence. The give and take with their limbs lasted about two minutes and then there was a grandiose embrace.

"Kire ... what the hell! I see that you have lost quite a bit of the power in your lungs. I could hardly hear you." said Keya.

"Lack of practice" replied Bhombol.

"Come, I will introduce you to my friends." Keya held Bhombol's hand and dragged him back to her friends, with the eyes of the onlookers on the platform following them.

Bhombol and Keya had grown up together till her father's transfer parted the two, stationing them in different states of the country. Bhombol was an orphan. His biological parents had hailed from the Sunderbans. A serious land dispute had led to both being murdered—a news that had hit the headlines in the early nineties. The police had been unable to nail the culprit. The killers were never caught, and the case soon got lost in the cobwebs of the police files. It was putative as another gruesome murder, under the influence of alcohol among the tribals.

Captain Talukdar and his wife, Parvati, were honeymooning in the region when the incident had taken place. They were moved by the sight of a four-year-old boy with a runny nose, grovelling in the dirt, long after the police van had left the scene of crime, after a perfunctory investigation.

Parvati had picked up the child and taken an immediate liking towards him. The child too wailed each time she made an effort to put it down. He clung to her bosom. She had instantly decided to bring the child home with her. Though the captain had initially objected to it, he relented later when he saw the growing bond between his wife and the child, and considered it as a gift from

God, since they had been unable to conceive a child of their own. Soon the child was going to school with Keya. Keya and Bhombol grew up together till the age of fourteen when Mr Mukherjee's (Keya's father) untimely transfer to Mumbai separated them.

Bhombol had an untamed spirit in him, right from his childhood, which his foster parents never tried to curb; in fact they encouraged it. He turned out to be a born sportsman and broke all school records in sprinting, and kicked the football high enough to touch the church bell for which he was often severely admonished by his principal. He was also a black-belt in karate. Today, at four and twenty, he was a strapping young lad with an indomitable zest for life.

Bhombol and Keya had tried to remain in touch, but their priorities in life, which kept changing in their adolescent years, let them drift apart. They were meeting at the Howrah Station, after ten long years.

"Wait Bhombol let me call mom." Keya switched her phone on and called her mother.

"Mom, we have all arrived safely, and things are so interesting here that we don't want to waste time on the phone. Bhombol has come to receive us and everything, is fine. We shall keep you informed about everything. Do not worry about us at all."

Keya had kept the conversation as short as possible. She remembered the words of Prof. Bhaduri—the mobile phone was suddenly redundant. Once the formal introductions were over, Bhombol whispered something into Keya's ears.

"The boat is waiting, for the last two hours"

"Guys the concert is about to start. Our chariot is waiting at the river." Keya too tried her best to remain calm, but her voice gave away the excitement in her veins. They were about to embark on an unbelievable journey to the Sunderbans, on a boat!

4 The Titanic

She was moored to the trunk of a rather stout tree that mushroomed out of the muck and frothy sludge, on the banks of the Hooghly River. The strong gust that blew over the river made umbrellas, held by portly women on the streets, turn inside out. It created yelps of disgust, and surprised others who witnessed this scene of comic distress. This wind was also strong enough for the *Titanic* to drift so far away from the banks that the tree trunk, which had a worn-out cinema poster of the film *3 Idiots* on it, bent sideways almost touching the water, and was about to snap in the middle. That would have been truly titanic. But suddenly, there was a calm. The wind eased; the Titanic floated a few meters back towards the bank; the rain stopped. Bhombol who was leading the way found this occasion ideal to surprise his newfound friends by introducing them to a Bengali beverage.

"Dada, my friends have come from Mumbai ... please serve them your special tea."

It was surprising, why Bhombol, who was more than twice the boy's age, addressed him as "dada", or older brother. But Kolkata had its own reasons for doing things and had remained a potpourri of strange customs. The small boy at the tea stall appeared to have acquired that epithet for his exceptional skills with the saucepan and the earthen cups.

Dada transferred the tea from one earthen cup (made of the local terracotta) to another making huge arcs with his hands. He raised and dropped both alternatively and let the tea flow from one cup to the other. This exercise lasted for about thirty-odd seconds before all the guests were served steaming hot tea to relish. Hazel had taken many pictures of Dada and his gymnastics with the liquid and the pots. Everybody noticed wide-eyed that Dada had not spilt even a drop of tea in the process.

Bhombol was the first to receive his cup and he touched his lips to the brim of the bhanr (as known in Kolkata) and made a loud slurping noise. Rahul, Keya, Hazel then got a cup each, and everyone seemed to enjoy hearing the intermittent loud noises that Bhombol made, each time he sipped from his bhanr. Bhombol enjoyed the attention he was getting and said aloud, "Hot tea is best enjoyed if you make some noise while sipping it," replicating the sound with more gusto to entertain his guests, who were in splits.

"I am not joking ... try it once and you will see." He endorsed.

For the city-breds, it felt a little uneasy to follow those instructions, at first. *Do not make noise while sipping tea*, is what they had learnt. Hazel's grandfather, who had bequeathed a stiff upper lip to his progeny, would have surely burst a blood vessel seeing his granddaughter make such demonic sounds while sipping tea on the riverbanks of Kolkata. But some aberrations are allowed on holidays, or life would be too boring. It was quite a sight, though, to catch Rahul, Imran, Keya, Hazel and Jassi all raise their cups of tea (Jassi's cup was empty as he did not drink tea), to this newfound learning. They paused for a fleeting second turning to look towards Bhombol, who was their mentor (as if to ask: *Are we doing this right*?) and then made a collective slurping sound, swigging in the tea right into their throats.

For Hazel, however, it was too hot to handle. She yelped in pain as the hot tea burnt her tongue, and she spewed an involuntary spray, almost, right into Jassi's face. Then she stood up, snorted and grunted and gulped some more air, and then burst into a loud guffaw when the embarrassment became too much to handle. Dada at the counter could not control himself either, and broke out into thunderous laughter. The rest of the gang joined in that infectious medley.

Soon, however, "the coastal tea party" was over and it was time to move on. Bhombol was the leader. He paused momentarily when he noticed that the Titanic was anchored in the muddy water, a meter away from the bank. This time it was not a whistle, but a scream, like Tarzan. He left the banks and went sailing into the air. The errand boy on the deck moved a little distance away to clear space for Bhombol to land on deck. Bhombol quickly gathered himself, and hurriedly placed a wooden gangplank to make a bridge between the Titanic and land. Rahul and the others all balanced themselves on the narrow plank, and soon they were all aboard the Titanic.

The Titanic was aptly named. It was a miniature version of the iconic ship. It was apparent from the first look of the vessel that the owner had very good aesthetic sense and must have been a sailor once. Keya struck a pose on the deck, the moment she got on board. Holding her fist in front of her mouth as if she was opening a concert, she said, "Ladies and gentlemen. I belong to a proud family of sailors and perhaps the only reason why I have not traversed the seas as one is because I was born a girl. Welcome on board. Our captain on the voyage is going to be Captain Talukdar and we shall always refer to him as 'Captain'."

Keya's uncle, Captain Talukdar, retired as a captain from the merchant navy after twenty-five years of service and had started a business of fisheries in Namkhana, an administrative division in Kakdwip village, in South 24 Parganas district, considered the gateway to the Sunderbans. As a sailor, he had led a regimented life for twenty-five years, and when he finally retired with a lot of money, he hoped to roll it in business.

But, that was a big mistake. Initial years in business resulted in severe losses as Keya's uncle found it extremely difficult to cope with the corruption prevalent in trading circuit and civilian life in general. Political interference in business, and a total unwillingness among his workers to work, were conditions beyond his control. Eventually, the trade union movement, and gross negligence and cheating among the people he trusted, sounded the death knell for his business, and he had to shut shop.

Captain Talukdar loved living life on his own terms; begging or pleading was out of his character. The locals usurped most of the land, and the fishing business thus collapsed. But, once a seaman always a seaman! The old adage had proven true in the case of the captain. He managed to salvage some funds from the monumental ruin his business had become, and bought a small boat. He planned to run the boat as a cruise liner on the Hooghly River, with Bhombol as his second mate. The business had started well, but soon that too fell into rough waters due to the interference of the local goons and politicians. The very people who had promised to help Bhombol turned a deaf ear, which spelled doom for the business again.

Spare parts of the ship would be stolen regularly, and the mechanics on the boat would be threatened if the demands of the cutthroats on the waters were not met. Captain Talukdar had braved the unruly seas and even had his occasional stints with pirates, but he found it extremely difficult to grease the palms of those in power for the smooth working of his business. Fed up with the system, he took a sabbatical to reorganise himself, and went on a holiday with his family.

Soon afterwards, things changed. The red brigade lost power. and the colour green was to be tested. The captain named his boat the "Titanic" and designed it himself; but it could only be used by the ones who could afford luxury. It was modelled after the iconic ship, but was much smaller. A mini theatre, a bar, a billiards room and a fashionable dinner hall, stylised the ship.

It was the Titanic's first sortie on the waters, and the captain had taken special care to be present for the five youngsters from Mumbai. He had plans to serve the Department of Tourism of West Bengal, and ferry tourists to the Sunderbans during the winter months. The captain had won a tender, floated by the government of West Bengal, and he was ready to put his best foot forward in his new business again. He had never done anything at a discounted rate, and he had plans to personally steer the ship during these tours. At least, that was the plan and it was to be tested today. Today, was the eponymous ship's first test ride.

A long Honda City, with black tinted glasses and a red revolving beacon on its roof, screeched to a halt outside the ferry ghat. Immediately, a few uniformed guards carrying automatic weapons and walkie-talkies got off another vehicle following it, and two really strong looking guards held open the doors of a VIP car.

A beautifully dressed woman got out. Mrs Chowdhury was originally from north India. She had had a rollicking love affair with Keya's youngest uncle. A movie-like sequence of events had seen a few failed marriage attempts at the registrar's office.

The reasons for these failures were varied. On one occasion, both the boys who were to be the signatories, and had been bribed, failed to turn up, and on another occasion (comically so) the bike they were escaping on, entered a pothole during the Kolkata rains, and turned turtle. The registrar had finished his power lunch and had left for the day when they arrived, soaked to the bone, cut and bruised.

Eventually, the family members had bowed to the determined resilience of the two lovers. Parvati had since then, for the last fifteen years, been the devoted quintessential Bengali bahu. Parvati, "Paro boudi" as she was lovingly known by one and all, also had it all. She could laugh, weep, scream, and generally give vent to all the human emotions known to mankind, at the drop of a coin. She was the providential drama queen.

Parvati got out of the car and ran furiously towards the Titanic in her sari, waving her hands to catch its attention. The two plain-clothed security personnel found it difficult to decide whether to follow her or not. It was quite a spectacle for the daily labourers and fishermen as well, who were collecting their nets and doing odd jobs on the banks.

Captain Talukdar had seen all this from the wheel room and had jabbed on a few knobs on the control console of the ship. The motor of the Titanic had huffed and puffed and then become silent. Keya had also seen Parvati get out of the car and run to the water's edge. She ran to the edge of the deck and started shouting.

"Mashi … mashi I knew that you would come. I was looking for you at the station."

Parvati was at the hospital the day Keya was born. She was born a premature child, but the doctors had taken special care and under the nurturing attention of Parvati, she had gained weight within weeks, and was out of danger soon. Parvati, or mashi as Keya called her, had been part of every milestone of hers since then. The formative years were, in fact, painful as Keya did not want to leave her mashi and go anywhere. When Keya was in the fifth standard, her father was suddenly transferred to Mumbai, where she had to pursue her education. Mashi had visited her a few times in Mumbai, and their love had only grown over the time.

"Hero, stop your 'vehicle' at once."

Parvati's statement was meant for the captain's ears who had already come to the edge of the deck and was craning his neck to hear more clearly. She called him "Hero".

"I cannot hear you!"

"Yes, I know you very well can, Hero. Come back to the shore at once, else ...."

Only Parvati could have pulled this feat in real life. She picked up a big enough boulder and threatened to hurl it at the Titanic. Captain Talukdar knew from the look on her face, and also probably from past experiences, that she meant business. Fearing that Parvati would let fly the missile, he ducked immediately, ran inside the bridge and jabbed on the control panels again.

The Titanic stopped her onward journey and seemed to be on a reverse gear. The two security guards who had come running to the edge of the water by now threw two stow lines, which flew across the rails and were secured on the capstons. With a little effort from the men, the Titanic was pulled back to the banks and moored to the tree trunk again. The two security personnel then disappeared not wanting to witness a family feud.

Captain Talukdar came ashore, balancing on the wooden plank. Meanwhile, Parvati organised the kumkum—a tray with haldi, flowers and incense and lamps—for a special puja. She had got a pujari along with her, who was missing from the scene of action, until then. But now as the puja paraphernalia was out, he sprinted from nowhere and started reciting the shlokas and the mantras with tremendous gusto. The rites were completed in a jiffy, and it was time for the sweet utsav. Rasogolla, sandesh, payesh, and jalebi, started pouring out from bags held by the security men and the five friends happily gorged on everything. They were still licking their fingers when Parvati broke the silence.

"This puja was done so that Ma of the Jungle, Bon Bibi, protects you from all evil and brings you back safe and sound. But can you please tell me, why you are going to the Sunderbans?"

"Paro boudi, can we carry some of these sweets with us?" Imran found the sweets far more interesting than Parvati's question.

"Yes of course you can. Sultan, please get out the handis from the back of the car."

Sultan, one of the security guards, ran along with Bhombol to the car and got back three round bronze utensils, deep and large, and kept them at the edge of the water.

"There is enough rasogolla and nimki in the handi to last you during the tour, but you still haven't answered my question. Why are you going to the jungle? It is full of snakes, and crocodiles, and the Royal Bengal tiger."

Rahul moved forward to answer.

"Paro boudi we have all heard of the Royal Bengal tiger and also know that it is a critically endangered species, and want to see it before it becomes extinct ...."

"But the little that I know about the Royal Bengal tiger ... there is a one in a million chance that you will see it in the jungle. Why don't you go to the Alipore Zoo and see it."

Captain Talukdar started laughing, but when he noticed that this was becoming embarrassing for his wife, he quickly cupped his hand to his mouth and walked away.

"Paro boudi, you see, we all want to do something different and out of the ordinary in life. We are going to the jungle for inspiration. I am a painter." reminded Imran.

"You want to paint the Royal Bengal tiger?" Captain Talukdar guffawed from behind the Honda City where he stood away from the scrutiny of Parvati.

Imran chuckled before replying. "You see the Royal Bengal tiger is our national animal, and it is about to become extinct. We want to take our chances and be part of history. We have all read about the Sunderbans and this a prize holiday for us."

Parvati acquiesced. What else could she say?

"Okay, but be very careful and don't mix with the locals too much. It is after the elections, and a time of change, so everybody is a little volatile and edgy. Enjoy yourselves, and remember to come home before you leave for Mumbai."

"Ahoy! The Titanic is about to sail." Captain Talukdar bellowed and got back on board double quick, treading on the wooden bridge.

"Bhombol is my second mate in this voyage, and there is one rule—in fact, the only rule that you must follow strictly on board—I am right, even if I am wrong. No arguments, please."

The Titanic sailed off. She cut through the mist that had gathered over the river. Keya was still waving at her mashi who stood on the bank wiping her tears.

5 Oh Captain, My Captain!

"Bhombol, you see, one can detect a mariner when one sees one. I have clinked many a glass over the Pacific and the Atlantic, but I haven't spilled a single drop. Its sacrilege my friend. Never, I say, never ever spill while you clink glasses."

Captain Talukdar embarked on the voyage by opening a bottle of whiskey that had matured for twenty years.

It was a striking sight with the skyline of Kolkata receding slowly and steadily in the background, and images of rural Bengal taking over simultaneously. The hatch to the main cabin being quite low the five friends had to bend sufficiently to get inside. What was waiting to welcome them inside was an enchanting world of art.

The interiors of the cabin were decorated like the Sunderbans. A picture of the "Land of eighteen tides and one goddess" on the walls, with rivers and small creeks running into each other, forming a labyrinth of waterways, with the forest around them, created an atmosphere of awe. Numerous islands rose above the rivulets, their heads covered with green foliage. They appeared like tiny green buttons. The flora of the area painted over the walls was so realistic that the branches of the trees seemed to reach out and touch them. The mangrove forests seemed to be growing like they had aerial roots, which held the trunk of the trees together.

The five friends, taken in by the surreal world of the Sunderbans surrounding them, turned around slowly. They were drawn by a magnetic pull from the last wall where they paused wide-eyed. On the wall, fierce and majestic, was a Royal Bengal tiger, towering over their shoulders—with its paws stretched out to strike, and its face elongated at the sides into a lingering growl.

The boat rocked a little and a thin shaft of the moon cut into the cabin, casting marvellous shadows on the serpentine branches, entangled with each other. One could almost hear the growl, such was the ambience. Below the image of the tiger, however, was a brilliant calligraphy: *Please Save Me* ....

Captain Talukdar walked into the room and caught the five friends transfixed—under the spell of the Royal Bengal tiger on the wall.

"This image is to prepare visitors for the real thing ahead." He broke the silence.

The captain took another large gulp from his glass and sat down on a chair.

"And right in front of you is the Royal Bengal tiger that seems to be really angry and growling at you, but if you look closely you shall realise that it is, perhaps, a big scream from a frightened animal ...."

"... Screaming for survival?" Keya probed.

The captain had had quite a few drinks and had become rather emotional.

"Won't it be painful if you realise that odds are all against you and that you have a predator stronger than you, all armed to slaughter you mercilessly, without a fighting chance for survival? What will you do? You can only scream aloud, but nobody is likely to hear you and help you...

"Life for me on the high seas was not like this. Even when we fell into rough weather and had to battle against all odds, we were never so hopeless. But that is not the case with the tiger. Poachers come with guns, the villagers come with poison, and sympathisers come with empty barrels of sympathy.

"You all here ... you all are going to the Sunderbans to see the tiger. Right? May be you will see one, may be you won't. When the trip gets over, you all will take your pictures to remind you of an exquisite holiday, but tigers will continue to die.

"Think how dangerous it is to be a rare species. The royal Bengal tiger is so priceless today that it doesn't really matter whether it is alive or dead—the last tiger must be butchered for its skin to adorn the walls and the floors of the rich and the famous only to make a statement of sorts.

"So, my young friends, do you think you can make any difference? Do you even want to? If you cannot save a tiger, if ever, a prayer escapes your lips, can you at least offer it for the tiger ... now that you know it isn't growling in anger. It's howling ... for a life!"

When the captain had finished his soliloquy, there was a painful pregnant silence in the cabin. Nobody really knew how to react as the words of the captain reverberated in the mind of the five friends. Imran was the first to speak.

"But captain how can *we* save the tiger?"

"Well, to begin with, ensure that you have enough energy and desire to save the tiger. That's half the battle won—especially now that you all are going right into the tiger's den. I request you all to try and do whatever is within your limits for this marvellous animal—give it a chance to survive, so that our future generations can hear it roar." The captain's voice trilled with passionate excitement. His eyes sparkled with what seemed like a drop of tear. Then he calmed down and spoke again.

"It's quite late and I think you all should catch up on some sleep. We shall anchor for a couple of hours when we reach Kakdwip, at daybreak. Goodnight."

The captain left the cabin a completely sober man despite his heavy liquid intake. The friends were left wondering what the jungle had in store for them. A feeling deep inside them told them that they were in for a treat—they were going to the Sunderbans, the largest deltaic region of the world, and this had all the possibilities of becoming much more than just a holiday.

The captain's short talk had profound effect on Hazel.

"We are not going to the jungle." She said disgustedly as she stood up and looked out of the window. "We are the real animals and we have created our jungle to live in."

"What do you mean?" Jassi asked. "We all know that Rahul sometimes behaves like an animal on stage, but why include us all in that tribe."

Keya echoed Hazel's passionate outburst.

"We as Indians should be proud of our heritage. Can't we save our tigers? All our politicians are paper tigers, roaring in the corridors of power and letting the real tigers die in the forest. It's so shameful. Let us today take a pledge that we shall all do something, however miniscule, to save the tiger."

Once again a pregnant silence engulfed the room only to be shattered by a roaring drumrole from the heavens above. Brilliant light limned the Titanic momentarily and two river dolphins, bouncing on the waters, dived back into the depths of the dark ocean.

Inside the cabin, one by one, all five friends came together under a collective huddle, much like the cricket team before the beginning of a match. But this one was not meant for personal glory. It was for the tiger.

At first it was a tentative whisper. "We shall save the tiger". Jassi said softly. Rahul, Hazel, Keya and Imran joined in, uttering the words in unison. They could all feel their blood churn within their veins as they jointly took the pledge—their bodies locked together moving rhythmically as if pampered and egged on by the upsurge created by these magical words.

Their collective voice rose in a crescendo in that cabin that night, and the two river dolphins surfaced again alongside the ship. They appeared to be dancing, celebrating this oath of honour, and the fact that the tiger had found five good friends.

The captain walked in again with a chart in his hand that had the course of the ship marked out.

"Here look. We have set sail from below the Howrah Bridge and we are sailing south down the river. Let's go to the bridge.

Once on the bridge, the captain placed the map on the console and pointed at it with his small stick.

"We shall hit Nurpur in a couple of hours, with Diamond Harbour to the left and Haldia to the right. Haldia is an industrial town, famous or infamous for its petrochemicals factory. Diamond Harbour is another small town and a popular weekend tourist spot, where the river meets the Bay of Bengal, on the banks of the Hooghly River, in the South 24 Parganas.

"Earlier known as Hajipur, this beautiful place was named Diamond Harbour by the British. The place was considered a safe resting spot for the ocean going ships, and it offered a spectacular view of the river.

"You will notice that the Hooghly River joining the Rupnarayan is like a shot of anabolic steroids, and the water body seems to explode suddenly and widen. We shall keep afloat sailing into the river Haldi until we reach the rivers Hatania Doyania and then drift further south towards Namkhana and the river

Saptamukhi. So get ready and enjoy the ride and lookout for the crocodile project at Patharpratima that we shall cross too."

Everybody marvelled at the knowledge of their captain and were excited, eagerly awaiting for the adventure to unfold itself and surprise them.

It was Poltu who first noticed the shimmering light, trembling above the water. Below the light was the faint outline of a solid structure that created immense curiosity in Poltu's mind as he lay curled up on the sand, inside the iron collapsible gate. He started barking instantly.

The Titanic, moored by the side of the river, was the subject of Poltu's prying eyes. He slowly eased in under the collapsible iron gate of the closed shop, and slithering on the mud, slipped through to investigate. A hop, skip, and jump over the puddles of muddy water got him to the edge of the water, in seconds. There he waited cautiously, looking at the stock-still vessel, intently, with extreme suspicion.

Misgiving intensifying, he nosed ahead vigilantly towards the water. Just then Bhombol walked out on the deck and released the chains and shackles that made up the workboat anchor, and it fell into the water making a huge splash. This sudden disturbance shocked the wits out of the probing Poltu on the banks, and he jumped a few steps back on the mud, frightened, and started howling furiously at once. And then all hell broke loose.

Domesticated and strays; dogs of various shapes and sizes ran out of dark corners and crevices. They came out of holes in the walls, from below tree trunks and over the pushcarts parked on the street, from wherever they were resting. Poltu's bark was enough to bring together a melee of mongrels that night, on the riverbank—short and long ones, cute and ugly ones, old and young ones, limping and zipping ones—all kinds, conjured up like apparitions, out of thin air.

There was also this three-legged one who was extremely committed and persistent in its barking. While others took some breathing time this one brayed on. Raucous, bawdy, feisty—what was heard by the captain and others that night on the river, was nothing short of a cacophony of howls, barks, shrieks, whimpers, woofs, growls and every other conceivable sound that could be produced by four legged mammals.

This exercise in vocal joint venture, demonstrated by all the dogs in the neighbourhood, created such a hullabaloo that little flickering lights showed up in the dark huts surrounding the trees, and soon, the entire village was up, in the middle of the night. It was not something the villagers could ignore, and soon, they stepped out groggily and followed the warning cries, to the edge of the water.

A potbellied man stretched his neck out and scanned the boat from head to toe. "Ki daarun dekhte go … Wow, it looks beautiful," he whispered.

"But, what is it? Let's find out." Asked another man and hastened towards the water's edge audaciously, but stopped after a few paces as he was not sure about investigating the matter alone.

A half-naked boy, struggling to find space within the crowd that was still growing, was picked up on the shoulders by his father. He looked at the structure on the water carefully and let out his own observation.

"This is a … ghoul. It will kill us all."

A rumbling of laughter started in the crowd and died soon into uneasy silence. The boy then got off his father's shoulder.

"Let's teach it a lesson," he said putting up a brave face.

He picked up a small stone and hurled it at the Titanic, with enough force for it to strike the side of the boat, making a shrill clanking sound. The captain knew at once that his boat had been hit. He ran out furiously on the deck and was shocked to see the entire village ganged up behind a barricade of dogs.

"What do you all want? Who dares to harm my boat? I am talking to you, not the dogs." The captain felt like diving into the water and encountering the crowd, but was held back by the friends.

Such a beautiful ship on the banks of the village was unheard of. Many thought that some raja or a maharaja, from alien shores, had come to visit them in the dead of the night. Nobody in the village had seen anything like this before, and few dared to go near the vessel alone. But it called for serious explanations.

When some people raised an alarm in the crowd that was impossible to ignore, Captain Talukdar had to bring out all his legal papers and ownership documents of the Titanic.

They had been reminded of the Purulia arms-drop incident, back in 1995, when a mysterious arms consignment was air dropped, in the dead of the night. The elders of the village commanded an inspection of the boat. Matters were solved in about an hour, but not before the captain took a dozen villagers on a tour of the river. That was a sight to behold. Villagers in lungis and dhotis, and women clutching small babies went on a joyride, aboard the Titanic!

The persistent animal, which had barked the loudest, also got a passage with the rest. It had walked up the gangway and had nosed around initially for food. But finding nothing of interest, relished the gentle movement of the ship as it started its joyride. If anyone ever saw a dog smile, it was that day.

The five friends took turns in patting and gently fondling their new friend, and it mewled in pleasure. Hazel named the dog Knockout who expressed no desire to disembark when the tour was over. While a little coercing worked with the villagers, Knockout had to be lifted bodily and transferred to land as it was time to move on to Bakkhali, where the Titanic's voyage would be complete.

None of the five friends knew how long they slept. The morning sun rose at around 5:30 am, every day, at this time of the year. They had crossed the crocodile project and the Mridanga Bhanga River. This river had derived its name apparently from the turbulent sounds it made, similar to a broken mridangam—a percussion instrument. They wanted to dock at Ramganga and the tour was going as per plan.

Bhombol carried the oblique rays of the sunlight on his shoulders as he crept into the cabin, carrying bhanrs of tea in the terracotta cups that they had already seen earlier that evening. Despite a lack of substantial sleep that night, all five friends were extremely fresh and got up quickly. Good thoughts and positive motivations were behind it.

"Chai chai … garma garam chai," he announced. "Jassi dada, you need not collect these anymore. You can safely have the tea and discard the cups. I shall give you truckloads of these before you go back to Mumbai."

Captain Talukadar was out on the deck, walking around at the stern end, and Bhombol was at the wheel on the bridge. Rahul came out first from the cabin carrying his tea, sipping it slowly.

"Hi, Captain, … did you finish the entire bottle last night?" Rahul had to bark out as strong gusts of wind swamped his voice. When the captain heard him at last he turned around and smiled.

"Well, you see," he spoke rather listlessly. "I always leave a few drops for Bhombol. My second mate does not want to drink in my presence."

The captain seemed strangely preoccupied, and Rahul wanted to find out the reason. "You … I mean … ah … you don't look comfortable … What's wrong?"

Before the captain could answer Bhombol came growling from inside the bridge.

"Captain, we are ten minutes from anchoring."

The captain looked at Bhombol. "Get ready to anchor, and make this quick."

The captain was not his cheerful self. His face said it all. There were long dark bags under his eyes and his voice was hoarse, and it was apparent that he found it difficult to speak easily.

Rahul tried his best to make him feel at ease.

"Captain, … is there something wrong?"

Captain Talukdar's eyes were moist. He swallowed a lump in his throat, and a shimmering crystalline drop of water formed and glistened at the corner of his right eye and began traveling down his cheeks. Rahul had to look carefully at the captain's face to discern that it was a teardrop. He could not believe that a man of his stature would need to cry. However, what surprised him more was the red blob that formed at the mouth of his right nostril.

Rahul took no time to decipher the urgency; both his parents were doctors. The captain was not only crying, he was bleeding from his nose as well. It was an emergency. The captain seemed to falter and then he buckled, all of a sudden. Had it not been for Rahul's superb reflexes, the captain would have crashed on the deck. He grabbed the captain's body with both his hands and put him down slowly on the floor.

"Paro, … these kids … but …," he managed to utter.

"Bhombol run ... get me a pair of scissors and a stretcher." Rahul had learnt the finer points of delivering first aid at a camp. Even at home he regularly gave injections and was also adept at checking pressure.

The captain was already frothing in the mouth. Rahul took out his handkerchief and dried his lips. Bhombol came in with a pair of scissors, and the others followed with the stretcher. Rahul quickly cut out the corners of the captain's shirt and the collar to free his hand. He motioned others to stay quiet, and sprinkled the captain's face with some water. The captain was unconscious, his eyes were blood red, and the veins near the temple had tightened and gorged.

The friends lifted the captain's body on the stretcher and carried him inside the cabin with some difficulty, bending low enough to get in. Rahul signalled for all the windows to be opened for ventilation. They lay the captain down on the bed, and the window over his head was also partly opened. Keya, meanwhile, stepped out to call her Paro mashi.

Rahul first felt inside the captain's mouth with a finger to see if there was anything blocking the windpipe and removed some paan that the captain had been chewing. He then placed the palm of his hand flat on the patient's chest, right over the lower part of the sternum and pressed it gently, at first in a pumping motion, once or twice, by using the other hand. When the captain still did not breathe, Rahul rose to take the next step.

"Who among you saw what I did with the captain's chest? Come on, hurry up!"

Imran raised his fingers, hesitatingly.

"All right, superb Imran. You carry on pressing down the captain's chest as I did, while I help him breathe."

While Imran took over pressing down the captain's chest, Rahul tilted the head back and lifted up the chin, all the time keeping an eye on Imran and what he did. He then pinched the nostrils shut with two fingers to prevent leakage of air. He took a deep breath and sealed his own mouth over the captain's. He breathed slowly into the captain's mouth for a few seconds, and everybody in the room could see the captain's chest inflate with air.

Parvati was woken up with the shrill sound of the land line.

"Hello!" Keya tried her best to remain as calm as possible, but her voice still gave away her anxiety.

"Keya, what's the matter? Tell me, is something wrong ...?"

"Mashi ... mashi ... Can you hear me?" Keya stammered.

A phone call at such an unearthly hour created panic in Parvati's mind.

"Tell me, is everything okay?" she asked nervously.

Keya was compelled to tell mashi the truth. Parvati tried to regain her composure and after disconnecting Keya's call frantically reached out to her brother-in-law. "Dada, we need a helicopter ... to evacuate your brother in Kakdwip."

Roughly around this time, the Titanic touched the shore with the ambulance waiting right at the mouth of the river. Quick phone calls to the local medical centre had ensured it arrived on time. Rahul and his other friends immediately carried the captain's body on a stretcher. He was awake and tried to put on a smile. Keya ran by its side, lightly grasping her uncle's hand.

The mobile phones had all of a sudden got a life of their own. They went abuzz. All and sundry, in Mumbai, had come to know that the five friends had reached Kakdwip and that they would have been on their way to see the tiger in the Sunderbans, but for the fact that the captain had had a heart attack.

The adventure had begun, but on a rather grim note!

6 The Coup at the Hospital

The army, navy and the airforce of the country is as much for defence as for humanitarian services. They provide aid to civil administration in times of emergency. Parvati considered Captain Talukdar nothing less than a national treasure and had requested her brother-in-law, a Commandant with the Coast Guard, to try and arrange for a helicopter to evacuate her husband. She would have flown in the chopper herself to fetch him, but unfortunately that was not allowed. She had to wait with her heart in her mouth till she could arrange some other means to reach him.

"We are not going anywhere till you recover completely." Keya's assuring words brought a smile to the captain's face. His right shoulder was still stinging, and the pain left him numb.

The ambulance ride was eventless. Even without a red beacon overhead, it arrived at the hospital in around ten minutes.

The condition at the district hospital, at Kakdwip, was not exactly exemplary. First, at this time of the day (6:00 am in the morning) nobody, not even the sweepers were in sight.

"From looks of this hospital it is beyond any doubt that it can turn a perfectly healthy human being sick, within minutes," Hazel seemed clearly uncomfortable and had passed her judgement. She looked at the numerous puddles of water here and there—an excellent breeding ground for mosquitoes—and sighed in disbelief. The walls had paan stains, and the few errand boys on duty seemed busy, smoking behind the main gate, hunched under the car shed. Despite the filth and the daunting conditions, numerous patients poured in. Lack of beds meant the sick were sprawled all over the floor.

A police jeep raced into the compound and screeched to a halt at the main entrance, leaving its engine to drone on. Two men in uniform calmly pulled out a body wrapped in a bedsheet from the rear. A baton-wielding police officer sitting at the front called out to one of the ward boys. Keeping his face covered with a kerchief to avoid the stench, he had a quick tête-à-tête with the boy and then signalled the driver to move on. Just as it whizzed out, an elderly woman came howling and started running towards the body, which the attendants were now preparing to move to the morgue.

"What do you want?"Mou, the nurse on duty, asked the friends nonchalantly.

"Well, to begin with, we need a doctor!" Imran said impatiently.

"You see the doctor on duty might be still in his room." Mou responded casually as she read the newspaper.

"All right guys ... enough is enough. If we cannot find any doctor, we shall operate on the captain ourselves. Keya's voice cut in like a military man on a mission.

Rahul did not believe what he heard and looked at her curiously. Keya winked; it made her look all the more beautiful, and Rahul got the clue. He blew her a kiss discreetly and got ready for action. The five friends played a quick round of Chinese whisper and reacted as if they had rehearsed this act countless times in the past. Rahul and Imran carried the captain's body very carefully and placed it below the lamp on the operation table and then the latter ran to the cupboard at the far corner of the room and took out surgical gloves and aprons. Rahul, standing at the head of the captain lying on the operation table, stretched out his right hand and spoke aloud.

"Scissors!"

Hazel and Jassi wrestled with the wires of the many machines that were lying idle on the tables nearby and somehow managed to get the monitor and some of the other appliances started.

Keya stood beside Rahul and lovingly patted the captain's forehead. "You shall be okay. I can hear the doctors coming," she said.

Mou had, meanwhile, jumped out of her seat like a bolt of lightning and run to the doctors' quarters.

"Five strangers are using the operation table. Come fast ... This is madness." She railed as she ran as fast as she could.

Normally, the staff quarters that housed all the doctors-on-duty remained noiseless, this time of the day. Everybody was either sleeping or inside the washrooms, slowly waking up to the day ahead. But today was different. Mou's message spread like wild fire and sent everyone into a tizzy—doctors, nurses, physicians, surgeons, all were rudely awakened by this unnecessary drama, threatening to cost them their jobs.

They came charging in from everywhere—from toilets, gardens, and canteens—running frantically towards the operation theatre. Everyone knew if the media came to know how complete strangers had invaded the operation theatre in the hospital because no doctors were available, the incident would snowball into something monumentally disastrous. The warden screamed as he ran and the rest followed like a cackling brood of lost ducklings.

Back in the operation theatre the captain was still unconscious and perspiring. The naked shimmering blade of the scalpel caught the light of the lamp and shone brilliantly between Imran's thumb and forefinger. It had started to descend when the chief medical officer, health (CMOH), burst into the room with two other doctors.

"Stop this nonsense. Who are you, and what do you think you are doing. Move away ... move at once I say, and let us see what the matter is."

Imran dropped the scalpel, fell to his knees on the ground, folded his hands and pleaded, "Please save our uncle. He has a cardiac complication, but there is nobody here to treat him... please save our captain."

"I request you to please vacate the room and let us work." The CMOH seemed to take charge now.

The friends left the room without further ado, but waited impatiently, pacing outside, in the corridor. Keya burst into sobs when she looked at the door of the operation theatre.

"Don't worry, everything will be alright," Rahul went and kept a comforting hand on her shoulders.

"What's happening inside?" A nurse came up and spoke aloud.

"Dear lady, our uncle has had a heart attack, and so your CMOH is cutting a birthday cake." Imran seemed to have lost his cool.

The nurse took a brief moment to comprehend the connection between a cake and a heart attack and then recognising the jibe walked away in a huff.

After an excruciating wait of another twenty long minutes, the doors of the operation theatre opened again and out walked the CMOH followed by two other doctors.

"The patient is out of danger. You can see him once he is shifted to the main ward." The CMOH took a brief pause, looked at the friends and asked "By the way, who administered the first aid?" he sounded serious.

"I did sir … both my parents are doctors so …." Rahul owned up.

"Excellent! If it wasn't for the timely aid, the patient could have been in trouble."

The sombre atmosphere lightened, and the CMOH explained the captain's situation.

"Captain Talukdar experienced what we call in medical terms as cardiac arrhythmia. Although most arrhythmias are harmless, some can be fatal. During an arrhythmia, the heart may be incapable of supplying sufficient amount of blood to the brain and other organs, leading to greater damage. The captain's situation was slightly serious, so we have treated him with a jolt of electricity in the form of cardioversion or defibrillation. He will be fine, but he would need to be under observation for a few days."

There was a collective sigh of relief. The CMOH shook hands with the friends and went back into another ward, and the friends started walking to the main ward where the captain had been shifted.

The main hospital ward, which housed all the patients, was enveloped in a surprising pall of gloom. An uncanny calm presided over the residential section, which was distinctly different from the cacophony and instinctive activity at the emergency area. There was a smell of imminent death here that sank under your skin. The captain lay in a single bed, in the middle of the main ward.

"Bhombol, we may have to forget the whiskey on the rocks for some time." The captain had regained consciousness and was talking softly to Bhombol.

The CMOH who had treated the captain walked in to check with the patient.

"Sir, you have been very lucky to survive this time. Do not even think about the bottle. You survived because the first aid administered to you was both perfect and prompt."

"Doctor ... when can he be released?" Keya asked the all-important question.

"Well, there are a number of tests due, so we shall have to keep him with us for a couple of days."

The captain heard what the CMOH said and turned away towards the window, crestfallen. He did not want to stay at the hospital.

Outside in the garden, the friends suddenly caught a glimpse of Parvati boudi, sprinting towards the building. She breezed in through the gate of the main ward and came screaming to the captain's side. She had used all her resources and contacts to get to her husband's side.

"How many times did I warn you to keep the bottle away? Oh my god! Hero, look at yourself. You look ashen. Come on, let's go home from this death hole, and you shall be fit and running in a few days ... Where are all the doctors? Who is in charge here?" Parvati wanted to know everything at once.

In the next few hours, Parvati turned everything upside down at the hospital, and at the end of it all her effort paid dividends. The five friends did as instructed by Parvati and took up the brooms.

The sight of five young people sweeping the floors surprised everyone at first, but doing good and seeing good being done is extremely contagious. Soon Parvati's charisma and personality compelled everyone to join in the cleanliness drive. The entire hospital staff became more alert and alive to the wave of change.

That day, it was proved that all it needed was a strong will to change things around. Around 10 am that day, there was no queue at the main emergency window. All patients were being either treated and checked, or told to come later; only the more serious were being admitted. What went on that day at the general hospital was nothing short of magic and cannot be explained in a few words.

It was finally time for the friends to leave.

"Captain, how can we go on a holiday when you are unwell?" Rahul asked, his voice crackling, full of emotion.

"Look my friends I will try and join you in the jungle if my health permits, but you cannot stay back with the old man here. What you all have done to the hospital proves that you are destined for bigger things in life. Rejoice and fly. The jungle awaits you with all its mystery … go and seek it my friends and befriend the tiger. It needs your help."

There was sadness in the captain's voice, but his eyes were joyful. He knew that his newfound friends were learning. Learning about life. Parvati started shedding copious tears and the entire hospital staff congregated to be part of the farewell party when the friends finally decided to leave.

7 Vande Mataram

The bus service all over rural India is intermittent and few and far between. In the Sunderbans, however, both the words *bus* and *service* have acquired a different meaning. The tottering rattle trap that moves on four wheels looks like a bus, but there is hardly any service. There were two such metallic jangling containers that operated between Bakkhali—one of the first villages of the region and a popular tourist spot—and Namkhana, on the fringes of the Sunderbans that had a visibly different terrain, its air salty due to its proximity to the sea.

Bhombol took charge of the situation as soon as he spied the so-called bus at a distance. "We have to get up real fast and grab our seats. Otherwise, it's going to be a long, standing journey," he warned everyone.

Hazel did not understand the reason for such a hurry as there were only four or five people waiting on the road below the pole, which had an arrow pointing down the road with "Sunderbans" written on a tin board, below it. A picture of something that vaguely resembled a malnutritioned tiger, adorned the board. That was all that was to the bus stop.

Bhombol pointed towards the far distance and asked a question. "Do you see that? Please, do what I say, or else you will not get a place to sit when you go inside."

The friends followed the movement of his hand and tried to catch a glimpse of a bus, but it was clear from their expression that they had not spotted anything significant.

"What you will soon see is what a bus looks like in these parts of the country. You know what overcrowded trains are like in Mumbai; now experience this."

All of a sudden as the distant rumbling noise of a moving vehicle became audible, an exodus of people emerged out of thin air. Men and women came streaming towards the pole from anywhere and everywhere, from secret hibernation. It was clearly unnerving for the friends. Their jaws dropped as they looked at the bus that was already quite full and came down the road quivering and trembling like an epileptic patient.

The swamping crowd had a nervous energy about it, which became palpably intense as the bus neared the pole. Like molecules in a chemical reaction, it bubbled and frothed, and then, at the very moment, when the bus finally pulled at its brakes, all hell broke loose. Deranged and maniacal men and women, started jostling, shoving, prodding and poking, either to get in or out. This exercise was not restricted to the two-legged variety; several four-legged ones who were being taken to the local market to be sold or slaughtered, added to the chaos.

Bhombol was, however, a champion at this. In a swift move he first jumped and held the railing that led to the carriage on top. "Pass me all the bags … fast," Bhombol shouted at the top of his voice. He tossed the bags, one after another with such consummate ease that it was clear Bhombol was an old hat at this. Rahul and his friends held on to their musical instruments; those could not be thrown about. Meanwhile, Bhombol attended to the cry of a small child.

"Dada … dada, please put me up there too."

Bhombol picked up the child and made him sit down among the bags on the bus's roof.

Once their luggage was safely tied to the carriage on top, the friends prepared themselves for the next battle. They clambered with the rest of the crowd to get a place inside the bus. Jassi was the first to squeeze in through the door, which enraged an old man who could not match up to his acrobatics. He started pulling at Jassi's shirt demanding an explanation.

Bhombol became the mediator, "Dada, cheleta kicchu janena … This boy is ignorant. They are from Mumbai and don't know the rules here."

Bhombol's words distracted the attention of the old man, and Jassi slipped past saying, "Sorry uncle," sneaking in to take a coveted window seat.

The other friends also shot into the bus like bullets from a gun. Rahul, Keya, Hazel, and Imran all bulldozed their way in and, amidst all the confusion, sat on top of each other on the same seats. There was no time now. Other passengers started bolting in, and in seconds there was not a single vacant seat left. But that was not the end of the harrowing drama.

"Dada, ektu side din to … Kindly shift a little." An old man pleaded with Rahul and abruptly collapsed beside him on the seat even before Rahul had moved.

The five friends were quite accustomed to travelling by local trains in Mumbai, which required ferocious stamina as well. But they had not witnessed anything like this before. Here you were allowed to do anything to grab a seat—butt head, punch, kick claw, or even tickle your way through—nobody seemed to mind. Everyone had a field day.

What made it bearable was that these actions of extreme brutality were interspersed with supreme acts of kindness as well. An old man stepped down from the steps of the bus to allow an old lady to climb up. Both smiled and became instant friends. The man was possibly flirting, but it was all in good humour. However, when it came to grabbing a seat, no finer feelings could overpower that single minded focus. Friendships were soon replaced with bickering.

Rahul felt a tickle between his legs, but he could hardly move as there was no space. Jassi who was sitting opposite him started laughing.

"A goat. There is a goat between your legs," Jassi pointed at Rahul, who let out an involuntary yelp, looking down between his legs and scared the kid back, beneath the seat, where it was struggling to curl up and sit.

Surprisingly, the driver and the conductor did not seem to be affected by the ongoing tussle on board. Within minutes, the former switched on the ignition, and the latter rang the bell twice to signal it was time for the bus to leave. Looking back behind his shoulder, he garbled out something that nobody understood, and the bus trundled on to its destination, once more. With half his body dangling outside the bus the conductor looked like a trapeze artist, calling out to all the people he could see, running alongside the bus, to join in the circus.

A woman seated in the middle of the bus, suddenly, gave out a loud wail, "Stop the bus at once. My husband is still running." She peeped outside the window and fiercely gesticulated to a man who was running through the paddy fields holding a bundle under his arms.

"Are taratari esho, bacchha hoe gyalo to … Hurry, else the baby will come out."

The bus service in rural Bengal is privately owned and the conductors get a commission on the number of tickets they punch, on each trip. Hence, conductors want to carry as many people as possible with total disregard to timings, passenger discomfort and safety.

The bus stopped again and Bhombol explained to Hazel the paediatric gravity of the situation. "That woman's husband is still running behind the bus, and they have to attend the delivery of their daughter-in-law. So the lady on the bus is urging her husband to run faster, so that they arrive before the baby arrives."

Hazel did not know whether to laugh or cry. She was relieved to see the flustered and perspiring husband catchup with the bus that had slowed down for him. He barely managed to secure his toe on the footboard, when the bus moved ahead.

If one looked at the moving bus from behind, one would have burst a blood vessel. It had a severe tilt on one side, towards the door where people hung holding on to a single rod. This excess weight was fortunately balanced on the other side, which had all sorts of paraphernalia hanging from windows—holdalls, tin cans, mud pots, cattle fodder, name it. Even newborn babies would have been accommodated, slung in gamchhas probably, had there been a brave enough mother to allow that.

Inside the bus, young ones stuck between the armpits of passengers, stacked together like sardines, gasped for breath. A stench of raw fish from an aluminium container wafted in to make it worse. Jassi noticed the man sitting beside the container and constantly slapping the water with his palms, to keep it in motion. Keya knew why this was being done and looked at Hazel's enquiring eyes and clarified.

"The fishlings need a constant supply of oxygen, else they will die and float on the surface. The man slaps the water to keep a constant supply of oxygen in the water. They are taking the fishlings to the fields to be released into the ponds. This is for fish cultivation."

She requested the man sitting beside the round utensil to show them what was inside. The man stopped slapping the water for a second and brought out his fist from the utensil and opened his fingers with the cup of his palm pointing up towards the friends. Hazel saw his hand teeming with tiny fish called charaa pona, jumping and swimming in the palmful of water.

"Our Captain Talukdar had a fishery that did not survive. Mother tells me that the Sunderbans are full of these fisheries." Keya informed Hazel.

The man put the tiny fishes back into the utensil and resumed slapping the water.

Rahul was convinced that the crying children would die that day in the bus. Hazel expressed the desire to carry a little one in her arms, but when the mother handed her the child, wrapped from head to toe in a handmade quilt, it started crying even louder. Hazel promptly handed it back.

"She doesn't like me." Hazel explained.

Bhombol had settled on the top of the engine cowling, beside the driver. Albeit uncomfortable because of the heat it generated, it ensured fewer people crammed in that area.

"Phot Jol … du taka … Phot jol … du taka … Phot water ₹2 … Phot water, ₹2," a vendor screamed at the top of his voice. Unable to make any elbow space through the crowd, he was the only one who had reconciled to sitting beside Bhombol, selling drinking water.

"Is it safe to have one of these to drink?" Imran asked looking thirstily

"Dada, ekta kholoto … Open one for me." Bhombol requested the water-seller. He opened one of the bottles making a *phot* sound, and that immediately explained the etymology of the word. Bhombol gulped down half the bottle that he got and handed it back to Imran.

Imran cautiously touched the tip of the bottle to his lips and then finished it all in one gulp. "It's quite nice actually though it's a bit salty. I'm sure you can't get sewage water in Mumbai for ₹2. First we had tea on the riverbank for ₹1 and now the water. It defies economic logic. In Mumbai, you won't get ten peanuts for the same amount! Are we travelling in the same country?"

The water-seller wondered what the discussion was all about as he desperately struggled to keep his balance thrusting out his hand to retrieve the bottle from Imran. The lurching movement of the bus did not help matters at all, and more babies began to cry.

A sudden drizzle produced a cool draught of air, but soon the rains got heavier and the windows had to be pulled down. After a breath of fresh air, it became more than suffocating inside the bus. In the midst of all the sighs and gasps and groans, a male voice rang out. It was a full-throated shriek that cut through the crowd from the back of the bus.

It rose above all the clamour, and drowning every discordant note, melded into the most mellifluous melody. Slowly but surely, every one fell silent and started enjoying the soothing tempo. Someone was singing in the bus! The words were totally alien to the friends. The other passengers inside the bus started passing coins from hand to hand, for it to reach the singer at the back. It was a mendicant baul who earned his daily living by singing.

Akbar Bidaye de ma, ghure ashi …
Bid me farewell mother, I will be back soon …

He was a young boy about eighteen years old who looked quite gritty, even though cheerful with a carefree attitude. The boy stopped to catch his breath, cried out "Vande Mataram" and started once again.

He was singing with an instrument called the ektara, which had only one string. The round dome at the bottom, fabricated from a bottle gourd, had two words written in Bengali: Amaar Desh (My Country).

This was the first time that the friends had an encounter with music on this tour, and so they were enthralled.

Rahul got up from his seat and started moving towards the back of the bus. A woman sat down on the seat he vacated, immediately, and flashed him a smile acknowledging his kindness. Bhombol anticipated something and got up too. He wrestled his way through the heads and shoulders, creating groans and yelps among the people and tugged at Rahul's shirt.

"Dada, what is it?" Bhombol was eager to know.

"That boy has a brilliant voice. I want to find out who he is."

"Dada … he is a mendicant, and you will find many such baul singers here in the countryside. Go back to your seat as people will start getting off now." Bhombol found Rahul's interest in the boy surprising.

No sooner had he said this, the bus engine backfired a few times, seemed to lose speed, kick-started again, and finally stopped by the side of a market, and passengers started getting down—essentially the villagers who had come to sell their wares.

"You see this is the market that the villagers come to buy and sell their fish. You can buy fabulous fish here." Bhombol explained, pointing at a group of foreigners, buying king-size crabs at the road-side stalls.

Hanshi hanshi porbo phanshi, dekhbe bharot bashi
Ekbar biday de ma, ghure ashi …
(I shall embrace the gallows with a smile, and all Indians shall witness it. Bid me farewell mother, I will be back soon …)

The song continued ...

All the friends had, by then, edged towards the boy at the back of the bus and taken seats around him. The boy's voice and the sound of his instrument had galvanised them and drawn them to him like a magnet. The boy gripped the neck just above the gourd resonator and plucked the string with the index finger of the same hand. With the other hand he strummed the string like a guitar, to produce enthralling notes. He took a breath paused and spoke in broken English that he must have picked up while interacting with the foreigners who frequented the Sunderbans.

"I sing Khudiram Bose song ... he gibh life for country ... young boy Khudiram Bose ... he want to kill British, but falsely kill other and he hang ... but he smile when he hang ... he also sing this song when he hang ... today whole free India sing this song ...."

Jassi had heard of Khudiram Bose and read about him in school. Bhombol waited till the song was over to tell Hazel more about him.

"This song nobody know bhere it is ... nobody know who write ... nobody know who phirst singer ... but in history this become Khudiram Bose song." The boy started singing again.

The boy managed to convey the story in his half-baked English. The song indeed was shrouded in mystery and had come to be attributed to Khudiram Bose the young martyr. It is also believed that Khudiram Bose had walked up the gallows with a smile and this song on his lips.

Koler boma tuire ḳore dariye chilem rastar dhare ma-go
Boro lat ḳe marte giye marlam areḳ englond bashi
Eḳbar biday de ma ghure ashi
(I prepared a bomb on my own and was waiting by the roadside
O mother. I wanted to kill the magistrate but killed another

Englishman by mistake. Bid me farewell Mother; I shall be back.)
Haate jodi thakto chhora, tor khudi ki porto dhora?
Rokto-mangshe ek koritam, dekhto jogotbashi.
(Would I have been caught if I had a dagger?
I would have slashed myself to death, and the world would have seen it.
Bid me farewell mother I need to go.)

The song mesmerised the friends. They brought out their own instruments and started tuning them. Jassi had been stroking on a metal tiffin box that he gathered from a vacant seat to set the beat, but when he found Rahul tuning his guitar, he dashed to the front of the bus and got his congo. It was easiest for Keya to join in. She had her flute ready and waited for an interlude. When the boy stopped to catch his breath and started strumming his ektara, she touched her flute to her lips and played a melody that blended in beautifully with what the boy was playing.

The boy was taken off guard for a second, but he accommodated Keya's melody into the music piece by playing his instrument a little softly. Music is such a leveller. It not only enriches the mind, but also broadens the horizons to accept others. The boy played second fiddle to Keya's flute for a few minutes and then took off.

Rahul joined in with his guitar and a musical jugalbandi started inside the bus which filled the air with magic. Hazel obviously could not join in as she was not carrying her keyboard, so she lent her voice. She started a westernised second-line vocal and it rang out as a part of the melody.

The baul boy held his instrument high above his head and strummed on it hard and Rahul provided accompaniment with his guitar lead. Everybody was improvising. Now Rahul lent his voice. It was the same tune, it was the same song, but he was singing a rock version of the baul number.

The Baul sang this song every day, but he never felt like this before. He almost felt feverish, he enjoyed it so much. When the song was over the boy once again screamed "Vande Mataram".

Keya's found it hard to control her emotions. She stood erect inside the bus feeling flushed. She was deeply affected by the song and echoed, "Vande Mataram". Her friends standing inside joined in one by one, "Vande Mataram".

A small child in the crowd copied their voice. "Vande Mataram", he squealed. Some passengers found this funny and made him repeat it after them, and each time their voices got louder. Men and women standing outside, buying fish or vegetables at the shops, turned around in surprise. Was it some election campaign, they wondered at first. When they realised it was a bus full of ordinary people like them saying "Vande Mataram" many endorsed gleefully rising their hands in the air, their fists clenched: "Vande Mataram, Vande Mataram".

The frenzy took little time to catch on and soon spread like a happy virus. The quiet boondocks had found a reason to celebrate. Rickshaw-wallahs, travelling with school children, stopped to see what was going on. One of them gave a toothy smile and said "Vande Mataram". The little children gurgling with joy, jumped in their seats and screamed aloud "Vande Mataram, Vande Mataram". There could not have been a bigger moment when just one word triggered so much patriotism in the hearts of the locals.

When the baul boy got ready to get off the bus, Hazel hurried to him and stopped him at the gate. She took out a five-hundred-rupee note and shoved it into his pocket.

"This is not money. This is my gratitude that I have met you. I name you Don!"

8 ABC Boudi

They were initially, modestly surprised and later, utterly shocked to see what a single one-rupee coin could fetch in this part of the country. For Hazel, especially, this was even more so, as she had only been exposed to the expensive lifestyle at the metros, during her stay in India.

"Hey, why are things so cheap here? Mumbai is like living in another world. Is this the same country?" She asked.

Bhombol, who was looking out of the window, turned around to answer. "You see, this is economics of scarcity. Things are cheaper here as people don't earn enough and can't afford to buy things that are expensive. In other parts of India, people can spend more as they earn more. So things are more expensive." Hazel was impressed with the explanation.

The rest of the bus journey was largely uneventful. A small child had started throwing up in the bus because of the jolts and jerks. Fortunately, there were not too many people travelling, most having got off at the market.

Hazel saw the innocent face of the sleeping child, resting her head on her mother's shoulders and wondered how lovely it would have been if one could remain a child forever. No responsibilities and no care in the world. The child did not even understand the many complications of life. The other friends were somewhat mute. They had been party to a momentous occasion of nationalism, and the word "Vande Mataram" still managed to give them a rush.

The bus let out a series of noises; its engine huffed and puffed a few times before it eventually stopped. The driver got off, looked under the bonnet and announced that there was some serious engine trouble that he could not fix.

This created some confusion inside the bus, and everyone started looking for alternatives to reach their destination. Only a mechanic could solve the problem, but the closest car garage was ten kilometers way. It was already quite dark.

A few passengers got off the bus and started walking. They lived in small villages on the way and were accustomed to such breakdowns. For the friends, however, that was not an option, at all, as the jetty was a good 25 kms way. They gathered from the conductor that the launch service operated only till 9 pm, so there was every chance they would miss the last boat if they were to wait any longer.

The next couple of hours were spent swatting huge blood-sucking mosquitoes that feasted fearlessly on them. A fire was lit behind the bus after some effort since the logs they collected were all moist due to the rain. A little petrol taken out of the tank was poured on the fire to ignite the logs, and soon they burst into a blaze.

The conductor and the driver took out bottles of coloured fluid, and from the look on their faces one could make out they were about to drink. When Imran smelled the liquid he made such a face that it seemed he would throw up.

"Dada, this thing is made from rice and smells real bad, but it is heavenly and is actually good for health." The conductor assured.

They waited by the side of the road, hovering around the fire, feeling hot and uncomfortable, but this was the only way that they could avoid the whirring mosquitoes. A truck was finally waved down by the conductor and the friends hitched a ride. An amount of ₹10, each, was not large by any standards in the night, for being rescued from the winged monsters.

It was pitch dark outside, and the pitter and patter of the rain on the truck's window was music to the ears. Forty-five minutes later the friends reached the edge of the water where they got off. It was a small creek that they needed to cross, to reach the other side. From there they had to travel further down and cross the river Hatania Doyania, to reach the jungle.

The district of the Sunderbans had actually started, but the area looked like a small town. That, however, did not interest the friends much. They wanted to enter the jungle. The small boat that took them to the other side of the creek swayed and bumped around even on the shallow waters so terrifyingly that an old man almost fell into the water.

From the talk of the other passengers on the boat they deciphered that the old man was a frequent traveller and this would happen to him regularly. The old man, they gathered, was a good actor who just feigned to lose his footing and fell over on purpose. He loved being made to sit in the middle of the boat, fastened at the elbows by men sitting around him. The world had so many captivating characters, churning out mundane pleasures, just to stay happy!

It was nearly 11 pm. On the other side of the creek, it was still raining heavily. A quick ride in the auto-rickshaw, also called a bhotbhoti sometimes, took them to the main jetty from where they would cross the Hatania Doyania. Jassi was keen to know why the vehicle was called bhotbhoti and figured it derived its name from the sound it made. He recollected the phot sound made by the bottles opened in the bus and immediately established the analogy. Later, he would learn that the boats on the river with engines out there were also called bhotbhotis.

"Ooh aap loog Bombaay shey haai? Aapko maalum haai Bombaay kaa pheelum industry mein shobshe boro boro maatha vaala log gulo shobkota Bangaali hai?!"

The driver's Hindi was heavily accented, but he insisted on using it. It was very amusing and everyone had to muffle their laughter when he spoke. The long vowels stretched every word to make them sound like a record being played at a slower speed.

He was obviously referring to the film industry of Mumbai and boasting about the fact that the celebrated brains of the industry were mostly Bengalis. The film industry of Mumbai had been indeed blessed with stalwarts who hailed from Bengal in the past. He also added that their chances of catching the last steamer were extremely slim and promptly revved the accelerator to race down the road.

The auto-rickshaw stopped on the road outside the jetty and they could see the shimmering water through the open gates. There was also a police chowki on the road that looked deserted. A stray dog ambled out of the chowki, disgruntled—probably, it had gone in to inspect the interiors and found no food and was all the more upset for not being able to report the matter to anyone.

The river looked bewitching with the rain falling on it. Light waves splashed along the banks, and the rain droplets created small ripples on the surface of the water making it look ethereal. Keya jumped off the rickshaw and ran up to the edge of the water, stalling for a second outside the police chowki. She felt it would not be really proper to be seen running around a police station. When she peeked and found it empty, she sprinted towards the jetty, holding out her hands beneath the pouring rain.

Rahul saw her from the auto-rickshaw and his heart skipped a beat. He had an irresistible urge to dash down and grasp her from behind. But he remembered he had promised himself to restrain his feelings during the tour. He would not allow himself to be carried away. At least, he was trying very hard. Rahul looked around and then called out to Keya, loud enough to be heard.

"Keya, I am told that the rivers in the Sunderbans have crocodiles. Be careful."

Keya immediately jumped back, a little disappointed. Bhombol and the others collected at the river's edge and were surprised to see no activity at the jetty.

"Why is nobody here? Let's ask the gatekeeper." Bhombol spoke aloud

The ticket window was half open, and the collector fast asleep inside. A drunkard sleeping outside the police chowki muttered in his drunken stupor.

"Shob bondo hoye gechhe ... It has closed for the night." The drunk got up and staggered on his feet.

"Ektu beshi kheye phelechi ... I have had one too many."

He looked towards the friends and asked, "Ki chaai ... What do you want? Dekhun bhai, ... aamra Bangali ... We are Bengalis ... We love our phish (fish), phood (food), phameely (family), phootball (football) ... aar ghum (and sleeping). Do not disturb us now. If you want the steamer, come back tomorrow."

It was obvious that the jetty service was shut for the today. The friends looked at the swelling river and gasped. The waves had grown in size as the tide was up now, and one had to speak aloud to be heard over the combined sound of the river and the rain.

"So, what do we do now? Spend the night on the road?" Imran sounded very concerned and serious.

The five friends got together and started thinking aloud when they saw a man approaching. The very sight of a man in the dark and in that desolate place sparked some hope in the minds of the friends and they moved towards him.

Kapil mama had aged prematurely. He was called "mama", or uncle, by one and all in the locality, even if they were not directly related to him. At 43, he already had bags under his eyes due to his frequent intake of country liquor.

Life had not been kind to him. The labour movement had robbed him of his earnings from the fields. But he was an educated man with a basic college degree. So when Ram babu, the local zamindar, expired six months ago, he volunteered to replace him as a tutor, earning just about enough to provide for his family.

Ram babu, had been a kind man who had a lot of land and a big house in the middle of the village. He had taken up the pastime of teaching the local children English in his sprawling house. The sound of more than a dozen children reciting the English alphabet, in chorus, could be heard from the road outside Ram babu's house every evening without fail. Thus, his wife had gained the sobriquet of ABC boudi.

Ram Babu was extremely dear to all the villagers, but his marriage to ABC boudi, a Bengali from Lucknow, had not gone down well with the locals. Several elders, who wanted their daughters to tie the knot with the handsome zamindar scion, felt spurned when he suddenly brought a wife from outside the village.

Unfortunately, adversity befell the family and its fortunes started dwindling soon after the wedding. A bad harvest for several successive years aggravated the situation, and the elders in the locality held ABC boudi responsible for everything. To top it, all Ram babu was diagnosed with tuberculosis. After Ram babu expired things got worse, and the locals were convinced that his marriage was the sole reason for all the bad luck.

Kapil mama was going past the jetty when he spotted some unknown faces around. It was a little strange to have five strangers loitering around at the jetty at that hour, and so he had decided to investigate

"Dada, is there a hotel where we can stay for the night? We have missed the last steamer and don't have a place to stay." Bhombol walked up and started a conversation in Bengali.

Kapil mama was still reeling from what he had heard at the clandestine meeting at the football ground. The scheming villagers and the local goons, in tandem, were planning to eliminate ABC boudi, spreading the news that she was evil and had to be therefore thrown out of the community. The villagers were obviously doing all this with an eye on Ram babu's property as his wife was the only beneficiary. The local off-shoot of the Aamra Bengali (We Bengalis) group had decided to raid ABC boudi's house that night. Kapil mama had not been able to openly disagree with the group without endangering his life. He figured a better option would be to somehow provide protection for ABC boudi.

Looking at the five smart young people, Kapil mama had an instant idea. They were godsent. If he could somehow get the youngsters to spend that night at that house, a dangerous incident could be averted.

"There is no hotel here, but I know the lady of a big house, down the road. You could get some space there tonight. Come with me, and I shall see what I can do."

After squelching through the mud and the water in the fields, for nearly fifteen minutes, they finally had a glimpse of the building through the trees. The moon was shining behind the house casting a halo on top of the roof, and the shonajhuri branches looked like strings of silver. The building stood like an ageing courtesan—faded, wrinkled, abused, and world-weary—having to stand the test of time and survive.

Kapil mama led the way. When he reached the house, he made a queer sound that woke up the watchman.

"Shalal shuorer bachha … ke dake … Son of a swine, who calls? What is it? Who calls me at this hour?"

Kapil mama was a well-known man, and the sight of him comforted the old man.

"It's me, Kapil mama … These youngsters have missed their last steamer and don't have a place to stay. If boudi kindly allows them to stay in a corner of the house for the night …."

Kapil mama stopped at the sight of a woman who appeared in the portico of the house, behind the watchman. She looked at them through the railings, wearing a white sari and holding a lantern that lit up her jaws and neckline wonderfully. She had long hair that reached her knees. The friends could make out that she was a beauty. The moonlight reflecting on her made her look like a fairy, standing at the gate.

A German Shepherd growled at her feet. The watchman trudged back to the portico and whispered a request to the woman. They had a short conversation in the dark. The woman darted a look at the youngsters and pointed behind the house with her right hand. Then she walked back into the house. The brisk strides of the watchman to the front gate was enough for the youngsters to guess that she had consented to the proposal. The gates were left ajar, for them to enter. Kapil mama also decided to stay the night with them.

The room that they had been allotted to retire was on the first floor. It had a single sofa, a bed with no mattress and lots of firewood. The wooden planks on the bed had been cushioned with folded bedsheets instead. They were also provided mosquito nets by the watchman without which there could be no sleep.

There was a clear view of the confluence of the two rivers, Hatania and Doyania, from the balcony, and it looked calm and serene with the rain having stopped. Kapil mama explained why the river had that peculiar name. Keya walked to the edge of the balcony and took in the beauty of the place. Hazel and Bhombol joined her.

Imran, Rahul, and Jassi jammed on their instruments, for a while, trying to play the *Akbaar Bidaye* melody that was still ringing in their ears when then they heard a different tune—a melodious female voice sounding sweeter than ever—wafting out from the dark tapestry of beauty and silence all around. Each word was being pronounced meticulously; they had a gravity of their own, and were in pure Urdu. It was Dr Iqbal's famous Urdu poem, they had all heard before.

Lab pe aati hai dua ban ke tamanna meri
Zindagi shamma ki surat ho, khudaya meri
Lab pe aati hai dua ban ke tamanna meri
(My desires come to my lips as prayers,
My life will be like the face of fire O lord)

Rahul waited for a few seconds and then moved towards the door. He had to find out who was singing in Urdu, in the jungles of Bengal. Almost as if on cue, Imran, and Jassi followed Rahul outside the door after throwing a cursory look at the girls who had snuggled into the sofa, and Bhombol who sat chatting with Kapil mama.

Just at that moment the German Shepherd started barking furiously from below the house. The howling stopped abruptly followed by what seemed like a yelp of pain as if it had been silenced by a desperate blow. The three friends stopped dead in their tracks on the balcony and wondered which way to go; the singing had also stopped.

"Ramu … Go and see what the sound is," It seemed like an order from the lady of the house.

Jassi put a finger to his lips to signal silence, and then all three moved towards the door from where the wafting sound of the song arose again. They reached the door and thought of knocking on it, but better sense prevailed. There was a long log of wood lying on the floor. Jassi signalled to help him put it up, perpendicular to the ground. Rahul walked forward knowing exactly what to do.

He put the tip of his toe in the middle of the log where there was a notch in the bark, to gain a footing, and then garnered his body upwards to lift himself up. He could barely stand on it but had a clear view through the ventilator. Jassi and Imran waited impatiently holding on to the log, balancing it upright from below.

The woman who was singing looked resplendent under the moonlight. Sitting on the windowsill she was looking out at the beautiful shonajhuri trees outside the window.

A sudden shrill ringtone, from Jassi's mobile phone, shattered the silence all around. As he fumbled trying to locate his phone in his pocket, the log wobbled under Rahul's weight and he came crashing down to the ground.

The large thudding sound silenced the singer. Immediately, the door swung open and there she stood looking down at them. Her expression said it all. There was a mixture of helplessness and anger on her face that made her look even more beautiful.

"Madam, … you sing so well … but in Urdu … we were curious … so we …?" Jassi stammered in shame. Jassi's mobile was still ringing inside his pocket.

"Answer your phone first." She said calmly and then turned around to walk back into her room. But a sudden clinking noise stopped her in her track.

It sounded like glass cracking, and it was right outside the window. The window was made of wood, but there was a glass flower vase that was standing on the windowsill, and a stone seemed to have struck it, shattering it to pieces. A few glass shards scattered on the doorway and Rahul picked up a small piece.

All of a sudden, everything turned chaotic. A fusillade of stones hit all the other windows and the metal railing of the balconies. ABC boudi ran back inside the room, but could not close the windows as pebbles and stones came crashing through them into the room. Imran, Rahul and Jassi ran inside and somehow closed the windows, stretching their bodies flat against the walls to ensure they did not come in the way of the flying objects. ABC boudi collapsed on her bed perspiring.

"They have attacked the house. They would never have dared to do it, if he were alive."

She started sobbing like a child and fell back on the bed when voices rang out from the garden outside.

"She is a witch. She has killed our babu. Kill her … let's put the house on fire."

More than a dozen voices were speaking in unison now, fuelling a tumult. They caught the voice of the watchman screaming, trying to stop the men. But he too seemed to have been silenced. His groan was a signal to what was to follow. Jassi pressed his eyes to the hole in the window and saw that the watchman had been felled with the blow of a scythe. The man who hit him was climbing the pipe of the building now.

"There is a man climbing up the pipe." Jassi sounded desperate.

"Don't just watch … stop him." Rahul ordered.

Jassi hurried to the balcony and counted the potted plants. He did not quite finish counting when he found one, small enough to be lifted up, but heavy enough to hurt, if thrown across. It was a foot-high pot with a tulsi plant sprouting from it. He picked it up and carried it to the edge of the balcony from where he peered down.

The man who had been climbing was stretching his sinews, and from the look of his face it seemed he was in agony. The climb was painful, and his fingers scratched on the rusted pipe and loose rust fell off it. Jassi walked up to the edge of the balcony where the flooring ended and his stomach touched the iron parapet. He positioned himself perfectly above the head of the man climbing the pipe below. He looked down to be sure that he was positioned directly above the man climbing the pipe and closed his eyes. He waited for a few seconds and then opened his eyes only for a fraction of a second to confirm the angle of the drop. Then he loosened his hands and let the pot fall out.

The man climbing the pipe had looked up that very instant when the pot hit his temples, and broke to pieces. He had not expected this at all; he lost his grip on the pipe.

It was a twenty-meter fall, and when he hit the ground he must have broken his spine as he could not move after it. There was a painful groan that continued for a few seconds and then there was dead silence.

Jassi ran back into the room and nearly bumped into Rahul.

"I saw what you did from the window. The man must be dead ..., but there are others. You guys hold on to them for ten minutes and I shall be back." Rahul shouted as he ran down the stairs.

The commotion created by those outside, and the sound of the pot breaking to pieces, had woken up Keya and Hazel. They had seen houses attacked by dacoits and thieves only in movies, but this was happening right in front of them.

"Something is wrong … where are Rahul and the others? They are not in the room," Keya was worried.

Bhombol and Imran dashed in, just as startled. Jassi, who had gathered some courage because of the hit he had scored with the tulsi pot, came running towards them and announced that the house had been attacked.

"The villagers have attacked the house. Rahul has gone to call the police, but we shall need to hold on as long as possible." Jassi sounded remarkably calm under the circumstances.

Rahul, meanwhile, had spotted a cycle lying idle against a shonajhuri tree. It must have belonged to the watchman, but who really cared? He jumped on it and breezed towards the police chowki, near the jetty. They all saw Rahul cycle his way through the shonajhuri trees towards the gate.

Bhombol picked up a kerosene can that lay inside the room and shook it to find how much kerosene it had. When satisfied, he ripped the bedsheet and asked others to help him tear it into long strips.

"Quickly, let's make some fire torches, or mashals, out of these log strips here. We need plenty of them."

When they had a bunch of them ready, Bhombol poured kerosene over and threw a burning matchstick on them. Tongues of fire, immediately, shot up towards the ceiling. Jassi was handed the first bunch. Imran and Bhombol followed him. The girls worked at a frantic pace to make more mashals, tearing up the window curtain and winding the cloth pieces around the logs to help them burn easily. Kapil mama helped them.

Jassi ran out with the mashals in his hand to the balcony. He found other villagers converging over the body of the man who had fallen from the pipe. He raised the burning mashals and hurled them, one after another, towards the group below. They looked like scattering balls of fire.

Bhombol and Imran attacked from the other corners of the balcony. Some of the burning missiles landed on dry grass and set them to fire immediately. The villagers panicked.

"The witch is attacking us. Run ..." Someone screamed from the garden.

Jassi regrouped with Imran and Bhombol in the room, and the girls comforted the woman on the bed. She was weeping profusely, and her tears had formed little circles on the bedsheet.

"Why are they doing this?" Hazel demanded to know.

"Kinkori babu wanted my husband to marry his daughter. And after my wedding they held me responsible for all the bad luck in the family. The harvest was not good; thieves stole most of the honey, and finally, my husband died of tuberculosis. Now they have come to get me. You see, I was a Muslim from Lucknow before my marriage, but I changed my religion. The locals do not like me. They want to usurp the property and the shonajhuri trees that were planted by my husband. Its wood is expensive and is used for furniture."

She could have gone on and on and on. But tears choked her and she stopped talking.

"But they loved me before my husband's death. It's only after his death that they have started eyeing the property. They gave me the name ABC boudi because my husband taught English to all the children in the locality. He was from Presidency College, Kolkata." She spoke in a mixture of pure Urdu, punctuated with Bengali

She stopped to pause and looked around questiongly.

"Where is your friend who had climbed the log?" she asked.

9 Brother Lobo and Bhor

Rahul had tried to reach the police chowki as fast as was humanly possible. He cycled over fields and then ran a distance over a small embankment that was filled with water, carrying the cycle on his shoulders. Then he came across a wall. The detour would have taken a while. He decided to throw the cycle over the wall first and then climb over it himself. He did all this all in absolute earnest not knowing that it was easier finding the crooks than the police in this part of the world. It took him close to fifteen minutes to locate the men in uniform.

The superintendent had been absent for the previous two days, and the sub inspector was sleeping. On being woken up he murmured sleepily that the officer-in-charge that night had gone to ease himself. Rahul had no other option, but to wait for the man.

The stray dog that had made the police chowki its own was also dosing below the sub inspector's chair. The officer who had gone behind the trees came out wiping his fingers on his trousers five minutes later and took an agonisingly long time to settle down on his chair.

Rahul tried his best to explain the emergency, but language was a definite problem. So he used dumb charade. When all that did not work, he threw a stone and hit the door to prove what had happened at the house. Fortunately, this woke up the sub inspector who wanted to know why he had been woken up, so rudely. Only after the errand boy had served him his morning cuppa that he agreed to dress up and go to the house to investigate the problem.

On arrival, the battleground looked deserted as the fighters had already fled. The police subjected a few locals to a round of routine questions, after which they concluded that nothing was seriously wrong. Kapil mama had stood at a distance when the interrogation of the locals was going on. He could not help but speak when he saw ABC boudi at the door of the house.

"Sir, this is a serious issue. I am sure they were thieves or dacoits who were not locals, but now this house needs security."

The police found Kapil mama's point serious enough to start a manhunt in the area.

"Okay, we will do what is needed, but can you identify the attackers?" The question was asked so feebly that Kapil mama did not hear it, so did not answer.

"Will you identify the attackers, if we bring them before you?" Another from the panel roared.

"Well, it was too dark, and we were busy saving ourselves so we could not see their faces clearly." Kapil mama clarified.

"What do you expect us to do then? Go to the market and ask people who came and attacked the house last night? We are also human, not gods." It was the police officer who had spoken.

Kapil mama realised this inane banter would lead them nowhere. After a few more meaningless questions he got up to make tea for his guests in the kitchen.

A meeting with the Panchayat ended up in being a farce. The Panchayat members had other pressing matters to attend; the attack did not seem to merit any further discussion—a forgone conclusion. Kapil mama knew that it would come to a naught.

The meeting ended with the conclusion that possibly dacoits across the border had attacked the house. But why the attackers had not left with any booty was left unexplained. Their effort in saving the lonely lady were nevertheless hailed and praised.

It was time for the youngsters to take leave again. The friends were rather tired as they had been subjected to a roller-coaster ride since their arrival at the Howrah Station. They had come to see the tiger, but what they had witnessed, since their arrival, was far more significant—a little bit of a tiger in so many people, in all its ferocity as well as its valiance.

Keya had been taking pictures with her Canon, but had not had the time to transfer the data on her computer. The plethora of characters playing out in her mind formed a brilliant montage. She made it a point to transfer all the files on her hard disc once on board the steamer. She wondered how the pictures would look. Would they be as exciting on the computer as they were in real life?

As they stood at the jetty about to board the steamer, the friends shook hands and hugged Ramu, with whom they had spent an eventful night, careful not to touch his freshly bandaged shoulder. The farewell at the house had been tearful with Ramu crying the most. It was strange to see a middle-aged man cry so inconsolably even though he had not known the youngsters for more than a day. He had got extremely attached to them, for what they had done that night to save his madam.

News of the attack had reached the Zila Parishad and it had donated a paltry sum to the old man, to buy a new cycle. He needed a new one to work on the fields as Rahul had forgotten the cycle at the police chowki, and it could not be traced. The friends also gave the man ₹1,000, for his medication, which thrilled him to bits.

When they reached the jetty, they could see the mangroves on the other side and felt a mysterious shiver in their veins. Somewhere on the other side, deep in the jungle, behind the bushes there could be a tiger poised to leap. It was waiting to be explored, and they could not wait anymore.

However, the friends were all fatigued. Their minds felt numb and their bodies heavy. It would be a forty-minute ride, and they wanted to catch up on some sleep.

For the friends this was no ordinary sleep. It was a state of semi-consciousness when the body is tired and the mind rewinds. Their minds leapt back and forth between myriad visuals with snippets from the adventures they have just had revisiting them as dreams. There were characters who were immediately recognisable, and others who were just figments of their imagination, but in all they captured the excitement of their journey, so far.

Rahul saw impressions of Bhombol whistling from atop the garbage can, and later, flying in the air over the wooden bridge and landing on the deck of the Titanic. Imran heard the notes of the song *Akbaar bidaye,* and saw images of the baul boy and his ektara. Keya saw the smiling face of the captain, sipping his drink behind the wheel, and Hazel saw the smiling face of the child resting his head on his mother's shoulder's, in the bus, but that got readily erased by the imposing portrait of the Royal Bengal tiger on the wall and Prof. Bhaduri speaking on the dais in front of it.

The sequences at the hospital were stitched together into a fabulous montage of visuals all ending well. Then there were the balls of fire flying in the garden, and the attackers scampering for cover. These vignettes were not rudimentary. They had perhaps been scripted by the Lord Almighty for a climactic conclusion.

They were all cherishing this half-awakened, tiredness induced slumber when the shrill sound of the horn shrieked over the silent waters and woke them up. They realised, they were only ten minutes away from the landing on the far bank.

The coveted land—the Sunderbans—lay unfurled, ten minutes away from them. It stretched out in front like a green canvas that one wanted to reach out and touch. And somewhere within its bosom was the tiger, waiting to be discovered.

The sound of a child singing wafted in over the still waters of the river and soothed their senses. It sounded like a small girl singing. Rahul got up and ran out on the deck to look. It was the beautiful rendition of a Rabindra Sangeet

Jokhon porbe na mor paayer chinha eei baate
(When I make no more a footprint on this road)

Imran had his body half resting on Jassi's and the latter found it quite a task to get out from under him. He went out on to the deck and stood behind Rahul, and looked out into the river. A much smaller boat floated on the waters, about twenty meters from the bank. There was a little girl dancing on it.

Gradually as the boat neared the steamer, the singing voice became louder over the water. The girl was singing as she danced. Hazel had learnt a bit of Indian dance forms in school, and she immediately figured that the little girl was improvising her own style, doing whatever she wanted with her hands and feet, and that made her look strikingly beautiful.

The image of the dusky ten-year old, dancing and singing on the boat, became clearer as the boat cut through the mist. The stunning visual was only occasionally marred by the girl's sneezing bouts—the only aberration in a picture perfect canvas. It was apparent that she was suffering from a severe cold and a running nose.

There was also something else that was seriously striking about the image—the man rowing it was a handsome foreigner in his mid-thirties. Wearing a priest's cassock and a pair of faded blue jeans, he looked like a strong man with his shoulder muscles pumped up and bulging above his collar bone. The foreigner appeared very happy in the little girl's presence and continued to row slowly. There was an unmistakable sign of divine satisfaction on his face.

"Natuda, tell your guests that I have come to receive them from the bungalow ...." The man seemed to know the people on the steamer to whom he shouted out in English when he was within hearing distance.

The sound of English was like manna to the friends. The white man rowed the boat and closed in with the steamer and then encircled the steamer slowly. The little girl was now stooped beside the foreigner, busily gesticulating and asking questions, occasionally, pointing at the boat and the people on it.

As the steamer neared the banks the boat too glided in smoothly beside it and touched the shore. The foreigner waded through the knee-deep water to the shore and tethered the boat to a tree trunk on the bank and came back wading through the water to the steamer. The girl stayed on the boat.

"Hello, I am Brother Lobo." He extended his arms and shook their hands. "And my little friend out there is Bhor. She wanted to see the steamer from all sides, hence I had to go around. "Bhor" as you know means the morning. She comes to wake me up every morning. I live in the jungles with the villagers and play football with the kids here. Sushil da requested me to come and receive you. Here is some bread and some shingaras. You must be hungry."

Samosas or shingaras are potato filled delicious triangular snacks, extremely popular and widely sold all over India, albeit extremely calorie heavy.

Sushil da was distantly related to Keya's mother and looked after the small resort in the Sunderbans that she owned. Mrs Mukherjee had planned it all rather meticulously. She had kept in constant touch with Sushil da right from the time the youngsters left Mumbai and ensured that he be present when they arrived in the jungle. She had heard of a foreigner who stayed in the area and played football with the local children, but had not taken a serious note of it. She had assumed he was a hippie who had come to the east, disillusioned with life in the west. When Sushil da had explained that he was a Christian missionary and involved in community service, she wanted the friends to meet him.

As the Brother bent low over the water and helped the friends wade across, Imran noticed a deep gash on one of his collar bones. It was an old wound that had dried. Imran wanted to know what it was.

"You were badly hurt it seems, Brother?"

"I was caught, and they wanted to leave their mark on somebody, so they chose me." The Brother smiled as he pulled at Imran and helped him up on the bank.

"Who caught you?" Imran sounded really interested.

"Ah, it was in Afghanistan."

By now all the friends were safely up on the bank and were squelching through the mud, sinking to their ankles at every step as they proceeded to climb towards drier ground.

"You fought in Afghanistan? We must hear those stories from you in the night." Hazel was very excited.

"No, I don't talk about those days anymore. It brings back horrible memories. It takes me days to recover. I'd rather talk about the battle of my own resurrection. I escaped duties, fled to Europe and embraced the Church. And here, I am in tide country. I get immense solace hearing the songs that Bhor sings to me, and I try and serve the locals in my own small ways."

Keya who was walking behind caught up, carrying the weight of the mud, stuck to her feet.

"But do tell us more about Afghanistan and its people." Hazel added.

"It was in 2001, when the US launched Operation Enduring Freedom. I don't want to get into the details of global politics ... but those were hard times. Once, I was on a mission, which resulted in the barbaric slaughter of innocent men, women and children, used as human shields by the terrorists. I was personally responsible for killing many ... even women and little children. That incident left a mark on my mind, and I started having sleepless nights ....

"Then I heard about the plan of drone attacks and refused to be a part of it anymore. I escaped the barracks and went missing. I, Albert Lobo, desperately tried forgetting my name and sought another identity, trying to forget my past. Albert Lobo is dead for the world. I, am Brother Lobo now. I live the life of a common villager here, devoted to community service. I also play football with the kids and love listening to Bengali songs. Let's talk about something else now."

It was obvious that the man's past had several significant scars.

Lobo originally hailed from Ohio. When his fiancée married another man thinking that Lobo was dead there was nothing left for Lobo to look forward to in life. Lobo sought solace in spirituality. He sought a place where he could get lost amidst the multitude, work for the society and redeem himself.

"So what brought you to the Sunderbans?" Hazel asked.

The Brother suddenly sounded much more cheerful.

"I had heard and read about this place and studied about this area many years ago. I had already embraced the monastic path and decided to live as a celibate, looking for a peaceful place to hide. I had wandered aimlessly for a few months, and then the tides pulled me here. I learned to play football and now coach the local children and play with them. In fact, my team won the local competition this year, and they got a small grant from the state government for the development of the sport. The world has finally stopped looking for Albert, the soldier. I am happy living here as Brother Lobo, among the villagers."

The steamer's pilot had crept up behind the friends and had been following them.

"And Lobo bhai is eespechal phisherman on ribher here. He always catch big phish when we phail … He will tell many stories, how he catch big big fish."

"Yes, I love the rivers and the creeks here. But at times my nightmares return to haunt me in the nights. I hear voices of children dying, and I see the gore and the blood … I escape to the rivers then, to find peace. I have to be careful of the crocodiles though," the Brother chuckled and lightened the mood immediately.

"Bhor is Sushil da's talkative ten-year-old daughter. He looks after the estate owned by the Mukherjee family, and she travels with me on the boat, dances and sings. In her I have found an outlet for emotions that were buried within. She is my catharsis and helps me forget the days on the killing fields. The moments I spend with her, looking at her locks as she prances on my boat while I row, I live my life again. She carries panta bhaat, a lightly fermented leftover rice, soaked in water to prevent spoiling, with salt, onion and chili pickles, and we stop our boat in the middle of the river and feed each other under the awning of the boat. Her songs soothe my mind and the blood-soaked, snow-capped valleys of Afghanistan vanish from my memory. These serpentine rivulets of the tide country, replace them. She picks up all her songs from her dad while he works and hums in the fields, and I learn them from her."

For the friends, all this information from Lobo bahi was revealing. They hungrily devoured the shingaras and the bread as they listened. Their appetite seemed to have increased in the salubrious surroundings, and they seemed hungrier than ever. The steamer's driver seemed to know the Brother quite well.

"He is bhery bhery good man … and he play bhery bhery good phootball. He is our Brother—Lobo bhai. The bhillagers believe him." The man hugged Lobo bhai as he spoke.

When the youngsters climbed upon the bank, they saw the local leaders campaigning for the by-election. The villagers here, like everywhere else, were fed up with their gross negligence towards their issues and the absence of basic amenities of public life. This time they were campaigning, riding the crest of the green wave that had abolished the red party from the state.

A small group of local party workers were going past in a cycle-rickshaw announcing the date of the elections in the village and also asking the people to vote for them. Small children ran behind the rickshaw as it meandered between the trees and entered the lanes, deep into the village.

The election van disappeared behind the trees, and the friends sat down at the base of a huge banyan tree that had its roots deep in the earth, its many tentacles surrounding the riverbank. Despite the rain, the sun was shining brightly over their heads, and the friends sat in the shade of the banyan tree.

"Brother Lobo, ... Bhor seems to be suffering from a fever, and the rain will not be good for her. Why don't you give her this?" Rahul was particularly concerned about the health of the little girl. He took out an anti-allergy tablet from his hip pouch and gave it to him.

They had to wait for a auto-rickshaw to take them to their destination. The friends sprawled wherever they felt like, taking short breaks. Bhor had warmed up to the youngsters, by now. In fact, they could not keep up with her persistent queries about this, that and the other. After inspecting Hazel and Keya minutely and learning everything she possibly could about nail polishes, eye shadows and mascaras, she riveted her attention to Jassi's mane. She could not reason how and why somebody who looked like a man would wear such long hair. She was obviously seeing a Sikh man for the first time in her life and was indeed bemused.

"Is he a man or a woman, Lobo?" Bhor whispered softly into the Brother's ears as she somehow understood that this wasn't a question she could voice, indiscriminately, for everybody to hear. Keya, however, sitting right beside the Brother overheard the question and took responsibility of clarifying her doubt, after muffling her laughter. She cuddled the girl into her lap and tried to rid her mind of all her confusion regarding Jassi's gender.

Bhor, ... you need not fear this person. He is one of us. He just has long hair, like a woman, otherwise he is a man. And he can do a lot of wonderful things. Jassi why don't you play a nice rhythm for her on your congo." Jassi was quick to the task and produced an immediate percussion roll with his fingers on his congo and Bhor took instant interest.

She drummed her fingers on his congo, which started a mild rhythm hoping to create the same effect. A volley of questions ensued: "What is this? What is that? What is its use? Why are you carrying it?" Brother Lobo was the translator. He butted in where understanding became impossible, but otherwise Bhor succeeded in conveying what she wanted quite well through her gestures and expressions.

Rahul requested her to hum the song she was singing on the boat, so that he could pick up the chords. Keya provided the harmony, and the song was sung again on the riverbank this time with background music. Village children, who were watching the spectacle from behind the trees, were encouraged to come out of their hiding places and enjoy the music. They thronged around the youngsters and stood in awe, listening to the new rendition of the song they had heard a number of times sung by Bhor.

Bhor was now inordinately curious about the guitar, and once the song was over she jumped at it. She had been watching Rahul intently while he was playing it and figured she could do it easily by plucking the strings. She pulled the third string so hard that it snapped. Rahul managed to gently take away the instrument, and Bhor was sorely disappointed with her toy being taken away. She sulked on the laps of Brother Lobo, for two minutes, and then quickly forgot it all and went back to playing with Jessie's hair.

"Bhombol where are the sweets that Paro boudi had given us?" Imran had tried controlling the rumblings in his belly due to hunger, but finally gave up.

"Don't you remember that we distributed them to the sweepers, so that they would sweep the floors at the hospital? I think the sweets are all over, but there could be a few nimkis or savouries left." Nimkis were the popular salted triangular shaped deep-fried snacks made from flour. Imran had taken a special liking for them, and when Bhombol got out a container, which had a few left, he devoured them ravenously.

A cacophony of worried voices floated in from the village behind the trees, and they noticed a man being carried out on a bedsheet, which was being used as a stretcher, by four other men. Bhombol walked towards them with a questioning look, when a van came out from the camouflage of the vegetation and stopped on the riverbank.

"Another young man, bitten by a snake." The driver informed the friends as if this was nothing out of the ordinary.

Lobo ran to the village to see what he could do, but the patient had been already taken to the local medical shop for treatment. This village had no hospital. There was just one dispensary with a medical practitioner, and the villagers treated most snakebites locally. Jassi stood up and walked a little distance to investigate, but Bhombol warned him.

"Dada, please be careful. The bushes here are full of all kinds of insects and reptiles," he said calmly. "I have spent my younger days playing marbles here, so I know."

Rahul, however, wanted to find the source of a noise he had heard and walked behind the trees, holding its branches. He said that he would be very careful and wanted to inspect the sundari tree that rose heavenwards out of the mud. He had done some reading on the Sunderbans before embarking on this trip and found this an ideal opportunity to explore a bit.

"The word 'Sundarban' most probably comes from the Bangla word for 'beautiful forest'. This tree that you see in front is one such. A large part of the forest is made up of these trees." Rahul rattled off the little knowledge he had about the trees.

"This tree grows in saline waters and has a very hard wood, which is excellent for building boats. Therefore, it is vulnerable to illegal felling. The boat we came in was probably made from the wood of the sundari tree." Rahul soon disappeared behind the bushes, striking the vegetation and making way with the branch of the tree that he was carrying, hoping it would make all the insects and reptiles scatter.

Even if they had the desire to follow Rahul, his friends could not do so as Bhor and her never-ending questions prevented them from venturing anywhere. She sat in the middle, circled by the friends and had a question for each of them. First the questions went clockwise, and once the circle was completed the sequence got reversed and started all over again. "Where have you all come from? How long will you stay? Where will you stay?" She wanted to know everything at once. And the friends equally amused, answered them patiently.

It was fascinating to see how a little girl from the jungle had become so comfortable with the city-bred youngsters, in such a short while. She did not know their language. They conversed in a mixture of garbled words and sign language, but it flowed like music, and they seemed to be playing a symphony together.

Rahul, meanwhile, had worked his way into the jungle and reached an open area. There was a single large bani tree, a few meters away from the water's edge. Its branches aimed skywards. Keya, too, had given her friends the slip and had quietly sneaked out of the group and was doing what she knew best—following Rahul. She saw him approach the tree trunk, hoist his body upwards, cling on to the body of the tree and pivot himself forward with force. Then with swift movements he started climbing the tree and was soon resting on a branch about seven meters above the ground. Keya ran to the base of the tree and looked up at Rahul. Safely perched, he looked afar, shielding his eyes from the direct sun.

What lay in front was a sight to behold. The Sunderbans stretched out in front of his eyes. He saw the entire span of the mangrove forest as it spread out in the horizon, all the time careful not to lose his foothold on the branch that was still moist due to the rain. The scenic ambience and the cool breeze hitting his face had a mesmerizing effect on the young man. He wanted to let go of all his inhibitions. He parked himself with his legs apart for a better grip and cupped his palms to his mouth ala Tarzan. Then he let out his war cry. It was a shriek that cut through the forests and travelled over the water, puncturing the silence of the region. In fact, he surprised himself with the sound he produced.

"Keya I love you." He was screaming. "Keeyaaaaaaa I looooooove you."

Birds and crows, nesting in the surrounding trees had been disturbed. Unaccustomed to a human voice, shouting so noisily, in broad daylight in the region, they took flight immediately. Crows flying out from the trees seemed to look back, mid-flight, to find out who had the audacity to shake the peace of the region.

Keya knew that Rahul was prone to these apparent acts of madness. There is a hidden pleasure in madness that only a mad man knows. That's how Rahul normally explained his actions.

Keya was a little surprised when she saw Rahul shouting atop the tree. She also felt touched. She felt like Tarzan's Jane. Rahul was now looking down and beckoning his Jane to climb the tree, and Keya was bubbling with the excitement to join him.

Rahul climbed down from his branch to help her up. He lifted her with his strong forearms and pulled her body rapidly up, to the lower most branch. From there it was quite easy, moving upwards. Rahul remained below her as she climbed one branch after another. Finally, once he had safely secured her on the branch of his choice, both looked out into the river. It was a heavenly sight. The stillness of the river contrasted the torrential upsurge of emotions in the hearts of the lovers on the branch.

They were no different from two love birds that sat on these branches each morning as the sun rose and set over the river. Then

Rahul turned around to her. The beautiful surrounding was still sinking in when Rahul kissed her. He pressed his lips against hers and she closed her eyes. The first kiss was short and quick, and they fell apart only to grasp each other again as if they wanted to have more of it. She could still see the river through a corner of her eyes and a lone boat that rowed in the middle. There was also a boat with a sail flowing in a river deep within her. The second kiss was more passionate and lasted a little longer, before they fell away.

Both recollected the time they had first met at college—the initial fire in them; the obvious parental resistance when they discovered the romance; the college festivals and the music when they developed a special bond, each cherishing the fact they were deeply in love. These instances seemed to strengthen their will and passion.

Brother Lobo, sitting with the friends in a circle, about fifty meters away at the riverbank, heard Rahul scream. He looked around curiously.

"What is Rahul doing?" He turned around and asked Imran.

Bhor's nonstop questions had not allowed them to notice that even Keya was missing among them.

"Seems like a declaration of love," said Imran.

"Whatever he is up to, he seems pretty serious." Brother Lobo smiled.

Imran had already begun moving forward through the trees when the others followed him. Hazel, Jassi and Bhombol cleared the bushes to make way. Brother Lobo helped Bhor who continued with her queries. Keya saw her friends from the treetop and waved at them, excitedly.

"Imran, look up, we are here." She shouted. She broke a small twig from a branch and threw it down which floated through the air for some time before it landed on the wet mud.

They would definitely remember their first kiss on the bani tree, for as long as they lived, but for now they had to descend and join the gang. Rahul had to hang above her and hold her like a pulley so that she would not go tumbling down. There were moments when her friends below felt that they had seen the last of Keya. She lost her footing a couple of times on the moist branches and slipped, but Rahul was holding on to her with colossal strength. He could not lose her, at any cost. The way down lasted a good fifteen minutes, and finally all the friends were together.

Bhor had become animated to see them up on the tree and started screaming and waving at them. She saw villagers climb trees every day to collect honey, but could not understand why Rahul and Keya had done that. Rahul and Keya were greeted like astronauts coming back from a space mission. They took the opportunity to describe the astounding vista from the top. Only Brother Lobo remained mute. He waited for the rejoicing and the excitement to get over, before he spoke.

"Rahul, I want to show you something … here take a look."

Brother Lobo looked through his pair of binoculars adjusting and focussing for the visual he had in mind and then passed it on to Rahul. Brother Lobo waited for a few seconds as Rahul aimed the lenses on the tree that he pointed. What he saw through the binoculars shocked and horrified him to the core.

He had read that the Sunderbans was famous for its honey. Natural beehives are structures occupied by millions of honeybees. As he looked carefully, he realised, most of the trees around were filled with beehives.

"Bees do not like their territory being invaded, and they can sting humans to death. You were lucky that the bani tree you climbed did not have a beehive, or you could have been history.

Look closely and you will notice that the others—kankra, karjan, dhudlul, hetal—have hives hanging from them. You were screaming and invading their territory, and bees do not like that. Thousands of bees could have come attacking, and you and Keya could have fallen from that height and met with a very bad accident, "explained Brother Lobo.

The friends were petrified. They took turns looking through the binoculars and saw beehives hanging from the branches of most of the trees. It was just a matter of chance that the tree Rahul had climbed had none. The Brother's words numbed their senses.

"I remember watching the episode on *Killer Bees* on the National Geographic channel."

Rahul realised how irresponsible his actions had been. They just had had a close shave with death.

"I am very sorry, Brother. I shall be very careful in future." Rahul's voice was heavy with guilt.

"I have seen life my friend and I know that life is precious. You do not have to restrict your natural instincts, but be a little careful."

Brother Lobo, however, did not want Rahul brooding with guilt. He patted him on the back and hustled the friends to the auto-rickshaws waiting for them.

10

The Road vs the Forest

The two auto-rickshaws stumbled through the muddy roads that cut through the vegetation like two misdirected oversized darts, not programmed for any particular destination. Nothing could be programmed here in the middle of the jungle. The road had to adjust its bends and turns as per the will of the vegetation that sprouted all around. That was probably the only rule of the jungle. It held on to the last vestiges of personal glory and right and did not allow the road to make its way forward at its will.

The tarmacked road—the metaphor for modernisation and industrialisation had become the bane of the forest. If both the road and the forest were to be personified then a superb drama of existence was being enacted here. The forest was the lovely maiden who was being imposed upon, and she did not want to be vanquished. She was fighting her own struggle for sovereignty.

The road was the equivalent of the historical figure of Alexander—the invader, the adversary. But the road had to still let the forest grow and spread where it liked and had to make way for it. In many areas what was referred to as the road was difficult to discern. The forest had grown indiscriminately and had reclaimed what was once hers. But it was evident that the region had been a victim of large-scale clearing and settlement to support one of the densest human populations in Asia.

This eco-region was under great threat of extinction. Hundreds of years of habitation and exploitation had exacted a heavy toll on its habitat and biodiversity. One moment, there would be a stretch of forest where one felt that civilisation could not exist, but suddenly there would be a clearing where small children would be spotted playing on the road—indications of the urban world cutting into the bosom of forest life with merciless ferocity. Some call it modernisation. Others term it deforestation.

Brother Lobo started a running commentary as they moved on.

"The Sunderban is one of the most densely populated regions in the world, and the population is increasing. As a result, half of this eco-region's mangrove forests have been cut down to supply fuel-wood and other natural resources. Despite the intense and large-scale exploitation, this still is one of the largest contiguous areas of mangroves in the world."

The Brother was speaking in a language which the driver did not understand. He patted the driver softly on the back and spoke in accented Bengali.

"Lalu ... tui chinta korishna ... You don't worry. Just take us to the forest resort owned by the Mukherjee family."

It was wonderful to hear the Bengali words pour out so fluently from a foreigner. The words were all quite clear, albeit with a slight American accent that made them sound even sweeter. Jassi tried standing up and signalled from the back seat, tapping the driver on his shoulder, wanting him to stop as he wanted to ease himself. The driver slowed down. Jassi was about to get out when the Brother held him by his elbows. It was a strong grip that left Jassi wondering how his fist would have felt, had it struck his jaw instead.

"Not here. Let's be fair to the jungle. Hold on for a few more minutes please," he said firmly.

The youngsters were impressed to see the concern of a foreigner for the fauna of an alien land. To this foreigner it did not matter whether it was his own or not; he simply cared for the sweeping verdure around him.

The auto-rickshaws had only briefly stalled for Jassi's call of nature, but they had to halt, completely, when they came upon a group of villagers, congregated in the middle of the road. They were discussing something animatedly, around some construction work that was in progress on the mud road. The three-wheelers could not go forward as the group blocked the way ahead. Brother Lobo leaned out and made a face that explained he understood what the mess was all about.

"I shall come back in a few minutes." He got out to make an enquiry.

He made his way through the crowd and people seemed to recognise him. They shook his hand and greeted him. There was a lady of about thirty years old with the anchal of her sari tied around her waist that made her look like a firebrand woman. She was leading a group who looked like protesters.

Brother Lobo walked up to the lady and struck up a conversation. He stayed there in the crowd, talking to the lady for a few minutes. Several others, young and the old, walked up to him and started explaining things, spiritedly. A few policemen in uniform, standing by, did nothing but watch.

Men who appeared to be construction workers sat on the roof of a truck playing cards. Below the vehicle the mound of sand looked untouched and had attained the colour of rust from the pile of red bricks which was wet due to the rain. A large concrete mixer was lying idle below the banyan tree in the corner, and kids played around it.

Rahul was curious so he climbed to the roof of the truck to watch the game of cards. He saw coins and a few soiled notes of small denominations, scattered on a dirty piece of chequered cloth, the gaamcha, on which they placed their cards. This game was called "teen-patti", a variant of the same was played in Mumbai too, but with much higher stakes. Rahul remembered his father playing with his friends during the Diwali season when the bets on the playing board went up to a few thousands. But here the workers were playing with paltry change. They were also drinking country liquor.

One of the players, suddenly, unnerved by something, stood up and started yelling. Rahul understood the seriousness of the situation when others also joined in the altercation. Within minutes what had seemed to be a harmless game of cards turned into dramatic scene from a potboiler movie, with threatening gestures, abuses and flaying arms.

One of the players, hurling a stream of expletives, grabbed the gaamcha on the ground, and then pulling it together quickly stuffed it deep inside his shirt. This meant that he had made the entire booty of coins and soiled notes his own. That ignited further remonstrations from the rest of the players. None of the other workers and villagers on the ground took notice of the shouting as they were busy gathering their equipment. There would be no work for some time, they realised.

Bhombol who had joined the Brother saw the wrestling on the roof of the truck and ran back. He knew badinage here easily turned to misunderstandings, and workers were prone to sudden acts of violence resulting in stabbings and killings, under the effect of alcohol. He quickly got up on the roof of the truck and separated the aggrieved workers who were now on the brink of physical assault. The workers continued abusing each other for a few more minutes, but then things calmed down with the exchange of a few coins and soiled notes.

Rahul and Bhombol helped in the transfer of the currency from one pocket to another and while doing this they noticed that 25 paisa coins were being exchanged. Back in Mumbai this denomination of coin had long been forgotten. Even 50 paisa coins were rarely used.

The disagreement over, Rahul watched the workers sit down satisfied. The dirty chequered cloth was laid down again and stretched, with a little more vigour this time; the card game resumed, the coins started tinkling in, casual banter and liquor flowed again. All's well that ends well.

On the ground, the volley of abuses, pushing and shoving was quite intense too, but the Brother stood firm. About a dozen people were armed with shovels and pickaxes and they had all the intention to turn violent. The heap of stone chips on the road was disturbed when somebody ran over it brandishing his pickaxe wildly that ignited other members in the group. Bricks from the pile started being picked up, hurled and thrown into far corners, and the women and children in the crowd also joined in. It was clear that they were not in favour of the construction work. But why the villagers were against the making of the road was not clear.

Brother Lobo did not move despite the pushing and shoving of the crowd and one could make out how strong he was to be able to do that. He stalled a burly man who came tearing in through the crowd and crashed on to him. But the man continued shouting at the top of his voice. The uniformed policemen on duty had decided not to interfere, perhaps jaded from past experiences. Then, finally, Brother Lobo took out a whistle from his pocket and blew hard. The sound cut through the forest like a sting of a bee, which made the crowd pause and wait. The whistle signalled it was time to stop.

The friends gathered later that the Brother's whistle had special meaning in the locality. He would whistle at the football ground when he refereed a game with his players, but he carried the instrument with him and used it on other occasions too, when something was really serious or terribly wrong. The unruly crowd settled down, people dispersed, the villagers kneeled down on the muddy path and others scattered behind the trees.

"Mon diye amaaye shunun … My friends, listen to me carefully." Brother Lobo spoke in fluent Bengali, so that everybody could understand.

"Nothing in the world can be achieved with force. I know as I have been compelled into trying to use force in life before and understood the futility of the same. I know that you all must be really worried that the city folk will take over your land. I understand your concerns, but this is not a way to voice your protests. You are destroying what is your own. What service are you rendering to yourself? Stop this nonsense. This man here will talk to you and note down your concerns. Please sign a petition, and it will reach the authorities concerned."

All the people gathered there listened with intent. When Brother Lobo stopped talking, a murmur started in the crowd. Someone walked among the people, holding a file. He looked like a government servant, but the villagers did not pay any notice to him immediately.

The Brother knelt down beside an old woman. He softly whispered something into her ears, and she felt reassured. He referred to the woman as "mother". Rahul and Keya and the rest of the friends had all gathered behind the Brother and heard him speak to the woman.

"Maa, … e shob ki hocchhe … This is not the right way. This road needs to be built. It will be good for the people here.

We shall not let the city rule the village, I promise to you that … but this road needs to be built. People here cannot travel to the hospital on time … supplies cannot reach the villages here during the rains. This road will solve your problems. Believe me, I am talking sense here. Please sign on this page, if you believe in me."

The old woman swallowed everything that the Brother said. She knew him well, for she had been teaching him how to speak in Bengali. Then she took off her huge spectacles and asked him softly, "What do you want me to do?"

Tears glistened at the corners of her eyes as Brother Lobo held the stamp pad with one hand, held the woman's hand with the other and dabbed her thumb on the pad. He then helped her raise her trembling hand and pressed her thumb on the paper that he held in the file. It was done. The protest had been inked.

The entire process was so smooth, with almost no resistance from the old lady. It proved beyond doubt the trust the community had on the Brother. The file then went around in the crowd with everybody trying to grab it.

The combined force of rural India, when harnessed and used for the betterment of society and channelised for the welfare of the commoners, created magic. The great revolutionaries of India had done it in the past, and Brother Lobo was recreating it, on these islands. Things were poised for change in tide country, and the Brother was a huge catalyst to that change.

11

Jasho

When the crowd calmed down, the police got involved. They made everyone line-up to put their thumb prints. The file was then duly sealed and taken to the local municipal office for the formal lodging of the complaint.

The youngsters were amazed to see the trust and faith the villagers bestowed on a white-skinned man. They were at first totally against building of a road in the middle of a jungle as they did not want the city folk to encroach and eat into their heartland. But Brother Lobo seemed to have influenced them with the realisation that protests needed to be carried out legally. Something they did not know but where clearly willing to learn.

With the chaos on the road having subsided the five friends felt little grumbles in their tummies that suggested they were famished. The last thing they had eaten were the samosas the Brother had got packed for them.

The sun was beating down mercilessly now, even when the air felt cooler at the water's edge. When the crowd dispersed and went home, the friends sat down in the shade of a banyan tree close to the river. The sides of the mud road dipped to the riverbank, and the water looked as if it was boiling. The rains seemed a thing of the past.

The lady who was leading the protesters came walking to the friends below the tree. She looked at the forlorn faces of the friends and decided to have a word with the Brother.

"Lobo bhai ... chelera to khide te more jacchhe nischoi ... I am sure the kids must be dying of hunger. Get them to my house. We shall hear all their stories, and I will cook something for them."

The friends could see her gesticulate, frequently pointing to her own mouth with her fingers formed into a cone that created new churnings in their bellies. They swallowed their saliva realising that she was talking about food.

The path down to Jasho's house was about fifty meters down the road. The friends walked the distance quite merrily as the mere thought of food excited them. When they reached her place they found it was a small hut by the side of the river, raised on four stilts. Houses in this region had to be on stilts to keep the mud floors dry and not get damp with the water that constantly percolated up from the forest floor.

Four to five boulders placed one on top of another led up to a shabbily assembled flight of stairs, cut out of bamboo. The sides of the staircase and the flooring were covered with old rubber sheets, and that rendered the house, no matter how old and shabby, a sense of dignity. Jasho led the group of friends to the base of the staircase and paused.

"Pola, ... O Pola," she was obviously calling out to someone from the house.

A ten-year-old boy peeped out from the window and came running down the flight of stairs and met his mother on the ground. She whispered something to the boy, and he ran back up the stairs.

"Lobo bhai, ... please make the guests sit on top, and I shall be right back." The transformation of this woman, from an activist to a homemaker was rather striking, but she was still in control.

The Brother led the way up, and the friends followed. Once inside the house, the friends were asked to make themselves comfortable on a madur, a handwoven reed mat, which the boy had laid out for them. Rahul felt the softness of the floor-covering made of bamboo reeds. He raised its end and looking at Keya through its mesh, winked. However, any kind of romance was not on her mind, and she looked away.

The house comprised two rooms, adjacent to each other. The one in which they sat opened out into another, and the door, in between, was ajar. Brother Lobo walked into the other room and stood beside the bed. It was not clear who lay, only a bandaged leg was discernible, propped up and tied to an iron stand.

"My husband broke his leg when he fell from a tree in the jungle." Jasho explained when she returned holding something in a cloth, which seemed like rice grains. She again whispered something into her son's ears, and Pola grabbed a small container and ran out of the house.

Keya walked to the window and looked out into the river and saw the boy land on the ground with a leap from the first floor, and run towards the small cluster of hutments at a distance. Jasho then came into the room.

"Lobo bhai, time is short and so I cannot make a big meal. You have to do with boiled eggs and rice …."

Pola came back into the house handed his mother a small container, which she kept quietly behind the haanri or handi, and into a round aluminium utensil, she poured the rice grains.

Keya had been watching all this from the corner of the room when a dust-laden book, below a pile of things, caught her eye. She picked it up and looked at the cover. She went forward and cornered the Brother at the window.

"Brother, it's quite clear that this woman has very little rice at home. Her son seems to have borrowed some oil from another house. It's going to be quite shameful for us to eat like this. And look what I found." She showed him a hardbound copy of Sunil Gangopadhyay's *Prothom Alo*—a book she remembered her mother reading at home. She herself had started reading its English translation, which she could not complete due to her exams.

Also translated into English, *First Light* is a book that like its predecessor, *Those Days*, brings history to life. Keya had been left wondering why history books in schools were not written as interestingly. Keya recalled how detail its research was and with what precision the writer had penned it.

"Who reads this book here?" Keya asked the Brother and he pointed at Jasho.

Keya was left numb with disbelief. A poor woman deep in the Sunderbans—a woman who had to borrow rice and oil from neighbours to cook a meal; a woman who a little while ago was the "Joan of Arc" of the jungle in a sari, now transformed to a mother, kneeling at the unoon, a home-made clay stove that used dung cake as fuel—read such an iconic book that the professors of the modern world were proud to read?

The friends had figured Jasho's was an extremely poor household, but what it lacked in wealth and prosperity more than made up with good intention and hospitality. To the friends she had already risen a few notches in their esteem.

"Byash ar kichu khon. The food will be ready in exactly ten minutes. Meanwhile, why don't you all tell us something about yourselves," asked Jasho to the friends who were sitting in a semicircle on the mat, muted by pangs of hunger she imagined.

"Acchha ami prothome shuru korchi ... Lobo bhai, apni pore anubad kore deben ... Okay, I shall begin first ... Lobo bhai, you can translate it later."

She started speaking in Bengali, and her words held the friends spellbound. The manner in which she spoke had an immediate impact on them, endearing them in a way that she seemed no more a stranger.

"To begin with ... let me tell you something about the jungle here. The Sunderbans is the delta region of Ganga, Meghna, and Bramhaputra stretching between West Bengal (India) and Bangladesh. It is the land of estuaries, creeks, big rivers, and smaller waterways, and it is the largest mangrove forest in the world. The mangrove forest is also home to the man-eating Royal Bengal tigers."

She immediately bit her tongue and stuck it out—to mean she had made a mistake. "I am sorry. I am wrong when I say they are habitual man-eaters. Very seldom do they attack humans but they can be, nevertheless, very dangerous. My father-in-law was a victim of a tiger attack when he entered the jungle to collect honey. But we are poor people, and our menfolk have no other choice but to enter the forest, even at the risk of never coming back.

"My husband is doing the same thing, even after his father was killed by a tiger. There he lies on the bed with a broken leg. He fell from a tree while collecting honey. But this does not mean that we shall let the city rule us, and that was what we were protesting about. We don't want to make way for a tarmac road. This land, this jungle is our home, we love it, and Bon Bibi is with us. She protects us from the wild animals, and I am sure she will also protect us from the city folk."

It was quite amazing how her voice suddenly gathered heaviness and acquired the timbre of the firebrand lady that she was. She had started her soliloquy very calmly, but got animated as she progressed. It was easy to notice that she had her pulse attached to the spirit of the jungle, and her entire life was woven around it. She had pointed to a small altar in the middle of the wall to her left when she uttered the words Bon Bibi, and everyone figured it was the Goddess of the Forest who had total control of the animals in the region.

Jasho could not hold back her tears. Her eyes had become moist and she raised the end of her sari or aanchal and hid her eyes behind the cloth, dabbing it to dry her eyes. This was the same aanchal that she earlier.had tied around her waist like a warrior,

"This land is also home to poisonous snakes, the rivers, and creeks are populated by estuarine crocodiles, making the place uninhabitable by humans. There is conflict between humans and the local wildlife, and it is mainly because of such roads that are eating into the territory of the tiger. Lack of resources on land and salinity of the rivers have made the fields unfavourable for good crops, so we totally depend on other resources like honey, fish, crab, wood and meat. Sometimes, the tigers find humans to be easy preys. So the government has given us these rubber masks for security." She held up a mask as she spoke.

"These masks look like a human face, and the honey collectors are supposed to wear them at the back of their heads. Since the tiger always attacks from behind, it saves the honey collectors from any sudden attack."

As she spoke, she wore the mask over her head so that she appeared to be a man from behind. Imran thought about making a sketch of the image later.

"But why does the tiger kill humans? You will ask. Will I not protest if people I don't know come into my house and dictate what goes on here? That is why we are protesting the making of the road. And so the tiger protests by attacking the honey collectors as they enter its lair.

"But what can we do? Each year, hundreds of people go into the forest with permits from the forest department, in the month of April. The honey collectors say that given a choice they would not ever enter the forest, but what do we do here? There is nothing here. No communication, no basic amenities, nothing, and now they want to build a road and make matters worse for us."

"The Aila, in 2009, further intensified the trouble here." Brother Lobo spoke now.

"The dreaded Cyclone Aila, hit Bangladesh and India, in 2009, bringing heavy rains and winds at over 120 km per hour. 40,000 people were evacuated to cyclone shelters. In the Sunderbans alone thousands of homes were broken, and people took shelter in nearby schools and Panchayat offices. There was an acute shortage of food, drinking water and clothes. There was also a gastroenteritis epidemic."

Jasho cut him short, "It is impossible to believe, unless you saw it with your own eyes what the Brother did for the common man, after the cyclone hit us. He travelled several kilometres into the jungle, to pick up the homeless and shift them to homes and shelters. I was with him a few times and so I know that his undying service to the people of the region has not been forgotten. If it were not for him there would have been many more dead on the roads, after Aila hit us. The villagers love him here."

Jasho removed the lid of the aluminium utensil, and the aroma of cooked rice and eggs wafted up, making the friends delirious with hunger.

"More of that later. Let's eat now." She put in the hanta, a ladle, into the rice and took out large helpings and placed them on the dishes in front of the friends. There was a watery dal in a container that she poured over the rice—making a dent on the rice mound with her ladle before pouring it—like a crater containing muddy yellow liquid in it. And there was mashed potatoes, mixed with boiled eggs, sprinkled with freshly broken green chilies, coriander leaves, and mustard oil rubbed in. The pungent taste of the raw mustard oil made it heavenly.

For the next ten minutes nobody spoke—the only pervading sound was that of slurping and rapacious eating, accompanied by the tinkling of the ladle and the aluminium pot as Jasho served more helpings of the rice and the mixture of egg and potatoes.

For Bhombol this was an ordinary experience. He often ate sitting on the floor, at home, in Kolkata, but for the rest it was a novel experience. Imran fumed as he had bit into a freshly broken green chilly in his haste to put in as much food as was humanly possible in one gulp. He snorted like a horse. Jasho noticed this.

"Danrao, danrao … hold on one minute. I shall teach you a local cure. Open your mouth wide."Imran acquiesced.

"No, that's not enough, much wider, open it real wide." Imran opened it as wide as he could and that drew muffled giggles from his friends.

"Okay, now hold your tongue out and stretch it right out of your mouth as far as you can." Imran tried doing so, and quite involuntarily an indecent noise from deep inside his throat emerged. He immediately tried his best to stifle it and shut his mouth.

"No, no … that sound is needed. Do not prevent it." Jasho demonstrated how by sticking out her tongue like Goddess Kali. "Aaaaaa …" She made a noise with her mouth open wide.

Imran replicated the action for a few seconds with his jaws opened wide, his tongue hanging out like a dog till saliva started dripping from its tip. He saw Keya and Hazel trying to hold back their laughter and shut his jaws suddenly. "Hey man … this actually works. I feel much better already. I think this stunt can become quite popular in the cities."

Once they were through with lunch, Jasho swiftly collected all the dishes, ladles, utensils, and tumblers. Pola put them together into a sack to be rinsed later, making clanking sounds.

The friends were feeling drowsy from what a heavy lunch of rice, mashed potatoes, and mustard usually induced. Imran was the first to roll backwards on the floor.

"Hey guys, good night. The food has really hit the spot." Soon one by one the friends fell asleep.

Jasho was fifteen when she got married. She was a student and went to the local Pathshala when her father met with an untimely death. Her education was prematurely nipped in the bud, and she was married off to a local honey collector. Though she could not pursue her studies due to her marriage, she had continued to borrow books from the dilapidated local library and read them voraciously.

The local librarian would keenly wait for the village girl to come and borrow books from the library; she was one of the very few who read in the jungle. An Englishman had started the library in a house that had been bequeathed to the villagers. Although there was no regular updating of books, tourists often left behind some new ones, and the local Gram Panchayat donated a few during the election time. So the library had grown and thrived.

Jasho had not allowed her unforeseen marital stature—a sudden invasion on her womanhood—to destroy her as a person.

She had also wisely avoided becoming the mother of half-a-dozen babies as was the norm with the other women in the region and kept her motherhood to the single ten-year-old Pola.

She would borrow books from the dilapidated library, sit and read them below the trees, whenever she could make time from her chores, carrying on reading in her bedroom, long after her husband went to sleep. She would often read out passages or incidents that she loved in the books, to her husband. He would enjoy them so much that one could find him mumbling passages in his sleep. This pleased Jasho, immensely.

As the friends slept, Jasho leafed through the pages of her latest book. In sharp contrast to the sleep on the boat that was induced by total fatigue, this was triggered by the intake of rice, a bhat ghoom or rice slumber as they call it, which takes total control of the faculties of the mind and the body and keeps it enchained.

Brother Lobo had trained himself to avoid these afternoon siestas that the staple diet of rice and dal induced in the mind. If one wishes to stay fit one should never sleep after lunch is what he believed and lived by. So he had ambled across to the other room where Jasho's husband lay on bed, and both played Bagh-bandi, the "capturing the tiger" board game.

It is a hunt game, played on an Alquerque board, where a bagh, or a tiger, is often spectacularly immobilised, not by bullets, but by mere goats. Two tigers attempt to elude and capture as many goats, while the goats try and trap the tigers by surrounding them. The tigers win if they capture enough goats, and the goats win if they manage to immobilise the tigers. Jasho's husband Nepal, preferred playing with the goats.

Lying immobilised and injured, with one leg held in a cast, Nepal would be overjoyed, celebrating each time he captured a tiger with his goats. It probably helped him vent some of the unspent anger on the imaginary tiger, and Nepal derived immense pleasure in capturing the animal that had killed his father.

Nepal was brilliant playing with his goats and won hands down most of the times. People refused to play with him, for fear of losing every time. Nepal realised this and would often allow his competitors to win a few rounds before he took over the board. Thus, Brother Lobo, too, was made to win a few times to have him hooked on to the game.

The Brother did not mind losing either. He understood the oblique symbolism Nepal attached to the game, how much it made Nepal happy to win each time, and how he kept his hopes and aspirations alive on the Alquerque board, with stone tigers and rubber goats.

Bhor had been quiet the whole while, which was a little unusual for her. The Brother had noticed this and watched her play khalna bati, a game of cooking with the utensils, from the corner of his eyes. She cut vegetables, some real and others imaginary and cooked her dishes on an imaginary fire, but the process created a lot of sound. Her sporadic sneezing along with the clanking sound made by the utensils, eventually, made enough noise to stir up the sleeping friends.

It was also time to leave. Brother Lobo thought it wiser to venture across the river when there was still enough natural light. Jasho would not let them go without paying obeisance to Bon Bibi, their protector of the forests. They all stood in front of the shrine on the wall, and Jasho closed her eyes and muttered her prayers and then applied tilak marks on the foreheads of everyone.

It was low tide, and the river glistened like a thin streak of muddy pathway in the twilight. Brother Lobo led the way to a boat that was floating on the water, about twenty meters beyond the wet mud. The wet ground touching the mangroves suggested that the water level came right up to the single bidi shop, at the edge of the road. This was tide country where entire islands and sandbanks disappeared under water, daily, only to reappear when the tide turned.

There was a young man in his late twenties on the boat, who welcomed the friends. He was wearing a white shirt with grey trousers that made him look like a corporate worker, in the middle of the jungle. Sumon worked as a forest ranger in the Gosaba region and had come on the boat to help the friends on this trip. Sumon was an educated man and spoke in impeccable English with the Brother. He assured them he would help the friends with his contacts in the region, to make their stay as pleasant as possible.

Imran noticed a few old, discarded whiskey bottles inside its awning and was surprised. Who could afford foreign liquor in tide country? He then remembered seeing honey being sold in whiskey bottles in old shacks that lined the highway and even the markets. The discarded liquor bottles must have belonged to the foreign tourists who came visiting the area, which were later used for storing honey.

A group of honey collectors, waiting for the boat, knew the Brother and hailed out to him. Before they set foot on the boat they collected around one of the shrines of Bon Bibi, dotted among the palm trees and thatched houses of the quiet village and said their prayers. In addition to the rubber masks that they wore behind their heads, the efficacy of which remains a topic of debate, the collectors sought blessings and asked for the protection of the forest goddess, Bon Bibi, who is worshipped both by Hindus and Muslims.

In particular, they ask her to protect them against Dakshin Rai, the demon king, and the arch rival of Bon Bibi. The villagers believe it is this demon, which attacks them in the form of a tiger.

After the puja was complete, the honey collectors got on the boat and sat inside the awning at the stern of the boat. The majhi (oarsman) held his hands in a namaskar gesture heavenwards and set sail.

12 Jungle at Last

There were two majhis on the boat and four honey collectors who were crossing the river along with the friends. Mujahir Aslam and Manzoor Sheikh were blood brothers. Ratan Palit and Abhiram Kundu were cousins. They were a third generation of a family of honey collectors, originating from the same family. Circumstances leading to inter-caste marriages had planted them into different religions.

The journey across the Panchamukhi River was largely uneventful, barring Bhor's questions that had resumed, proving that she was probably feeling a little better, but her sneezing bouts continued undiminished.

"Are these friends going home with us? *Hanchoo*! How long will they stay with us? *Hanchoo*!"

Rahul touched her forehead and grimaced. "Brother I think we need to take her to the doctor. She seems to have a little fever."

Sumon heard what Rahul said and advised, "Yes, why not? There is a small dispensary across the river, a little distance away, so let's take her there once we cross the river."

Sumon's actions amplified his concern. He crawled on all fours, entering the awning at the stern of the boat, with enough dexterity to suggest that he was used to doing this. He used this boat, which was owned by the forest department, for patrolling the area after dark. He knew the Brother and Bhor's father Sushil da quite well and so had decided to use his clout and ferry the friends across the river.

The four honey collectors on the boat were singing a folk song attributed to Bon Bibi. Rahul and the others enjoyed the song and Bhombol explained the words.

Bon Bibi, mon bibi, ma bole daklo ke jon bone …

(Bon Bibi somebody cried out her name in the forest …)

Sumon came out of the opening, holding a rolled up sari in one hand and a crumpled bunch of clothes in the other. He walked up to the Brother and handed over what he was carrying. The Brother unfurled the sari, and then in one lyrical move covered the girl from head to toe; the other crumpled ball of clothes, consisting of under garments, a couple of singlets and one gamchha, he placed under Bhor's head as a pillow.

The bare-bodied man rowing the boat looked on solemnly and smiled when Bhor stretched out underneath the sari. Her lithe body could be seen curled up underneath the translucent material made of coarse cotton.

"My wife knows Bhor, and they sing songs together. She will not mind. In fact, she will be quite pleased that she had been draped with her sari," the majhi exclaimed.

The piece of cloth, which had once been the woman's sari, had marks and blots on it suggesting it was being used for other purposes on the boat—perhaps to mop the floor of the boat. The friends remembered how Jasho had also got out a similar worn-out sari, from a dilapidated suitcase, and laid it on the floor, and spread the lunch over it. There were no newspapers readily available to be used as throw-away dusters, in these parts.

Bhor grasped the thin sari and turned around on her back, slithering into the corner of the boat, and from her face it appeared that she was much more comfortable this way. She lay in the corner, coiled underneath the sari for a few seconds and then began humming the song *Jokhon porbe na mor payer chinha ei batey*—as if to sing herself to sleep. She only uttered the first two or three words and then murmured the tune without the words, and it was clear that she was not quite herself.

The splashing of the oars on the sides of the boat and the soft lapping of the waves repeated itself as though giving an uncanny, yet a definite rhythmic beat to her song. The humming gradually grew inaudible as Bhor slowly fell asleep. The friends were uncomfortable with this sudden quietude. Bhor had become so dear to everyone that they worried to see her so uncharacteristically quiet.

The other bank, which lay roughly one hundred meters away, could be seen. The smog that had descended over the river made the line of trees look like a string of silver, gleaming through the darkness. The light was not good anymore and the crescent moon looked like a shining sickle hanging above the trees—as though the jungle had committed a crime and would be punished that night, with a savage blow, severing the stillness with ferocity. The floating sickle moon tonight, a device only to inflict injury, made the ambience eerily scenic; this oddity in the rich tapestry of beauty and silence made the friends anxious and uncomfortable.

The boat sailed noiselessly for a few more minutes, gliding through the waters towards the banks, then the splashing of the oars stopped. The oarsman, who had smiled when his wife's sari had been used to cover Bhor, threw a tethering lasso on the group of Avicennia, Sonneratia and Pneumatophores or breathing roots, which grew out of the ground.

Pneumatophores grew slower and became woody, reaching heights of 3 m at times, but these were smaller in height, not more than 50 cm tall. The widely spread out horizontal roots, below the ground, from which these grew, improved anchorage in the unstable mud, and they were now being used for anchoring the boat.

The two majhis then lit a fire each. The first man held a piece of wood about the length of a forearm elbow, and the second wrapped a piece of cloth around it. Then they poured some kerosene on the cloth, and within minutes, there were leaping tongues of flames from the mashal. They did the same thing to a second one, and then both the majhis held their mashals high in the air to not only help everyone on the boat to disembark but also discouraged any wild animals on the shore. Then one majhi jumped on the bank and fastened the rope tightly around a root and called out for the others.

One by one, all the people on board got off. The loose mud gave way under their weight, and their ankles sank into them as they moved forward towards the shore. There was a forest officer on the bank, carrying the permits to enter the main tiger reserve. This area was out of bounds for tourists, and those without permits were fined by the government. Sumon went straight to the man and they started a conversation in the local dialect. He appeared a little unnerved at the end of the short conversation. He was holding a file in his hand that he had taken from the other man and was looking at it intently. Then he walked up to Brother Lobo.

"Lobo bhai, there is a slight problem. The forest officer here has been able to manage three passes, and so all five cannot enter the tiger reserve area. He says that he tried getting five passes, but could not. The man who stamps the passes wanted a bribe, but the officer did not have the money."

Sumon was talking in Queen's English, which the officer did not fully comprehend, but nodded his head in sync with every important word uttered. His face had an expression of helplessness and he nodded a little more furiously when he heard the word "bribe"—he had understood that single word in the entire sentence spoken. By now, all the friends were standing at the foot of the mangrove trees, but the group of honey collectors had moved away and were sitting on the mud a little distance away. They hardly moved and remained huddled together smoking their bidis a little distance away from the rest.

"Sumon, it appears that these honey collectors are not really interested in befriending us. Why is that? Why are they sitting so far away?" Imran wondered.

The look on Sumon's face suggested that he was uncomfortable with the question, which had caught him off guard. His face attained a tinge of red, and the man who a while ago had looked so full of life on the boat, suddenly, seemed disarmed. He mopped the sweat on his brow, taking special care to single out a blob that had trickled down to bridge of his nose and was sliding into the corner of his left eye. He stopped its progress with a dab of his handkerchief and rubbed his eyes with it as if wanting to erase some visual. That done, he neatly folded the cloth and put it back into his trouser pocket. This action had given him ample time to think of an answer. He gave out a huge sigh and let out the words.

"These honey collectors gather the honey from under the noses of man-eating tigers. Given the perils confronted by the men who enter the tiger's lair to harvest it, it is perhaps the costliest honey in the world. Yet, the honey collectors of the Indian Sunderbans, this unadulterated tide country, find themselves at the very bottom of the economic and social heap.

"Despite or, perhaps, because of the hard-scrabble existences they live, they are often looked down upon by other villagers and government officials. Confronted by increasingly enforced regulations designed to protect the tigers and the delta itself, it sometimes appears as if both mankind and nature are conspiring against them. These men are not considered equal by others, and hence, they have somewhat reconciled themselves to their fate and left their destiny into the hands of Bon Bibi. They are happy to keep their distance from the common folk as they do not want to stir matters as that would only make life worse for them. It is easier to live in solitude than be castigated."

While others wondered about the problem with the passes, Imran was left moved by Sumon's sudden outburst, and though he spoke softly, his words hit him hard. It also set him thinking. Apartheid! It lived even in our midst. The Khap Panchayats established their own Talibanistic rules of life in north India; the entire country had its own regional evils of caste system and differences according to race or lineage. We denounce it in public and shun it at parties, but it lives around us like a parasite, growing into an epidemic. Imran was left with a lump in his throat that he found hard to swallow.

"Look it is dark now. We are close to the Mukherjee family resort where we shall retire for the night," informed Brother Lobo. Nothing really can be done tonight, so let us not even think of the passes we don't have. Let's all go there and shift our luggage, and tomorrow at daybreak we shall think of our way ahead."

His words had a steely resolve and timbre that he must have acquired from his days in the army, and it discouraged any protest. He knew when and how to take control.

The forest officer had brought with him a couple of cycle thhelas to transport the luggage to the Mukherjee resort in the dark. The thhelas were four feet by four feet wooden platforms, fixed on the rear wheels of a tricycle. And it worked brilliantly in carrying luggage and even people at times.

Bhombol found one of the men driving the thhela very familiar; he brought back memories from the past. He quietly walked up to the cart and stroked the person on the back. The man looked around, squinted in the dark, looking closely at Bhombol's face. The thin shaft of the moonlight cast a glow on Bhombol's face through the trees, but the driver could not recognise him at first. Gradually, his expression changed as he rubbed his eyes with the back of his fists, his face acquiring a look of inexplicable disbelief and joy. Tears started rolling down as he held Bhombol by the sides of his body, looking at him from head to toe. Then at last he spoke.

"O ma, koto boro hoye gechish tui … My god, you have really grown."

Then they embraced each other, and neither would let go until Brother Lobo spoke.

"It's getting late. Let's go."

A couple of uniformed guards carrying rifles followed the officer, their presence lending an air of gravity to the journey. The guns seemed to add a different edge to their adventure, which until then, had been just an exciting roller-coaster ride. The gun-toting men appeared to be from some other planet with absolutely no emotion. Bhor oblivious to it, reached out to fondle with their rifles, which caused some alarm, and they reacted gruffly, scaring Bhor a bit. Brother Lobo, immediately, pulled the girl towards him and cuddled her to his bosom. There she lay comforted and closed her eyes to rest.

13

Marshall Estate

The Mukherjee's had a long lineage and history in Bengal. Their origins lay in Khulna, in East Bengal, and the family members had mushroomed all over undivided Bengal, till the partition of geographical boundaries separated two sets of people who had lived together for hundreds of years. The two partitions of Bengal—first in 1947, with the creation of East Pakistan, and then in 1971, with the birth of Bangladesh—had resulted in, perhaps, one of the greatest exodus of humanity across land and water.

A Bengali nursery rhyme written by Annada Shankar Roy, soon after Independence, captured the anguish of political freedom gained at the expense of home or homeland.

> *Teler shishi bhanglo bole khukur pore rag koro,*
> *Tomra je shob buro khoka bharot bhenge bhag koro . . .*
> *Tar bela?*
> (When, unwittingly, a bottle of oil breaks in the hands of a little girl, she is admonished,
> What about the adults who deliberately create rifts and divide India?
> What then?

An act of reckless and an irresponsible demarcation across the map of the country resulted in the exile of the two communities—the Hindus and the Muslims—to two different countries and Bengal lost on its plural existence. Even today, hundreds of people try and cope up with their newfound identities, and some still feel ostracised in their own country. For some, there is home, but only in memory.

The Sunderbans, too, had been part of this grand division. Offsprings of the Mukherjee family that included Keya's uncles, aunts, foster uncles and aunts grew in numbers, and most of them being Hindus had shifted their base to West Bengal in India. A few, however, stayed back in Dhaka and maintained a casual contact with the extended family.

Keya's grandfather had been given this resort by a British general who wished to contribute towards humanitarian services in tide country, after the partition of Bengal. He had vetoed the idea of partition of Bengal and had decided to stay back in the jungle, even after independence. Keya's grandfather knew the English man and had served him well. The British general had been bitten by a poisonous snake, and he died on the way to the hospital.

"Ranjan, look after the people here. Look after my house and use it for the benefit of the people if you can." His last words were in the arms of Mr Ranjan Mukherjee.

Ranjan Mukherjee had been involved in the good work started by General Marshall in the area. So nobody had protested when he occupied the premises of the bungalow and took control of the functioning of the trust that General Marshall had started, even though it raised an eyebrow or two as they were jealous of the man.

Mr Mukherjee had named the bungalow and the surrounding area "Marshall Estate" and started a small dispensary that distributed medicines for the locals initially. For the next two decades the property was used for various community work by the locals, and also for the local Durga puja, by Hindus and Muslims alike.

After Keya's grandfather expired, the legal tangle involving the land dispute of the estate flared up again and spread among the locals. A few of the locals had their own vested interests, and wanted to usurp Marshall Estate for their own dastardly designs. The general had left some money with Bhombol's grandfather, and hence, he held himself morally responsible towards the estate. He got involved in the local land dispute, trying to secure the estate from the nefarious intentions of some of the locals who wanted to wrest control of it by all means.

Because Bhombol's grandparents enjoyed intimate relations with General Marshall, his parents continued to serve in the dispensary and at the estate too. Those who wanted to usurp Marshall estate could not accept the automatic ownership rights that Bhombol's parents seem to have acquired over Marshall estate over a period of time.

2nd Jan 2001

Shyamol was a daily worker, employed with the contractor, making dam at the embankment. It was said that the new dam would vastly reduce the problems of the locals. Shyamol had gone to collect his dues for the day, but the contractor was drunk and he could not find his assistant either. Night had fallen in tide country; nobody travelled alone at this time, but Shyamol had to return home.

Suddenly, a shadowy figure came out from behind the tree and blocked his way. The stranger wore a turban made of a gamchha on his head and he brandished a sickle. His wrists were unsteady, and the blade of the sickle caught the beam of the moon and gleamed as he twisted it in his hand. He was probably not entirely accustomed to doing what he had been tasked to do. There were beads of sweat on his forehead, not entirely due to the temperature that had plummeted over the last few days.

"Shyamol ... tomake niye jete eshechhi ... I have been sent to take you ... we had warned you many times before, but you did not listen. Now time is running out. But that does not mean they have sent me to kill you. You have been given one last chance to save your life and your family. Amar shonge chalo kotha ache ... come with me ... we need to talk."

He spoke as though he had rehearsed the words many times over, without once pausing to breathe. He had probably mastered the phrases with practice, or could have been deliberately rushing through the lines to come to the real thing as fast as he could.

Shyamol considered scooting, but to run in the jungle at that hour had its own hazards. He was much stronger than his adversary, but picking up a fight when he was dog tired, in the middle of the jungle, was not what he wanted. Instead, he followed the man and reached the end of the road that dipped suddenly to the riverbank. There was a hut at the edge of the water, set up on bamboo stilts with a flickering light, probably from a candle, lighting up the interiors dimly.

When the footsteps of the two sounded on the dry leaves outside the hut, the candle was blown out. Shyamol was allowed to enter the hut first. Looking back, he could see that the door had been bolted, and the man who he had followed was standing with the sickle in hand.

There were about six men, in lungis, sitting hunched on their knees smoking bidis in the room, suffocating it with the smoke. Shyamol did not smoke regularly, but he felt a throbbing in his temples due to the smoke and waved the air in front of his eyes with his hands. The man sitting in the middle of the group offered him a bidi.

"Oto natok korte hobena Shyamol ... Enough of your antics ... The Britishers have left the country with their cigarettes ... Come on, here, have a bidi ...."

Shyamol took the bidi from the man and lit it. It was easier smoking in the room than breathing the air and it helped calm the senses too.

"We are giving you a last chance. We shall also give you ₹10,000, in cash. Go to Kolkata and start a new life and leave us alone. That estate is not yours, so don't seek it."

Nyata you go and fetch sister. Tell her to carry her luggage and we shall put them on the first boat in the morning."

Nyata, the eighteen-year-old boy addressed, opened the only window of the room that had been bolted shut and jumped out. Shyamol saw him ride a cycle through the fields and pick up speed once he reached the mud road.

"Ta ki mone hocchhe ... so what do you think? Is ₹10,000 okay, or do you want a little more?" This time another man smoking a bidi had started asking the question, but before he could complete it a staccato cough took over, and he started struggling with his words. He was given a glass of water.

"Ami taka chai na ... I don't want any money and neither will I leave the estate ..."

The sickle hit him at the back of his head.

It had been rehearsed.

If Shyamol agreed, ₹10,000 had been arranged and the boatman had been paid in advance. But there was another backup plan at the very first refusal. Shyamol fell to the ground and blood started oozing out from the gash behind his head, which instantly disappeared on the parched mud floor, leaving a mere trickle. Then the others pounced on the body and in a barbaric act of violence, hacked it to pieces with axes, kataris, knives and rods. The pieces were then swiftly transferred into a large gunny bag. Then they waited for the wife.

One hour later, two gunny bags were taken some distance into the river, on a boat, and were dropped into the water. The crocodiles must have had an underwater feast that day as the two-gunny bags were found in the mangroves with hardly anything left in them, barring a few bones and tissues, some days later. No identification was possible from the remains, but a lungi and a sari found in the house, soaked in blood, helped the police trace it to Bhombol's parents. The villagers claimed the case had been left unsolved on purpose as it would have opened a can of worms.

Captain Talukdar was honeymooning in the region, soon after the double murders, when he and his wife Parvati found the little boy, Bhombol, who was being looked after by Shikari dada. The legal tangle involving the Marshall Estate had continued for years till the courts stayed any verdict on it with a stay order. Due to Shikari da's goodwill in the locality, the courts had allowed him to use a part of the estate for community work, and lately Brother Lobo had started a Holy Communion movement from the estate. The dual murders had been forgotten, only casually mentioned by the oldies of the locality when they were in a drunken state.

Marshall Estate was not a huge house by any standards, but the look of it still had a semblance of the days of the Raj. There was no electricity in most of the Sunderbans as there were no grids. Those who could afford had to do with the solar panels that tilted heavenwards during the day. Marshall Estate had one such array of panels installed on its terrace that produced just about enough electricity for two lamps and two fans to be used at night. Keya's parents had installed the panels some years ago and Sushil da had been tutored to use it sparingly.

The main entrance to the building was through a huge archway that led to the iron gates. The thhelas got in and parked themselves near the main garden. Here they were unloaded and the drivers took the thhelas behind the house and chained them to the fence.

It was 9 pm, and the chowkidar of the estate Sushil da, who was Bhor's father, was nowhere to be seen. Together, all the friends unloaded the thhela. For Bhombol this was a homecoming he never imagined would happen. He waited for the driver to come back after he had secured the thhelas.

"Gaachh ta kothaye? Where is the tree?" Bhombol asked the man.

It was strange question that took the man by surprise and set him thinking. He waited for a few seconds while allowing the question to sink in, and then his face formed an expression that showed ambivalence. He ran forward and grasped Bhombol and started crying on his shoulders. He did not let go of the boy, and the latter had to wrench his body out of his grip.

"Where is the tree?" Bhombol asked again.

The man simply pointed towards the back of the house. Wasting no time, Bhombol ran behind it and looked around the area. He looked to his right, then to his left, and was left confused as he was not sure of the place anymore. He rubbed his eyes to bring back the memories of his childhood. He spent a couple of minutes standing in front of the fence, making sure that he did not do something totally stupid in front of his friends.

He then walked up to a tree and felt the bark kneeling down in front of the stem and rolled his palm over the trunk. He poured some water at the base of the plant from a vessel that he had picked up from the front of the house. Shikari da saw all the friends looking at Bhombol with curiosity and cleared all doubts.

"He is our Bhombol. When he was a child, before the murders happened, Bhombol was a little four-year-old boy, running around naked. He and I had planted a tree here. He remembers that and feels nostalgic."

Bhombol saw the tree from the top to the bottom and then came back and joined the crowd.

"Shikari da ... how much money has the tree borne?"

Everyone was left confused with this question. How could a tree bear any money?

Shikari da, or Hunter da, had got his name as he use to work as a guide for the hunters who went into the forest in search of game back in those days when hunting was legally allowed, and though that as a practice had long stopped, he still lived with the name.

"Bhombol as a child used to like those small five-paisa coins still in use those days. In fact, he liked them more than the fifty-paisa coins. So, one day, I asked him to plant a five paisa coin into the ground and told him that when he grew up the plant would bear fruit and he could have as many five paisa coins he wanted." As he spoke Shikari da's eyes became moist and he reached out and touched Bhombol's cheeks.

"Baba, can my boy speak in English?"

Bhombol was quick to respond, and he made sure he spoke in English as that made Shikari da very proud.

"Yes, of course, I can Shikari da. I can speak as well as any other city kid. But I am sure they can't plant money plants as well as I do." Bhombol was laughing one minute and then seemed overwhelmed with emotion and continued.

"Shikari da, the plant may not have borne any money, but with all the nurturing I received I am ready to bear the fruits. I am educated, strong and able and I can work and earn my living today. I am going to use all that I have … all that I can … for the betterment of this place that is my own. That is how this plant has borne its fruit … in me today."

The friends were moved. Bhombol had indeed been lucky as he had been picked up from the dirt and adopted by free thinking men, but there were thousands of others in our country who were not as lucky. It remained to be seen what the lucky Bhombols of today gave back to the society.

Everyone looked around for Sushil da, but he could not be found. Then Brother Lobo blew his whistle. It was a loud shrill sound that cut through the darkness, and within seconds Sushil da appeared at the terrace corner, waving a white cloth. A mark of surrender.

"Khabar ready … Food is ready. Let's have dinner." Brother Lobo spoke with authority and started walking into the house.

Jhor, the Storm

Murgir jhol and bhat... Chicken curry and rice—that was for lunch. Sushil da was a fabulous cook. The chickens multiplied within the estate, and the rice was from the local paddy fields. Sushil da sat alongside the friends, serving them with the long hataas or ladles, taking turns to drop heaps of chicken and rice on the plates even when the friends did not want any more. This was a familiar custom in Bengal. They would go on serving till the person was stuffed and bursting at the seams.

Sushil da himself sat with the others and ate. Watching him eat was a sight to behold. He would shred the chicken pieces into small bits, mash the potatoes, mix them into the rice with the curry and roll them all into neat palm-sized balls. Then, he would hold the balls a couple of inches close to his mouth and pop them in with reasonable accuracy. Most of the balls entered the mouth smoothly, but at times they missed the target and struck his nose or his lips, breaking up into little bits of chicken mixed in rice and potatoes, which scattered around soiling his neck, often falling on others sitting around as well.

In the end, when his plate was empty, he started a process of licking the plate that could only be termed a ceremony—so precise and grand was it in its execution. He would rub his palm on the plate, first clockwise and then anti-clockwise, and then lick them right from his wrists upwards to the tips of his fingers. All this would be aided with tremendous sound effects that could put snorting horses to shame. This done, he would finally raise the plate, hold it in front and lick it dry.

Keya was very amused watching Sushil da and was fondly reminded of a very famous poem by Tagore in which he describes the pleasure of eating a porridge, in which a mango cake, a ripe banana and a Bengali sweetmeat, sandesh, have been added—a favourite combination of delectables that can only be relished in utter solitude while producing "hapush hupush" sounds. Even the crawling ants go moaning hungrily over the empty plate.

Even though this was chicken and rice, and not the Bengali delicacy described in Tagore's immortal words, the poetic comparison was unmistakable and could not be ignored.

Hazel and Keya had been given a separate room to retire for the night that was on the first floor, and Bhor decided to wriggle into the bed with the two girls. The other room was on the ground floor, beside the balcony, overlooking the main gate, big enough to accommodate everybody else.

By the looks of everything on offer, this estate could pass as quite a functional 2 star hotel of the cities. It did not have bathtubs or geysers or air conditioners, but the food was fantastic, and the mosquito nets were properly stitched. Bedsides, lanterns were in place as electricity was unpredictable.

The Marshall Estate was the only building in the locality with facilities to generate electricity, and all the other village houses had to make do with hand fans and lanterns. Brother Lobo took out a pack of cards and laid them out on the floor. He was playing a game called Patience or Solitaire. Imran started drawing a sketch of the Brother playing the game on the floor with the light of the lantern shining on his face.

He requested the Brother to move as little as possible and saw that his model acquiesced with total honesty. Brother Lobo held his pose—both hands cupped below his chin holding it up, eyes fixed on the floor on the cards—and relaxed only when he had to move cards in the game.

The Brother had been playing for over half an hour and had managed to secure the game, but then he realised that Imran had not spoken at all. A faint snoring sound had begun to grow, progressively, louder. He looked aside and found Imran fast asleep with his pencil held between the index finger and the thumb, still resting on the top of the second eyebrow of the sketch that was only half complete. Rahul, Jassi, and Bhombol were sleeping silently on the cot that had the mosquito nets covering them.

The Brother smiled and helped Imran lie down on the floor that had been covered with a quilted cloth. He packed his cards and lay down beside Imran with his head resting on a pillow and thought about the happenings of the day. He would do this every day. It helped him sleep well. It was his form of meditation.

Suddenly, a gush of the wind upturned one of the lanterns on the balcony wall. It fell on the ground, rolled to the far corner and struck the railing, breaking into small pieces. The rain had started once more. The wind blew in through the railings of the main gate and the balcony making a noise that normally signalled arrival of monsters in B grade Bollywood flicks. The doors started swinging ferociously, banging hard against each other.

Brother Lobo was the first to get up when a deity on the wall, made of wood and shal pata, came crashing to the floor and hit Imran. Within minutes wind speeds rose to alarming levels. Thatched palm roofs from adjoining village houses were uprooted from their bamboo bases, colliding against each other in mid-air and were flung to far distances.

The bamboo door of the chicken shed, wrenched free from its hinges and went and struck the iron main gate, and the hens scattered, some died, instantly. The estate reeled under nature's wrath, and one shuddered to think of the helplessness of those who dwelled in the huts at the riverbank. The waves of the river were known to rise to great heights and smash into the huts and damage them. The Brother came screaming down the corridor.

"Sushil da, take care of your daughter and the two girls. I shall be with the others."

He fastened the main door of the room and moved the wooden chest in the middle of the room against it for extra weight.

Sushil da was sitting on his bed holding his daughter tightly to his chest as she was now shivering from fever. Keya and Hazel clutched onto each other and tried to shut their minds off from everything they saw and heard around them. They could hear the sound of wailing children and men scampering around shouting in a language they did not understand. There was a total pandemonium all around with no indication of ending any time soon.

Sushil da heard a frantic banging on the main door of the house, on the ground floor, and Brother Lobo seemed to open the door and move out. He left the relative security of the bed, went to the window and peered down. He saw the Brother talking to a man at the door.

"Lobo bhai, ... Lobo bhai, my wife is in labour pain, and she has to be taken to the hospital. What should I do?" The man was screaming at the top of his voice so that he could be heard over the howling winds and the fury of the storm. Sushil da could hear him faintly from the first floor.

The Brother did not wait to hear any more. He bolted the door from outside and slipped out and ran across the garden getting drenched in the rain. The man followed, struggling to keep up with him. With the Brother sprinting across the garden, the wind relented slightly and the rain eased. But it appeared as if strangers had attacked the estate and left with the booty. Then the proverbial calm before the storm descended.

The tempest must have lasted about twenty minutes. The hangover of the wrath of the calamity still hung in the air, and a pungent salty smell of the wind that came roaring over the oceans, lingered on. It was impossible to imagine that a place could be so ravaged and left squirming and battered, within minutes. Wind speeds of over a hundred kilometres an hour had left the entire village devastated and traumatised. The friends tried forgetting the storm and took succour in sleep, all huddled together with Sushil da and Bhor in the same room.

They woke up to the incessant cackle of the hens in the garden, early next morning. The hens seemed confused, expressing great woe for having lost their shed and also, perhaps, mourning the demise of their companions.

There were also the sweet calls of the Asian koel, a large, long-tailed, cuckoo. The male of the species, glossy and bluish-black, sat on a branch with a pale greenish grey bill and a crimson iris. This was a bird that had a melodious voice, but it did not know how to build a nest. They were known as brood parasites who deposited their eggs into the nests made by crows, and the crows worked as surrogate mothers raising their young. A crow also cried out from another branch in sync with the koel as though it had recognised the trick and would not be fooled again.

Sushil da brought in steaming tea that was served again in the earthen pots. The tea was refreshing, and after everyone had a second helping, Keya noticed that Brother Lobo was missing.

"Where is Lobo bhai?" She asked.

"Someone came calling from the village, late at night. Something urgent. He must have stayed back." Sushil da replied as he poured out the tea.

Then they heard the sound of the bolts unfastening at the door. Sushil da went running down to enquire. Brother Lobo was standing there with another twenty-year-old woman with him. Her eyes suggested that she had wept the entire night. The Brother walked in without a word, and the other woman kept standing at the gate.

"Sushil da, give the woman ₹20, from the collection." The Brother was referring to the paltry funds that the people who comprised the Holy Communion had generated.

Saying this he hurried inside, and one could see huge bags below his eyes, bearing testimony to the fact that even he had not slept the whole night. He went straight for the room where the others were sipping tea. He seemed to be in a rush, not his usual calm self—something he did subconsciously when he was angry.

He was hardly ever angry, but today he was. He poured himself a cup of tea and gulped it down without even greeting anybody in the room. Then he tried to pour another and found that the tea pot was empty. Sushil da, meanwhile, had come back to the door and saw the Brother looking for more tea.

"Lobo bhai, … please wait for a while, and I shall get some more tea."

Saying this, he left the room for the kitchen on the terrace. The Brother rolled up the sleeves of his shirt and walked up to the window and sat on the sill. He could see the damage the night's storm had done to the village down below.

Hardly anything was left of the chicken coop. The wired barricade of the coop was lying a few meters away and half-a-dozen birds lay dead with their feathers entangled with each other. In the middle of this destruction onc cock still followed a single hen around, probably seeking a shoulder to cry on.

From the window, one could get only a partial view of the damage to the property, but the wailing of the children and the cries of the older women reverberated in the Brother's ears who had just come back from the village.

The anger in the Brother lent the room a strange seriousness. Hazel and Keya felt an odd discomfort around him; the tea they were sipping did not taste good anymore. Nobody really knew what to do or say as the Brother sat on the windowsill, looking at the huts beyond the estate's fence that were razed to the ground. The destruction was visible everywhere.

Sushil da appeared at the door, waited for a few seconds and then walked up to the Brother and poured him another cup of tea.

"What has happened Lobo bhai?" He tried to maintain softness in his voice, hoping to calm the nerves of the Brother.

A few seconds of painful silence ensued. Then, he started speaking in a cracked voice, filled with emotion.

"Sushil da, I feel so helpless at times. There is nothing I can do. There was a man who wanted to convert to Christianity the other day. I told him that it wasn't necessary; all he needed was to be a good human being. The man had stolen some honey from a local contractor and his wife had reminded him that it wasn't a good thing to do.

"Tai ami oke bollam je theek ache tui giye khoma cheyye ne ... So I had told him to go and apologise to the man, return his money and say he was sorry. He did that, but the contractor got him beaten up by his men. That angered the man and he swore revenge. He had come back home sweaty and vengeful when he found his wife in labour. He came running to me last night, during the storm. The women from the village helped out despite the storm, and we somehow transferred her to the local dispensary. But it was too late. The local hospital ..."

The Brother was now weeping profusely even as he was speaking half in Bengali, breaking into English sometimes. He did not try to hold back his tears but continued speaking.

"The local hospital had no facility to perform a caesarean section; the woman died on the bed delivering a stillborn. The woman who had come with me, last night, was her sister, and they needed some money to burn her body." With this the Brother fell quiet and there was an eerie silence in the room.

Finally, Bhombol got up and walked up towards the window. He placed his hand on the Brother's shoulders and pressed it gently. Then, one by one, all the other friends came up and surrounded the Brother, holding him gently. Nobody said anything. They formed a human coil, a knot with their arms and their bodies; falling over each other, grasping each other.

The Brother's words had touched a raw nerve. Sushil da and Bhor were the only two left who were not part of this human knot. Then Sushil da walked up and fell over the heap of bodies, and Bhor did the same not knowing why everyone was falling over the Brother.

Towards the main gate, on the road going into the village, a group of village lads, all from the Brother's football team, inspecting the dead chickens by the gate, looked up to find this curious sight. Why everybody had fallen over the Brother was a mystery to them, but they found it rather amusing. They started jumping and laughing, expressing their solidarity—A reason to celebrate amidst the total devastation and squalor. There could not have been a better visual vignette in black humour.

15

The Dispensary

"Let's take Bhor to the doctor." Rahul could not let the matter rest anymore. He had seen the girl sneezing when he first met her and had given her a tablet, but the incidents of the last day and a half had engaged them totally in other pressing matters. But now the child was shivering under the bedsheet and Rahul could not take it anymore.

"Yes, of course, we must immediately," Brother Lobo agreed.

The journey to the local dispensary led through the small town and the market. This was deep inside the main tiger reserve sanctuary, and the sides of the road were earmarked with photographs of the animal on poles.

Most of the poles, however, had fallen to the ground, and the destruction in the locality from the storm the night before, was very visible. Uprooted trees lined the sides of the road, naked babies roamed the paths, and dead carcasses of cattle floated on the muddy banks, below the road. Damaged houses, with dented hopes of people, lay in a monumental ruin, and paramedics, holding long pipes, fumigated the area. The combined screams of the people in pain and the cries of the women in grief created a painful melody, impossible to ignore.

Brother Lobo was riding one thhela, with Sushil da and Bhor. The second had Rahul at the wheel with the friends sitting behind. The two thhelas travelled through the line of destruction and suffering on the streets and approached the dispensary.

The sight of the dispensary from a distance was deplorable. Hordes of people were gathered at the mouth of the emergency ward. It was clear that there were too many patients and not enough doctors. There was a peculiar smell of disease hanging in the air.

The Brother got off his thhela in the middle of all this and carried the body of the child on his shoulders.

"Wait … Wait … Where are you going?"

The ward boy could not see the Brother's face from behind, amidst the throng of people. When he realised who it was, he immediately apologised.

"Please forgive me Brother Lobo. I could not see you … Why have you come again?

He was obviously referring to the Brother's earlier visit to the hospital, the night before, when he brought the pregnant woman who died.

"This little girl here is sick. She needs treatment, but not to worry. I understand that you all must be under a lot of stress."

The relatives of the sick and the ailing were hounding the doctor on duty and he was himself probably feeling sick.

Suddenly, a fight started. A man came charging in through the crowd shaking his fists. He vented his anger on the door by kicking it a few times and then left as he understood the futility of it all. The door remained shut for the next ten minutes and only opened when the man inside spotted the Brother through the window. There were also the local ward boys who took some eager customers behind the walls and thrust out their greasy palms for doing them a favour.

Meanwhile, Bhor was being readied on the diagnostic table. When she saw the house surgeon and the doctor picked up the syringe and needle to take her blood, she started weeping. Brother Lobo grasped the girl and held her close to his chest.

"Don't worry shona (darling). It is just a tiny pin prick and then we shall start singing songs again."

He started humming a song Bhor had taught him. A young nurse on duty tied Bhor's forearm with a rubber band that made the vein on the inside of her elbow bloat. Bhor pressed her eyes close as the doctor punctured the vein with the needle. She gave out a yelp and started crying. The Brother patted her cheeks with her palms and whispered into her ears.

"It is over ... we shall go home now."

The friends were all loitering around in the courtyard of the hospital when Rahul seemed to hear something from inside and rushed forward.

"That's Bhor crying, I think. That's her blood being taken for the tests, or could also be an injection."

"Have we come here to do a study on the medical facilities available in the Sunderbans? First, we did what we could at the hospital at Kakdwip, and here again we are at another hospital." Imran sounded unhappy.

"Nobody told us to do what we did at Kakdwip. Why are you being so cynical?" Hazel frowned.

Jassi did not want to take sides. He walked up and stood between the two.

"Where is the confusion? We all like the child and so we have come here. We can't change the system here overnight. But at the end of the day we came to enjoy a holiday and we seem to be doing just the opposite."

Rahul wanted to carry on the conversation, but Brother Lobo came out, swinging the door open, with Bhor's body slung over his left shoulder and walked straight up to the thhela. He placed Bhor on it and sat at the wheel. For the others it was enough indication to move. Imran got up with Bhor on the Brother's thhela. The other friends huddled into the cart behind Rahul's.

Rahul looked at Imran attending to Bhor, sitting on the cart on Lobo's bhai's thhela. He was patting her forehead. "Don't worry baby ... everything will be okay."

The journey back was through the same market, but now the kids of the locality had all gathered around and they started running behind the thhelas. Two kids jumped on the one the Brother was riding, for a joyride, but the Brother stopped immediately

"What happened Lobo bhai? Why did you stop? Come on, take us a little further down the road," One boy pleaded.

The Brother did not want to harm the sentiments of the kids but he could not let them ride on the thhela and become a hindrance as Bhor was sick and had to be taken indoors to rest as fast as possible. The sky was blackening and he knew that they had to be indoors before it started to rain again. So he explained:

"Look my friends, your sister here is really sick, and she has to be taken indoors before it starts to rain. I suggest you help me do that. Give me a little push, so that I can get home fast."

The road got into a slight uphill curve and immediately the two kids jumped off the thhela, and all of them started pushing the cart from behind. Hitching a ride on Brother Lobo's thhela would have been interesting but pushing it together was even better. They pushed the thhela, running behind it, screaming all the while.

"Lobo bhai ... Lobo bhai ... Lobo bhai ..."

What a fantastic sight this was for Rahul and the others to watch from their thhela. Fun and celebration, in the middle of remorse and destruction! Hope, amidst sadness. Keya took some pictures again.

She had captured the emotions of the children when they were excited and jumped on the cart, when they had jumped off, and now the look on their faces when they were pushing the cart.

Kids all over the globe, were probably the same. The Brother took out little sweetmeats from his pocket and distributed them among the kids. They accepted the small gifts and knew that it was time to leave. They shook the Brother's hands, raising quite a din. Then the Brother took out his whistle and blew hard on it, and the kids immediately fell into a line.

"... The game is over now ... go back to your houses."

At the estate, Sushil da carried Bhor inside. He came out soon afterwards and stood in front of the Brother as though waiting to be told what to do. Then he asked the most obvious question.

"What has happened to my girl?"

The Brother understood his feeling and patted the man on his shoulder and calmed his nerves.

"Sushil da, a blood test will have to be done. These things take time."

Then he took out a crumpled paper ball from his pocket and opened it. A few medicines fell out into his palm and he gave them to Sushil da.

"Give her one each in the morning and evening, after dinner, but remember like last time don't give her all the tablets at the same time ... that will not cure her immediately."

Sushil da smiled and went back into the house along with Brother Lobo. The five friends, meanwhile, gathered around some of the honey collectors who were getting ready for the Bon Bibi puja at the shrine.

16
Bon Bibi

The honey collectors had made a small clearing within the line of trees that surrounded the fencing and were giving finishing touches to a tiny replica of a hut with mud and leaves. They placed a little line of seven earthen mounds, freshly decorated with flowers, beside one another. The five friends walked up to the trees to inspect, but Keya remained behind, at the door of the estate.

Ratan Mondol and Abhiram Mondol, the Hindu honey collectors, placed the Hindu deity, Bon Durga or Bon Devi, wearing a crown and garland, carrying a club and a trishul (trident), and her vahana (vehicle), the tiger, on a wooden platform.

Her Muslim followers, Mujahir Aslam and Manzoor Sheikh, venerated her as Bon Bibi or Pirani. Her predominantly Muslim image, beside the first one, had braided hair. She was wearing a cap with a tikli, loose salwars (instead of a sari), and a pair of shoes. Both the Hindu and Muslim images had a boy on the lap, called Dukhe by her worshippers.

The honey collectors started reciting poems that began with the chanting of the invocation of Bismillah. "Ma Bon Bibi, Allah, Allah" mingled effortlessly with "Ma Bon Devi, Durga, Durga"—the words of prayer the honey collectors paid obeisance with before venturing out into tiger territory.

Mujahir and Manzoor, stroked their beards and sat arm-in-arm with Ratan and Abhiram. The Muslims had no qualms in praying to the same deity, with the Hindus.

"For these islanders, Bon Bibi goes against the distinction of caste, class and religion. This is the reason why those who work in the forest—woodcutters, fishermen, and crab collectors, and the like—stress the fact that they have to consider all jatis, sects, and casts—whether Brahmin or Malo, rich or poor, Hindu or Muslim, or even human or animal—as equal.

"Tigers and humans share the food from the forest, and they both depend on it for their survival. Tigers eat fish and the deer; the villagers like the honey and need wood from the forest—they both depend on the jungle for their sustenance. These facts not only make tigers equal to humans, but it also 'ties' them to humans." The Brother's words explained the entire role of the jungle in the lives of the honey collectors and the mighty Royal Bengal tiger in a context that was seldom revealed with such simplicity.

The honey collectors had come out from the shrine once their puja was complete and were distributing a local sweet. They started collecting their wares as it was time to go into the jungle.

Keya stood a little away from the shrine and waited for her friends to join her. It was an ideal time to talk to the honey collectors about the local customs.

"Could you tell us, what is the significance of this worship, and how does it help you?" Keya asked the honey collectors as they approached her.

The four of them looked at each other, probably wondering where to start. Roton and Abhiram started speaking at once. Then Roton stopped and let his Brother continue.

"Didi ... this land of ours is called the land of the eighteen tides, and the stories here are fascinating. We believe in these stories."

He pointed at the shrine that they were worshipping and his voice acquired graveness because he was referring to something that they held sacrosanct.

"There you see, the most important goddess in the region—Bon Bibi (Lady of the Forest). But she did not come down from the Himalayas as Durga or Ganges to help her people. She is the only Hindu goddess whose origin is not in India. Her story begins in the second holiest city of Islam—Medina."

"A Hindu goddess from the holy place of the Muslims? Interesting!" Hazel was amazed when Bhombol explained to her what they said.

Abhiram felt extremely eager to narrate this story to the friends who did not hail from the region. It gave him immense pride. He started speaking so fast in his excitement that he stumbled on his words.

"Yes, that Medina ... Legend has it that once upon a time there lived a Sufi fakir, Ibrahim, who was childless. The Archangel Gabriel spoke to him and promised Ibrahim that he would have children. Two children were born to Ibrahim at once—Bon Bibi, and her brother, Shah Jongoli.

"When they got older, the Archangel Gabriel appeared to them as he had appeared to their father and said that they had been chosen for a divine mission. Gabriel said that they should leave their homeland and come to India. They obeyed and started their journey as Sufi mystics.

"But in the land that Gabriel had chosen for their divine mission they met a very evil demon—Dokkhin Rai. This demon had a passion for human flesh. When overcome by desire he would take the form of a tiger and hunt human beings.

"Bon Bibi, along with her brother, quickly overpowered him. However, they did not kill the demon, but urged him to promise that he would avoid devouring human flesh. Bon Bibi also divided the Sunderbans and drew up the boundaries of places where people should live. She left the other parts of the jungle for the demon."

Keya and Hazel got so involved in the story that they did not see Jassi sneak up behind them, slither on the ground on all fours and disappear into a mound of hay and cattle feed—covering himself totally under the heap, so that nobody could see him. From underneath the fodder he started a soft growl, mimicking the voice of an animal.

In the beginning, the honey collectors did not quite hear it. When the growl persisted, Abhiram, who was narrating the story, stopped and looked to his left and to his right. The sound Jassi made was indeed so much like a tiger that it even took the honey collectors by surprise.

Abhiram looked at Roton. Nobody said anything, and though it was highly improbable that a tiger would be lurking in the area especially when it was not even totally dark, a big cat's growl out in the open created tremendous suspicion and uneasiness among the honey collectors. They hurriedly started gathering their puja paraphernalia.

Keya who had seen the entire drama tried her best to remain calm but dug her nails into Rahul's forearm as she knew that it was Jassi who was making the sound.

"What is he doing? This is such a bad joke." Rahul had a mixed expression.

"Dada, how effective is this puja?" Rahul did not know what to do, so he tried to change the topic of discussion.

The honey collectors were whispering in hushed tones and did not pay any heed to Rahul. The sound of the growl grew in its ferocity as if the animal had been cornered and was finding ways to fight. The honey collectors surmised foul play, but they nevertheless grouped together in a corner and recited the verses dedicated to Bon Bibi in a chorus.

All of a sudden, Jassi came out of his place of hiding roaring out menacingly, mimicking the movements of a frontal charge of a tiger with raised hands into the air, pawing and clawing the air, and rushed ahead towards Keya. There was a brief pause when nobody spoke, and then Keya started giggling and Rahul also smiled and the friends started chuckling about how well Jassi had recreated the cries of the tiger, but the honey collectors were not at all amused and started leaving without a word.

The friends found this quite odd. Keya became serious and walked up to Jassi who was sulking by now, realising that his little jest had displeased the honey collectors. For a while there was total silence. No one knew what to do. Then Keya took the initiative.

"Jassi, I think what you did was not quite right. Even the mention of the word "bagh" here in the area is not allowed. And you have played a prank on a subject that these honey collectors are really edgy about. You need to apologise to them." She made her point.

Jassi had played a prank in good spirit and had meant no harm. But since the honey collectors were praying for their safety in front of Bon Bibi and asking for protection from the animal that they dreaded, this prank was quite misplaced. He had mindlessly reduced their faith to a mere joke. Brother Lobo would have taken exception to Jassi's behaviour too, had he been around. Jassi realised his fault and walking up to the honey collectors, begged for forgiveness. Sushil da, standing behind him, translated his words.

"He says he is extremely sorry. He did not understand what he was doing. Please forgive him."

Jassi held on to Abhiram's elbow so forcefully that the poor man dropped all that he was holding. Jassi continued to mumble his apologies even as he bent down to pick up what he had dropped.

"I will pray that you are safe and sound and come back tomorrow, so that we can taste the honey that you get back." By now Jassi was crying.

"Dada, please forgive me. If you do not, this holiday will be meaningless." He again fell at the feet of the man folding his arms in a gesture asking for forgiveness.

Roton immediately bent down and held Jassi by his shoulders.

"Aare aare ki korchhen. Come on, what are you doing? We will be okay. Don't worry" Next he held his fingers to his lips and curled his lips.

"Toomra to janona … You are unaware of the customs here, so it's not your fault. No one even utters that word here. Go sleep well tonight, and we shall see you again tomorrow evening. If you are lucky, we shall be back will lots of honey. Now we have to leave."

Coming out of the house, Brother Lobo noticed the commotion near the shrine. He was told what had happened, but the Brother could see that Jassi was really penitent, and so he did not broach the subject again.

"You see, here in tide country, both Hindus and Muslims fall at the feet of the same goddess. Isn't that wonderful? The Hindus of the region have no qualms in hinduising Bon Bibi. But she remains for them, in the local language of the region, a Molla Debi, or a Muslim goddess." The Brother changed the topic.

Rahul was amazed at this. It also made him a little philosophical. He had often thought to himself: Who or what was God? Did God have any realistic explanation in science? He struggled to understand the conundrum and concluded that religion was only a convinient safety net. Men fell at the feet of a power, or a protector, only in distress.

He remembered a seminar at college with some environmentalists who had organised an interactive brainstorming session with the students. The moot topic was the atheistic assumptions of how matter and cosmos had come into existence and how it had metamorphosed to its present state.

During the seminar, they had also been introduced to several theories by world-renowned biologists and environmentalists about how life had evolved from mere hydrogen, through many stages. These abstract theories made him question the presence of God even more. Was God a man-made power then? Did God make man or did man create a power that he named God for his own convenience? Rahul and his friends had wondered and debated on these issues, for weeks after that seminar. And today, all these thoughts came back again as he looked at the shrine of Bon Bibi.

He saw Abhiram and Roton along with the two Muslims, Mujahir and Manzoor, leave the estate and a cloud of remorse enveloped him. There was also a lump in his throat he could not swallow and something deep inside told him that this was not the last he had seen or heard of the honey collectors.

In the far away horizon, a molten sunset glowed like a fried egg, and its strange orange colour lent a beautiful hue to the trees. The sun itself was descending beyond the trees, taking with it the incidents of the day, over the river, probably to be churned again at the bottom of the river, to emerge the next day in more radiant colours. Fifty meters away, beyond the trees, was the river. Rahul felt an urge to sprint across the estate's garden, jump over the wall and dive into its waters. There he wanted to swim for hours and rid his mind of the quagmire of confusion. But before he could budge, a man came running into the estate holding something in his hand, looking around for a place to hide. He eyed the friends for a second and then shot across the garden, darting through the vegetation and by his speed and his clever manoeuvrings he appeared to be extremely agile.

But why was he running? What was he trying to escape? There were no answers yet. The man was in a tearing hurry and had started climbing the water pipe going up the Marshall Estate bungalow and was soon out of view. There was no place to hide on the terrace, but at least he could not be seen from the ground.

Within seconds, there came rushing into the estate, a dozen villagers, all heavily armed with kataris, shovels, and axes, looking for him. However, when they could not find any trace of the man inside the garden, they re-grouped in a corner discussing their next step. There was a stout man, who appeared to be the leader of the group, directing everybody else.

"Dyakh to Molla … Molla you look for the bastard behind the trees. Let's kill him today."

Molla promptly ran behind the trees, making way through the undergrowth, savagely with his axe, making huge arcs with his hands as he moved ahead. One shuddered to think what would happen to man or beast hiding within the shrubs. Little trees and bushes were felled with each strokes, but he continued his destructive forward march. The leader who had ordered the search, saw Rahul and the friends standing in the open area and decided to walk towards them.

"Who are you?"

Fortunately, the Brother came to their rescue.

"Ki hoechhe? What is the matter?" Brother Lobo asked the man.

"Lobo bhai, this man has been hounding us for days stealing our honey and our wax and today we almost caught him, but he escaped. We saw him come into the estate, and he must be hiding somewhere."

Saying this, the man scanned the area in the garden, hoping to find the man. Meanwhile, Molla had managed to damage nearly the entire garden with his axe, and had stopped for further orders.

"Remember that if you make so much noise while you are searching, the man will escape. Search silently, but kill him if you find him." The leader gave him clear instructions.

"Nobody will kill anybody, in this estate." The Brother's words were like an order and the leader immediately lowered his voice.

"But Lobo bhai, we are poor people and he is stealing our honey. Our children will remain hungry."

"We can solve all that even without fighting. If you kill him today, somebody else will steal your honey and wax tomorrow. Will you kill him too? How many will you kill? Killing is not the answer. Go back home, and we will solve the problem tomorrow morning."

The group of villagers spoke amongst themselves in hushed whispers for a few minutes and finally left.

Hazel took Keya by her arm and started walking towards the shrine.

"No, I can't go near the shrine." Keya said in a whisper.

Keya did not want to say the words aloud as the Brother was within earshot. When the Brother walked towards the building to look at it closely, Keya pulled Hazel aside and whispered.

"Hazel, I am chumming. I am not allowed to enter the shrine." Keya made a face. "It is a custom with us Hindus and even Muslims here. Women cannot enter places of worship during their menstrual cycles."

"But you are so educated, do you have to follow it? "Hazel was curious to know.

"Well, that's a long discussion. In earlier times these customs developed around notions of hygiene. They are not relevant in modern days, but sometimes we follow these customs to respect popular sentiments."

The Brother was looking at the top of a tree that grew adjacent to the building's terrace and seemed to have spotted something at the top.

"Ebaar neme esho ... You can come down now."

There was silence all around and the youngsters wondered whom the Brother was speaking to.

"They have left and it's safe now, so you can come down from the terrace." The Brother repeated a little louder.

Then a little movement on the terrace caught their eye. Somebody or something was moving at the edge of the terrace. After a few seconds they noticed a man slowly raising his head. How the Brother figured that the man had been hiding there nobody had any idea, but what happened thereafter caught everybody's fancy.

The man came to the edge of the terrace and flung his body into the air and caught hold of the branch of a tree that was closest to the terrace. He swung like a monkey from branch to branch, slithering down, and was on the ground in no time.

He promptly came and sat at the feet of the Brother like a tamed animal, an honest dog that had only one master. The Brother bent down and held him tightly to his chest. He started crying on the Brother's shoulders and everybody could hear him sob.

"Lobo bhai, my daughter wanted to have bhat (rice) and there was nothing in the house to feed her. She has fever too, and there is no medicine. Lobo bhai, you tell me, what can I do to feed my children? When I see the other kids eating I cannot rest as my children are hungry at home. So I stole some honey from the fields and some wax. That would have fetched me some money tomorrow morning from the markets."

The man was crying even as he spoke and made no effort to stop his tears. The youngsters noticed a pair of thick silver anklets that the man wore around his ankles. Then he bent down to touch the Brother's feet, but the latter stopped him from doing so. Then he shot across the road outside the estate and disappeared into the mangroves.

Sushil da immediately confronted Lobo bhai "That man, Kinu, is a drunk. He is not even married ... Who will marry such a drunkard? And he has no children. He steals only to drink. He is a swine, Lobo bhai ... Why do you waste your sympathy on such a man? Now come inside, or the mosquitoes will eat you alive."

The rest of the evening was spent in silent speculation. They had an early dinner and retired for the night. The girls slept in one room and the boys had huddled into another on the first floor. Bhor had crept into the sofa with her dad.

It was a well-earned sleep and the mosquito nets helped. Sushil da had cushioned the beds quite well with extra pillows. Soon Bhor was talking in her sleep. She was muttering the names of the friends, probably trying to memorise them.

Kinu, utterly drunk, sat a little away from the estate gate, deep into the night, counting small pebbles and humming a bizarre folk tune that lent the atmosphere a mysterious air.

17

The Bhotbhoti

It was eight in the morning. It was a little odd for the bhotbhoti owned by the forest department to remain anchored at the mouth of the river, so late in the day. Usually, the forest rangers would stop by at the village to pick up rations in the afternoons or when they ran out of diesel. By dusk they would leave silently.

Sometimes, the officers on duty would retire for the night and watch the many palas, or the Bon Bibi musicals, enacted by the jatra parties. They would spend the night at somebody's house after dinner and leave in the morning. But today, the boat remained moored on the bank, long after daybreak. The kids gathered on its deck and raised a ruckus.

The five friends were still sleeping at the estate when the sounds of the children shouting wafted into the bedroom like music to their ears. The playful sounds of the children and their cries of "Chai … chai … garma garam chai," was all really very soothing. Bhombol served bed tea, which was even more comforting. They had slept really well that night.

The Brother did not waste any time at all.

"Listen, I need to give you all a crash course about today's expedition over the river, and I expect that you will all listen carefully. We have been given a bhotbhoti, a big boat with an engine, by the forest department, to go into the jungle. You can see the mangroves and the flora from the river, but you cannot get off the boat. That is too dangerous."

Imran jumped at the word danger. "Why is it dangerous Brother? Is it for the crocodiles?"

"No, not for the crocodiles? If we were to go out on a dingy then there was cause for concern from the crocodiles, but this is a bhotbhoti. I suggest we go to the riverbank where I shall explain everything."

The girls had been given the washroom on the first floor and the boys got in together into the toilet on the ground floor and created quite a noise as they rinsed their bodies with water. Within the next twenty minutes they were all packed, ready to leave.

They were carrying their bags and the ration: rice, dal, and vegetables had been stocked up for a couple of days, and the chicken and the fish could be bought from anywhere on the way; crabs, too, were abundantly available.

Bhor was not running a fever anymore, and the drugs given to her had worked. The blood sample, however, had been sent to Kakdwip to be tested. As soon as she started feeling better, she resumed her questions.

"Why are you all leaving? Can one of you, Keya or Hazel didi, stay back? When will you come back?"

When she saw all the luggage being hauled, her eyes became moist. Then the tears came streaming down her cheek and did not relent until the Brother picked her up.

"Okay, okay, you can come with us to see us off at the river."

The Brother carried her on his shoulders and took her out of the estate. Others followed him, walking down the brick road that dipped to the riverbank. Sushil da followed them with the rations.

The tide was beginning to swell, and they could soon see the bhotbhoti, a little distance from the shore, prancing on the water. They would have to squelch through the mud to get to the bhotbhoti. The Brother started talking, and though his voice remained friendly it had acquired a tone of seriousness.

"Look my friends, we have only three passes to enter the tiger country, but I shall request Sumon, the forest ranger who has given us this bhotbhoti, to see if he can allow all of us to travel, but before that you all should listen to me carefully." He pointed to the bhotbhoti on the river as he spoke.

"There is no apparent threat from the tigers in the middle of the river, but still you will notice that the windows of the bhotbhoti have steel rods." He pointed to the rusted iron rods that had some garlands hung around them. Imran could not wait anymore.

"Why the iron railings Brother? Are there pirates?"

The Brother resisted an urge to laugh out, but this was a serious matter.

"You see the Royal Bengal tiger is an extraordinary swimmer. Though there has been no attacks known on bhotbhotis, tigers have been known to swim across rivers when the tides come in, and that can be more than twenty kilometres both ways. So why not remain secure? We do not want any surprises. You shall remain in the middle of the deck, at all times, and never do anything stupid. We shall never get off the boat on the shore as that is not allowed."

At this point, they spotted the four honey collectors they had met earlier, carrying a small dingy on their shoulders and squelching through the knee-deep mud, walking to the bhotbhoti. There were two younger boys with them now.

"Who are the other two, Brother? Are they all coming with us? Why are they carrying the small boat on their shoulders?" Hazel had to know.

"Our bhotbhoti cannot enter the smaller channels. It is too narrow for it to turn. So they are carrying the dingy to enter the mangroves. They will get off somewhere down the river and go into the jungle on foot to collect honey."

"And what protection do they have, Brother?" Rahul wanted to know.

"Well, they have the rubber masks you saw at Jasho's, a few crackers, divine faith in Bon Bibi and immense hope. That's really all, and often that is not enough."

"Hazel do you know of any Royal English tiger back home. I mean a distant cousin of the Royal Bengal tiger?" Bhombol's comment made every one laugh.

"Well, I don't know anybody personally, but I promise to find out when I get back home. But Brother, from what I see, these honey collectors have to battle against heavy odds to survive." Hazel joined in the banter.

"But you see, they have no option. This is their only means of survival." Brother Lobo ended the debate with a kiss on Bhor's forehead and handed her over to Sushil da.

"Promise not to cry. I will be back, before you know," he said.

The forest department rangers on board had laid a wooden plank that rested on the gunwale. The other end was embedded a foot deep in the mud, and one by one everybody walked up in a single file and boarded the bhotbhoti.

"Okay, now come and show me your permits." The forest officer on board demanded.

One by one, Mujahir, Manzoor, Ratan, Abhiram, and the other two boys all lined up and took out crumpled cards, about the size of one's palm, folded in plastic packets to avoid contact with water, and showed them to the officer. The officer saw all the permits taking special care to hold them against the sun to ensure the presence of a watermark that was the security guaranteeing it was not a fake one. Next, he wanted to see all the passes of the guests. This was trouble, and Brother Lobo took Sumon aside for a quiet conversation. "Sumon, we just have three passes but there are six of us. I am taking personal guarantee that they will be safe and will not get off the boat. Can you please allow all of us to go on this tour?"

Sumon got really embarrassed. He had spent many nights with the Brother discussing world politics and his past and knew that the Brother meant what he said.

"Rest assured Brother, I shall keep this to myself. But please ensure you come back within the specified time limit. There are people among the higher authorities who do not like me and they will not hesitate to make a mountain out of a molehill, if they get an opportunity."

Brother Lobo had devised a schedule for the tour that would get them back to the spot, by a certain time in the evening to collect the honey collectors. He needed to confirm it.

"Shono Mujahir … tahole … As decided we will come back to the place where they drop you at six this evening." He referred to his wristwatch and continued. "That gives you about ten hours to collect all your honey. Is that okay?"

"Ye … ye … es … Lo … lo … bo … bh … bh … bhai." Mujahir agreed.

He nearly spat out the word "bhai" as though he was irritated with the way the words seemed to tease him, coming out with such reluctance each time he opened his mouth to speak. It was decided that the honey collectors would be let off a little distance away from the other shore as the bhotbhoti would get caught in the silt if it went in too much inland.

The bhotbhoti must have been sailing on the waters for twenty minutes when the engine coughed a few times, let out a loud hiss, backfired, let out more steam, and then stopped. The honey collectors sat huddled together at the stern of the vessel singing Bon Bibi songs and playing cards. Sumon and the other forest ranger came out of the wheel room and stood in front of the friends as if about to give a speech. The other forest officer kept his gamchha over his shoulder and was constantly fiddling with it, rubbing his face and his eyes and his nose, trying to dry the sweat. The boat was drifting in towards the bank with the current though the engine was dead, and soon it was, twenty meters away from the bank.

"Now you guys can lower your boat and go to the bank. We cannot take the boat any further." Sumon spoke to the honey collectors.

The honey collectors immediately got up, flicked their bidis overboard, which made little hissing sounds as they hit the water. The friends were resting in the hold of the boat and came on deck to enquire why it had stopped. Imran had Lobo bhai's binoculars hanging on his neck and he pressed his eyes into the lenses and scanned the shore.

"I cannot see any bagh on the bank."

His comment was jocular, but he immediately remembered that uttering the word "bagh" in front of the honey collector was taboo, and so he lowered his voice in the middle of the sentence while uttering the unspeakable word.

The honey collectors, meanwhile, had lowered their boat by the side of the bhotbhoti. It hit the water and started bobbing on it. Then, one by one, they all lowered their bodies into the dingy carrying all their accoutrements. They were carrying little knives, a couple of saws, some round aluminium utensils, and their rubber masks.

The six of them started rowing the dingy, which started drifting towards the mouth of one channel that had remained hidden until then. They also had their rubber masks on by now. It seemed they were rowing backwards with their mask behind their head. Then one of them, suddenly, turned around to wave at them. One face turned around to reveal another. This sudden appearance of a doppelganger was bizarre.

"Lobo bhai, it's so easy to understand that these masks are not real. How useful are they to ward of the clever tigers?" Imran was curious to know.

The Brother let out a huge sigh, which proved that he too was a little circumspect about the usefulness of these masks.

"These honey collectors work in places that are most vulnerable to tiger attacks. They virtually invite tiger attacks by crawling through dense tangle of mangrove vegetation, unarmed and even separated from one another by thick screens of undergrowth. But what can they do? They have no other option!"

Lobo bhai had become very knowledgeable about the practices of the locals and other habits of the people in tide country. He also derived pleasure in discussing these habits and customs.

"Remember what Jasho told you in her house? When stalking, the tiger takes care to choose the moment of its attack. Case studies carried out in the Sunderbans have noted that victims have always been attacked from behind—from the unguarded side when they are not alert. If you put a mask at the back of the head the tiger probably thinks that the victim is looking back, so does not attack. Fooling the extremely cunning and clever tiger is not an easy task, and it's still debatable whether this impersonation works, but initial findings have indicated that people wearing these masks have seldom been attacked."

Imran painted a picture in his mind of the dense foliage, and the honey collectors crawling in the underbush, proceeding towards the beehive up on a branch. He also picturised a tiger lurking behind them, camouflaged brilliantly by the mangrove trees. Though this was only a painting in his mind, the sheer authenticity with which he imagined it gave him a chill, and he immediately erased the vision from his mind with a quick blink of an eyelid. He could do that as it was just a figment of his imagination, but he wondered what Abhiram and Mujahir would do. They would not notice a stalking tiger if it came from behind.

"Lobo bhai, can't somebody insure their lives? Can't somebody come forward and protect their lives against tiger attacks with an insurance policy?" Imran broached an important issue.

The Brother heaved another sigh of helplessness and exasperation, and unlike him seemed a tad annoyed.

"Why don't you do something about it Imran? Why don't you take up the cause? You all come from affluent families, so why don't you all contribute a nominal sum from your pocket money—from the large sums that you spend on burgers and junk food and at hookah bars, or from the money you spend on presents that you buy for your girlfriends.

Can you not take a pledge today that you shall do something for these really unfortunate people? Can you promise that, God willing, tomorrow if your paintings sell like hot cakes, and decorate the walls of the rich and the famous, you will ensure that a nominal amount goes out as a premium, for a life-insurance policy, for these hapless honey collectors? If tomorrow the music album that you sell becomes a hit, will you remember these people and donate some money from your earnings? Can you do that?

"Touch your heart and try and answer the question as it is a pertinent question, and needs a pertinent answer. What is social responsibility, and who is accountable? We have to ask ourselves first!"

Brother Lobo rarely lost his cool, but the way his fingers clenched the iron rods of the bhotbhoti, after he completed his soliloquy, one noticed the distress taking over him. He waited for a few seconds and then looked out into the river and took a deep breath trying to swallow the lump in his throat. He closed his eyes in meditation for a few seconds.

"I am sorry … please forgive me. I got carried away … It is all God's will. Come on let's go down and eat something."

Meanwhile, the small dingy had touched the muddy banks and the honey collectors got off. They were sunk into the soft mud to their knees. They pushed and shoved the boat into the green mangroves and hid it. Then they came back out of the canopy again ready for their mission—to fetch the deadly honey from the trees right in the tiger's lair. If they were lucky there would still be six of them carrying back the honey!

18

Tiger Attack

With the rubber masks tightly secured behind their heads, the six honey collectors crept on their knees and entered the labyrinth of mangroves, in absolute silence. Abhiram was leading the way as he was the most experienced of them all, with each of their masks tightly secured behind their heads. He paused knee deep in the water and stayed rigid for a second. Any movement around had to be judged with caution. He peered down into the water and saw a fish swim through the folds of his lungi, brushing against his inner thigh. The touch of the fish to his skin sent a shiver through his body. The others watched the fish cruise through noiselessly and get lost between the submerged roots.

Then they proceeded down their journey, fleetingly looking up to inspect the top of the higher trees, glistening above the water. They would have to wade through the water for another ten-odd minutes before they could start hunting for the beehives. Here in the water they were slightly safer, but deeper in the jungle when they would have to stand up and look around, the threat from the tigers increased greatly.

No words were exchanged while wading through the knee-deep water, and each one went through the chores as if on cue; their actions all well-orchestrated and rehearsed. There was no improvisation. Improvisation was too dangerous.

Roton's face brushed against the bark of a mangrove thicket, and the rubber elastic band that fastened his mask got entangled in its branches.

"Danrao ... danrao ... ufff ... these branches are like death," he said.

Abhiram and the others surrounded Roton and started beating their drums and bellowing on their buffalo horns, while the latter wrenched his mask free from the tangle. They knew that if there was a tiger somewhere in the area it was impossible to have gone unnoticed. Scent formed the basis for territorial behaviour of tigers, and they depended a lot on this faculty. It was better if they remained on the move always, but if all of them were stationary at a single point the chances of an attack greatly increased.

Mujahir and Manzoor came around and Roton and Mujahir started lighting a torch fashioned out of the leaves and the twigs that they were holding. It seemed that they were all in a hurry to fetch the honey and escape, and Roton was now blowing on his buffalo horn really loud. This way they created enough noise to deter the tiger from attacking.

The other two boys, meanwhile, had ventured a little deeper into the forest to look for the hives. These two were much younger boys, probably in their mid-twenties, and they looked a little unsure on their feet. The others made as much noise as possible with their drums and horns. Their loud screams, along with the beating of the drums and the buffalo horns, were enough to scare any animal. Whether it could scare the tigers of the area was to be seen.

To produce this caterwauling was, however, tiring. So the honey collectors took pauses, breathing heavily to regain composure. These moments were used in lighting up small crackers that they had carried with them. Roton held up the cracker as the others lit it with the torch.

"Dada, akta chaank dyakha gyase ... Brother, we have spotted one hive ... It's up on a tree, and it's this fat and looks really rich." The two youngsters who had gone deeper into the jungle came out and announced victoriously.

One of them held his hands in front of his chest, holding both his palms close to each other to denote the width of the hive. Abhiram and the others looked at each other and moved forward. By now they had reached a part of the jungle where the trees were higher than the shrubs, which they crossed twenty meters behind, and though the vegetation had thickened, movement was a little easier.

The mud below their feet was harder; they did not slip anymore. The breathing roots and shoots, sticking out from the mud were not so sharp as to prick their heels as before. They could walk erect now, and they continued their onward journey through the growth. Roton was now leading, and he was clearing the way forward by swinging his da, a sickle, in huge arcs to make way through the branches and the twigs.

Roton noticed a secluded grove, deeper into the forest, a little distance away from the river. The beehive was sitting on a branch about ten-feet high, and it was quite a picture. It was interesting to note that though the vegetation had thickened with shrubs, the rest of the foliage all grew together in a cluster looking like a coppice. Honey bees, especially, looked for such clusters where their hives would not be threatened by gusts of wind. Even from below they could see teeming bees resting on the hive and hundreds more swirling all around it. Abhiram and others quickly took up positions—Roton took out dry leaves and twigs from his jhola, the side bag he was carrying, and placed it right below the hive on the ground; others continued to beat the drums and sustained the cacophony. It was hard to even think how a tiger could appear in this serene setting and spoil the equipoise of peace and tranquility. Everything looked so picture perfect, there did not seem to be any danger at all.

The mound of dry leaves and twigs at the bottom of the tree, below the hive, was lit at once. It crackled slowly building up into a fire, and the smoke started snaking upwards. When the first wave hit the beehive, the commotion created was immediate. The bees resting on the hive took wing, scattering and scurrying into the air, but hovered around nearby. The area around the tree was soon under a covering of these orange-winged insects, circling around their home that was being attacked by aliens.

While the rest maintained the clamour below, Abhiram started climbing the tree. He was a master at this and was soon half-way up, carrying a saw and a wooden basket. A couple of bees rested on his face and shoulder. They stung him, but he was used to this; his focus glued to the prize that was hanging a couple of meters up.

Roton climbed after him, carrying a few aluminium buckets tied to his lungi. Both were feeling the sting of the bees on their foreheads. Fearing attacks on their eyeballs, they squinted now and then. The honeycomb right in front of them kept them going. When he finally reached his destination, Abhiram secured himself on a branch in front of the hive, brushing off a couple of bees that were still resting on it.

"Are nibhe gyalo to … the fire is almost out … light it again." He shouted at others who stood below.

The two youngsters heard what was said and did what was required. One of them started fanning it furiously with a palm-leaf fan, and the other boy knelt down on his knees and blew at the fire from close distance. Mujahir and Manzoor got themselves busy gathering more twigs and dry wood.

Up on the tree Abhiram and Roton, both, looked at the hive right in front of them. The wax was bubbling with the red liquid. It would easily fetch a ₹1,000, at the market, and if they were lucky the wax could fetch some more. Both Roton and Abhiram first tied their own bodies to a strong branch of the tree with their gamchhas, leaving enough slack in the rope for some movement. They were tied to the tree from their waists, and could easily stand up or sit down.

Roton held the hive with one hand and placed the aluminium handi below it. Abhiram severed the hive at a place where it was attached to the branch with the end of the saw and brushed the side of the hive, puncturing it. The golden syrup percolated out of the sides of the hive, flowing gently along the sides of the wax body and collected into the handi. This was the sight that they all cherished—rewards for hard and risky work! Mujahir and Manzoor resting against another tree, with their head turned skywards watching Abhiram and Roton, relished the process.

The fire was dying again below the tree, so the boy kneeling beside it took off his mask and went closer to the fire. He inhaled a lung full of air and blew at the twigs with a huge guffaw of breath, and the dry leaves and the twigs immediately sparkled like gold as the fire took grip. He had to move away at once as it got too hot and the leaves flew around, and the fire spread to the far corners of the mound because the other boy was fanning vehemently with his palm-leaf fan.

About fifty meters behind the fire was a line of sundari trees that had a thin opening between them leading deeper into the forest. There was a slight rustle in the vegetation, and then suddenly, the forest came alive without warning. The vegetation separated, the trees gave way, and golden yellow black stripes dazzled, in the blink of an eye.

The cat must have been stalking the boys on the ground for some time and had waited for the opportune moment to strike—for that precise instant when the boy crouched on the ground, hunched in front of the fire. He was wearing no mask either. The tiger crept out stealthily from the bushes and was on his back in a second. His weight felled him to the ground, immobilising him immediately, and one bite to the back of the neck must have killed him, instantly.

Mujahir and Manzoor, a little distance from the boys with their gaze still upwards a while ago, were left speechless, shaking in fright. The other boy with the palm leaf in his hand did not know what to do. He had only a burning twig in his hand that he was shaking, involuntarily, but the animal had smelt fear. It was such an enormous animal that everybody was dwarfed by its presence.

The tiger, stirred by his movement, reached out and pawed at the boy's shoulder with a huge swipe of its thaba or paw, and a ferocious growl that left a gash on his shoulder and sent him sprawling to the ground. Mujahir started running and went as far as the river screaming like a mad man.

The injured boy lay on the ground, inert for a while, and then managed to wriggle his way painfully into the trees, while the tiger turned around to concentrate on the first one it had attacked. Another quick bite to the neck, and there was a brittle sound of the spine breaking. It then dragged the body into the mangroves, leaving a trail of blood.

The entire sequence, right from the time when the forest came alive and the yellow and black stripes leapt out, till the time when the tiger dragged the victim into the mangroves, did not take more than thirty seconds. Abhiram and Roton, fastened to the branches, held on for dear life. They had had a bird's eye view of everything and were shaking in fright.

Each one was trying to grapple with the situation and its rude lessons—a honey collector had been killed—he was not wearing the mask; another had been grievously maimed and Bon Bibi had failed to protect them.

Abhiram and Roton were numb with fright. They slowly sat down on a branch. The handi that had the honey had also been fastened with a gamchha to a branch and that kept it from slipping and falling to the ground. Both wondered about their next step. What should they do? They could not gather enough courage to come down from the tree, but they knew that they would eventually have to do that.

Once the body vanished into the bushes, silence cloaked the surroundings, leaving an uneasy stillness in the air. The injured boy's body lay on the ground, half hidden by little shrubs, and he was, probably, bleeding to death.

It all looked so improbable now. Abhiram and Roton wondered how they would face the villagers back at the village; what would they say when the boy's mother wanted to know about her son. Though the compensation claims were the last thing on their minds now, yet they knew that they had to find traces of the body, or whatever was left of it, as the government authorities would want photographic evidence of the kill to substantiate compensation claims.

But climbing down was a very difficult thing as thoughts invariably went to the tiger lurking in the bushes. They waited on the treetop wondering what had happened to the others in their group. The river was about a hundred meters from the tree and they knew that if they stayed together and moved quickly towards their boat then probably they could make it.

Manzoor had followed Mujahir to the river who was acting very demented by now, splashing around in the water, beating his chest and crying. Manzoor took hold of him and hid under the shrubs, trying to calm his endless prattle. Meanwhile, Abhiram and Roton looked at the area around and finally decided to climb down.

It was high tide now and half the island had disappeared underwater and the distance to the water's edge was greatly reduced. When they were all about five feet above the ground they jumped down and rushed forward making all the noise they possibly could. Abhiram beat furiously on the drum, Roton blew on his buffalo horn. Manzoor dragged Mujahir from their hiding spot and rushed towards the rest, with earsplitting shrieks.

Everyone, immediately, ran to the injured boy who was lying in a pool of blood. Roton unwrapped the gamchha around his waist and dressed the wounded shoulder as quickly as he could. He then swiftly turned the boy's gamchha into a sling to support the wounded arm. Without wasting another minute, they picked up the boy in a semi-conscious state and, lugging him from one side scurried towards the river.

Together, they ran towards the river with renewed vigour, generated out of desperation, their bodies getting bruised by the mangroves, but nothing stopped them. With great difficulty they dragged the boy along, who could barely run, buckling under the excruciating pain in his shoulder. They pushed him from behind and shoved him forward gently, careful not to touch the bleeding wound.

The tide was now at its highest, so as soon as they hit the water they had to start swimming towards the boat. The salty water touched the raw wound, and the boy gave out an ear-splitting scream fainting instantly. The breathing roots that were bare and sharp before were all submerged underwater, but they brushed against their knees and their ankles cutting and bruising them. They had no option, but to push through the water carrying the unconscious boy along.

The boat was rocking gently and swaying with each incoming wave. It bobbed and bounced as they approached from all the sides to get up all at once, such was the state of their despondency. Roton signalled others to hold the boat, while he climbed in. They swiftly moved the body of the boy next. Despite the remarkable circumstances and the chaos, Abhiram had remembered to carry the honey, which he held above his head. The honey was transferred next—a prize they had won, but at what cost?

19 Experiences

They rowed the dingy silently. Nobody spoke. They looked back at the island where they had to leave one of their companions behind. They had no clue where the body had been dragged. Abhiram, Manzoor, and Roton at the stern, looked quite lost. Mujahir babbled to himself, still quite distraught. The vast stretch of vegetation and undergrowth of mangroves, through which they had waded and swam into the island, was now reduced to a mere mudflat bubbling in the water. Here, in tide country, stretches of land mass and solid surfaces disappeared and vanished, while newer ones appeared daily. The daily tides had their own ownership rights in the region. They could alter or preserve the geography to their own whims and fancies. Nothing was the same every day in tide country.

The injured boy lying on the boat was probably dying. The gash in his shoulder was still oozing. He lay within the awning of the boat groaning and writhing in pain and crying helplessly. Outside the shade, the others sat in a bunch. This was the first time that someone from their group had been killed. The handi containing the honey lay in a corner, resting on the bow of the boat. The injured boy, inside the semi-circular tent, suddenly gave out another painful shriek. Roton dashed by his side and crouching under the awning, offered him some water.

"Here, drink some water."

Roton raised the boy's head and poured some water down his throat, but that seemed to aggravate the pain, and he let out another piercing cry, turned over, resting prone, face down on the floor. Though he hardly had any strength left in him, for executing such a body twirl, probably the pain due to the sudden movement, compelled his muscles to move.

Facing the bow of the boat, he could now see the aluminium handi containing the honey. Its very sight brought back ghostly images of the golden and white stripes of the tiger, and he almost heard it roar. Images of his brother's body toppling forward under the weight of the huge cat flashed before his eyes, and he closed his eyes and started crying. The sight of the utensil had brought back those troubling vignettes, and he could not bear them.

He tried to wriggle his way forward, crawling on his belly, out of the covering of the tarpaulin to approach the handi. Roton stood aghast. It was a miracle enough that the boy was alive. He had not imagined he could garner so much strength as to move forward, on the bobbing dingy, towards the bow. His movement disturbed a number of aluminium pots that were lying tied together and they scattered and struck each other as the boat begun to rock due to the sudden movement.

What was he trying to do? A little perplexed, the boy waved his hands in the air and shouted.

"Bhango … bhango … shesh koro … Break it … finish it," as if he was trying to break the handi, which was still quite a distance from him. But why would the boy want to throw the honey overboard? Had he gone mad? They rushed to the bow of the boat circling around the awning, trying to calm him down. He struggled a little and then crying out in pain started weeping inconsolably, like a child.

"This is not honey this is my brother's blood ... son of a swine, the tiger ... if only I could lay my hands ..."

Tears drowned his voice and exhausted him, and his blabbering grew quieter. Tears still ran down his cheeks, incessantly, even as he passed out. Roton felt the pulse below the neckline.

"He is still alive, but don't know how long he will last."

There was a sense of helplessness in Roton's voice. He sounded peculiar trying to force the words out. However, its message propelled them to row a little faster as they knew that time was running out on them.

A faint but the unmistakable sound of a bhotbhoti wafted in. There was hope, yet. They saw the vessel sailing, in the distance. Everybody on the boat started screaming and shouting, waving the utensils to reflect some light if they could. Abhiram and Roton stopped rowing, took off their white singlets and started waving them over their heads. They had no idea that waving a white cloth was a sign of surrender, but they had unwittingly surrendered to their circumstances.

Be it their combined shouting, which was pretty loud despite their fatigue, or the reflection of the aluminium utensils, they managed to catch the bhobhoti's attention. That probably proved that hope drove humans to greater limits of achievement than hopelessness. Hope was so much stronger than fear.

Brother Lobo was standing looking out into the river, with the wind blowing through his hair, when he saw the dingy wobbling on the water, about a hundred meters away to his right. The other friends were looking into the water for the fish that swam behind the boat. There were a few more fishing boats on the water, but one attracted attention as there seemed to be some commotion there. It was about five in the evening and the water had started to acquire a reflected orange hue due to the sun that had started its descent over the horizon. The Brother looked at the boat, shielding his eyes from the rays of the sun that hit his face, and knew immediately that something was wrong.

"Sumon take the boat a little faster towards the dingy … I suspect there is some problem."

The two forest rangers in the wheel room directed the vessel towards the dingy, and within minutes the bhotbhoti was circling it. Mujahir was crying and he stopped waving the cloth. Everybody on deck could see the body of the injured boy lying inside the awning in the middle of the boat. The forest rangers immediately threw a rope to the dingy, and it was tethered close.

Mujahir started crying even louder now, trying to convey something, talking incoherently, but because he stammered, it became impossible to understand him. But that he was speaking to the Brother was evident from his actions. A wooden plank was laid between the dingy and the boat and the injured was taken on board, and the Brother knew at once that he was in a serious condition.

"Sumon, get the bhotbhoti to the nearest island as fast as possible. We can all listen to the story later."

The forest rangers along with Sumon had their walkie-talkies that came to use now. Sumon, at once, switched his on and spoke into the mouthpiece.

"Sector 1 calling SHIS … Sector 1 calling SHIS …"

Keya and the other friends, watching all this silently, were struck with pain as they could not fathom the reason why things had gone so wrong on a holiday they had earned. Imran gathered some courage to close in and inspect the situation.

The Brother looked at Imran, and even before he said anything his expressions said it all.

"It's a tiger attack. One honey collector has been killed and one mauled. We have to get first aid urgently, or he will die too."

"Why did I have to talk to them about tiger attacks? That must have attracted bad luck." Imran felt his innermost thoughts had been manifested. He felt enormously guilty. Rahul was the first to speak.

"You need not feel guilty about this Imran. In fact, I think this should give us some reason to get a few things organised."

Hazel and Keya moved away from the path of the stretcher, feeling nauseous.

"Brother Lobo, it's nice to see that at least they have these walky-talkies during emergencies, but who is he speaking to?" Rahul enquired.

"Have you heard of the French writer, Dominique Lapierre?"

All the friends nodded in the affirmation. Who did not know him?

"Almost everyone knows about his book *The City of Joy*, but very few know of his contribution for the betterment of the people here—he was conferred the 'Sunderbans Award' by an NGO, for his immense contribution towards the underprivileged in rural areas who he believed could also be part of nation-building. Lapierre has donated the entire royalty of his best-selling book to Southern Health Improvement Samity (SHIS), the NGO involved in extending medical assistance to people in the 54 islands of the Sunderbans. Sumon called the medical boat of the SHIS, for assistance."

Rahul wanted to go in and check on the injured boy, but Brother Lobo warned him against doing so.

"Sumon has been able to reach the medical patrol boat of the SHIS. They have a speedboat service, and if the boy is lucky then it will reach us any time now."

The Brother had not completed his sentence when a purring sound was heard over the river and a speedboat came screaming down the water towards the bhotbhoti. It was quite clear that the people on board the speedboat were well trained. They had their own stretcher. Two medics ran in with saline drip bottles, and within fifteen minutes the boy was transferred to the speedboat, which sped away.

The friends were really impressed with this prompt medical service. Keya walked up to the Brother and flashed a smile, and the Brother gave out a sigh of relief as he spoke.

"Wow … so I see my lady can smile too! Come on, let's be hopeful. If the boy is lucky, he will survive. Luck does play a very important role in the lives of these people here."

As the speedboat sped away into the distance, Keya pursed her lips and shut her eyes, and prayed for the boy's survival. The sun was about to set on the river, and the area took on a resplendent look that words cannot describe. The sky was brilliantly illuminated with an orange glow, and the sun descended wearily over the river. The waters had turned gold too and the meeting of the circular golden ball, and the still waters was like a divine embrace.

The sun would be an overnight guest of the waters and then would rise again the next day with all its fury, recharged and well-fed, to lord over the tidal islands again. But now it was tired. It was slipping readily over the horizon and the bhotbhoti was actually riding into the sunset. This was also the time when dozens of fishing boats were returning or the fisher-folk were drawing in their nets, standing on the decks.

For Rahul and Keya this moment was infused in romance. The surroundings were like a dream, but the incidents of the day and the sight of the injured boy stymied the desire to give in to thoughts of passion and excitement that the scenic ambience created in their bellies. Keya hunched on one side of the boat and watched the water silently lapping at the sides of the boat, and Rahul came and stood beside her, touching her fingers softly.

"What are you thinking?"

Keya was still thinking about the injured boy and wondering what his chances of survival were, but the golden sunset was wrestling with her mind, trying to consume all her thoughts. It was a tug-of-war between the malice of realism and the throbbing pulse of fantasy.

"Rahul, something tells me that the boy will not survive. I caught a glimpse of his wound. What are his parents going to say?"

This was the last thing that Rahul expected Keya to say to his question. He made a face as if he had been given a dose of cod-liver oil to swallow.

"Keya, I know this is not the best thing to say right now, but do you see the sunset over the river?"

He pointed in front of him. The sun was in its final phase of decline; a slow and steady crawl at the edge of the horizon, and one could almost hear a woeful sigh in the air as it disappeared over the horizon that had caught fire. The fishermen on their boats were all silhouetted against the golden horizon, and the mind could not be kept in check. It was a beautiful sight.

The others were peering over the side of the bhotbhoti looking down into the water and were talking to a group of fishermen who were finding it difficult to haul in their nets. Something big and heavy had obviously got caught in the netting. A middle-aged man stood up on his small dingy and held up a large fish dangling at the end of a rope, over his head, to exhibit the catch. The Brother was bargaining the purchase with him.

"How much do you want for that?"

The Brother would never be unfair to the fishermen here nor would they in return charge him anything exorbitant, but still they bargained as that was the usual norm. Nothing would be exchanged without some negotiation.

"Three-hundred rupees for this one." The fisherman held up his catch for the others to see.

"I will give only two hundred. My friends want to taste the hilsa here, so I am buying this, else I don't need it."

The fisherman stayed adamant, for a while, and finally sold his catch for ₹200. There were others on the boat who were scaling, cleaning, and cutting the fishes and neatly packing the pieces into polythene bags before handing them over. Meanwhile, a few other fishermen were still struggling with their nets and had got tired trying to haul them in. This was a little surprising considering that all the others had hauled in their nets. After a few minutes, the fishermen sat down in the middle of their boats and one of them commented.

"Ae shala kumir dhora poreche naki? Have we netted in a crocodile?"

There was a short splutter of laughter among the other fishermen, and then there was a sudden movement on the water behind the boat. A silvery body leapt high up from the water in an arc and landed back about ten meters away. A few seconds later another silvery rubber-like body did the same, adjacent to the first and soon one could see two lithe shark-like creatures, bobbing up and down, jumping back in arcs, creating a rhythm with their movement that nobody could avoid noticing. The friends on the bhotbhoti got really excited, and Keya started taking pictures. Hazel started jumping up and down on the deck.

"River dolphins!" She screamed.

The Brother walked up to the side of the bhotbhoti and saw the movement of the creatures on the water. These aquatic mammals had a restive nature. They would surface momentarily necking each other as if exchanging views and dive back into the depths of the water. As though there was something deep in the waters that they were discussing on the surface. Their posture and behaviour spoke a thousand words if one cared to listen, and the Brother was listening.

The other fishermen were quite accustomed to sighting these marine mammals in the waters, but Brother Lobo had derived a more meaningful conclusion from the behaviour of the dolphins.

"You know what? I fear something, and sadly, I think I am right. The dolphins seem really disturbed at something. They are agitated!"

As the Brother spoke he took off his shirt and was soon standing bare bodied on the deck of the boat. His shoulder and chest muscles bulged on his hirsute chest. Next, he took off his trousers. Why was he taking off his clothes? In the water below, the two dolphins orchestrated their dance number, leaping out and diving back, a fair distance away. They seemed to be dancing but the Brother felt otherwise. He muttered under his breath.

"Something is wrong ... Who among you swims well?"

Both Bhombol and Rahul, who were more than average swimmers, raised their hands, but they were not sure if they wanted to jump into the crocodile-infested water.

"All right, let me find out first."

Saying this, the Brother jumped over the gunwale and dived into the water as gracefully as an Olympic swimmer. When he hit the water he cut through it with minimal splash, such was the artistry and perfection of the dive. The friends ran to the side of the boat and peered down and tried to locate him.

The water was heavily silted and it was impossible to see more than a few inches beneath the surface. Soon the water settled down and calmness returned to the surface. But virtually everyone's eyes were on the surrounding waters, trying to spot the deadly crocodiles that infested these waters.

Brother Lobo resurfaced in a couple of minutes and threw out a mouth full of the saline water. He was coughing gently and was a trifle breathless and the friends on the deck had to make an effort to understand what he was saying.

"Two dolphins are caught in the fishing net about twenty feet below. They are struggling, and they will cut themselves to death. I need some help."

Though the fishermen standing on the other boats did not understand English, they somehow figured out what the Brother meant, and one of them immediately jumped into the water and joined him. Bhombol was standing right in the middle of the group. He was wearing pyjamas and he dropped them instantly baring his thighs. An epic leap over the gunwale of the boat, and he hit the water too.

Bhombol and Brother Lobo swam side by side, descending into the depths of the water. Bhombol was a trained swimmer, but even he was a little intimidated by the sudden feel of the water and its salinity.

Something heavy and slippery brushed against his shoulder. He was thrown off guard, and he collided against the nylon netting of the fishing net in the water, struggling to regain his strokes, and whatever had hit him dived further below in front of him. He could see it clearly now.

It was one of the dolphins they had seen bobbing on the surface. He also saw the Brother and the fisherman swimming beside him, but for a few seconds his vision was blurred as all the aquatic life moved vigorously within the nylon ropes, and he held on the net to regain his balance under water.

He had been driven down into the water due to the sudden impact of the dolphin's body and was holding the fishing net and clinging to it for support. That disturbed all the fish caught inside, and the net swayed at the sides.

Then they saw the two river dolphins trapped in the net struggling to get free. They were excited and clueless and had lost all sense of direction and were darting about erratically. Each time they hit the nylon netting they became even more vigorous. The two dolphins that had dived in from the top, reached the one's trapped and necked each other through the netting. It was tremendous to watch how animals expressed their concern and affection. Those free were sympathising and lamenting the condition of the trapped, but they were helpless.

Then the Brother came knifing through the water and held the net with his hands, and the fisherman beside him took out his da (sickle) from the folds of his lungi, neatly tied to his waist. He held the da, or the cutting instrument, to the edge of the net and waited for the dolphins trapped inside to swim a little further away from the net.

The fisherman waved at the Brother with his palm, signalling to him to go back, and the Brother pedalled back. Then with a huge heave he severed the netting and the loose nylon threads fell at the sides, letting out hundreds of fish that were now free.

Schools of fish swam to freedom touching their bodies and swimming over Bhombol and the Brother. The two dolphins, however, waited in the water for some time weighing out their possibilities. Then one made a dash for the opening in the netting and came out, and the Brother swam to the side, making way. The free dolphin then turned around as though beckoning the other to follow. The one inside the net then came forward behind the first one, and both swam to the surface of the water to freedom.

When the rescued dolphins surfaced, a little distance away from the bhotbhoti, the five friends on the deck gave out a huge cheer. They watched in wonder the four dolphins who started circling the Brother and the fisherman, touching them with their noses and brushing their bodies.

The four were no doubt expressing their indebtedness for being freed from the shackles of the net. This time their movements seemed more lyrical as they jumped and leaped in the water in beautiful arcs, no longer restive, but in perfect harmony. The Brother and the fisherman found it difficult to stay afloat; so vigorous was their expression of thanksgiving. Then, all at once, they headed for the deeper waters.

For the friends this had been a magical spectacle to witness, and it was majestic to see the four river dolphins bounce and dance further into the river, carrying the twilight on their backs. But Imran being a painter had seen a little more.

Imran shut his eyes and imagined. He saw the dolphins pause in the water with their necks raised together; synchronising into a salutary posture; holding up their bodies high above the surface of the water as if they were all woven together by an invisible thread in one straight line. Here they hung together, frozen for a few seconds, time standing still, on the canvass of imagination.

When he opened his eyes, Imran saw the dolphins jump and skip on the surface of the water and then dive back again, creating the ceremonious arcs that are so distinctly synonymous with this aquatic species.

It was a seamless transition between the rainbow coloured realms of fantasy and the monochrome palette of the real world where he saw the dolphins, disappearing into the deeper waters of the ocean, jubilantly.

20
Back Home

One of the most difficult things in life is to convey the message of death and tragedy to the near and dear ones. Once back to the Marshall Estate, Brother Lobo and the friends would need to encounter the parents and the relatives of the boy who had been killed and the one who was injured.

The bhotbhoti was about to hit the riverbank, and it was totally dark. They were not expecting anyone to receive them at the jetty, which was a relief. But to their great surprise forest rangers had got news that the Brother had entered the reserve forest with honey collectors and that he did not have permits for all. So they were waiting to receive them at the jetty.

This was bad news. The forest rangers and other officers looked out for such opportunities to make some quick money, and Sumon knew this very well. So when he saw his colleagues waiting for them, he knew at-once that trouble was brewing. Sumon walked up to the Brother.

"Lobo bhai, all does not seem well here. My colleagues have come to receive me, and I think I know why."

"Whoever is on board, please be ready to show us your permits," the voice of one of the forest rangers speaking on a megaphone, rang out, harsh and intimidating.

The Brother knew that this meant serious trouble. He also suspected that the way ahead would not be easy since a personal vendetta against Sumon was at the root of it. Once the bhotbhoti was moored on the banks, Sumon went and spoke to his colleagues and walked back to the Brother.

"This is more serious than I thought. I know the man speaking on the megaphone. There is a high-level investigation planned already, and they want to serve me a show-cause notice for allowing three extra members to enter the tiger reserve without passes. That there has been a tiger kill on the tour, has compounded the matter. I suggest you all carry on and I shall come back in the morning with all the details."

The Brother and the friends slipped away in the dark and soon they were all sitting at the Marshall Estate, trying to think of a strategy to break the tragic news to others. Sushil da already knew about the tiger kill and was really concerned.

"The entire village knows about it already. Sumon is in real trouble. He needs this job for his family, but he could be sacked."

This made the Brother feel really guilty as he had coerced Sumon to allow the five friends to accompany them on the tour.

They had barely settled down, and the friends were cleaning up, when a forty-year-old lady came rushing through the gate of the estate. She threw herself at the feet of the Brother and started howling. Eventually, another group of women emerged and tried to pull her away. She was the mother of the one who had been killed. Fortunately, the boy was unmarried. There was an unhealthy custom here to socially ostracise the widows of tiger victims. "Tiger widows" as they were called, were considered cursed and were forced to live in isolation, away from the rest of the village.

Several villagers had also collected with emotions running high. Sushil da managed to ask them to leave when he realised that things could get out of hand, and they walked away grudgingly, throwing back glances at the group of friends as they left the estate.

Sushil da had earned some goodwill in the locality over the years and that helped. But the youngsters knew that there would be more trouble at daybreak. When they were getting ready to retire Lobo bhai spoke again.

"Fortunately, the boy was unmarried. The wives of a tiger victim are considered unlucky in society, and they live forever, praying to break the spell. Some tiger widows have even been spotted begging on the streets of Kolkata. The society considers them bad omen."

Sleep was the last thing on the friends' minds that night. Imran sat up erect and felt extremely uneasy, almost sick. He accidentally upturned the bedside lamp and came out of his mosquito net to retrieve the glass lamp that was beginning to roll below the net. The disturbance created on the bed woke up Rahul, Bhombol, and Jassi. They did not like this rude awakening, in the middle of the night.

"What the hell do you want?" Jassi sounded exasperated when he saw Imran slipping below the bed.

Imran held his forefinger to his lips and frowned in retort. Jassi bent low and craned his neck as far as he could out of the mosquito net to peep under the bed, and saw Imran grab the lantern that was rolling away. Once it was placed back on the side table, the four of them sat up and started a discussion in whispers.

In the faint light of the lantern they saw the Brother pacing up and down the corridor, which looked resplendent, bathed in the moonlight. He was wearing his cassock, which shone brightly. There was a glow around the Brother too because of the reflected light. The friends slipped out of bed and walked up to the Brother who was more than surprised to find the friends up at that time of the night.

"Haven't you gone to sleep?" The Brother asked.

"How can we sleep when we have not yet seen the tiger?" Rahul hit the nail on the head. They had come on this tour to see the tiger, but they had not even come close to doing that. They had not even smelt the tiger.

"By the way, you look different in your cassock. Why don't you wear it all the time?" he added.

"I only wear it when I am delivering sermons at my local communion, but sometimes when the mind wanders and I am confused, I wear it. It gives me a lot of peace and strength within. As for seeing the tiger … you see, it's not that easy to see the tiger. In fact, it's a one-in-a-million chance that you will ever see the tiger, here in the jungle. Not until …"

He looked out into the trees and fell silent. There was a certain redness on his cheeks and a seriousness to his face that suggested that he was deep in thought. The friends were a little confused and they grouped around the Brother.

"Until what, Brother?"

Lobo bhai heaved a rather long sigh and then turned and looked at the friends and smiled as he spoke.

"Until you to see the tiger in you!"

His words did not make sense. *Tiger in you*? What did that mean? The Brother was again looking far out into the darkness. He turned around fleetingly, giving out a loud exasperating gasp and walked into the house. He had a wry smile at the side of his lips.

21 Retaliation

The boys were fast asleep when they heard some disturbed voices outside the house. The Brother, who was resting on the sofa, sat upright and looked at his watch: 5:00 am. It was still dark outside, but there was a golden glow to the darkness that was a precursor to the rising sun. The Brother ran to the balcony as he heard a voice shouting below. Somebody was running on the road below, screaming.

"Bagh beriechhe ... bagh beriechhe ... There is a tiger ... a tiger in a house."

Lobo bhai saw a man running below the house and a mob of a dozen people running behind him; each one was carrying either a da, a pick axe, a sickle, and other formidable weapons. The Brother was sure that there was enough reason for concern, as he knew the behaviour of the people here.

He came back into the room and quickly put on his gumboots. That made some noise, so the three boys got up on the bed. They had to be quick if they wanted to keep up with the Brother. Within minutes all four boys were ready and they bounded down the stairs. Bhombol stopped outside the girls' room and banged on it hard a few times.

"Keya, ... chol chol ... If you want to see a tiger ,come on fast ... it seems there is a tiger that's strayed into the village ... Hurry up."

There was a little noise inside the room and Keya's voice rang out.

"You leave we shall follow in a few minutes."

"Be very careful. Don't do anything silly in your excitement. This is a jungle not a zoo." The Brother's words rang out loud in the minds of the four boys standing outside the house from where they could see a mob streaming down the road.

The villagers were rather agitated and angry and almost everyone was carrying something that could be used as a weapon. They ran down the stone path and were soon near a cluster of houses, surrounded by mangroves. The river was behind the houses and they could see about a hundred people all approaching a hut, some distance away.

A large keora tree grew behind the house and the hut was nestled within its trunk and branches. It was up on bamboo stilts and was flanked by paddy fields to the west. The crowd gathered at least twenty meters to the east. Scores of others were walking up the mud road from the riverfront and from behind the trees, to join the rest of the crowd.

There was an opening in the wall of the house and one could clearly see the animal inside. It was a beautiful animal and its hide shimmered in the first rays of the sun falling through the interstices of the adjoining trees, but it was shaken and terrified, and was pawing aggressively in the air and growling menacingly. Each growl threw back the crowd that was now clearly baying for blood. The shouting of the crowd agitated the animal even further and it was clear that the big cat was extremely scared and was looking for an escape route.

It tried darting out of the house, but stopped dead on seeing the crowd outside and went back in. The villagers were now closing in from all the sides, and there was no escape possible.

Everybody started throwing stones, axes, sticks and whatever else they could lay their hands on into the house, and by the look of things the house would be in shambles soon from the barrage received. Brother Lobo came running and stood in front of the crowd with his back to the house.

"Daanran ... daanran ... wait ... wait ... We will inform the forest officials and they will come and the tiger will be tranquillised and taken away."

But nobody would listen to him now. Nobody wanted to wait and listen anymore.

The tiger had strayed out of the forest in the dead of the night and had entered the compound of an isolated hut, lying at the wee end of the village. It had approached the pond in front of the house for a drink, lying low on the paddy fields all the while, and then slowly approached the hen coop.

Dawn was about to break when the old woman had gone out, carrying her lantern, behind the trees, to ease herself. She was half asleep when she noticed the dazzle of gold between the trees.

She had frozen in her tracks on seeing the huge animal, half hidden behind the banyan tree and raised an immediate alarm. The sudden din had frightened the big cat who had turned around and immediately pounced on her. By the time the son had rushed out to inspect, he found the tiger dragging the blood-soaked body of his mother into the bushes.

In that moment of despertion and anxiety, not knowing what exactly to do, he had grabbed the iron rod used to bolt the doors, lying on the beaten mud floor, and swung it maddeningly, hoping to hit the tiger on the head.

The tiger had leapt back and attacked the man next. With a furious swipe of its front thaba it had killed him instantly. The iron rod had struck the lantern lying on the ground, setting fire to the fodder that lay in a heap towards the rear. The big cat was now trapped. There was fire at the back of the house and a crowd in front. All its escape routes were blocked.

The tiger's roars had been heard by other villagers, and men and women had started collecting on the fields around the house. Many villagers had preferred to keep their doors shut and prayed, while others kept watch. When the damage was eventually counted it was two humans, three goats, and a few chickens killed! Villagers started gathering around and the frightened animal found itself trapped in the kitchen of the house where it had moved to take cover.

The fury of the crowd was uncontrollable now as they moved ahead towards the Brother, brandishing their weapons, but he stood his ground. A man wielding an axe came running from behind the mob and hurled his weapon at the house with all the force he could garner. After he threw the missile, he fell down to the ground from the after effect of the force he had applied. The Brother ducked just in time, or he would have been hit.

The weapon must have reached its destination and hit the animal inside as there was a loud growl. The sides of the house plastered with the wet mud from the riverside had tin coverings. Parts of a boat balanced on its mud walls. They shook vigorously and fell to the ground.

"Saala bagher bacchha, amaar bhai ke mereche … The swine has killed my brother." The man who had executed that deadly blow cried out in anguish.

He was the brother of the boy who had been killed by the tiger in the forest.

Everybody was furious now. They did not even want to understand that the animal that had killed the boy in the jungle was a different one from the one that had strayed in the hut.

Logic did not apply; they were being driven by an unappeasable urge to kill the tiger now trapped inside the house.

Slowly, the crowd grew, and now they were actually about a hundred people all really angry and furious wanting to kill the tiger. The two girls, Keya and Hazel, came running to the area and were shocked to see the crowd.

"What are they going to do?" Hazel was terrified. Keya had still kept her cool.

"Well, nobody would want to answer your question now, but I guess we shall know in some time."

Keya spoke as she moved and found a vantage point on a pile of bricks that gave her a nice view of the scene of action. The Brother had moved to the corner, making way for the crowd to move ahead as he could not control the throng of people that was rushing forward with their weapons. Bhombol and the other three boys, who were with the Brother, had been pushed aside rather recklessly by the mob. The crowd was advancing, surging ahead to kill.

There was one strong man who had climbed the keora tree that branched above the roof of the hut. Once safely balanced, he let through a noose, made of thick jute rope, and lowered it through an opening on the roof into the house, until it touched the shoulder of the tiger. He tied the other end of the rope firmly to the branch of the tree. It was all visible now as the missiles thrown by the mob had broken away the mud walls of the house. What was left was only the frame—some pieces of tin walling, few palm leaves, half-broken pieces of wooden planks and lots and lots of dry leaves and hay that made the roof.

The tiger was edgy and anxious and paced around nervously for a while, and then coiled up in the corner of the house when the noose came and strung itself around its neck. At a certain point, the villagers all started shouting and the tiger leapt forward in a desperate attempt to escape again. But the noose tightened, and the rope, held by the tree, steadily began to strangle it. The man peeped through the crack on the roof and heaved at the rope. The noose tightened even further around the neck of the animal inside, and pulled it up.

Somebody was waiting for this opportunity outside the broken wall of the hut and he savagely hacked the head of the animal with his axe. Others poured in and, within minutes, they had clubbed the beast senseless. Keya could not believe her eyes and screamed aloud in pain.

"Stop this ... Don't kill it like this" Her voice was drowned by the collective roar of the crowd billowing ahead furiously.

It was the beginning of an end and it was a painful sight to witness. The tiger was strung to the branch of the tree and its body was visible to all. It was a massive beast, almost 8 feet long. And it was being pounded, butchered, hacked, smacked, torn and wasted by the crowd.

People with sticks and stones, axes, and metal rods all joined in furiously, venting their anger on the animal. Soon the animal was rendered motionless, and the man on the tree came down and looked proudly at the kill. Many were still throwing stones and other missiles at the body of the animal, long after it was dead.

The man who had climbed the tree then cut the rope and the body of the tiger was dragged to the rice fields and the mob followed to see. Few in the crowd still threw stones and sticks at it, from a distance. Right then an auto-rickshaw stopped on the mud road behind the trees and two forest officials walked out with their tranquillising guns; all too late.

"Who would you want to help, and how do you want to start?"

The Brother stopped and asked the question, walking on the estate garden, looking at the friends who had been all shaken beyond words. Nobody spoke as nobody knew what to say. They had seen the mob mercilessly kill a tiger in front of their eyes and they were helpless. One member of the critically endangered species in India had been mercilessly butchered, in front of their eyes.

They all knew about the atrocious slaughter of whales and dolphins in the Faroe Islands, which belong to Denmark. To initiate into adulthood it is mandatory to kill a dolphin or a whale, and this senseless slaughtering has been practiced since at least the 10th century. Nearly 1,000 dolphins are killed annually in the "grindadráp' whale hunt—typically occurring during summer months. They had seen the photographs on the Internet, and some social organisations had held meetings and seminars against the brutal ritual to educate students in their college. But this was the first time they had witnessed first-hand, a mindless killing of an endangered species of the animal kingdom by human beings, and that left them speechless.

"What do you want to do—help the villagers or help the tiger?" Brother Lobo sounded disgusted.

Bhombol stood up and walked to the Brother.

"Brother we are all educated and fortunate enough. These villagers are not. If not for the tiger, the Sunderbans would have vanished already and disappeared. But there is a crisis here. The tigers are straying out of the jungle due to declining food reserves, and that is why such man-animal conflicts are rising. But I am sure there is a way for a safe co-existence for all."

"I believe what we saw today was a maniacal reaction of a mob to avenge the tiger killings yesterday. But I think we should seriously look into the insurance cover for the honey collectors and the other villagers who work under such dangerous conditions. That would be a good beginning. If the threat element for the villagers reduce they would look at the tiger a little more kindly and compassionately," Imran added.

The Brother listened to Imran and then patted him on the back.

"I am sorry that I got a little carried away and spoke to you harshly the other day, but what you say makes sense. What exactly do you have in mind?"

Imran had a smile at the corner of his lips, but he did not answer the Brother's question immediately.

"We can brainstorm several possibilities but do explain first what you meant when you used the expression 'tiger in you'?"

The Brother sat down on the grass. He was looking like the typical parishioner, lecturing to the friends now.

"Look my friends, ... why have you come here?"

Everybody was silent.

"Come on, tell me? What is the single motive of your visit?"

"Lobo bhai, we wanted to see the tiger. But not like this. Not when the tiger is being killed. We wanted to see the tiger in all its glory." Jassi spoke out.

Lobo bhai started laughing a little sardonically, but what he told them next would hold them in good stead for the rest of their lives.

"My friends, I have found peace in this country, and I daresay I shall find my salvation out here too. I have realised that the locals are all wonderful people, lovable, and caring, but they have nothing. They are so poor that the majority of the people cannot even afford a single full meal in an entire day. As for the tiger, it is a solitary animal. There is only a one in a million chance that you will see the tiger in the jungle. You can spend days and weeks, on one of the tiger sighting tours of the tourism ministry, and hope like mad that the tiger comes to drink at the river."

Hazel was very restless.

"Can't we go into the jungle and hope to see it there."

The Brother was smiling.

"You are all behaving like kids. We went out into the jungle today. Did you see the tiger? You know what happened to the two honey collectors who saw the tiger in the jungle."

Bhombol stood up and took control of the situation. He took pride in the fact that he was originally from the region and hence knew much more about everything here than the rest.

"Well, most of those who have seen the tiger have not seen anybody else in their lives." Bhombol made the conversation lighter.

The others did not know whether to laugh or cry. The Brother remained silent. Then he spoke again.

"What I want you to do is to see the tiger within yourself. That would be some sighting."

This time he explained what he meant by it

"Look my friends everyone is born for a cause. This is your calling. You have come here on a holiday, and you have seen the hapless lives of the villagers—the poverty on the banks and the illiteracy all around. If you feel for them and can do something for these poor villagers, the honey collectors and the fishermen, anything that would help them improve their living standards then you would do yourselves proud. That would be like sighting the tiger within yourself. And if you manage to do that, god willing, your dream of seeing a real tiger in the mangrove may also come true. That is my belief. I have not seen the tiger myself in the jungle, but I am willing to try."

Keya was waiting to explode. Her emotions had swelled up within her like a ticking time bomb, and she felt like screaming again as she had felt at the Howrah Station, the day she arrived.

"All right then. This is our battle, so let's fight it. We shall write emails to LIC and other insurance companies and hope to sell a socially-relevant policy that could begin the process. Rahul you can write out the first draft, and we will all sign it and mail it to the authorities. Let's see who owns up to some corporate social responsibility. Let's find the tiger in us. "

Keya tried opening her laptop but realised that its battery was totally discharged. Sushil da offered to charge the set at one of the few shops that had solar-powered energy. The friends then got together and started drafting a handwritten letter.

It was a wonderful sight. Five city bred youngsters, all peering over a foolscap paper, under a tree, trying to write a letter that they hoped could bring about a little change in the lives of some hapless villagers who the larger society did not care for.

Sumon the forest officer entered the house, and the Brother got up to receive him.

"Lobo Bhai, they have suspended me. They were waiting for a chance and now since a tiger has killed someone I am being made a scapegoat. I can do nothing now, but I need this job."

The Brother knew that he was indirectly responsible, for the tragedy that had fallen on Sumon. He could not afford to lose the job. The Brother tried to remain as calm as possible but, menacing thoughts crossed his mind. Was this the cul-de-sac of Suman's career?

"Don't worry, God will find a way."

Sumon knew that the Brother was trying to make him feel at ease even if the situation seemed hopeless.

"I don't know what to do, Lobo bhai." Sumon sounded desperate.

"Look Sumon, I would suggest that you don't leave the region now. These youngsters are trying to do something for the villagers, and I think they would need your help. Anyways what would you tell your parents if you went home now? I suggest you get your luggage, and move in with us at Marshall Estate. We shall all try and do with whatever supplies we have, and hope that things will take a new turn."

Sumon agreed. He could not go home now, as he would indeed have to answer to his parents about this unwarranted visit. He could not dare tell them that he had been suspended. He decided that he would keep low profile and not stick his nose unduly into things that did not matter to him directly.

Meanwhile, the letter was ready, and Hazel read it out loud.

Dear Sir/Madam,

We are a group of friends out of college touring the forests of the Sunderbans in the south of Bengal, for the last few days, and would like to share with you our experiences.

We came here to see the Royal Bengal tiger, but what we have seen has shaken our innermost being. The dismal living conditions of the farmers, fishermen, the crab collectors and the honey collectors have compelled us to write this to you, out of sheer guilt and shame.

In a country that boasts of economic growth and a rising GDP, year after year, simple villagers fall victims to tiger attacks as they have no option but to venture out into the tiger's lair, without weapons or protection, only with the blessings of the local deity, Bon Bibi. Only yesterday, another one honey collector has been killed and one seriously injured. These villagers who are totally dependent on the forest, for their sustenance, have no option, but to remain a victim of their circumstances.

The LIC, is an Indian state-owned insurance group and also the country's largest financial institution from whom even the Reserve Bank of India takes loans. We request you to kindly inspect the conditions, and consider starting a group insurance that would insure the lives of these villagers working under these hazardous conditions. We propose that the policy be named the "Bon Bibi Policy".

Surely, if corporate houses can sponsor Pace Foundations for fast bowlers and football academies, they must have some social responsibility, for the impoverished and backward citizens of our country. We are working here trying to find other ways to make the lives of these people worth living, and hope that your organisation will look at helping us in our drive.

Thanking you,
Yours sincerely

They all signed the letter, and when Sushil da got back the laptop sufficiently charged, Keya typed the letter out and saved it as a word document on her desktop. She browsed through Google and got an email id of the General Manager of LIC. She was about to shoot him the mail when she had another idea. She would send a copy of the letter to "Didi", the chief minister of Kolkata. She left the file as it was on her desktop and opened another window on Google. Getting the official email id of the Chief Minister of the state of West Bengal was not a problem at all. She got all the information that she wanted quite easily.

They all gave her the thumbs up. She attached the letter to the mail with a covering note and jabbed on the send button. An icon, *Sending,* appeared for a few seconds and then it changed to *Message Sent*. The friends gave out a yelp of joy. Never before had they a reason to celebrate sending a mail. They were thrilled on being able to start a process.

A villager walked up to the main door, holding a packet. The Brother called him in. He was the man who had taken Bhor's blood sample to the city, and he had got back the test results. The Brother tore open the envelope which contained few printed sheets with figures and tables that only doctors and medical students could comprehend. But right below the sheet, at the bottom, was written in bold red letters the words that any educated person could understand at first glance.

Name of Patient: Bhor
Age: 8 (Eight) years.
Elisa Test: HIV

22
Trouble

Sushil da did not know why he had been called into the room and made to sit on a chair, while everyone sat around. Had he done something wrong? He had tried his best to take care of his guests as he was indebted to Keya's mother. The ₹1,000 salary that he got every month was just about enough to take care of Bhor's education and all his other needs. In return, he took care of Marshall Estate, and that prevented the sharks of the area who had an eye on the property, from usurping the place. Land disputes often led to a lot of trouble in the area.

"Sushil da, when did your daughter first fall sick? "The Brother spoke with a very soft voice.

"About a year ago she had very high fever. I got very scared that night. That was the last time when she was really sick." Sushil da's voice was heavy due to sadness and also due to excessive smoking.

"What happened after that?" Imran sounded like a detective taking an interrogation and immediately changed his style as he realised it made Sushil da uncomfortable. "I mean how did you treat her?"

"I took her to the Ramganga Municipal Hospital, and they took her blood for testing. In two days the doctors said that she had malaria, and they gave her some really bitter medicines. In about a week she was fit as the medicines worked really well."

Keya probed further. She spoke in Bengali and that made Sushil da feel more comfortable.

"Tarpor … What happened after that?"

"My daughter was never really a sick girl, like her mother. But after this malaria she went through one bout after another, falling ill at the slightest reason. She has been having a running nose ever since …"

Sushil da could not complete the sentence. He had an attack of vigorous coughing. He had to stop talking to catch his breath. He covered his face with his gamchha to muffle the sounds, and the coughing subsided.

"I don't know what happened after she had the malaria. She recovered from the ailment pretty quickly though. But what is wrong, Lobo bhai? What do the blood test results say?"

They realised that Bhor had been infected with a contaminated needle from the hospital, and she was now a HIV positive patient. For the friends this was the most shocking bit of news, in a long time.

They were aware that HIV spread through blood transfusion and infected needles, but to have actually seen a patient from such close quarters created a sickening feeling in their stomach. And Bhor was such a lovely girl! And so innocent! Why her? All these questions were clamouring in the minds of the friends, and the room had been gripped in ominous silence once more.

The silence confused Sushil da even further. But he had to be told. They could not keep the truth from him. Bhor's condition would soon deteriorate, and he would eventually know from the doctors which would be worse.

"Lobo bhai, what is wrong with my child? Tell me … Bolun na."

Brother Lobo came and sat on the floor beside Sushil da. He put his arms around his shoulders to comfort him.

"Dada, your child has been infected with a disease from the hospital. There is treatment, but it is very costly. But you need not worry. We shall do our bit to get her treated. In today's world all diseases can be treated."

Sushil da somehow understood that these were mere words of consolation. He tried swallowing, but there was a lump in his throat. Then he had another furious coughing bout. His eyes started watering and he pressed the gamchha to his mouth and shook under the vigorous coughing. Keya's eyes suddenly fell on the chequered gamchha on the floor. It was tainted with blood.

Outside on the road, a loudspeaker was blaring the election manifesto of a local party, over a microphone.

"Bondhugan ... Friends, the time has come to stand up and be counted. This region of the country ... "

Sushil da collapsed on the ground under the violent coughing, and had to be carried to the bed. The Brother sprinkled some water on his face and forced a smile. In a few minutes, the coughing subsided, and Sushil da sat up on bed.

"Sushil da, how long have you been coughing blood?"

The Brother was very blunt in his question. Sushil da was embarrassed like a young boy caught stealing a candy. He made a sorry face and hid his face with the pillow when suddenly a loud ruckus and banging on the front door gripped everyone's attention.

"We are from the party office, and we have come to talk about the voting."

When the Brother opened the door, half-a-dozen men came into the room, and the chief candidate spoke at once.

"Namaskar, Lobo bhai ... I do not want to sell myself. You know that we have been tirelessly working for the benefit of the locals here, and we have come to request that we can work much better and more constructively if we come to power. Oh, I see Sushil da is sick here. What is wrong with you, dada?"

"He has tuberculosis. And he had been hiding it from others till today." The Brother looked at the man straight in the face. He looked away, such was his glare.

"Oh, I see. Don't worry dada, I have my connections at the hospital, and you will get a bed easily. Send someone to our office for my signature. But please, vote for us in the elections ... Lobo bhai, please ask the villagers to vote for my party, so that we can serve them." Then he turned around and looked at the friends.

"You must be the guests who are staying here. Everybody is talking about you. The five really handsome boys and girls from Mumbai! So, are you enjoying yourselves here?"

Bhombol was about to reply, but Brother Lobo signalled him with his eye not to prolong the conversation. There was a lot of commotion outside the house. They spotted the two forest rangers, who had been at the jetty to receive them the previous evening, walk into the estate premises. There were other villagers at the gate and among them was the woman whose son had been killed by the tiger.

The villagers seemed to be accosting the rangers as they came in, and there was some pushing and shoving. The woman was crying aloud all the while. When Brother Lobo walked out, the jostling finally stopped. The forest ranger brushed the Brother aside and walked to the shade of a tree.

"Sala suarer bachcha, chhobi debe na! Bloody swines. If they don't have photographs of the victim, they will not get the compensation. What can I do? That is the rule."

Now the candidate sensed an opportunity to take charge of the matter and spoke out aloud.

"Leave all this to me. Don't worry, once I get elected all these rules will change. But please, vote for me. Ma, you come to our office, and we will sign a document that will help you."

"This is ridiculous. How can someone get photographic evidence of a tiger-kill when the victim has been dragged into the jungle by the animal? This is all a ploy, for not giving the money." Rahul was livid.

The candidate who was leaving heard this. He was really impressed with the fire in the boy and turned around and walked to Rahul.

"Bravo, bravo, … the youth of the country speaks! We have all the information about you. We used to know Prof. Bhaduri, you see. He was posted here as a forest ranger. Sadly, he was attacked by a tiger and had to retire. Do you know him?"

The friends were surprised at the mention of Prof. Bhaduri. Then they recollected that the professor had worked in the region as a forest ranger and the locals knew him. But Rahul had ignited mutinous sentiments in his friends, which had, hitherto, been lying dormant. They burst forth like a volcano.

"Look, we will stand by the boy who has been killed. We knew him. He was such a nice boy … really young. We will take the matter to court if needed, but we will ensure that he gets the compensation from the state." Imran pursued the matter.

The candidate and his supporters shook hands and exchanged pleasantries with all the friends and left the estate. On the way out, they crossed the mother of the boy who had been killed, at the gate with few other villagers. She threw herself at the feet of the candidate howling like a child.

"Baba, please do something. We need the money badly. We will all die of hunger."

The candidate passed some casual comments, and then they all left in a hurry. The crowd that had gathered outside the gate stood wondering what to do next when Brother Lobo came out and beckoned them.

One by one, the men and women collected at the estate garden, and soon there were about a hundred people on the lawn. Rahul and the friends recognised the strong man who had climbed the tree and let in the noose through the roof of the house. He was still carrying the rope in his hand. It had become a priceless souvenir. The Brother turned around from the crowd and spoke to the friends.

"My friends, this is your day. This is your moment. Seize it. Address the villagers. Tell them what you feel from the inner core of your heart, and this would be the beginning of a mission. Your mission to nurture the tiger within yourself."

The friends felt goosebumps, all over. They looked at the expectant faces of the villagers and felt a rush of adrenalin inside their veins as if their energy were to burst out like a forest fire. They felt like champions already. Then Keya walked up and to the crowd, and then sat down on the ground. She spoke in Bengali and like a true orator touched the sentiments of the locals by talking in their own local language. At first they did not take serious notice of the girl, but slowly her words caught on and people started collecting in numbers. They all sat down and listened to her with rapt attention.

"You collect the honey from right out of the tiger's mouth, and we relish it with our porridge; our country proudly acknowledges the tiger as its national animal; the Sunderbans is an ecological wonder—but you still starve. Many people from other parts of our country do not even know about your fight for survival every single day here. And, when a tiger kills one of you, the authorities ask for pictures of the kill, to substantiate the compensation claims.

"This cannot go on. You all are our brothers and sisters. If we promise to unite then we can shake the authorities right down to their foundation, and truth will win. We are trying to gather support from some powerful people so that you don't have to go into the jungle without protection anymore. We shall bring about change on these islands. But for that we need all your support. Because it is you who will bring the change. We shall go to the office of the regional forest department tomorrow. We shall all go as *one*. Our protest is non-violent, and we shall hold a hunger strike if needed, but we shall get the compensation that is due to this lady."

As long as Keya spoke, nobody in the crowd moved even an inch. They listened to her so attentively that the men did not even light their bidis, lest they miss a few words. And when she finished they all clapped in unison. The applause was so loud that birds from the adjoining trees took flight.

A little distance outside the estate was a keora tree, and a bicycle was parked at the base of its trunk. A plain-looking man, wearing a lungi, standing behind the tree, smoking a bidi, also clapped at the end of the speech. Then he threw the butt of his bidi into the river, got up on his bicycle and pedalled down the brick road.

The spokes of his cycle caught the glint of the oblique rays of the sun that was beginning to dip to the west. He took a bend around a cluster of keora trees and picked up speed. He was the same man who had led the attack at ABC boudi's house.

23 Mumbai, a Reminder

The St. Andrews auditorium at Hill Road was half-filled for the show, that evening. Prof. Bhaduri was the secretary of an NGO, "Alcoholics Anonymous", which organised lectures and chats, for those interested, on weekends. But these lectures were largely unattended, so Prof. Bhaduri had devised a plan to attract the commoners and others who mattered.

Prof. Bhaduri had very strong reasons to battle alcoholism. He had suffered as a child due to his father's addiction. His mother had tried to compromise with the situation for years, but then she finally left her husband and brought up her son all by herself. Though Prof. Bhaduri grew up without any contribution from his father, his mother more than made up for that with her perseverance and dedication. He was given enough love and attention and the best of education to grow up into a wholesome person.

When he was old enough, he had the misfortune of witnessing the death of his father on the streets—an alcoholic, heckled by people and considered a good-for-nothing parasite by the society. This left a permanent scar in his life. He refused to drink even socially and resolved to do whatever he could to fight alcoholism in society.

The Alcoholics Anonymous lectures and chats were usually held before a musical program to pull in the crowd and ensure their participation. Prof. Bhaduri, an avid admirer of Hindustani classical music himself, greatly looked forward to them. This evening the renowned tabla maestro, Bikram Ghosh, had a fusion percussion display with the amazing percussionist, Taufeeq Qureshi. The program had created quite a hype over the week and ticket sales had picked up.

Before the show, Prof. Bhaduri addressed a small gathering, of around twenty-odd people, on the ill-effects of alcoholism—the usual—how it was not only bad for the health, but also a cause for the ruin of a family.

The speech was followed by a short Q & A session, which he moderated and then the show began. Both Bikram and Taufeeq were personally known to him, and he enjoyed their jugalbandi immensely. They were doing this for charity.

Prof. Bhaduri's wife had joined him that evening and sat beside him in the third row. Due to some medical complications they had remained childless and could be seen hanging around together all the time. Though Mrs Bhaduri did not understand the intricacies of classical music, she enjoyed being in the crowd and always accompanied her husband to these shows.

The show ended amidst thundering applause, and after a customary exchange of greetings and pleasantries between those who knew each other in the crowd, everybody started filing out of the auditorium. Normally, one met many known faces at these concerts—the regulars at these entertainment programs.

Prof. Bhaduri was one of the last to leave the auditorium along with his wife as he was from the organising committee. He had to attend a few formalities after the show. When he finally sat behind the wheel of his five-year-old Maruti Esteem and looked at his wristwatch, it was 9:30 pm. There were the last few youngsters who were walking down the lane in a group, but other than that the streets were rather empty, and the lane was dead and quiet.

The buzz on the Hill Road, shining under the street lamps, flitted in, and the neon signs of its shops were clearly visible from where he stood. Prof. Bhaduri switched on the ignition when through the rear view mirror he saw a bike racing up behind him. It stopped for a moment, and the driver raced the accelerator, but the bike did not move. It stirred the stillness and made such a lot of noise that it practically woke up everyone in the neighbourhood.

It must be one of the youngsters in the area who had a beer too many, he thought. He waited for the bike to go past, but it came forward and paused beside their car. Both the driver and his pillion had their helmets on, so their faces were not visible.

What followed took place so quickly that Prof. Bhaduri had no time to react. When the bike slowed down outside his window, Prof. Bhaduri thought for a moment that the biker wanted to ask him something, so he started rolling down his windowpane. But the biker then pulled out something and hurled it forward towards the car. Prof. Bhaduri ducked instinctively and heard something crash through the windowpane, narrowly missing him and his wife. The biker then raced down the road and disappeared around the bend into Hill Road.

It was a small Fosters beer bottle, which fortunately did not hit Prof. Bhaduri. His immediate reaction was to pick up the broken bottle and fling it outside.

"Don't touch it. It might be a bomb," his wife screamed. Prof. Bhaduri took a moment to gather his wits together. The bottle was empty except for a small chit of folded paper that had been stuffed into it. A message ... A warning? Since it was a beer bottle Prof. Bhaduri's first thoughts went to the drunkards in the area. They had tried to create trouble before and would continue to do so.

He picked up the bottle and pulled out the piece of crumpled paper. Scribbled in Bengali were the words:

Call the kids back, if you don't want them killed!

Prof. Bhaduri read the words aloud to hear them. He next closed his eyes in deep contemplation. Anger rose within him as bile, and he grit his teeth, but he did not allow his emotions to be wasted in exasperation, so he steeled his nerves. He rested both his hands on the steering wheel deep in thought for a while. His wife was surprised to see a thin smile form at the corner of his lips, at first. But then just as quickly, his face tightened, the muscles on his cheeks bloated, and the sides of his ears became red. His face formed a steely resolve as he turned around and looked at his wife who sat flabbergasted.

"Don't you worry. These are just small fish in the pond. The crocodiles are panicking, and it's them I am after. This also proves that my children are doing a few things right. So their party will continue."

The Prof. started mouthing a percussion tempo rhythm he had heard at the show. "Dha dhin dhin dha … dha dhin dhin dha … na tin tin ta …" His car keys inserted into the ignition was still swaying like a pendulum—its keyring was a miniature ektara.

He turned on the ignition and reversed his car into a lane to turn around and go home.

24

The Funeral

Back in Marshall Estate, the dead body of the second boy was brought in and laid on the garden. Excessive bleeding had killed him. The boy's mother and few other relatives came howling and threw themselves at the body. It was a sorry sight especially because the youngsters had known both the boys and spent some special moments with them on the boat.

The villager's took Sushil da to a corner, and they seemed to discuss something important. The rangers from the forest department were busy clicking photographs, but Jassi saw that Sushil da was visibly distressed after his interaction with the villagers.

The cameras now needed flash bulbs as the light was dipping fast. The sun was setting over the river, and there was a golden halo behind Keya's shoulder when she walked up to Sushil da.

"What is the matter Sushil da?" She enquired tentatively.

Sushil da gave out a sigh and sat down on the ground.

"The rangers from the forest department have given orders that the body can be cremated, but the problem is they don't have money to buy firewood for the rites. All the wood readily available is wet from the rains, and hence unusable." Sushil da broke down and started coughing vigorously again, and Keya could see that his condition was turning worse by the minute.

The youngsters had funeral pyres burning within them since the time they had learnt about Bhor's illness. They found it hard to bear the conditions of these villagers who were enmeshed in a vicious circle of dire poverty, which had forced them to a hand-to-mouth existence—buying firewood for the last rites seemed like a luxury they could ill afford.

Imran who had held himself responsible in some way for the death of the two honey collectors had been thinking, for a while, about the various ways they could help these poor villagers when a lecture, in his economics class in college, on microfinancing came to his mind. He remembered his teacher's words—how microfinancing was one of the great success stories in the developing world in the last thirty years and is widely recognised as a sustainable solution in alleviating global poverty.

"Remember, the age old adage: What cannot be done by a single person in years can be achieved by a group in minutes. Strength lies in numbers! Little drops make the ocean, and if the combined wealth of the community can be harnessed and put back in use for the society then it can work wonders," he had said.

But how was it possible to make the villagers understand microfinancing here, in this tide country? Imran thought. The Brother saw Imran sitting all by himself and came and sat beside him on the ground.

"What are you thinking, my friend?" He asked.

"Microfinancing. That's what I have in mind. Look Lobo bhai, these people have no money to even buy food, forget about firewood to cremate the body of the dead. But maybe if everybody contributed a little we could form a kitty that could be used by all and sundry to improve their life."

"Lovely. Here is my contribution. Let's start in a small way with a collection from the villagers" The Brother handed ₹200, towards the kitty. Imran dug into his pocket and fetched a few coins and one soiled two-rupee note.

"I am afraid that is all I have for now." Imran's contribution totalled to ₹2.50. The friends concealed their laughter on seeing the offering, or rather the lack of it! They too contributed whatever they could, and the total now swelled to ₹520. The Brother wrapped the money in a shaal leaf, stood in front of the crowd and placed the leaf on the ground.

"Look friends, we have collected roughly ₹500, a part of which will be used for the cremation of the bodies. If you all contribute a little more we can create a fund for you to help you in the future as well, for using this money for more productive purposes. You do not have to got to a moneylender."

The crowd hesitated as they had their own doubts and questions regarding donating money. Nobody moved for a few minutes and then the mother of the boy came forward. She opened the knot in her anchal, the end of the sari, and a few coins fell to the ground—₹3.50! She dabbed the end of her rheumy eyes with the end of her anchal and went and deposited the money with the Brother and then sat down on the ground—that started a shower of coins.

Those who were not carrying any money ran to their houses to fetch some. Others who lived across the creek promised to pay later and helped collect all the money. For the youngsters this was another delightful extravaganza to behold—impoverished villagers all contributing whatever they could to build a fund for themselves.

Kids ran out from lanes and by-lanes carrying coins that they had collected from their parents—not to buy toys, but for firewood, for someone's last rites! They did not understand the deeper meaning of what they were doing, but they were, nevertheless, happy doing this as it seemed as pleasurable as buying kites or marbles.

The elderly ran out of houses, holding on to their lungis, racing up to the estate garden to donate generously, as per their means. Most of them could not even afford a square meal, but they still answered to a call from within and added to the kitty for the welfare of the village.

Probably, this was the call of the tiger. The tiger within! The tiger that does not only kill but safeguards the forest from encroachment, the tiger that is worshipped by the villagers! Soon there was so much money on the ground that everybody was amazed and speechless.

The Brother called a villager and spoke silently into his ear, "Go and find out from the dom, the in-charge of the crematorium, how much he would need for the firewood. Come back fast."

Lobo bhai deputed two villagers to count all the money, and they sat on the ground and segregated the coins of the different denominations and left them standing in a heap. The entire village had got wind of this "money donation camp", and there were a couple of late entries too.

Two elderly ladies came into the estate and untied little knots at the end of their saris, and coins of small denominations like 25 and 50 paisa, poured forth. There were others in the crowd, far too poor to contribute, but they participated with great eagerness. They helped count the coins and heap them neatly. Finally, the Brother blew on his whistle to signify it was over for the day.

The collection from the villagers totalled to ₹375. The villagers looked at the money, and a murmur started in the crowd. They were discussing their achievement. Nobody believed that they could ever collect such a fabulous amount.

This amount was miniscule to the five friends from Mumbai, and that only indicated the inequality in wealth distribution in India. ₹375 could hardly fetch a family food for the entire day, in Mumbai, but the same amount meant a lot here for the residents of tide country.

The man who had gone to fetch news from the dom's got back information that the wood would cost around ₹100. The Brother kept that amount to be used for the cremation and entrusted the balance with an old lady.

"Ma, here, please keep this with you. It has roughly ₹800. Tomorrow we shall all go to the bank and open an account in the name of Bon Bibi. That bank account will lead us to microfinacing."

"No. I cannot keep the money." The woman replied. "I don't understand anything of this. I don't even know how to count. It is best that you keep the money with you, and we shall all use it when we need it with the promise that we shall pay back on time and use the money again in times of our need."

Brother Lobo hugged the woman. He was quite emotional. "Ma, despite your illiteracy you have summed up a huge banking practice or economic movement that can be beneficial to our villagers here." Then he turned around and addressed the villagers.

"This gamchha has roughly ₹800. I shall keep this money with me and it can be used for our people at times of our need. But it would be used like a loan, with the promise that the money shall be paid back, so that it can be used for others during their need. Bhombol, get a note book to record all these transactions" Bhombol promptly ran into the house and got an old note book that he was using to maintain a dairy.

A man came running forward excitedly, but was hesitant talking to the Brother, at first. It was not exactly an appropriate moment, but he could not restrain himself.

"Lobo bhai, I needed to buy some seeds. The harvest would yield a huge profit if I can have some right now. I can keep my cow as a guarantee against the money if you want. I am illiterate. I do not have an account and cannot avail a bank loan. Do you think you can help?" He whispered.

"Certainly. That is the real purpose of collecting this money. Borrow it for productive purposes to help you grow economically. Pay a little money every month—that is all that is required. The kitty will grow slowly and you will have your own village bank, right here. We do not need the cow as a guarantee. Your word is enough. Just make an entry here.

Imran was handed Bhombol's register, for the first entry for the microfinancing project, in tide country, to be made.

"Imran, first help this man write his name and his contribution, the amount he is taking as a loan and the due date that he promises to return the sum. Next, write down the names of all the villagers who have contributed today and the sum against their name. I shall work out the mathematics later and explain the principles of microfinancing to all."

"Lobo bhai, this is tremendous news. If my job is done, I shall contribute what I can to the common fund surely after the harvest. I need to go and share the good news with my son." The man had tears in his eyes. He ran back like a child when he wins a medal at his school sports day.

Brother Lobo looked back at Imran who was writing down the names of all the villagers who had contributed that day, and both knew that they had initiated a great movement. They had witnessed a watershed event among the impoverished villagers; a process that could greatly alleviate all their economic troubles, and hopefully, become an epoch-making episode, in the region.

The sun was setting over the river, and it cast a divine golden hue to the surroundings that evening. There was an aroma of tremendous achievement in the air, and the young friends could feel it in their veins. They had started sensing a rumbling in their tummies; a feeling of ecstasy that one wanted to reach out and share. They felt as if a sluice gate had been opened within them and good faith and feelings were pouring out. They felt a thrill they never realised in their lives before. They had never felt such tremendous bliss before.

The tiger within them had awakened! Darkness was falling, slowly cloaking the surroundings, swallowing the far things in the horizon first and then the nearer mangroves on the riverbank. But there was golden light in the form of hope in the horizon.

That evening, around 8 pm, the firewood that had been bought was piled up near the riverbank and the body was cremated. The soulful shrieks of the mothers tore through the studied silence beside the riverbank. But, after a while, even she stopped. The sound of silence that enclosed the surroundings seemed more deafening and made the night darker.

Lobo bhai was holding a gamchha that had all the money collected, bundled in it. It had been put to great use, and from now on a systematic savings habit would have to be inculcated amongst the villagers. He was certain that slowly they could garner enough resource to improve their lives.

Sushil da had to be taken to the hospital, but he was too weak to squelch through the wet mud on the banks to reach the boat. There were many volunteers who were willing to lift him on their shoulders. Sushil da started smiling, seeing so many people wanting to transfer him to the boat. But they made it a little uncomfortable for Sushil da as they tossed him around from shoulder to another, aggravating his coughing bout. The Brother did not like this.

"Enough with your games now," he thundered. Sushil da was immediately put down comfortably on the boat. Bhor had also been carried to the deck for a last parting kiss. Sushil da held his daughter close to his chest and gave her a squeeze, and she started weeping.

"When will you be back, baba?" She asked.

Sushil da could not hold back his tears. He knew that any effort to speak would make him cough again, so he did not. He held her tight to his chest. The siren of the bhotbhoti sounded, and many people got off.

"Be good. I will get you some candies from the city," the Brother waved at Bhor. Signalling her to wipe her tears, he climbed up on the bhotbhoti to accompany Sushil da. Rahul went up behind him. He had been tasked to get fresh supplies from the city.

The bhotbhoti reversed at first, turned around, and then picked up speed going upstream, leaving Bhor to look at it from her new vantage point—over Bhombol's shoulders.

None of the villagers looked back at the dying embers of the funeral pyre. They had learnt to move on from one tragedy to another.

25 The Hospital

The bhotbhoti skimmed the waters for ten minutes when Rahul's mobile phone let out a beep. He looked at his handset and realised that the signal had been restored, but the handset was almost discharged and hence useless. However, a system-generated message appeared on screen: 10 missed calls. Rahul found that Prof. Bhaduri had been trying to call him. Immediately, there was another call from the professor himself.

Rahul tried answering, but the line got disconnected. The phone switched off, yet again, as the battery was completely discharged. Why would Prof. Bhaduri call so many times? Was there an emergency? Rahul wondered.

The bhotbhoti docked at the jetty, at the end of the journey. The hospital was a quick ride by the auto-rickshaw. The two rickshaws bumped on the gravelled road that had holes and pits including open manholes at regular intervals, and each bump induced fresh coughing bouts for Sushil da.

It was pitch dark now, and in fifteen minutes they drove in through the gates of the municipal hospital at Raidighi. Brother Lobo went straight into the front office. Rahul saw that the place had electricity and looked around for a plug point to charge his handset. He spotted one below one of the doctors' table, in one of the empty rooms. He bent low and plugged in his instrument.

He then called Prof. Bhaduri. There were a couple of rings, and Prof. Bhaduri answered almost immediately.

"Hello Rahul … Where have you been? I have been trying to reach you." The professor's voice was loud and clear, but had a surprising calmness to it.

"Sir, there is neither any electricity, nor any signal where we are staying. I just saw your missed calls. I have come to the hospital and am calling you while I am charging my handset."

There was silence on the other side, and Rahul thought he had lost the professor.

"Hello … hello …"

"Why are you at the hospital? What is wrong?" Prof. Bhaduri's voice sounded a little stern.

"Professor, Marshall Estate's manager, Sushil da, has fallen sick, so we have got him for treatment to Raidighi hospital. Don't worry we are all fine."

"I know Sushil … take care of him and listen … has anyone threatened you? Be a little careful about where you go and take care of the girls. When do you come back? Start planning for it."

Rahul wanted to continue the conversation, but the lady doctor who came into the room saw him huddled under the table and gave out a shriek. That attracted a dozen more curious eyes that came looking under the table.

"I was just charging my mobile phone", said Rahul, emerging from below the table.

There was a sudden flush of relief in everyone's face, and the murmurs changed to gurgles of laughter.

"Sister, will you please keep an eye on my mobile here?" Rahul requested the sister-on-duty, and she smiled agreeably.

Sushil da, lying on a gurney, was being taken into the hospital. His face had aged overnight, and eyes looked like two black beads. He continued to have an occasional coughing bout, which he tried to muffle by covering his face with the corner of the bedsheet draped on his body. The Brother, holding his hand, walked alongside the stretcher, leaning over him from time to time.

"Brother, I leave Bhor in your custody. Please take care of my daughter." Sushil da made an effort to speak aloud, despite the lack of strength in his voice.

"Sushil da, don't worry. She is the reason I live in tide country. You take care of your health, and we shall take care of your daughter."

The Brother's words induced a faint smile at the corner of Sushil da's lips, but he took control and curbed his emotions, scared that any attempt to smile would throw him into another fit of coughing. By now they had reached the corridor beyond which entry for visitors was prohibited. The typical stench of the interiors of a hospital engulfed everyone. The medical-ward boys took over the gurney and took it inside. Sushil da made a last effort to raise his head to wave a finger at Rahul who was also following him and then the gurney turned a corner and disappeared from sight.

Rahul had a sinking feeling within him: was this the last time he was seeing Sushil da? But then his mind wandered and he remembered Prof. Bhaduri's phone call, and suddenly everything else became unimportant. Why had he asked them to be careful?

"What are you thinking?" Brother Lobo tapped him on his shoulders.

Rahul knew that he had to discuss the issue with someone and the Brother was perhaps the ideal person. He tried to keep the explanation as short as possible and that made him hurry through the sentences. The Brother had to make an effort to follow him.

"Rahul please repeat what you said, and relax." The Brother placed a comforting hand on Rahul's shoulder. Rahul took in a deep breath to calm his nerves.

"Brother we have a problem. There is a professor in Mumbai who was posted in the Sunderbans as a forest ranger, but he had to retire as he was injured by a tiger. We know him quite well. I was talking to him when you found me under the table. He is a man always in control of himself, but I could sense that he was a little worried about us. He was saying that we should be careful of where we tread and take care of the girls. I couldn't finish the conversation. I am worried. I don't know why he said that. He is also not one to try and call me ten times, unnecessarily. Why did he seem so distressed?"

Despite Rahul's frantic state of mind, the Brother kept his cool. He waited for a few seconds to decide what to say and then spoke.

"All right, call him now. I want to speak to him. Where is your mobile?"

Rahul and the Brother started walking back to the doctor's chamber when they encountered a large volatile crowd outside the gates and found it impossible to get through. Something had gone very wrong.

There was a woman, wailing aloud, thumping her chest with both her hands, and others were trying to console her. The hospital staff stood huddled with a few errand boys running up and down. The crowd was getting hysterical and violent, and there was an obvious need for some security.

Rahul and the Brother tried to barge in through the crowd and eventually succeeded. Rahul heaved a sigh of relief.

"Wait, I will get my mobile," he said, and at once dashed towards the room he had left his mobile for charging. Rahul was on his knees trying to locate the phone when to his horror he found the charger lying unplugged beside the switchboard. His mobile was missing. Rahul panicked.

"Madam, my mobile phone is missing. I had left it here in your care," Rahul asked the nurse on duty whom he spotted outside the room.

The nurse seemed equally harried. She was trying to escape the marauding mob.

"I can do nothing. There has been an emergency here. An operation has gone wrong, and a small boy has died. I had to go to check. I wasn't here. I am sorry." Saying this she ran into another room, leaving Rahul totally helpless.

The crowd outside seemed to be swelling. Amidst the ruckus of voices, which was baying for blood, it was hard to attract Lobo bhai's attention. Frantically waving his arms and screaming at the same time, Rahul ran towards him.

"Lobo bhai, my mobile has been stolen."

"There is not much you can do here. A child has died at the hospital due to the negligence of the doctors and the villagers are very restive and angry. Word has got around that truckloads of villagers are gathering on the ground outside, with stones. Soon there will be total chaos and we shall miss the last boat back to the island. Let's leave, and we will plan our next move on the way."

Brother Lobo was as calm as ever. Rahul looked around helplessly, realising that going back to Marshall Estate was a far more important choice to make. They managed to escape the fury of the crowd and slipped out to some comfort, outside on the lawn.

When Rahul and Lobo bhai were rushing out of the gate of the hospital, somewhat confused by the chain of events that had suddenly swamped them, a pair of peering eyes, of that of a frail looking man smoking a bidi, followed them through a hole in the main wall.

Mohan, who had masterminded the attack on ABC boudi's bungalow, had also heard Keya's speech on the estate grounds. And today, he had been given other orders …

Scare the youngsters enough, so they leave the islands immediately.

The youngsters were becoming an unnecessary irritant to the politicians on the island. They were offering practical options to the villagers towards the path of self-reliance and making them voice their grievances. This had to stop. Mohan had to devise plans to stop them from incurring any further damage. He was also polishing Rahul's mobile phone with a soiled cloth when the phone rang in his hand, and the name of Prof. Bhaduri appeared on the screen. Mohan, immediately, disconnected the call and switched off the handset.

26
Is this Love?

The unrest at the hospital had spilled out on the streets. Policemen were stopping vehicles and frisking travellers. The ferry services at the jetty were also disrupted. Going back was near impossible.

"Under the circumstances we cannot make any enquiries about Bhor's treatment at the hospital. It is better that we stay here at some hotel tonight and come back in the morning."

Lobo bhai found the easiest way out, but Rahul was not ready to submit. He tried reasoning with the Brother.

"I understand the helplessness of the situation Brother, but going back to Marshall Estate is also equally important. Is there no other way we can go back."

"Not unless you want to swim back." Brother Lobo replied.

But Rahul was steeped in gloomy introspection. He was thinking of Prof. Bhaduri's phone call and was concerned about his friends. However, the Brother prevailed upon him, and they moved into a local lodge the Brother knew well. They were given a single room on the first floor that had a double bed.

Sleep wasn't easy that night. There were numerous outbursts in the mind as it reviewed all the situations and developments—Bhor's current medical emergency; the facilities for treatment available for HIV patients in the locality; the obvious fear of imminent death that came with any thoughts related to the disease; there was Sushil da's tuberculosis, and nobody knew what was in store for him at the hospital; the LIC insurance policy for the villagers, which they were eager to initiate, and to top it all there was Prof. Bhaduri's incessant phone calls.

Who were they to suspect? Had he not mentioned some kind of a threat? Rahul had no clue about the form of the threat, but he suddenly started doubting everybody. Sixth sense told Rahul that the rest of this trip would not remain a simple holiday on the river. He even somehow established an unreliable connection with his stolen phone and the professor's words regarding a threat. They had disturbed a hornet's nest; they were in the midst of a highly violent situation of extreme perplexity where there was a surprise at every turn and intrigue beyond each tide.

Rahul toyed with the idea of lodging a complaint with the local police about his stolen phone. Brother Lobo suggested that under the circumstances doing so would be pointless as all the uniformed guards and the policemen were busy controlling the violent agitation of the villagers at the hospital. In all this chaos a stolen mobile phone would hardly be considered important.

Eventually, Rahul reconciled to his fate. He did not remember Prof. Bhaduri's mobile number, but he knew Keya's mother's number by heart and decided to call her from Brother Lobo's phone.

Getting Prof. Bhaduri's number from Keya's mother was easier said than done. She fired a volley of questions. Only Bhor in her usual self could out do her. She had to be first convinced that they were all well and enjoying the holiday just as she had planned.

"What time do you eat your breakfast? Does Sushil da cook it himself? What time do you have lunch?" Followed by several mandatory instructions: "Never go out after dark. Do not mix unnecessarily with the locals, and never, ever, have any unsolicited things to eat when they are offered. They were known to mix harmful things in the food."

After a laborious innings spent at listening to what was, largely, a one-sided harangue. Rahul finally got the professor's number.

Next, he called him. The professor made his point, in brief. He also wanted to know the names of the people who the friends had come to know on the tour.

"Remember, this is an educational tour for you and not an investigation. Get ready to come back home." The professor disconnected the line abruptly even before Rahul could ask for some explanations on what he meant.

Rahul looked at the Brother who was not his usual cheerful self anymore. The incidents of the last few days had taken its toll on his unshakable character. He looked tired and weary. On the contrary, Rahul seemed battle hardened and ready for more.

"Prof. Bhaduri is a good man. You will like the man if you ever meet him. He has immense knowledge of the Sunderbans and was posted here as a forest ranger once, but he was attacked by a tiger and had to retire prematurely."

"Is he related to you all?" Brother Lobo asked.

"Not by blood, but he taught us at the college, and we look up to him" Rahul added confidently.

Till late in the night, Rahul kept tossing around in the bed, his mind wrestling and seeking explanations to the professor's concern and the threats he had mentioned. He noticed the Brother get out of bed and walk to the window.

The Brother looked out into the river from the window. He suddenly yearned for a cigarette though he had kicked the habit some years ago. He closed his eyes in meditation, standing at the window for a few seconds, to regain his composure. It was a full-moon night and the sight was heavenly.

The still water glistened under the moonlight, and even the trees on the banks were bathed in gold, and a couple of small fishing boats, returning home, looked like golden marbles floating on the water. He let out a huge sigh as he spoke. He had heard several comments about Prof. Bhaduri. He had reserved his. Now he spoke.

"I have heard about this Prof. Bhaduri you are talking about. Local stories circulating in the villages about the man are indeed mysterious. Some say that a tiger didn't maul him. It is believed that he had hurt the interests of some locals due to some actions that he had taken while he was posted here. It's difficult to ascertain the truth, after so many years, but the fact that he is talking about threats now means something is brewing. We can only wait and watch, but there is nothing to lose if we become careful. But I think that you all should be a little careful and not venture out alone in the night and, in general, be alert."

Rahul suddenly felt even more concerned about the safety and security of his friends. He missed Keya. Was she thinking of him too? He was half asleep when a striking visage—a lady in a yellow sari sitting on a window ledge—arrested his mind. He sat up instantly. They were in Raidighi and this was where ABC boudi lived.

He felt an uncanny urge within, to jump out of bed and run across town to her bungalow. But it was late in the night so better sense prevailed, and he decided to wait for the dawn. The mind tossed around on a bed of dreams in slumberland for some time and then wafted into suspended consciousness. Surprisingly, he slept soundly that night.

Though Rahul's sense of direction was not very good, he had no trouble in locating ABC boudi's house the next morning. They passed the police chowki on the way, and Rahul recognised the stray dog that had made the premises its permanent home, nosing around. He remembered how he had come racing on the cycle, the night ABC boudi's house was attacked.

Rahul felt a thrill in his veins when he met Ramu at the gate of the bungalow and walked into the house. The house instilled in him a sudden rush of adrenalin. He felt like a victorious soldier coming back to the place he had won in a battle; memories flooded him—the fire balls, the man dropping down the pipe. He felt elated and excited. He had told the Brother the entire story about how they had come to meet the lady of the house and the incident of the night.

"Are dada babu ... why did you not inform me that you were coming. I would have come and fetched you from the ghats on my cycle ... my new cycle."

Ramu was as friendly as ever; however, when he saw the Brother, he raised his eyebrows. He did not understand why a foreigner was accompanying Rahul and wondered who he was. He walked up to Rahul and whispered into his ears.

"Who is he? I didn't see him when you last came here."

Rahul decided to introduce them to each other.

"Brother Lobo, this is Ramu kaka, and he makes the most fabulous khichdi you have ever tasted."

The Brother joined his hands in front of his chest and uttered the word, "namaskar," speaking in the perfect Bengali that took Ramu by surprise, which was instantly apparent on his face.

"You must be wondering how he can speak in Bengali? He has been living in the Sunderbans among the villagers, for the last many years. Haven't you heard of him before? The villagers call him Lobo bhai," Rahul quipped.

"Oh, tai bolo … Say that. I did hear of a Christian borobabu … a white man who helps the needy and the poor in the jungles. I never thought that I would ever meet the man. I have heard that you can play 'phootball' too. Is that true?" Ramu stooped to touch his feet as a mark of respect that greatly embarrassed the Brother and he immediately pulled him up by the shoulders and embraced him.

"Are ki korchen … All this is totally unnecessary. Come on, will you make some of your khichdi for us?"

"I will make the most wonderful lunch for you." He ran inside, announcing their arrival on the top of his voice. "Shyamol … go get some fish from the pond … Boudi, come and see who has come to our house …"

When ABC boudi came into the living room, she was wearing a normal cotton sari and her hair was tied in a bun behind her head. Rahul noticed that she had combed her hair neatly and remembered how she had looked the first time when he saw her at the gate with her hair loose. Her face lit up seeing Rahul; naturally so—the friends had played such a huge role in ensuring her security that harrowing night.

Rahul and Brother Lobo sat down after greeting her with folded hands, and she sat on the sofa opposite them. An errand boy came in with two glasses of coconut water. Rahul gulped down his share immediately and reached out for the second glass when he saw the Brother, transfixed in his position, admiring the lady of the house. He was rather moved by the beautiful lady, and Rahul was rather thirsty.

"Go get two more glasses." ABC boudi broke the silence, and the boy left the room to fetch more coconut water.

ABC boudi then looked at Brother Lobo and spoke in impeccable English.

"Brother Lobo, I have heard of all the commendable work that you are doing in the Sunderbans. We are really grateful to have you in this house today. What would you like to have for lunch?"

The Brother was speechless. He had never imagined that a local lady could speak such good English, but he replied in Bengali.

"Please do not embarrass me. I have found my happiness in this country. Whatever you will cook for lunch would be fine as we are really hungry."

Though ABC boudi had heard that the Brother could speak Bengali, his meticulous accent, impeccable speech and choice of words took her by surprise, but she thwarted a cry of wonder that formed inside her throat with a smile. The Brother tried to capture that smile in his mind not willing to let go of that easily.

Lunch was sumptuous as expected—freshly cooked rice along with ghee; a mixture of mashed potatoes, green chillies and mustard oil; fresh fish caught from the pond, fried into crisp pieces that went very well with the dal. Then there was the fish curry. They naturally overate. A chatni rounded things off. They got up after lunch feeling a tad sleepy.

The Brother had been struck though. He could not take his eyes off the lady and looked up many a times even as he ate. She was the most beautiful person he had ever seen in his life. Her past and her experiences that he had heard from Rahul had greatly touched him too. But sadly, it was time to leave soon, for they had to hurry back to catch the bhotbhoti.

Rahul enquired about Kapil mama and was told that he had left Raidighi—he had taken up a teaching job in Kolkata. The pressure on him to run his family had become severe, and the locals he had angered were up in arms against him. So when an opportunity came calling from Kolkata, he had grabbed it immediately.

Once on the bhotbhoti, the Brother fell asleep. Rahul was quite surprised at this. The Brother was not prone to siestas after lunch, but then he must have been relieved after a tumultuous string of events. Sushil da had been hospitalised, and whatever the outcome, at least, the man would get some treatment. Rahul had fallen asleep too, which he realised when the bhotbhoti's blaring horn woke him up. He looked for the Brother on the bench he was sleeping on and found it vacant—he was leaning over the railing and peering over the waters.

The sun was setting once again over the river, and the Brother was silhouetted against the golden sky. Rahul walked up behind the Brother and heard faint sobs. The Brother was sobbing. Why was he crying? Rahul touched the Brother gently on the shoulders, a trifle unsure, and again heard the faint sobs above the purring engine of the bhotbhoti. The moment he felt the touch on his shoulders the Brother seemed to force himself back to his usual composed self.

"What's wrong, Lobo bhai? Are you sick?" Rahul knew that something was wrong.

"It's nothing serious … The stench at the hospital and the sight of the sick has shaken me a little … I will be okay. Don't worry it's a passing phase."

Somehow, Rahul was not convinced.

27 Beaten Dry

Marshall Estate was not the same without Sushil da. A woman from a nearby village was available for cooking and cleaning of the house, but everyone felt Sushil da's absence. That evening the friends had an early dinner and collected at the garden, to play Antakshari, a musical game.

Imran moved away to sit below a tree as he wanted to complete the drawing of the Brother that he had started the first day they arrived at the estate. He sat below the tree with his sketch book. The incomplete drawing of the Brother, sitting on the floor with his chin cupped in the cradle of his hands, stared back at him from the sheet. A small kerosene lamp allowed Imran to draw sitting on the grass.

Imran made sure that the Brother wore a cassock. They had hardly seen the Brother in the official uniform of the parish, but Imran had an image in his mind of the Brother in his cassock, and he started translating that image on to paper. The white robe draped his back, covering the muscles underneath the folds of the cloth. Imran ensured that the cassock had enormous pockets. He remembered that the priests in his school always had enormous side pockets in their cassocks.

A faint cry arose from behind the bushes. Imran looked into the darkness trying to figure who or what it was. He noticed a dim outline of a man in the darkness who took a couple of steps forward, and the glistening moonlight falling on his shirt lit up his face too. He recognised him at once—Kinu! The man who they had saved from the villagers.

Kinu made a soft swishing noise with his lips, similar to the ones made by roadside Romeos in Mumbai, to draw his attention, gesturing him to follow him. Imran quickly tucked the sketch book under his armpit. Behind the trees, Kinu was sitting on the grass, looking distraught. He spoke in broken Hindi to convey what he wanted to.

"Wo log aapko khonj ta hai ... they are looking for you. He is contesting the elections, and he says that he has very useful information about the voting."

"Who is he and what does he want from me?" Imran asked innocently, confused about what Kinu meant.

"They know everything about you all—where you come from and everything about your families. He says that there will be trouble if you don't meet him now. Come with me and I shall take you to him." Kinu's reply further confused matters for Imran.

Imran thought about informing his friends that he was going out of the gate, but then decided otherwise. He was within earshot of his friends anyway.

Once out on the main road, which was made of beaten mud and bricks from the local kiln, Kinu lit his hand torch, flashed it ahead and walked on briskly. The beam of light cut through the darkness and fell on an ox cart, about 20 meters ahead, in the middle of the road. The road was lined on both sides with trees that threw long shadows on the path, and the mud felt cool despite the soaring temperatures of the day.

Imran saw a ten-year-old boy sitting in the cart. The lad looked animated when Kinu approached him, but Kinu slapped him so hard that he yelped in pain, jumped off the cart and ran away in the darkness. Rahul quickened his steps towards the cart. He felt a tinge of nervousness, being alone in the darkness. Why did Kinu have to slap the boy, he wondered.

He had almost reached the cart when something fell on him from the trees above, and as he wrestled to free himself, he got further entangled. After a while, he could not see anything. It was a heavy net used by the villagers to catch big fishes.

The weights hanging from the netting were heavy and made his movement difficult. Imran found himself chocked by the sharp strings of the net that clung to the skin of his throat. Three men jumped down from the tree to the ground and started hitting Imran with bamboo sticks. "Bloody swine ... leading our men astray. Now the crocs will feed on your body."

Imran screamed in pain, but two more men pinned him to the ground and threw blankets over the netting, and muffled his shouts. Then they picked him up and threw him to the back of the cart. One of them paused, for a while. He called Kinu who was standing looking as if sedated and gave him two soiled twenty-rupee notes.

"Buy yourself the best chullu (country liquor), tonight. You deserve a drink."

Kinu took the notes and disappeared into the darkness. Imran had been hit on the head and the shoulder, and he had passed out. He was also bleeding badly.

At the estate garden, the game of Antakshari had picked up momentum. Bhombol sang aloud the lyrics of the song made immortal by the late Shammi Kapoor.

Yaaahooo! Chahe koi mujhe junglee kahe ...

When it was Rahul's turn to sing he stood up and looked towards Keya.

> *Waada karo nahin chhodoge tum mera sath ...*
> (Promise you shall never leave me)

This was one of his favourite songs from the film *Aa Gale Lag Jaa*, starring Shashi Kapoor and Sharmila Tagore. He decided to enact the song romantically pulling Keya out from the group. She offered no resistance and was only too happy to play along.

Both pirouetted and sashayed around the garden singing together gleefully without the faintest inhibition. When they had finished they paused, holding on to each other, breathing heavily. It was a moment of magical revelation between the two, and they spoke a million words without uttering a single one. Enchained in eternal present tense, they both felt and heard each other's blood pumping in and out of their veins. When the others started clapping, the epic moment of love was broken, and they walked back to the group.

Ganesh, hiding behind the bushes from the riverbank, had watched Imran being beaten and carried away. He was lightly stroking his right cheek that was still stinging from the slap he got from Kinu.

Earlier that evening when he had spotted the cart parked in the middle of the road, what got him interested was a pair of canvas shoes lying unguarded, on the bamboo awning over it. It would be very useful on the playgrounds, he had thought.

Ganesh was the star centre-forward of the football team that Brother Lobo coached.

He had felt an irresistible urge to try out the canvas shoes. He had leapt up on the cart and retrieved the pair, which were wet. They were also a size too big, but some stuffing with hay and cloth could work, he imagined. He had barely pulled the second one in when Kinu appeared from nowhere. The slap was sudden and unexpected, but he was relieved to find Kinu least interested in the shoes. He asked him to leave with them right away.

The shoes belonged to Kinu. An hour earlier when Kinu sat with his legs dipped in water, wondering where to find some money to buy a drink, two men came with a weird offer.

"Come with us and we shall give you a job to do. If you do it well, we shall give you money for your drink." They had been very explicit, and Kinu was happy that he had a chance to earn his drink.

Now hiding behind the bushes Ganesh saw the cart drive away in the darkness. He got up to inform bother Lobo about it. He felt his cheek burn and he remembered the slap again.

"Wait till Lobo bhai gets you!" He thought.

Ganesh sneaked out from behind the bushes and went up to the spot where the cart had been parked. He picked up the sketch book lying on the wet mud road. He had noticed that there were three men on the cart. One man was riding the cart sitting on the ox's shoulder and the other two were keeping watch over Imran's body wrapped in the net at the back of the cart. He had also noticed that the cart was carrying a small boat. He decided to tail the cart from a distance to check where it was going.

Ganesh saw the cart stop at the mouth of the river from where a mud path dipped to the water's edge. He lay flat on the ground and saw two men get off the cart and carry Imran's body to the edge of the water. The third carried the boat. Ganesh was lying face down on the road and the mud was moist.

He remembered how in films dacoits put their ears to the ground to hear far off sounds of galloping horses in the desert. His nose felt cool as it touched the ground, and he turned on his side, lying still, with his ears to the ground.

He lay still for some time when rustling sounds in the mangrove made him look up. One of the men had disappeared into the foliage. He returned carrying a stone so huge that he had to struggle with it. He carried the boulder some distance and then put it down and started shoving and rolling it to the edge of the river. The second man then went into the mangroves.

Ganesh did not want to wait anymore. He had to act fast. He realised, by now, that Imran's life was in great danger. He waited for an opportune moment for the three men to have their backs to him, and then he got up from his prostrate position and ran as swiftly as he could towards Marshall Estate.

28 Rescued by a Tiger

At the estate, the game of Antakshari was over. When the friends realised that Brother Lobo was not sitting among them, they set out to look for him. Imran was missing too, and so they assumed the two of them had gone somewhere together. The maid, who was sleeping in the corridor, was awakened by the friends looking for the Brother. She pointed upstairs, signalling that the Brother was in his room.

The friends tiptoed up the wooden staircase to surprise the Brother. They reached the door and tried to push it open, but it was locked from inside. Hazel and Jassi quickly looked inside through the window and saw the Brother sitting on his chair, hunched over his writing table. Was he sick? Why was he not moving?

"Brother ... Brother Lobo. Are you okay?" Keya called, softly at first.

The Brother remained motionless; the friends waited quietly. When the youngsters were about to lose patience, he suddenly got up and walked to the door. The latch was released noisily, and the door flung open. The youngsters barged in.

"Brother Lobo, what's wrong with you?" Rahul asked.

The Brother went back to the chair and sat down again. He actually seemed to collapse into the chair. Looking outside the window he let out a huge gasp of sigh. Rahul knew that something was wrong, so he walked to the Brother's side and put out a hand on his shoulder. The Brother kept looking out of the window and did not move. Rahul whispered softly.

"Brother what's wrong?"

The Brother did not utter a word but sat still in the silence. Everybody knew that he was deep in thought. Then he turned around, desperately fighting back his tears, but they streamed down his cheeks, and he could not help but grab Rahul. He held him tightly for a moment and let go.

Words flowed as if they had been kept captive for long and were now set free at last. This was his catharsis.

"My first war was the one I fought in Afghanistan. Then, I gave up the life of a soldier to redeem my soul of hatred—that was my personal battle. I have lived here among the villagers, worked towards their betterment and played football with the children; I have been happy. But suddenly I face another crisis.

"As a Brother, I am in the process of preparing for the sacrament—as part of a religious order. I am to be called to priesthood soon, and I had intended taking a vow of celibacy. But after all these years, for the first time, I feel an uncanny tug at my emotions. When I saw that lady at the bungalow, the other day, strange emotions flooded me. I have no idea what is happening to me Rahul. This is a new war which I must fight."

Rahul did nothing but listen silently to the Brother unwind as he wept. He felt his shirt getting wet with his tears, but deep inside he felt great joy. Joy for a man who was suddenly in touch with his pristine emotions that made him look more human than ever.

As a handsome man in his mid-thirties, with the best of his intentions, Albert Lobo had wanted to embrace a life of celibacy, to devote himself to the Almighty. But now he had met a woman who made him question his choice. This was his personal battle. This is what made us human, made of blood, sweat and tears.

But the Brother was not ready to let go yet. His self-respect, his belief in the Church and his decision to become a Brother were not taken in haste, and hence his mind was not ready to yield easily to this sudden surge of new emotions invading his soul. And so he was weeping. He was fighting himself, questioning himself—he was not ready to give up on himself, so easily.

For everyone else in the room this was an experience that they would carry for the rest of their lives. They had never, ever, imagined that the Brother, who they had come to be known as a man of principle, of supreme mental and physical strength, confidence, unflappable boldness, calmness, courage personified, could be so utterly shaken by an emotion like love. But deep within, the friends were happy.

Around this time, Ganesh came sprinting to the main estate gate and nearly collapsed due to fatigue. He had been running for almost ten minutes. Hazel saw the boy from the window and cried out.

"Brother, isn't he one of your star footballers—that boy at the gate?"

Brother Lobo was too immersed in himself to react immediately. He saw the boy through the corner of his eyes, panting at the gate, and somehow he knew all was not right. He got up wiping his tears and ran out of the room. In quick bold strides he bolted down the stairs followed by the friends, and in no time they were at the gate of the estate. Ganesh was out of breath, but managed to rattle off all the vital information.

"They have taken your friend to the river ... they have also beaten him badly ... I think he is bleeding ... hurry up ... you have to save him."

The Brother was instantly back to doing what he did best—marshalling his troops.

"Bhombol and Rahul, go get the cycles from the rear of the bungalow; girls, you wait here."

He ran inside the house and came out sprinting even faster. He was carrying two pistols. He handed one to Jassi and the other he kept with himself.

"Jassi, you stay back with the girls. Do not hesitate to use this but only if there is an emergency." Jassi stood holding the pistol in his palm, and it gave him a chill. It was the first time he had ever held a firearm. He tightened his fist over the magazine grip.

Rahul and Bhombol followed the brother on their cycles, down the mud path, with Ganesh sitting on the Brother's carrier, but even then, it was quite a challenge to keep up with the Brother who rode at least ten meters ahead of them.

Far away, lying on the boat, Imran began to move a little, entangled underneath the fishing net. His skin burnt where he had received the cuts in more place than one. The cut in his throat ached the most and he could feel the blood drip out and wet his collarbone. Then, he felt a hand underneath his waist. It propped him up and a rope was flung around his body over the netting.

They were tying him up!

Moving inside the net brought great pain to his back and shoulders, and he remembered that he had been clobbered with sticks before he had passed out. There was a swelling, the size of his fist on his left temple that blurred his vision. Squinting hard, he could make out two burning torches. They were being carried by the two men on the boat, while the third had an emergency light. Why would they be carrying fire torches when there was an emergency light available? He groaned painfully and now saw the two men carrying the torches, jump off the boat. They buried their lighted sticks into the soft mud.

Suddenly, Imran felt some additional weight tug at the side of his waist. He realised what they were doing. The men were tying weights at the sides of the fishing net.

He would be thrown into the river; the weights were to drown him!

The thought of being eaten by the crocodiles at the bottom of the river startled him. He let out growls of anguish and tried to wrestle free through the net.

The man beside him on the deck, tying the net around his body, was whistling a tune, and he slapped Imran hard on the face when he tried to move. He did not know the words of the song, but the tune sounded eerie because of its timing. Even as Imran stopped all movement, he could see far out into the river and remembered his friends.

He felt some movement and realised that the boat was being pushed into the water. The still waters of the river, the injured body and the pained mind conjured up joyful images of the five of them doing a musical concert. He would die now, he thought, and the feelings of being in a concert calmed his senses for a while.

The man on the boat uttered something in a disgusted tone, probably a Bengali invective, and suddenly the movement of the boat seemed to stop. Then, the two other men joined in, grunting as they pushed together. With tears streaming down his face, Imran lay resigned to his fate. He desperately tried thinking of ways to escape but could not.

He lay tied up on the deck of the boat with weights at his sides. He was being pushed to the water. Soon he would drown and be eaten by crocodiles! Wasn't there anything anyone could do? The men pushing the boat sounded a little frantic, and Imran raised his head a little to see what was happening outside the boat.

He clearly noticed a few flaming torches among the trees, in the distance, on the opposite side of the river, away from the water. Torches, from different directions had started collecting together like little drops of mercury that flow and merge as one. Scattered human voices also started growing in unison. It all looked surreal to Imran. Could he be hallucinating?

Imran looked away into the mangroves by the side of the river, and was stunned. He saw a spark of yellow and white dazzle in the mangroves about fifty meters away from the edge of the river. The mangroves moved and the men at the boat started shouting at each other. The collective voices of the people and the balls of fire now made sense. They were villagers carrying torches, and running towards the river. They had grown in strength, and were much nearer now.

"There, I can see the tiger in the bush." Someone shouted.

Normally, the mention of the word "tiger" would send shivers down anybody's spine—such was the ferocity and fear the image of a Royal Bengal tiger generated. But it had no effect on Imran as he writhed in pain, tied up to be drowned and eaten by crocodiles, which was no less scary. He had lost all sensation to differentiate the fear factor associated with either. Imran lay immobile and helpless, inside the fishing net.

His vision was hazy and restricted, but he could still make out the gold and the black stripes moving around within the mangroves. It darted from one end to another, and then, everything stood still.

Two burning red dots suddenly glowed in the darkness and made him nauseous. Imran was looking directly at the eyes of a tiger that was not more than twenty meters away. He remembered that the eyes of the tiger appeared to glow as it reflected light. It was reflecting the light from the torches buried in the ground and that meant that it was directly looking at the boat.

The three men must have seen the eyes too, and that is why they had panicked. They dashed frantically for the road through the bushes, and Imran was left all alone. This was it then, he thought. They had come to the Sunderbans to see the tiger, but Imran had never imagined that the circumstances of the sighting would be so frightful and tragic.

The voices amidst the trees became a collective roar by now, and somebody in the crowd threw his burning torch into the trees, and the fireball scattered on the ground. The villagers had been chasing the tiger. It must have strayed into the village and caught the fishermen unawares.

The burning eyes of the tiger remained stationary, for a few seconds. May be the tiger was weighing possibilities of an attack. Would that be worth with so many men carrying burning torches?

Then suddenly, there was again some movement within the mangroves. The black and golden stripes dazzled momentarily, and then, the burning eyes disappeared, followed by a loud splash in the water.

Imran made a painful effort and propped up his body on the rim of the boat. He could clearly see the tiger now swimming away to the other side. Only its head remained above the water and the body surged ahead, and within minutes the cat disappeared into the fog.

Imran had been saved by the tiger! His body ached menacingly and he fainted on the deck of the boat. On the riverbank a dozen villagers gathered together with torches, and Brother Lobo, Rahul and Bhombol also cycled up in the nick of time.

"He is on the boat, tied in a fishing net." Ganesh pointed them to the direction and led Brother Lobo to the boat.

29

A Confession and a Prayer

They discovered Imran on the boat, battered and bruised beyond words. At first, they had taken him for dead as he did not move, or react to any stimulus.

Rahul had sprinkled some water on him in his haste, which made him immediately winch in pain. He started groaning and tried turning around, but his sides ached, and he gave up the effort.

"What have you done? That's salt water and painful for his wounds." Brother Lobo admonished Rahul.

They immediately washed Imran's wounds with fresh water that a villager got from a hut on the banks. Imran screamed as much as his aching joints and muscles allowed him and his voice cut through the river and must have alerted a few fishing boats that were bobbling on the water, blissfully unaware of the death row already played on the banks.

The Brother knew from experience that moving an injured person without precaution could do more harm, as brittle and injured bones could break further on being moved haphazardly. They transported Imran's body out of the boat, with extreme caution, and laid him down on the riverbank. A cycle cart was organised and he was immediately taken to the clinic for a check-up.

Fortunately, the injuries were not so serious. His head had got miraculously saved despite the indiscriminate bludgeoning by the men. His face and most of the body was plastered, and he was ordered two days of absolute bed rest. The cut in his throat needed two stitches, and Imran sportingly smiled as the doctor stitched him up. But the doctor suggested that he should get a scan done of his forehead, as a precautionary measure.

Rahul, Keya, Jassi and Hazel were flustered. They saw how badly Imran had been beaten and were left numb with fright. Keya was sobbing in a corner and Rahul felt anger creep up within his sinews; his jaws tightened.

"You wouldn't believe who led me to the cart that evening," Imran spoke with a wry smile on his face.

"And who was that?" Everyone was curious to know.

The Brother came walking to the side of the bed and kept his hand softly on Imran's head. He was desperately trying to fight back his anger.

He was the man who came running to the estate the other night. We saved him from the villagers."

The Brother looked away and sighed.

"Kinu? Goodness me! Well, at least, there is a lead." Rahul growled in anger.

"Getting angry is very natural, but one needs to be very careful now" Brother Lobo said in a slow, deliberate drawl.

"Anger will not resolve anything. It will discharge needless negative energy which can be harmful." Brother Lobo's words sounded like a sermon and Rahul was in no mood for it.

"What do you expect us to do, Brother? Our friend has been badly injured by those bastards and we are all sitting around doing nothing." Rahul took everyone by surprise by the wrath in his voice.

"Rahul, you want to see the tiger? Don't you? Here you have an opportunity to see the tiger within you, and I suggest that you do not lose this opportunity. Tomorrow at daybreak we shall all pray. We shall pray for ourselves, we shall pray for the villagers, and we shall pray for those who have harmed Imran, and we shall pray for the tiger. But that does not mean that we shall not hunt the culprits." With these words the Brother walked out of the room.

That night, all the friends, except for Imran, had a sound sleep. Imran groaned in pain when the maid applied a hot paste of the edible raju chuna and turmeric on his temple, which they claimed to work as a superb antibiotic. Turmeric was used in these parts of the country for its healing powers. Imran had also been given a glass of milk with turmeric dissolved in it to drink in the evening.

Shuffling noises woke up Rahul, late that night. He found Brother Lobo opening the door and letting some people into the house. In the shaft of the moonlight that fell into the room Rahul could see that the Brother had changed into his cassock. His white robe was shining brightly in the dark making the atmosphere rather serene. There were three men who had followed him into the room.

One was carrying a Baul's ektara—that was Don. The other was, surprisingly, Kinu. The third was an unknown man. The Brother signalled the men to remain silent and whispered under his breath.

"There is someone injured in the room and everybody else is sleeping. Find yourself a corner to rest and we shall talk in the morning. Lock the door from inside, and don't let anybody in."

Then the Brother himself sneaked out of the estate.

The soft mud felt like a cushion below the Brother's feet as he hurried towards the church. He was wearing his gumboots. That secured his feet against the snake bites. Today, he was walking faster than usual. He was on a mission, but one that was a little different from the many missions he had been a part of in the past.

Oddly enough, the death sorties played out again and again in his mind now—trickling blood, bomb blasts, wailing children, broken limbs and the rat-a-tat-a-tat of gunfire; he also remembered the woman and children who died in his hand.

The Brother took a deep breath, trying his best to shake the gory visuals off his mind, and quickened his pace. He had about a dozen Christian followers in tide country and they would collect on weekends in the dilapidated brick structure hidden by the mangroves.

The mangroves would grow even after being cleared on each visit. They would also be inundated daily by the rising tides and appear again when the waters receded.

The Brother trudged along separating the undergrowth with a long wooden branch of a tree. He reached the church and pushed aside the leaves and weeds that had collected around it. Few more bricks had fallen loose from the wall to the west of the church, but that could be easily taken care of soon.

A few meters away the soft waves of the river lapped on the sides of the mud bank and the roots of the mangroves cherished its touch. Brother Lobo went down on his knees in front of Christ and lowered his chin in prayer. He confessed. He confessed that he was in love with a woman.

In the morning, the Brother's football team came running in through the estate gate. The Brother blew on his whistle softly, and they immediately started filing into groups. Eventually, they lined up in two rows in the order of increasing height on the field. Ganesh was the tallest, and thus he stood right at the back and the friends took position with their musical instruments on the ground floor balcony of the estate. They whispered into each other's ears in soft monosyllables. Rahul strummed on his guitar and Keya played a few impromptu notes on her flute.

The local music club had an old and worn out harmonium, and Hazel immediately grabbed it when it was carried into the estate. She had been already introduced to this Indian musical instrument in Mumbai and had learnt to play it.

The prayer started. Brother Lobo had taught his football team this song from the film *Guddi*. Though it was a film song, he really loved the words. They sung it all together. And the musicians joined in, in perfect harmony. Don started the song with his heavy baritone voice and it sent shivers down Hazel's spine as she played the chords on the harmonium.

Humko mann ki shakti dena, man vijay kare
Dusro ki jai se pehle, khud ko jai karein ...

"It says—help us cast away all differences of cast and creed ... keep us away from falsehood, and fill our hearts with truth ... when troubles befall us, bless us, so that we can tread the path of spirituality and perform all duties ... make us confident and fearless ...," Bhombol explained the song to Hazel.

Among the three who had been given shelter in the night, Don was singing with his ektara. Kinu, who was deeply repentant, stood in line, singing the song as well.

The third unknown spectator had been sent by "Didi" as an answer to the email sent by the friends to the West Bengal state government. He had come to inspect the grounds for the proposed

LIC policy, for the fishermen and the honey collectors. Perhaps, he was the answer to their prayers. He also sang along, and by the look on his face it was apparent that he was singing for the first time in his life. But nevertheless he lent his voice.

Brother always sang the song with the kids on the football ground, before the start of a game, but today he had tears streaming down his cheeks. Deep inside, he felt as if he was letting off a huge load!

30

Hope and Agony

The local political party was campaigning on the municipal football ground. Loudspeakers had been fixed on wooden poles, and the young and the old had gathered on the field, listening to the speech of a man wearing a dhoti. Two old farmers flanked him from both sides. The man spoke on their behalf, voicing their feelings. In the far corner of the ground few kids kicked around a football, totally unmindful of what was being said.

"In the last two years we have brought to light the basic problems of the farmers in the village. To those who didn't have money to sow seeds, we have given them loans ...."

The speech continued, but the speaker could see from the stage that Kinu, walking briskly through the assembled crowd, was whispering something into people's ears and visibly diverting their attention from the speech.

"Bishtu da, some people have come from Kolkata to help us. They are waiting at the estate. Lobo bhai has sent me to call you all. Let's go."

Kinu knew them all by their first names and could influence them easily. Though the villagers seemed a trifle hesitant at the beginning, eventually a few in the crowd got up and started walking towards the estate. From the stage the speaker noticed all this, finished his speech in a hurry and left in a huff. Other villagers, too, started rising and moved towards the main gate of the ground where Kinu came and joined them.

At the estate, Bhor had become livelier. She struck up a conversation with the messenger who had come from Kolkata, and found special interest in one of his shirt buttons. Subodh Maity was an agent working for the LIC of India and had been an active worker for the Trinamool in Kolkata. He was now wearing one of Brother Lobo's shirts and Bhor was stitching one of his shirt buttons that had come loose.

There were about ten fishermen and honey collectors gathered on the municipal ground, and Subodh addressed them from the steps of the estate. Speaking from that elevated vantage position, his words assumed grater gravity.

"For those of you who venture into the forest ... the West Bengal Government along with LIC have come up with a solution."

Subodh explained to the villagers that Didi's party was ready to look into a group insurance in association with LIC for the honey collectors and the fishermen in the area, but to do that they would need to fill up application forms. The forms were distributed and the villagers got together to discuss the pros and the cons of the project. Outside the estate, two men on cycles stopped to cast a casual look into the garden. They took a quick head count and left.

It was 3 pm when Prof. Bhaduri got off the boat at the jetty, limping slightly. Hardly anyone at the jetty remembered him now, but back in those days, when he was posted here, almost all the fishermen referred to him as "dada".

Prof. Bhaduri hailed for an auto-rickshaw, and noticed that there was some confusion at the jetty. A gunny bag had been located in one of the dumpyards and there were people crowding around it. A few policemen were also to be seen. The auto-rickshaw wrestled its way through the mob when a man, with his mouth covered with a gamchha, came running out from the dumpyard and started vomiting, right on the road.

"Bhoyonkor … it's ghastly." The auto-rickshaw driver was probably speaking to himself.

"What is the matter?" The professor asked the driver.

"They have found a severed head of a man in the garbage dump. Dada, I don't know anything else, but the youngsters, who have come from Mumbai, will know. They are causing all the trouble here. Where will you go?"

"Take me where the youngsters, from Mumbai, are staying."

The police were already at the estate when Prof. Bhaduri's auto-rickshaw stopped outside the gate. Shikari da, at once, recognised the man who alighted from the three-wheeler. He came forward and bent to touch the professor's feet. The professor immediately grabbed his shoulders and stopped him in the act.

"Aare Dada … why did you not inform us that you were coming. I would have gone to receive you." Shikari da was excited.

"And please take the kids away, at once, else there will be disaster." Shikari da's voice had an anxious urgency. He wanted to say so much, but it was not the right place or time. He helped the professor walk into the estate, carrying his luggage behind him. Prof. Bhaduri noticed two police officers deep in conversation

"Illegal activities had gone underground, but these kids have fanned the fire." Shikari da continued.

Keya saw Prof. Bhaduri from the bedroom window and came sprinting out, nearly tripping over the balcony railing as she came bounding down. One of the policemen found this very funny and chuckled. The other policeman walked up to Prof. Bhaduri and spoke to him.

"Who are you, and how are you related to these youngsters?"

"I will answer all your questions. May I go inside, first?"

Keya brushed aside the policeman, nonchalantly, and helped Prof. Bhaduri inside. Once inside the room, Prof. Bhaduri was surrounded by all the friends. They all wanted to speak at once.

"We are going back tomorrow," announced the professor.

The friends were taken aback and fell silent. But Brother Lobo walked into the room abruptly and punctured the silence with a deluge of information. He had not noticed the professor's presence.

"They have identified the body ... I mean there wasn't much of the body ... just a head."

There was shocked silence all around, and Brother Lobo finally noticed Prof. Bhaduri amongst them.

"You must be Prof. Bhaduri ... Sorry, I didn't notice. When did you come?" Brother Lobo reached out to shake hands with the professor.

Shikari da interrupted this exchange of pleasantries and spoke furtively.

"Kinu left the estate about four hours ago after he collected the villagers from the ground. Now the police have recovered two gunny bags from the dumpyards. One has Kinu's severed head and the other his bloody clothes. His body is still missing."

Shikari da tried to remain as matter-of-fact as possible. But he was speaking about the death of someone he knew dearly for many years. His voice wavered towards the end and cracked, and he had difficulty completing what he had in mind.

For everyone in the room, death had come too suddenly again. Like a leaping tiger, the latest revelation pounced at them from nowhere and left them benumbed. Kinu, who, even a few hours ago, was breathing and walking beside them had been terminated! The friends were dazed with shock and disbelief.

"Obviously, somebody's interests must have been badly hurt. I suggest we do not discuss the matter further and let the law take its course. We shall remain indoors for the next couple of days and decide what to do next." Brother Lobo advised.

Prof. Bhaduri listened to the Brother's words carefully and nodded in agreement. He had heard of him earlier and had begun to respect the man for his work.

"Brother Lobo, I agree with you. Besides, this was supposed to be a holiday for these kids, but it is turning out to be a death trip. I am beginning to get concerned."

"Prof. Bhaduri, I understand your concern for us, but you must also realise that we have not directly caused any harm to anybody." Hazel confronted the professor.

"We have interacted with the villagers here in the most amicable manner possible, and our experiences with them have been most eye-opening to say the least. This killing is a stray incident that has nothing to do with us."

Bhombol looked at both the Brother and the professor. He cleared his throat and walked to the middle of the group. He wanted Hazel, whom he had begun to like a lot, to hear what he had to say.

"Madam, I do not completely agree with your views. I agree that you have been quite enamoured by the villagers here, but we aren't totally disconnected with this killing. You, or rather "we" have, indeed, harmed the interests of the local politicians here during election time. We are facing its backlash now.

"Kinu pulled out people from the crowd who were listening to an election speech, and got them to our estate to listen to our programs instead. So, it was *we* who were leading the villagers away—luring them to freedom, should I say, far away from the nefarious clutches of the politicians.

"What would they do then? They couldn't get to us easily, so they got Kinu. They did it to my parents more than twenty years ago and they are doing the same thing now. Probably not the same people, but with the same intention. And please don't think I am shaking in fright here, but I think we should calm down and take stock of the situation."

What Bhombol said true and Prof. Bhaduri added to it.

"These are very dangerous people here. Directly or indirectly you have got involved in some underworld activities here. I know that for a fact—I have lived with something burning inside me, since I left these shores. It is, probably, time to go home."

It was a moment of uncomfortable silence and some bitter truths to mull over and grapple with. What should they do? Safety seemed synonymous to cowardice now, and they hated the idea of having to leave the villagers in a lurch, forcing them to go back to their dismal life after fanning their hopes. They felt like traitors. Yet, the gravity of the situation demanded that they did not do anything foolish to further endanger their lives. How would they defy Professor Bhaduri whose arrival on the islands signalled that there could be some serious concerns around. They were at a difficult crossroad, unable to fathom the best way forward.

Amidst that eerie silence, walked in the mother of one of the boys who had been killed by the tiger, carrying a bunch of forms. She looked like a lady possessed. She put the papers down on the table and spoke to the Brother and spoke with great deliberation, slowly, but surely.

"Lobo bhai, ... I brought the forms. They are all signed .... The word has spread. Other villagers are on their way from far-flung islands. People feel there is hope. We need hope. This is more important than the elections here. They will all sign. I have lost my son and will not have this loss go to waste," Her voice choked with tears, but she continued, "I am willing to go anywhere you want. No honey collector will enter the jungle, ever again, without a valid insurance."

Brother Lobo put his hand on her head affectionately and assured her gently, "Yes, we will not let this hope flicker and die. We need your strength of conviction behind us."

Bhor ambled into the room and jumped on to Rahul's lap. She had a lot to share with the friends too.

The Brother looked at Prof. Bhaduri and said, "Please, I need to talk to you alone for a few minutes." Saying this he took him aside.

"Sir, I have some clue about what you have gone through here, years ago. Your story is almost like a folklore here and is proudly narrated by the villagers as a case of extreme courage with no personal gains. A rare combination. These youngsters have similar qualities. When I first looked at the youngsters, on the steamer, and interacted with them, I understood that these youngsters have not come here merely on a holiday. They have been sent. This is their calling."

The Brother had got the professor interested. His briefing lasted for fifteen minutes, and he told him almost everything about the experiences of the friends on the islands over the last few days—their interactions with the villagers, how they freed the dolphins, about Jasho, their crusade to start a LIC policy for the honey collectors—everything, barring ABC boudi. He mentioned the woman casually and narrated how they had managed to save her on the night of the attack. Prof. Bhaduri listened silently.

"Brother you have been a part of a process that I cannot nip in the bud. I don't have the right to do that. But there is grave danger here, and I am not only talking of the tiger in the jungle. That is the least of our worries. We have to save the tiger, but before that we need to save ourselves. I am ready to stay back here, but for how long?" Prof. Bhaduri was now speaking to the Brother as if they were friends for years.

"Sir, allow us to get this LIC policy on its way, and next week after the elections they can go back. By then, I think, they would have seen the tiger within."

Prof. Bhaduri's face lit up immediately. His inner-most thoughts had found a resonance in Brother's words.

Whether Prof. Bhaduri wanted to leave or not was immaterial as the police had left with strict instructions in writing that nobody could leave the estate premises till the investigations of Kinu's murder was complete. Everyone was under imposed house arrest.

As for the friends, the incidents had played out at such a vigorous pace that they could not immediately mourn Kinu's death. But that night, when they retired, thoughts of Kinu crossed their minds. Kinu had no immediate relatives and was virtually a loner, and that is why the police investigation on his killing could not gain any momentum. Who cared about the needless death of an alcoholic sloth, in an overpopulated deltaic backwater, in a forgotten part of the country? But for the friends he was someone who had become important. They remembered Kinu descend to the ground, slithering down the branches of a tree from the terrace, the first time they had met the man. And now the man was no more. Why was he killed? All the visuals and questions made sleep difficult for the friends that night.

Raimanagal is a tidal estuarine river around the Sundarbans, in South 24 Parganas district, in the Indian state of West Bengal and

Satkhira District in Bangladesh. The region is, as is the case with other border areas, prone to illegal incursions and other nefarious activities like cow and medicine smuggling. Bangladesh is a huge market for smuggled Indian drugs and cows, and the BSF is often, infamously, in the news for shamelessly torturing Bangladeshi smugglers caught crossing over.

Sumon had a licensed revolver and often patrolled the waters to nab such culprits. His suspension order had been withheld with the help of some political clout, and owing to his past goodwill he had been let off with a severe warning.

Tonight, Sumon was standing at the bow of his bhotbhoti, scanning the horizon with his naked eyes, for any suspicious movement on the waters. The river narrowed ahead into a small channel, and his motorboat cut through the river stealthily.

Deep inside the narrow channel that suddenly opened out to the left and tapered further and disappeared into the mangroves, another boat was cleverly camouflaged. It was carrying a load of a dozen cows in its belly.

Sumon had not seen the boat yet and wanted to light a smoke desperately, but he knew that any light on deck would alert anybody hiding in the darkness. He ordered the engine to be put off and slipped below to the belly of his boat and lit a cigarette. He pulled hard at the end of the filter and felt the smoke enter his lungs as he inhaled.

Looking out through the port hole in the wood on the side of the bhotbhoti, he saw the mangroves rustle. Then, he saw a light glow within the vegetation. Somebody was there, and he was probably smoking a bidi. He went back to the deck, and got his other guards together.

"There is some movement in the mangroves, and I suspect it is a boat. Let us not hurry. We can catch them off guard."

The guards got their emergency lights together and stood in a line. They took out their revolvers, for protection. The broad beam of the combined battery lights fell on the semi-submerged tendrils and took the men on the boat totally by surprise. There were three men on the boat.

The sudden glare of the beam of light fell on one of the cows in the belly of the boat, and she bayed aloud. Another followed, and soon the darkness was rent with the combined cacophony of the baying of all the cows from the boat. It was a medium-sized vessel with its sides battered due to age. The bow of the vessel thinned sharply like a soldier's bayonet. Sumon weighed the possibility of taking his bhotbhoti into the narrow channel. Then, he directed it within a few meters of the other vessel and fired in the air. The smaller boat in front was now swaying to one side because of the sudden movement in its bowels and tried surging ahead on the channel to escape.

"Hands up. Keu palate cheshta korbe na ... Don't try to escape."

Sumon spoke in Bengali as he was sure they were Bangladeshi smugglers. He made sure that he himself stayed low on the boat along with his other guards as smugglers often carried firearms. But this was an easy surrender. May be the men on the boat were too tired. There was complete silence for a few minutes after which a white cloth waved on the boat on the head of a stick—the raid was over.

Sumon threw a jute rope to the boat to soldier on it and went on board with his guards. By then, the three men had lined up on the deck without any revolt, whatsoever. Two of them were in their early twenties, and the third one was a teenager. Sumon remained on the deck with his gun, while one guard frisked the skinny men for arms. The other climbed downstairs to check the hold of the boat.

There he spotted seven cows, all in shackles, their toes tied to each other and bleeding down to their bones due to constant pulling from either sides. There were a few buckets full of fish and crabs. That was all that was there on the boat.

The guard below finished his inspection and was proceeding towards the ladder to climb when his legs brushed against a polythene bag and he stumbled. He pointed his emergency light to the floor and saw a pair of naked feet of a man dangling out of a polythene bag. The ankle was broken, and half the bone dangling at the heel had a silver anklet strung around it.

The guard knelt on his knees to inspect further. A fetid stench immediately hit his nostrils, and he covered his nose with the corner of his shirt. The malodorous smell was coming from the polythene bag so he brushed it with the corner of his emergency light, hard enough for it to roll to one side. It tore in the middle revealing the contents inside.

There was a torso of a man lying on his side inside the bag, but he could not see the head. In fact the torso had no head. It had been severed from the rest of the body. It was a headless corpse, decaying in the belly of the boat. The guard held his face, fighting off the unbearable stench, and he felt paralysed, unable to get up.

"Sumon da … come and see what I have found." He struggled to speak.

Sumon had already handcuffed the three smugglers on the deck. As he moved forward he saw a few bubbles by the side of the boat and peered down the edge of its wooden sides.

The two men who had disposed of Kinu's head at the dumpyard, carried the body on the boat. Further down the river they had picked up three young fishermen wanting a lift. The extra luggage would not matter and they could be used to fool the forest guards. They had taken the boat deep inside the mangroves and given the fishermen some fried fish and a few bidis to smoke on the deck. Below, in the hold of the boat, they had waited to remove the anklets from the body before dumping the body into the water. But, suddenly, lights shone through the mangroves, followed by the sound of a gunshot in the air.

The two men had quietly slithered down the sides of the boat and lowered their bodies into the water and remained submerged, only occasionally sticking their noses up over the water level to breathe. That had created little bubbles in the water. From there hiding position they could see Sumon and the other guards who stood on the deck with the fishermen who had surrendered.

Deep in the waters, about a hundred yards away, totally submerged and hidden within the mangroves, there was, however, another twist in the tale. It was a five meter long beast who had been rendered uneasy by the sound of the gunfire. The crocodile noticed two pair of human feet dangling at the side of the boat. It waited silently in the water, for a perfect moment to attack.

When Sumon peered over the edge of the boat to inspect the bubbles in the water the crocodile had already started skimming through, moving towards its prey. One bite at the thigh and the femur bone had snapped in two. The body had been wrenched off its hold on the iron shackles at the sides of the boat and dragged into the depths of the water. The animal had brushed the other man's waist and he had jumped above the water screaming in fright.

"Kumeer … It's a crocodile and it has taken Aslam …" The man who had jumped on the boat started howling and collapsed on the deck.

For Sumon and his guards this mission had been an easy routine of meek surrender. And the crocodile helped to nab the culprits. The fishermen were innocent and were let off with a warning. The prized catch was the man who had clambered back to the boat from the water in fright. He was a seasoned history-sheeter. This mission would go a long way in revoking Sumon's orders of rustication from duties. But the biggest gainer was Prof. Bhaduri.

Brother Lobo had been summoned to the police station. The friends accompanied him, along with Prof. Bhaduri, to identify the culprit. They entered the police station and were led into the room where the arrested man stood handcuffed against a wall.

"Do you recognise this man?"

The friends and the Brother were seeing the man for the first time in their lives, but Prof. Bhaduri looked uncomfortable. He also looked as if he was deep in thought, trying to ferret out something from the recesses of his memory. Then, without a word, he limped up to the man and slapped him on the face.

No one had expected such a dramatic enactment of frustration from Prof. Bhaduri. It happened so suddenly that even the police were taken unawares. Prof. Bhaduri, however, calmed down and started speaking. It was evident that he was letting off the steam he had stored within him, for the last so many years.

"Do you know the pain that I have borne for carrying a burden of a lie for more than ten years? I haven't slept peacefully ever. I have lectured on tiger killings and my own past, spoken lies—blatant lies—knowing that I could not do anything. But I waited impatiently for this day as I knew that my destiny would lead me to justice. And now you want to harm my children?"

Prof. Bhaduri had to be restrained. It was not easy as he was so emotionally aroused, having had his life on a rack for so many years. Now a dam had broken. A group of smugglers and poachers ruled over the islands when Prof. Bhaduri had been posted there as a ranger. As a conscientious vigilante he had managed to hurt the interests of the criminals who then sought revenge. He had waited patiently with an albatross hanging around his soul, for so many years. It was payback time.

The arrested man was being led away when he suddenly wrestled free from the clutches of the policeman and came running towards Prof. Bhaduri.

"Saala shuarer bacchha ... Bloody swine. We should have killed you that day. How many times we warned you not to meddle in our lives, but you would not listen. Now you will see what happens to your family ...." The man was wrenched away by the other cops.

This incident led to a few other arrests of smaller groups all over the island, revealing a can of worms. These were all second-generation smugglers and criminals, sons and nephews of poachers and drug traffickers, from both sides of the borders, who had wreaked havoc on the pristine archipelago of the islands of the Sunderbans. Most of the incidents went unreported, but this time the holiday of the youngsters ruffled many a feather and things got out in the open. The arrested men revealed the diabolic nexus.

Back on the estate that day, a special police party came visiting. They had serious faces but noble intentions. The leader of the group was a representative of the West Bengal Government and he was carrying an official letter written by the State Minister of Environment and Forest.

Dear Prof. Bhaduri,

We are pleased to inform you that there has been an official investigation ordered, and the case of the attack on your life and your subsequent voluntary retirement has been reopened. Rest assured justice will be delivered soon.

We apologise for the inconvenience and the trauma caused to you and your family over the last so many years, and would like to make amends.

We offer you an honorary designation to head an official committee that will look into measures to safeguard the Sunderbans, for the future generation, and look into executing projects to alleviate the problems of the locals.

Your vast knowledge about the area and the intimate relations that you enjoy with the locals here would be invaluable to us. We would be honoured if you accept this honorary position and resume duties at the earliest.

Honourable Minister for Environment and Forest,
Government of West Bengal

Shikari da came running in.

"Have you heard the news? The locals are all rejoicing. They are least bothered about the elections. Word has leaked out that Prof. Bhaduri is coming back to work again. The tides are turning."

Truly so. Things started moving really fast on the islands, thereafter. Police presence became instantly visible, ensuring peace was not tampered with. The next few weeks would see a cleansing operation in the island that was long overdue.

The friends breathed easier. As for Prof. Bhaduri, his pride had been restored. Honey collectors and fishermen started pouring in from far-off islands with their identification papers to register their names for the LIC policy, jointly started by LIC and the state government. They converged at the Marshall Estate, filling in their papers.

The Brother looked at Bhor's face and touched her cheeks. Some medical practitioners were on their way from Kolkata with an AIDS treatment program that was to be started at the Raidighi hospital. But the Brother was not only thinking of that. ABC boudi was on his mind and he smiled as he remembered her face.

31 The Way Ahead

The friends wanted to go on one more tour down the river before they left the islands. But the elections were around the corner, so most of the bhotbhoti's were employed on election duty campaigns, for the parties.

Marshall Estate looked like an army garrison. The friends had excitement writ large on their faces, as they had been honoured with the success of their LIC policy drive. Villagers were pouring in from far-off islands—from Sajnekhali and Canning; from Piyali and Gosaba. Impoverished villagers who had been compelled to live lives in a constant toil suddenly found hope. So they congregated at Marshall Estate wishing to give thumbprints to the cause.

The friends divided their duties. They had decided to keep up the excitement generated in their veins with adequate action. They had grand plans for Marshall Estate. First they renamed it "Marshall School". Bhombol was to be the overall in-charge and its would-be martial-arts teacher and the principal; Keya and Hazel took responsibilities of the curriculum. They wanted to start an education drive that would rid the area of all petty crimes and get the parents of the kids involved too.

Brother Lobo saw a group of men campaigning for their party and announcing their election manifesto outside the estate and got an idea. He went towards Shikari da who was squatted on the grounds with Don, Bhor and a few others. He squeezed himself beside Bhor, attracting everyone's attention.

"Shikari da. How long have you lived in this area?" The Brother wanted to come to the topic only after he had engaged the man in a conversation as he feared outright resistance if the matter was thrust upon him.

"What do you mean, Lobo bhai? I have never been anywhere else ever. I have been to Kolkata and crossed over to Bangladesh a few times, but that is it. I have played marbles here on the mud and lived all my life here on the islands."

Shikari da became excited even as he spoke; he was talking about his own land—the rivers and creeks here were his blood vessels.

"Right, I know that, and I also know that nobody knows this area as well as you do—you know the people; they know you; you are so familiar with their lifestyle and their problems. So there's so much you can do for them." Brother Lobo interjected.

"Na, Lobo bhai. I can't do anything to help them. We are an impoverished lot." Shikari da spoke helplessly not knowing what was coming.

"Why not? If you have the will, there has to be a way."

The others also did not know what the Brother was getting at, so they sat looking inquisitively, shifting their gaze to and fro from the Brother's face to Shikari da's, like watching a tennis match. There was a pause as the Brother waited for Shikari da to get his scattered wits together and reply.

"I have the will, but I have no power."

"Then get the power."

"How? I cannot buy it from the market."

"No. Not from the market. You can acquire that."

"How?"

"Win the elections."

Shikari da heard what the Brother said, but since he could not fully comprehend what it meant he kept silent.

"What do you say?" The Brother probed.

This exchange of questions and answers between the Brother and Shikari da was heard by all sitting on the ground and everyone seemed excited by its prospects.

"But, Lobo bhai, I don't understand politics." Shikari da was shamelessly honest and that was his strength.

Brother Lobo saw a woman carrying some clothes to wash to the edge of the river, and he called out to her.

"Didi, yes, I mean you ..." He shouted and the woman turned around with the basket on her head

"What's the matter, Lobo bhai? I don't have time as the children will soon be back home, and I will have to light the unoon (the clay stove) in the house and cook."

Brother Lobo shouted back. "Didi, Shikari da wants to talk to you for a minute. Please wait there."

Brother Lobo pushed Shikari da to go and talk to the woman.

"Go, speak to her, and ask her about her troubles. Find out what she needs in her house, and tell her that she needs to vote for you. Your election campaign starts here and now. Go hurry up. Go get your first vote." Brother Lobo's words were simple, yet meaningful.

Shikari da stood bewildered for a minute, still unsure of himself. He, then, ambled to the woman who had let down her load of clothes on the ground and waited for him. Imran and Keya followed Shikari da, at a distance.

"O Shonar ma ... mother of Shona ... There is an election due, do you know that? Tell me about your problems, and I shall try and solve them. But for that you need to vote for me at the municipal elections. I am representing your dreams. Will you vote for me?"

"I am not interested in politics. I am too occupied with my own problems." The woman spoke her mind. Shikari da grabbed the cue easily.

"But that is what I want to know. Tell me about your problems. And I will try and solve them. Okay, tell me what is the single thing that you cherish? I promise to try and give that to you if you vote for me."

"Are you speaking the truth? Do you promise to give me what I want the most, if I vote for you?" Shikari da suddenly had all her attention.

"Yes, of course. I promise that I will try and give you what you want. Come on, tell me. What is it you want?" Shikari da was speaking like a seasoned leader the only difference being he was absolutely sincere about it.

"Build an English school here so that my grandson can study in it. He will then be able to get a good job in the city. That is all that I want. The rest we can take care." The woman joined her hands in a plea as she spoke.

Shikari da did not know how to react. Imran and Keya, who had followed him, came to his rescue.

"Didi, we promise that on Shikari da's behalf. The English medium school will be made. And we shall teach English to all the kids here. Marshall Estate will be Marshall School from now. But will you vote for our Shikari da? He needs to win the elections to do that."

"Yes, you tell me what to do, and I shall do everything if you start the English school. Now I have to go home." The village lady picked up her pile of clothes and started walking back home.

When Keya, Imran and Shikari da turned back towards their friends they were almost running with excitement. They could not believe they had started campaigning for the first election of their lives. And they had also got their first vote.

"Go, get some blank sheets of paper for me. There is so little time and so much to do." Imran was screaming out of excitement.

Village children were put to the task of getting blank sheets and joining them with glue to make a big enough banner. They ran merrily from house to house collecting old copies and tearing out pages from them. They, then, sat down at the estate garden and started sticking them with homemade glue, which they had forced their mothers to make out of wheat flour and water.

"What will our election symbol be?" Rahul was eager to find out.

"A drum. I think it should be a drum as we want to make a lot of noise, so metaphorically it makes sense." Jassi wanted to sound as impressive as he could, but nobody bought his argument.

"This is not the time and place for metaphors. Let's speak in the language of the villagers so they understand what we say. Let's draw a tiger with a small girl sitting on it. That will immediately make sense. *Bhor*. That should be the name of our party." Nobody had anymore suggestions. Bhombol had put an end to the debate with his reasoning.

Imran sat and drew out the emblem for their party, a symbol to vote for. Within an hour the election campaign had been finalised. The party emblem was a little girl sitting on the back of a tiger.

However, all good intentions conceived on the estate ground had to be given some formal recognition by the election commission. The name of the candidate had to be filed with the election office along with a security deposit. Brother Lobo did not want to touch the money they had collected to start the village microfinance project. He took permission to use part of his church fund, instead.

The electorate paid for their candidate to file in his nomination, which had to be some kind of a record in independent India. The candidate did not have much of a choice either. He was genuinely representing the hopes and aspiration of hundreds who had contributed towards the security deposit.

It was decided that the election campaign would involve a tour down the river, and its details had to be finalised. There was a villager who opted to hire out his bhotbhoti for the tour, and it was decided that they would leave at daybreak.

The Brother, however, had another idea. Whether he had carefully thought out this one, nobody could say, but it was a master plan.

"I have noticed that the women of our region stay away from civic needs and do not come forward with their problems. If we could somehow get the women involved and get their support, then, it could be a big benefit."

"What are you hinting at Brother?" Imran wanted to know.

"Ah … you see … we need to enter the kitchens and get the women out, and to do that we need women to speak to the women." The Brother explained.

"And how do we do that?" Rahul sounded serious.

What the Brother said after that made the friends smile—what a clever idea, indeed, they thought.

"I was thinking … you know … if we could request Jasho to help—and the other lady from the bungalow at Raidighi—if we could get them both to help in our campaign … you see women can only get the other women involved, in such things."

I can convince Jasho, but I don't know the lady in the bungalow too well. Somebody has to speak to her." Having revealed his intention, the Brother started plucking the string on Don's ektara.

There was no time to waste. The friends divided into groups and duties were charted. Imran completed few smaller pictorial pamphlets and signages to aid in the campaigning and few villagers went to the nearest town to print them. Jassi, Rahul, Keya and Hazel stayed back at Marshall Estate to complete the formalities about the LIC policy. Bhombol accompanied the Brother.

First, they went to Jasho's house and asked her to help. She agreed immediately. She was distantly related to Shikari da and was ecstatic when she heard he was contesting for the elections.

"This is what this area needs the most. One of us should be in charge, so that he understands all our problems. Shikari da is the perfect man to do the job" Jasho was euphoric.

With Jasho on board, the thoughts of victory were being discussed even before the campaign had started. That was some optimism! After the three had finished their second cup of tea at her house, they decided to go to ABC boudi's house.

Jasho, Brother Lobo, Bhombol all sat in the room and Ramu got glasses of coconut water as usual.

ABC boudi sat on the sofa, deep in thought, as Ramu served the guests. They had already broken the news to ABC boudi and explained to her in detail about their plans. She had to give it some thought.

It was dark, already. The room was lit up by a lantern, burning on the window ledge, behind ABC boudi. The Brother found it impossible to look away from her beautiful pensive face in the half-light. Smitten as he was, he felt pangs of love pounding against his ribs. He did not want to confound her with his emotions and be hasty. What if she refused to join the campaign? That would be disastrous for him.

The Brother felt edgy and could not hide his impatience anymore. The visage of the woman he was in love with enveloped his mind. He found it impossible to steer himself away from it and think of anything else. He could not possibly sit before her and not look at her, so he rose and walked to window and decided to fiddle with the lantern behind her.

He stood there lost in his thoughts, for a while. His heart beating faster than ever, he bent low looking at the glass shade. He caught a reflection of his face and a glimpse of her long hair, tied in a bun. He suddenly realised that he had been looking into the glass too long for comfort and hastened to think of other things to do. He pressed down the rusted knob on the sooty kerosene container at the bottom and lifted the glass. He lengthened the wick first, lowered the glass and watched the warm glow of light bathe his beloved. Then, he shortened the wick and saw the smooth curve of her face disappear into darkness.

That drew a backward glance from ABC boudi as the room suddenly brightened, and then, darkened, and the Brother's heart skipped a beat. Was he doing too many things, all at once? Bhombol looked at the Brother too, at the window, fiddling needlessly with the lantern and felt pangs of unrequited love—thoughts of Hazel crossed his mind.

ABC boudi looked away and listened to Jasho digesting all the information ardently. Then suddenly, she spoke and the Brother was on alert.

"But, what am I to do?" She asked.

The Brother pounced at the opportunity and spoke aloud.

"To begin with you need to travel with us, to different villages. The fisherwomen and the crab collectors' wives would identify with you being there and they would become accessible. And then we can go deeper into the villages … speak to others … spend time … you know … quality time …."

Bhombol knew that the Brother needed assistance, so he prodded Jasho with his elbow. She got the signal and begged ABC boudi for help.

"Didi, we need your help. We can also sing on the boat together. This is how we can get the village folk together and ask them to vote for Shikari da. Please, don't say 'no'."

Jasho completed what she had to say and looked at the Brother who was still standing at the window, following each word carefully.

"Ramu, go get some tea for us and add some ginger … that will be good for the journey. And pack your luggage too. I won't travel alone." ABC boudi rose from her sofa even as she spoke.

Brother Lobo felt like screaming in joy and the lantern tinkled in his fingers. He released his grip as he feared that he might crush the glass. He was very excited with the prospects of ABC boudi joining them on the campaign. They would travel on the boat, and he would have all the time with her.

Back on the estate grounds the thumb-printing campaign was well on its way and the kids started filling in for the martial arts coaching camp to be conducted by "Bhombol Sir". Imran had also painted an image of Bhombol poised in a karate pose, and they had distributed them locally. That created an immediate buzz and the kids started filing into Marshall Estate with numerous enquiries.

Marshall Estate looked like the army headquarters before an important mission. This was Brother Lobo's base camp. When Bhombol trooped into the estate along with ABC boudi, Jasho, Ramu, and another boy who accompanied them from the jetty, helping out with the luggage, there was a small crowd waiting to greet them outside the gate.

The mother of one of the village boys blew a conch shell, and another welcomed them with a tray of flowers. Boron kora! This was a symbolic Bengali gesture of welcoming guests or a newly married couple. Bhor was there too with a smaller conch shell and she tried blowing hard on it but failed to create any sound. Everyone laughed and got into the estate.

This was Shikari da's army, and he would fight the elections with their help. The twenty-odd kids who had registered for the martial-arts program included the players from Brother Lobo's football team and many more from the vicinity. They could not wait and started throwing their arms and legs in the air.

They kicked, jumped, landed, rolled on the ground, jumped again, and made short war cries that karate fighters used while fighting. Bruce Lee was still popular here, and they replicated his screams. These sound effects were probably more important than the actual physical contact, for the kids wanting to enroll in the martial-arts training program.

Bhombol lined them up for a pep talk, but they were too tired already due to the needless screaming and kicking. It was decided that Bhombol would remain on the estate, to begin the program with the kids, while the rest would go on the election campaign. This would also be a holiday tour, so they decided to carry their musical instruments. They would try and woo the electorate with their music—that was the plan. Prof. Bhaduri had to be convinced, and he agreed to let the friends go on the trip only if he went along.

Marshall Estate had been turned into a multi-purpose village school, which had a martial-arts class on the estate garden, an adult-education program for the illiterate women of the region, and also an optional music class.

People could afford these services as everybody was making nominal contributions. Ramu helped out with all the paperwork and collected the donations. The villagers had been requested to contribute blank sheets from their homes that they would otherwise dispose. All names of the applicants—whether they were kids for the martial-arts program or the adult-education campaign—were written down.

An assortment of paper sheets of all shapes, sizes and colours were collected on the centre table. The Brother looked at the heap of assorted papers of different shapes and smiled. They carried a lot of hope in them. Hope in the form of names and thumb impressions. The Brother knew deep within, however minuscule it was, a beginning had been made. And he believed, together, they would move ahead for bigger things.

They set out at noon. The sun clawed down on their shoulders, but dark clouds also loomed large. They hoped the heavens would cooperate with just about enough rain to make the journey comfortable, yet possible. A heavy downpour would make things extremely difficult. Don immediately strummed on his ektara and sang out.

Bager daake ontor kanpe,
Na dori aaj baghe re
She achhe mor hridpure je
Aar kaare na dorai na re
(The mind shivers at the call of the tiger
But we are scared no more
As the tiger calls from within
So I fear no more)

It was a heavenly feeling. The mind raced ahead, riding the crest of the waves that lapped the sides of the boat. One by one, all the friends joined in with their musical instruments. The words were unimportant and they hummed along lending their voices to Don's song. ABC boudi sat at the stern of the boat with the end of her sari covering her head as a cowl or ghomta.

She did not sing at first, but as the boat went into the river and floated away from the banks she started humming the tune under her breath. Brother Lobo kept looking back at her, but made sure that he did not catch her eye. Soon everyone was singing on the boat. Few kids ran alongside the boat on the banks, shouting and cheering, and Shiraki da's political electoral campaign was well on its way.

A schedule had been planned for Shikari da and his team that would extensively traverse the adjoining areas of Kultali—Maipith Baikunthapur (2.5 km); Achintyanagar (10.8 km); Kankandighi (13.5 km); Raidighi (16.7 km), Nalgora (17 km), and also to Patharpratima (21 km) and Mathurapur II (22.1 km) and Mathurapur I (29.2 km). How long the trip would take would depend on how they would be received at each port. Anything was possible, so they decided to keep an open mind and tackle situations as they arrived.

Initially, they were welcomed everywhere because of their music. They docked their boat at the jetty and started singing. That drew the village folk to the banks in numbers like teeming bees to their hives. Shikari da spoke to everyone and tried to understand their problems. A lady stood in a corner clutching two children, and her face spoke a thousand words though she did not utter a single phrase.

They gathered that the lady had been driven out by her husband who was an alcoholic. Now she was a homeless woman with two kids. Shikari da offered her the safety of the boat and she readily came aboard. She was his cadre. She would work in the electoral campaign. They distributed many leaflets, and Shikari da spoke to the locals, heard their problems, and moved on. Jasho and ABC boudi went into the homes of the villagers. The women spoke out their hearts to them.

An old man came walking to the edge of the river, smoking his bidi and said, "My son wants to go back to the forest to fetch honey again. Your signature campaign is a blessing."

Shikari da grabbed the opportunity immediately. He hugged the man and addressed the crowd.

"Shono, shono, shobai shono … Listen everyone. This is the beginning. We need to know everything that you want. We need to know all your problems, so we know what is to be done. So come with us and share them. We can't change everything in a day, but we can at least make an effort."

There was a huge roar from the people collected, and a woman grabbed her son and spoke to Shikari da.

"What are you saying, Shikari da. I swear on my son here that I will vote for you. I shall also tell the entire village to vote for you … I promise. Wait, hang on, I want to come with you and join the campaign."

Saying this she jumped onto the boat as it was leaving and shouted out at her husband. "I shall be back in the evening. Please, look after the house."

As the bhotbhoti sailed out, heading deeper into the river, the older women blessed in unison. "Durga, Durga …"

Word had spread to different villages that Shikari da had started his election campaign, and he was received warmly as he was a local. At Maipith, there was an old man who had come to the river's edge accompanied by his two grandsons.

"Lobo bhai, my two grandsons have gone mad. They want to go to the Tata Football Academy. Where will I get the money for that?"

Shikari da pounced at the opportunity. "Dada, we cannot send our boys to the big coaching centres, yet; however, we can have our own. Lobo bhai has his football team ...."

"Dada, you get me half-a-dozen kids interested and I shall come here personally and start a football-coaching centre. I would love to do that." Brother Lobo picked up the cue.

They moved on the Baikunthapur and heard the pleas of a lonesome woman.

"We have no electricity, and all our chickens get stolen after dark. The thieves are amongst us, but we don't know what to do. It's also too dangerous to walk out after dark to keep a check always."

Jasho came and held the hand of the woman and went into her house. There other women collected and voiced all their problems. Alcoholism was an acute problem and people regularly beat up their wives. Jasho and ABC boudi organised a meeting with the elders of the society, on the ground. Three women who had been beaten by their husbands were lined up. ABC boudi then stood up and spoke. Many knew her as the wife of the zamindar at Raidighi.

"I speak to all the men here. Why do you beat your women? Is it because you feel it is your right, or is it because you are stronger?"

The heads of the men in the crowd dropped in shame that day.

"Now I speak to the women. It is within your right to stop all work in the house if you are beaten. Do as I say: Don't cook; send your children away to other houses to eat. I am sure you wouldn't mind staying hungry for a day along with your husbands. But that is how you have to assert yourself against such a shameful act. Not with sticks and stones but by your actions."

The men beating their wives were identified and made to take an oath in public that they would not beat their wives anymore. Then everyone got on their boat again and moved towards Mathurapur.

For the friends this tour of the villages was an education in itself. They saw the emaciated faces of the villagers, devoid of emotions, who would gather in numbers, when the boat docked on the banks. Don would start one of his Baul songs that pulled in the crowd.

"Dada, you must taste our local tea without milk—with lime instead of milk." Don requested.

The friends had the lime-tea on the riverbank, and would not forget it ever. The way the villagers had reached out was deeply touching.

Their trip lasted for three days. They entered the homes of the locals, addressed small assorted groups below trees and on football grounds, and drank tea at dingy tea stalls beside cycle stands, and spoke in the language of the villagers. Shikari da was one of them and many villagers knew him. Everybody was joyful that he was contesting the elections.

During the trip, the friends were regaled by several funny anecdotes. In one of the villages they were told how a tiger had left the villagers in total panic. For many days nobody went out after darkness out of fear. Every morning they took stock of missing things. Hens and honey, freshly cut paddy stacked in barns, and even firewood and wax started disappearing. The Panchayat collected at the football field and it was decided that a watchtower would be built.

Finally, one night the tiger got caught. It was entering a tinned coop that housed a dozen chickens. The owner pounced on it the moment he found the tiger had a walking stick. What came out of a black-and-yellow-striped shawl was a lame man. A crowd collected instantly, and the man was given a sound thrashing. Life returned to normalcy, at last.

Prof. Bhaduri was a great help on the trip. The elders of the region had heard of him, and some knew him personally. During these three days on the trip, the Brother and ABC boudi had become quite friendly. The Brother had played his cards really well, not rushing into anything that would make her uncomfortable.

The Brother was also deeply involved in the election campaign and remained engrossed with his work all morning, but in the night when he retired, his thoughts always returned to ABC boudi.

That last night, when they were staying at a villager's house, the Brother was restless and unable to sleep, so he got up to take a stroll outside. Surprisingly from where he stood outside the mud house, he had a clear glimpse of ABC boudi in the room, lying beside Jasho, deep in sleep; her long lustrous hair loosely gathered in a bun. A flash of the bare skin below her nape brought back the pangs in him, and he hurried away.

Early next morning, the campaign had to be stopped prematurely as a fisherman got the tragic news of Sushil da's death. He had gone to deposit his load at the Raidighi fish market when he got news from the hospital staff about how Sushil da's condition had deteriorated and he had died in the night. The coughing had subsided mildly, when the medicines started having its effect, but then he had contracted cerebral malaria.

Sushil da's body was brought to Marshall Estate and was kept in the main courtyard, for almost one entire day, till word reached the friends. It took almost four hours for the Brother and the rest of his party workers to wind up everything and get back to the estate. Many villagers had gathered at the estate garden as they knew Sushil da and were paying their last respects to the man. Many, however, kept their distance from the corpse, as they feared that the deadly contagious virus was still potent in it.

For the five friends, who had become particularly close to the man, in the short time they spent together, it was surreal to behold him only as a body that would turn to ashes soon. The truth had not sunk in, yet. They remembered the food he cooked for them, all his childish stories, the love and warmth they all shared with him. How soon a man, who once had a name, a life and a presence all around, had turned to an inert corpse and was referred to as "the body"—it was sad to imagine.

Bhor was nestled in the Brother's arms sobbing, inconsolably.

"Your father will always be with you. If you look up, you will see him." The Brother pointed towards the sky and Bhor looked up and saw many stars glittering in the dark night.

"There, he is in that corner—the brightest. Remember, he is always there, watching over you."

Bhor cuddled up close to the Brother, and he started humming, *Jokhon porbe na mor payer chinha ei bate,* softly under his breath ...

> Tarar paane cheye cheye nai ba amaae daakle ...
> (Looking at the stars you might not call my name)

The words attained a different meaning. In the dark night the Brother and Bhor sat together singing along, looking up at the sky, with tears flowing down their cheeks.

32
Marshall School

Keya called her mother when she found the signal restored on her mobile and broke the news of Sushil da's death. Instant shock, remorse, and a hundred questions ensued. The moment she heard about tuberculosis, Mrs. Mukherjee feared the friends may have been infected already.

"Come back at once!" She bawled over the phone, and only after she had spoken individually to each one checking that nobody showed any symptoms whatsoever—no one even had a mild cough, or the remotest indication of a fever—did she relent.

Then she was given the important news—the transformation that the Marshall Estate was to undergo—it was to become the *first* English-medium school, in the heart of the jungle.

The building was big enough, and teachers were ready—Albert Lobo, ABC boudi, Prof. Bhaduri, Bhombol, and the five friends, to begin with. The curriculum was to include martial-arts classes and special coaching for the elderly. The finance and the paperwork would be looked into under the supervision and advice of Brother Lobo.

It was a great idea, and Keya's mother could not refuse. In fact when she consented to the idea, standing on her terrace, in Mumbai, her eyes were moist. Her students were indeed doing something wonderful.

When the first batch of students came in through the gates of Marshall School that morning about a hundred-odd people had gathered on the mud road outside. The gates were thrown open to the celebratory sound of conch shells and twenty-odd kids dashed into the school, screaming. They were neither carrying books, nor school bags; they ran bare foot, carrying heaps of aspirations—here they had been given an opportunity to learn English!

An hour later sounds of A, B, C ... rang out, echoing in stentorian chorus and Marshall School resonated a mood of festivity. Behind the building where Bhombol had set up his martial-arts camp, he and Brother Lobo conducted the warm up exercises with twenty more kids in their mid-teens.

On the courtyard, Bhor sat counting her marbles. She had made many new friends, some of whose parents had enrolled for the adult education program in the evening. Her tears had not dried, and she would run to the Brother for a hug ever so often. But her young mind had so much more to process. The hullaballoo all over the estate left her distracted, and she was not so lonely anymore.

Bhor had taken a special liking for ABC boudi. The English alphabet greatly interested her and she memorised the first six letters from A to F and rattled them off at a furious speed. After the letter F, however, she would falter, pause, and look heavenwards, seeking divine help. When she found no stars in the daytime, she would run to ABC boudi and hide behind her sari.

ABC boudi, too, found this talkative little girl too lovely to resist, and she personally taught her the alphabets making it mandatory for her to write them down during her recitations. And Brother Lobo would keep looking at them. He would hide behind trees and notice how comfortable and happy the two were in each other's company. He would smile and take deep breaths and walk away to speak to the villagers. That evening when boudi had finished with her last batch of students and was walking back indoors, Bhor ran up to her almost colliding with her on the courtyard.

"Aare ki korchish? What's the matter? Why are you so excited?" Bhor called her mashi and she derived a lot of pleasure from that.

"Mashi, ... look what I have made."

She pulled out a crumpled piece of paper from the folds of her frock and spread it out. It was a drawing of a boat with a man wearing a cassock, rowing it. At the stern, there were two other passengers. One was a little girl in a dance pose, and the other woman was wearing a sari, with her hair loose by her sides. She had also named the vehicle. In deep crimson crayons were the letters "BOAT" written in capital letters by the sides. An arrow pointing to the lady in a sari read, "ABC".

ABC boudi knew at once what the little girl was trying to say through her drawing. She noticed the great sense of security, love and thrill Bhor exuded in her company.

Bhor waited for a few seconds and then pulled back the paper and ran with it to the Brother. The Brother was sitting on the ground making plans, for the next day, when Bhor came and thrust the sheet to him.

The Brother's eyes lit up when he saw the paper. "Wow ... lovely ... but we should do this for real. Let's go and do this on the river."

The Brother was also speaking his mind. He was also looking for another opportunity to be with his beloved and do what he loved most—row his boat. Bhor, however, pulled the paper away and ran inside the house to show it to the friends.

Jasho had been noticing how the Brother had grown unmindful lately, looking dreamy and rudderless, to say the least. The unshakable figurehead who worked tirelessly for the benefit of the villagers was showing a more vulnerable side. And then she noticed how disoriented and edgy he had become at ABC boudi's house. He had kept staring at boudi's face and had got up and fiddled, needlessly, with the lantern, at the window. Jasho intuited the rest. The Brother's metabolism was undergoing a change.

Jasho walked up and sat on the grass beside the Brother.

"Lobo bhai, you are fighting something, within yourself … aren't you?" Jasho asked hesitantly and there was a mischievous smile at the corner of her lips that she found hard to shield.

What was she hinting at? The Brother looked into Jasho's eyes and found her smiling. The Brother had read somewhere that a woman was a natural mind reader. Did ABC boudi know about his feeling too? And then he recalled that he had spoken his mind to the friends. They might have told Jasho. But suddenly, he was a little shaken at the enormity of his feelings. Its consequences stared him in the face, for the first time.

He, a Christian Brother, had developed personal feelings, for a lady who was a divorcee and had once been a Muslim, widowed only very recently. Was not there too much of a social stigma and a complicated protocol to overcome? His mind was also, fleetingly, engulfed in shame. He had to speak to someone mature, and so he decided to speak to Jasho to get some clarity.

"I cannot help myself, Jasho. All my interests—the church, the river, the villagers—all converge in her. Try as much as I would to fight my feelings, they haunt me, and I am somewhere loving even the pain of this struggle within me. Am I doing something wrong? I have confessed, and if the Lord wants to punish me, so be it. I don't know what to do."

"Don't worry, Brother. You are perfectly all right. I shall speak to her. But it has to be done discreetly and with care. This cannot be rushed. Have faith and carry on with your normal activities, and leave the rest to me. These things happen to human beings, so don't worry." Jasho said gently.

With these words Jasho walked towards the estate building, and joined Bhor and ABC boudi in the courtyard. Bhor was holding her drawing, and she would not allow anybody to go inside unless she explained to everyone what it meant.

A photographer and a reporter from Kolkata had come to interview Prof. Bhaduri. The interviewer, a girl in her mid-twenties held a Dictaphone close to Prof. Bhaduri's face to record the conversation.

"How does it feel to be back were you belong?"

"I had never left this place. I may not have been here physically, but my mind was rooted in these mangroves, which are so dear to me. These rivers and streams reside in my blood. They are my life." Prof. Bhaduri was speaking from his heart.

The news of his arrival and the recent incidents involving him had spread to Kolkata. The journalists were looking for some sensational news. Prof. Bhaduri spoke like a classical singer—first analyzing the notes in a slow and deliberate "alap", picking up speed gradually into a "bilambit", and finally gushing out in a "jhala". How long had he waited for this day.

"I have waited for this day with bated breath. I knew that truth couldn't be kept subdued eternally. And now my students have helped unearth the facts and bury the story. I was never attacked by a tiger. There was no man-eating tiger here during my posting. But there were sharks and serpents of other kinds."

He bared the details of how the political goons ruled the islands during his posting—information buried in his bosom for many long years. When he finished he was almost out of breath. Then he noticed that the photographer was carrying a picture in her hand. It was the photograph of the man resting his left leg on the carcass of the slain tiger that had supposedly mauled the professor. He paused looking at the snap.

"I don't even know whether this man had ever held a gun. Look at his face—he would have urinated in his pants if he ever saw a tiger. What a shame!" He felt like tearing the snap, but paused a bit and signalled to the photographer.

"You there ... you want a sensational snap, right? Here, shoot this ... you will have one for your cover page."

The photographer got ready with his lens and focused on the professor. Prof. Bhaduri held the snap between his fingers and seconds later it was torn. The photographer clicked a number of times as the professor tore the picture to shreds.

The interview was over. The newspapers, next morning, would carry an emotional story of a government servant who was falsely framed and forced into retirement about ten years ago. A photograph of the man tearing a snap to pieces would accompany the article on the front page.

It was six in the evening. Darkness was beginning to cloak the surroundings fast. The daily classes were over and the students were running back home, happy and fulfilled with the day's activities. The woman entrusted with the duty of cooking, served cups of steaming hot tea along with a mixture of moori or puffed rice and green chilies—of which everyone took generous helpings and happily tossed down their throats.

When it was time to go to bed, everyone trooped into their respective rooms to retire. The Brother had his own place on the first floor where all the men slept together, and the ladies had two rooms on the ground floor to share. Bhor was the only one who could sleep anywhere she liked and usually went hopping from one room to another, finally settling down with Keya and Hazel, or Jasho and ABC boudi.

Bhor spent about an hour with the women listening to stories and then suddenly got up.

"I must go to the other room. I want to hear their stories now."

"It is so late. They are all asleep by now. Carry the sheets and pillow with you, if you must go," Jasho reasoned with Bhor.

Bhor trudged out of the room covered under the sheet, dragging the pillow, looking like a ghoul.

The boys had indeed fallen asleep, but the Brother was praying. The wait was getting unbearable for him. He had resolved to take his destiny in his own hands. His eyes still closed in a prayer, he sensed some ruffling beside him. Bhor had slithered into the space between him and Prof. Bhaduri, making herself quite comfortable with the sheet and the pillow. She waited for the Brother to open his eyes. The moment he did, her questions started.

"Lobo, who will win the elections?" She whispered.

She called her "Lobo", and the Brother found that quite endearing. Even the young girl had somehow gathered that winning, or losing these elections was important.

"I don't know. Now go to sleep. We have to get up early again, tomorrow."

"You go to sleep, first."

The Brother curled up beside her and patted the girl on her head, trying, to put her to sleep. Soon, he was lost in a dream. He found himself in the mountains of Afghanistan, its snow-capped valleys reverberating with gunfire. Then abruptly the countenance of ABC boudi reappeared and brought back a smile on his face. It was like balm. But that also woke him up.

Imran was snoring and the others were all fast asleep. The Brother had an urge to take some action right then. He nudged Bhor.

"What's the matter Lobo?" Bhor asked sleepily.

"Listen, can you call mashi?" The Brother tried to remain calm and make it sound like an ordinary task.

"Why now? She must be sleeping." Bhor obviously did not understand why mashi had to be woken up in the night. She closed her eyes as though she had gone back to sleep, but then she opened them again and spoke as if she had forgotten to say something important.

"The corridor is too dark. I cannot walk alone."

The Brother almost leapt out of his bed and landed noiselessly on his toes on the ground. He picked up Bhor, nudged her out of the room, and followed her. They tiptoed down the wooden staircase that creaked alarmingly, and Bhor jumped the last two steps to reach the ground floor. Brother Lobo did the same. From here they could look into the room where the girls were sleeping. Fortunately, ABC boudi was sleeping closest to the window.

"Give this to her, but don't make any noise, or wake up anybody." The Brother hurriedly gave her a sheet of paper.

Bhor silently pushed open the door and crept in, and Brother Lobo crept back into a dark corner of the corridor. He could peer out from there and see what was going on in the room.

Bhor walked into the room and knelt beside ABC boudi, sleeping on the bed. Warm breath fell on her face and she startled, but Bhor instinctively placed her palm on her lips and stopped her from crying out.

Bhor gave her the page that the Brother had given her and pointed to the corridor outside. Then she ran back out of the room and was picked up by the Brother in the darkness and escorted back to the room.

"You sleep. I will finish some urgent work and come back." The Brother put Bhor down and left immediately.

Meanwhile, ABC boudi opened the folded page and turned it back and forth a couple of times. There was nothing written on it. It was a blank page. She looked outside the window questioningly. Then she spotted Brother Lobo walk out of the estate gate in a cassock. He was headed towards the edge of the river where he finally sat down. The white cassock glistened brightly in the darkness as the moonlight reflected on it.

ABC boudi smiled to herself. She fished out a small mirror from underneath her pillow and looked into it. She wiped a dark spot below her left eye, settled her hair above her forehead and got off the bed. She looked at the other women fast asleep in the room and quietly moved to the door.

The Brother sat silently, breathing in and out, without bothering about the pests and insects around. He playfully threw small pebbles into the river. Its soft plopping sound cut through the silence and reached ABC boudi, who stood hidden behind a thicket.

Soon she heard him humming: *Bager daake ontor kanpe / Na dori aaj baghe re* ... It was the song that they had sung on the boat, while they had gone campaigning. Even as he sang the Brother turned a few times looking at the bungalow. Was he looking for her?

He had not noticed ABC boudi approaching him stealthily. But suddenly, he felt a movement around him and got a start.

"You sing quite well. I heard you on the boat, but this is even better," she said. She picked up a small pebble from the ground and threw it into the river, softly joined in the singing as sat down beside the Brother.

Back in the house Bhor had become restless waiting for the Brother, so she woke up everyone else. Jasho and the girls emerged one after another, and a quick search revealed that both the Brother and ABC boudi were, in fact, missing. They huddled together in the balcony wondering what to do when they heard the faint sound of a duet coming from the riverside. They spotted the lovers, singing, lost in thought, by the river.

"Oh my god! This is so romantic. How did the two plan this?" Keya felt an urge to ask. The friends, however, decided to leave the two alone and go back to sleep. But they could not convince Bhor to return with them. She ran towards the river.

Bathed in moonlight, the two lonely souls continued singing without a care in the world. Bhor joined them and sat cuddled between the two and sang along.

"What is this?" ABC boudi pulled out a sheet of paper from the folds of her sari and showed it to the Brother.

It was the blank sheet of paper that the Brother had given her. The Brother was at his wits' end as he struggled to answer, but she did not wait. She quickly made a couple of folds with the paper, turning it back and forth, and soon the paper took the shape of a small boat. She handed the boat to Bhor.

"Go and put this on the water. It will float away."

The Brother's heart was pounding. Had he spoiled everything in his hurry? He thought. Bhor carried the small boat on her palm and lowered her body at the edge of the water, and released the boat into the river, which floated away.

All three sat quietly and watched the boat float away. Surprisingly, it did not capsize. Within minutes it got lost deeper into the tentacles of the mangroves and its half-submerged roots and melted into the river.

Brother Lobo tried to trace the route the boat had taken down the water. He craned his neck, looking into the mangroves as the boat disappeared into the floating tendrils.

"I am hoping the boat will find its own destiny." ABC boudi's words sounded deep and prophetic.

There was silence again and the Brother struggled to get a few words out.

"I have something for you, too." Bhor sensed the Brother's discomfort and wanted to break the silence.

It was another piece of paper—a little soiled. The Brother felt the edges of the paper and opened it. It was the previous drawing of the boat. He flattened the crumpled piece of paper on the ground and noticed an addition to the drawing. The letters O, U, R, had been added in block letters, in the same font, to the left of the word "BOAT". It was a different hand, but an effort had been made to make it look the same.

"What does this mean, Lobo?"

Bhor was curious, as "OUR" was a new word in her dictionary.

The Brother gleefully grabbed Bhor sitting beside him, wanting to conceal him inside his heart if he could.

"Lobo that is hurting," she cried feebly. Brother Lobo released his embrace and looked back at ABC boudi who was smiling shyly and avoiding direct eye-contact with him.

Brother Lobo's eyes pricked with involuntary tears.

33
Love and Results

With first light when the cocks started crowing, Ramu kaka was the only one who had completed his morning ablutions. No one had noticed a boat float out into the river, at the break of dawn.

The Brother was at the stern rowing the boat, and ABC boudi sat at the bow tying her hair. Bhor was dancing in the middle of the boat. It looked exactly like the drawing. Nobody spoke. There was no need for words. The oars splashed at the sides, creating ripples in the water, and then ABC boudi started humming the tune of the prayer *hum ko manki shakti dena* … that the Brother had taught them to sing. They looked beautiful as a family as the Brother rowed away deeper into the river.

Suddenly, Bhor collapsed in the middle of the boat, holding her head. The Brother stopped rowing and rushed to catch her and held her to his chest. Her body was burning.

"She has fever. I think we should head back." The Brother reversed the boat and headed back for the banks.

The friends had all got up by now, and they could see the boat heading back towards the bank, cutting through the mist over the water. The Brother stopped rowing a couple of meters from the bank, and the boat drifted in with the current. He lifted

Bhor in his arms and waded through the ankle-deep water and hurried towards the estate.

On reaching the bungalow, Bhor was put down on the bed. ABC boudi wet a cloth and applied it on her forehead. She had been told about her ailment and had wondered why and how the almighty in heaven had such unfair rules and destinies for those on earth. She had asked the question to herself, time and again—why her, such a pure soul?

Bhombol and Ramu left for the hospital. Ramu knew the locals so he would be of great help. The others stayed back as there was such a lot of work to be done at the base camp. The elections were scheduled in a few days, and there was also a rally and a program organised at Kultali.

That evening about a hundred people collected for the election rally, but with Bhor's sudden relapse of illness, the wind had gone out of their sails. They were merely going through their motions and nobody seemed genuinely interested anymore.

Jassi tried fiddling with the khol (a local percussion instrument made of leather), but the rhythm sounded boring. Even their candidate Shikari da looked lost in thought as he sat below the stage, looking into the mangroves with the wind blowing through them.

The Brother, too, was forlorn. The happiest night in his life had turned sour. Everyone in the group already knew about Bhor's illness, but the tumultuous events of the last few days had led their minds away from it. With the sudden relapse, the reality of the situation dawned again and weighed them down.

Bhombol and Ramu reached the hospital and found that the hospital walls had been repainted. The agitation of the public had its effect. The state government had taken special notice of the crib deaths, and many things had been overhauled at the hospital. A new HIV-treatment centre had also been initiated, but very few patients and relatives had lined up for its services as there was a stigma attached to the dreaded disease, which kept even the infected from owning up.

Ramu kaka was carrying a copy of Bhor's blood report, which he showed at the clinic. What they said was reassuring. Bhor needed first-line therapy, and owing to her age and timely detection could live comfortably with proper medical treatment, for years. That was a relief. For the therapy to begin, she would need to be examined and undergo a few clinical tests. She would probably need to start antiretroviral drug treatment, but nothing immediately.

Two medical technicians from the hospital accompanied Bhombol and Ramu, on their trip back to Kultali. They were carrying a medical kit for Bhor's initial treatment. When they were leaving the hospital they observed a newfound zest among the workers. They had been granted incentives for their extra effort and everyone was going about their chores very cheerfully.

Bhombol and Ramu left with a lot of hope. Before leaving Bhombol called Keya's mother. He was told their graduation results were due in a week, which meant their holidays would be soon over. They had overstayed their ten days holiday by a few days, anyway.

Back at Marshall School, wedding bells were tolling. The friends had arranged for the Brother and ABC boudi to get married as a perfect parting gift for them. But it was easier said than done. ABC boudi had no doubt accepted the Brother's proposal, but there were too many loose ends still to be tied: What about her in-laws? Was it not important to inform them? What about her own estate? There were many critical questions to be settled, yet.

Jasho saw ABC boudi pacing up and down the corridor and decided to join her.

"I know that your mind is like a sixteen-year old now. So where do you plan to go for your honeymoon?" Jasho gave her a broad grin and asked.

Her smile was contagious and ABC boudi smiled back. "Jasho there are a hundred more important things on my mind now ... much more important than the honeymoon. I mean who will plan everything. What is the need for a wedding, so quickly?"

"What do you mean, where is the need? The villagers love you both and want you to be together. We must celebrate this grand occasion."

ABC boudi was blushing. Hazel and few other women came running in, and holding her by the hand led her to the centre of the garden where a small awning had been constructed with banana plants. Under it, ABC boudi was smeared from head to toe with turmeric paste and bathed with turmeric water and beautified.

The friends had lined up with their musical instruments, meanwhile, and played lilting melodies, popular in Indian weddings, complementing the celebratory mood with appropriate background music. Jassi had gone wild with joy. He played on and on, drumming on his congo long after ABC boudi had been taken to the main courtyard for the ceremonial wedding. The Brother was at the mercy of Shikari da and other men, inside the estate. He too had haldi all over his face and his shoulders, and now it was time for the formal wedding to commence.

The choice of the wedding ceremony was not left to the bride and the groom anymore. A vote had been taken and the consensus was that the marriage rites would be observed as per Hindu faith. A Hindu purohit had been called from the village to conduct a simple rite. A Christian priest had been invited, as well, who stood behind Brother Lobo rather grimly, in his cassock, lending some seriousness to the proceedings.

The bride and the groom were made to go around the fire with the purohit chanting in the background. The friends and assembled villagers clapped merrily when the ceremonies got over. Long wavering high-pitched sounds, resembling a howl, emanated from the congregated women. They took the friends by surprise, at first.

"Ululululululu!" The ululation continued for a while. Hazel and Keya tried to move their tongues inside their mouths, but could not manage it that easily. They finally gave up and enjoyed the proceedings. Jassi continued to play his congo, which had been hanging from his neck, adding effect to the grand finale. When Jassi ended his percussion solo, the priest solemnly pronounced the couple married with the usual "now the groom may kiss the bride," line.

There was a roar of laughter from all who understood what it meant. And when Shikari da translated the sentence for those who did not understand into Bengali, it drew even more laughter. ABC boudi nearly died with embarrassment.

The marriage done with, it was now time for the gala feast. Imran and Bhor had painted out invitation cards for the villagers. The card said it all in Bengali.

Lobo bhai gets married to ABC boudi.
All are invited for the ceremony and a contributory feast.
You are requested to get your favourite dish—to be shared with others,
at Marshall Estate gardens, on 6th evening.

It was a sight to watch. Villagers from far and near—men, women and children, young and old—all trooped in and congregated at the estate garden for the feast of their life. Each family carried their best dishes and some banana leaves to eat them on.

The guests came dressed in their local costumes, but they had tried to make the moment special with whatever little makeup they could afford. Kohl had been used to paint the eyes black and alta to smear the feet red. Married women chewed paan to render a red colour to their lips. Even the men had tried to look as fair as possible, applying powder on their faces, for the special event.

There were prawns and crabs, and a dozen variety of fishes, and assorted vegetables. Every family carried enough rice for themselves. Shikari da had made special arrangements to serve country liquor, especially fermented for the occasion, which was preserved in a huge vessel behind the bungalow.

A formal reception was also meticulously planned. Two garden chairs decorated with the local flowers had been placed in the garden. The bride and the groom sat on them and gleefully accepted all the best wishes that the villagers gave them. When it was Shikari da's turn to bless the married couple, he walked up and fell at the Brother's feet and broke down in tears.

"Dada babu, ... God from the heavens above has weaved this magical story for you two, and for us."

"Don't embarras me, Shikari da. I have found a new life among you all." Brother Lobo could not control himself either and had tears flowing down his cheeks. He grabbed Shikari da and hugged him tightly. Meanwhile, ABC boudi was attending to the pleas of the other women and the band had resumed, providing entertainment for the evening.

Never before in this region had a wedding been enjoyed with so much fervour. The Brother suddenly noticed, while the garden was buzzing with women and children, the men were largely missing.

"They are all behind the house." Shikari da clarified. The bar had been set up behind the house and the men were busy wetting their throats before dinner. When everyone had almost finished eating, the men at the bar had to be literally dragged to dinner. Few of them were already tottering on their feet.

The Brother realised there would be several guests who would not make it beyond the estate gate that night and would prefer to stay back and relax. The newly married couple, as is the custom, were not allowed to sleep either and were kept awake for the bashor—the celebration on the night of the wedding. So the revelry continued through the night.

With the first morning light cutting through the trees around five in the morning, when guests were still singing, the boatsman at the jetty came with an important news—there had been a fresh tiger kill on an island.

34 The Honeymoon

The bereaved family and their relatives were sitting on the mud floor when Brother Lobo walked in with the five friends, Jasho, Don and ABC boudi. They found the woman whose young son had been killed by the tiger in a semi-conscious state, inside the room. Other women were sitting beside her, fanning her. ABC boudi promptly went in to comfort the women. The menfolk had all collected with drums and mashals, ready to cut down the mangroves.

"Lobo bhai, … I had told my son to not go out after dark, but he did not listen. How can we keep our children indoors? That is not possible. We have to kill the tigers, or else they will kill us all." The boy's father kept mourning.

The Brother knew that this was an uneducated man who had lost his son to a tiger. It would be impossible to make him see sense, so he took a different route.

"Okay, we shall kill all the tigers, but first we need to trap them. We have called the forest rangers, and tonight you all shall be informed on the future course of action."

When the crowd dispersed, the friends sat down with the Brother wondering how to control the marauding crowd that was getting violent by the minute. Then, the Brother came up with an idea

"Why don't we put up some skits for them? That usually works marvellously with the simple village folks."

He took out a sheet of paper from his pocket and a pencil and started taking notes.

"Jasho, what according to you is the single largest reason for these tigers straying?" He asked.

Jasho was absolutely certain of the answer and did not mince her words.

"If I take away your home, won't you be angry? Will you not go crazy and roam the streets? I mean we have no business to come into the jungle. The tigers live here. We are encroaching, if we enter the jungle."

The Brother and the friends devised a small skit to address the villagers regarding the problem with the tigers—why they strayed and what had to be done. The friends contacted the local drama club and approached them for props. A few local actors agreed to join in too. Imran painted black and golden stripes on a bedsheet, offered by them, and made a hole in the middle of it. He stuck his head through the hole and was ready in his tiger's costume.

Don started strumming on his ektara, singing out a lilting melody attracting a crowd around him. When there were enough people, the Brother addressed them.

"Without the tiger there will be no forest. And without the forest you shall all perish. Tonight, you shall all know why. Come and watch our pala (play) tonight and enjoy."

Soon, a bhotbhoti docked at the jetty carrying Sumon, his men, and Prof. Bhaduri.

"Sumon bhai, this has to be done in absolute silence. We are dealing with an animal with an acute hearing sense. Please leave your megaphone on the boat as there is no use for it here." Prof. Bhaduri reminded as he limped down.

Some labourers came down the bhotbhoti, carrying iron bars, pieces of wood and branches of trees and a goat, on their shoulders. The uncle of the deceased boy took all of them to the spot where his nephew had been attacked. It was a twenty square meter area, totally hemmed in by houses from all sides. The proximity of human existence to the place of the kill was indeed frightening.

It was decided that the trap would be laid at the centre of the clearing, and the labourers went about building it in absolute silence. Prof. Bhaduri informed them that though Royal Bengal tigers were known to frequent the spot of the attacks they were extremely clever.

The friends watched in amazement how the sidebars were buried about two feet into the ground first. Once secured firmly, the cage was built on this foundation. Other iron rods were quickly joined together, and soon it took shape of a cage. It was about six feet by ten feet, and it was covered with vegetation once they had completed fixing the iron bars. The cage was almost invisible after that, and the trap seemed to be a part of the environment. The goat was placed inside the cage, its neck locked to the iron bar at the end of the cage, for it to collapse the moment the tiger went in to retrieve the goat.

By six in the evening, the friends had been able to rehearse once. Since there was no electricity small fires had been lit for the show, fuelled continuously by kerosene to keep them alive. A small arrangement had been made at the side of the stage for the musicians to perform live. It was like the quintessential theatre of the olden days where the musicians performed live alongside the actors. Everyone would take turns to either sing or act here.

Don started a song with his ektara. A crowd of about a hundred-odd people had collected to watch the skit. The story began with a hunter entering the stage with a gun. It was

Hazel dressed as a boy looking for the tiger. Don's singing lent background information and music to the visuals. The next few minutes the hunter scouted the stage, the make-believe forest, for the tiger, but could not find it.

Then the light dimmed on the stage and the hunter decided to rest below a tree. Bhombol, dressed as a tiger, pounced on the resting hunter and killed him. The audience sat speechless as the chords of the harmonium played out a melancholy melody.

In the next scene a group of hunters were shown holding a high-level meeting where it was decided that the forests would be cleared, to flush out of all the tigers. Don sang a few soulful baul songs to reiterate how the forest was the home of the tiger and how human beings were encroaching on it. In the next scene, the hunters were seen approaching the forest with weapons. They were stopped at the fringe of the forest by a beautiful girl (Keya) who offered them wine and entertainment. But the beautiful woman transformed into a tigress during the course of a song-and-dance sequence, and started to plead with folded hands.

"Please spare us from your anger. We are really scared. Please spare me as I am pregnant and have nowhere else to go." The tigress wailed and the crowd sat mesmerised. They had never heard a tiger speak before!

"You have been attacking us and our children when our backs are turned to you and stealing our animals, and now you ask for forgiveness?" Hazel the hunter mimed as Brother Lobo spoke in the background in his booming voice.

"We don't like human flesh. We would rather eat the deer and the goats, but there is no food left for us in the jungles, and we cannot cook rice and vegetables like you. That leaves us with no choice, but to attack your cattle and your dogs. But believe me, we have got fed up with the conflicts and would rather stay inside the jungle, if only you will leave us alone." The tigress pleaded again.

"But why do you have to come out of the jungles, at all?" the hunter asked.

"What can we do? You are taking away our jungle. We are helpless. Please don't come into our jungle, and we shall not come out. Believe me, we don't want to fight. We are scared of your guns. Please spare us, we beg of you."

"Okay, in that case we promise to give back the jungle to you. Do you promise to stay back and never come out?" the hunter asked. "We shall only roar inside the jungle. We promise. You leave us alone and you shall never see us. We promise. God promise." There was a roar of laughter from the crowd when they heard the tiger swear in god's name.

The skit enacted the entire man vis-a-vis animal conflict in an entertaining way, and the crowd rose to its feet happily clapping at the superb performance by the youngsters. The villagers had been educated, and they had found the songs and dances very entertaining.

After the skit was over, Hazel spotted Don sitting, all by himself, below a tree. She walked up to him.

"Where did you learn your music?" She asked and sat down beside him on the ground.

"From the people we meet. We are itinerant singers. There is music in everyone if you care to listen." Don explained.

"But where do you stay?" Hazel was curious.

"In your heart." Hazel was taken aback and his words left a deep imprint on her mind.

"We are moner manush, people of the heart. We believe that all the strength you need to conquer the world is within you."

He broke into another mesmerizing melody strumming on his ektara.

"I have been sent here—to clear all mistrust and seek truth." Don suddenly paused his song and spoke.

"Who has sent you?" Hazel was puzzling over his words a trifle nonplussed.

"The boss." Don pointed heavenwards with a mischievous smile on his face. "He is everybody's boss. He has sent you too."

"I would rather listen to your songs than speak to you. What you say, at times, makes no sense."

Hazel suddenly remembered that there were more important things to do. "Let's go. The others must be waiting." She pulled Don and they walked back to the village.

Those who waited till the skit ended were told about Shikari da and his election manifesto. The election banners and other leaflets were distributed. The crowd was thrilled to know that Shikari da, another poor villager like them, was contesting the elections. They all identified with the man.

The villagers started homewards in small groups discussing what they had seen and heard when a ferocious growl emanated from the mangroves. The roaring became a prolonged agitated call from the area where they had planted the trap. Sumon and the other forest officials decided to proceed with caution.

"I request that women and the children to go back home," Sumon announced, beckoning only a few strong men to stay back. They carried battery torches and moved towards the clearing stealthily. The dry leaves made crunching noises below their feet. Prof. Bhaduri, the Brother, and the friends followed them from a safe distance, huddled in a group. Jasho, ABC boudi, and Don returned to take care of the bereaved family.

There was a brief pause in the roaring when all of a sudden a heavy metallic sound startled one and all. Everyone stood silent for a minute. The mangroves had thickened and they had to separate the twines to get a clear view ahead.

What they saw through the mangroves curdled their blood. The cage had been uprooted from where it had been dug into the ground. It lay upside down, about twenty meters towards the river, with a full-grown tiger trapped inside it. The animal was extremely restless and was hurling itself to the sides of the cage. The goat was lying, half eaten.

The friends did not know how to react. Everyone was left stunned and immobile. They did not know whether to move forward towards the cage, or retreat. They had come to the Sunderbans to see the tiger, but to see it caged was most traumatic.

"Hurry up, we need to put the tiger to sleep fast otherwise it will get badly hurt with this constant hurling against the iron rails." Sumon spoke very excitedly. His colleagues had already started readying their tranquilliser guns.

The friends noticed that, indeed, the animal was bleeding on the face due to the constant bludgeoning against the rusted iron rods of the cage. The two armed guards were now ready with their tranquillisers, and they wrestled their way through the mangroves towards the cage, when one villager ran back towards the village shouting out in absolute frenzy.

"Bagh dhora poreche ... The tiger has been caught!"

The two men with the guns were trained tranquilliser experts. They filled in the liquid, measuring the dosage of the drug, taking extreme precaution as a little less or a little more could have dangerous repercussions. Too little and the tiger could wake up even before it was relocated into the jungle, and too much of the drug was harmful to its central nervous system. The two men moved ahead towards the cage as the animal was still restless inside and continued its blitzkrieg against the cage.

Sumon, Prof. Bhaduri, and Brother Lobo directed the strong beams of their electric torches through the mangroves and hit the cage. The light beam fell on the face of the tiger blinding it momentarily. Immediately, it made a stronger effort to leap out of the cage and struck the iron railings of the roof. Blood trickled out from the wound on its face and it sank to the floor tired, but still roaring. Then the men fired two shots and waited. Prof. Bhaduri looked on with great sadness in his eyes.

"This animal walked the earth over a million years even before man. A symbol of power grace and beauty, this tiger is a mesmerising supreme predator. And look how we have managed to cage its indomitable spirit. Look how we are crushing it and compelling it to be at our mercy."

The first shot hit the tiger in its hind leg. It squealed in pain, but even before it had stopped crying, the second shot hit him on the shoulder. For a few seconds it became fiercer inside the cage trying to run around in circles, confused and agitated, but then the drug started taking effect. Within minutes, it cowered to one corner and stretched out, trying to fight back the anesthetising effects of the drug. Then it collapsed on the floor. The professor continued talking as the friends fell silent viewing this epic drama.

"This is the biggest of the big cats and must be around two hundred and fifty kilograms."

Its tail that was almost three feet long was sticking out of the bars. It twitched a little before it went completely limp. Sumon waited for a few minutes more and then cautiously approached the cage. The friends stood around and saw the majestic animal lying motionless within the cage and wondered how strong it must have been.

The men who had tranquillised it went to work at once. The cage was opened after ascertaining that the tiger was totally unconscious. They carried out few tests on the body of the tiger with their medical kit and even attended to its wound on the face cleaning the injured area, first with mercurochrome and then applying bandage. One of the men was holding a long stethoscope with hearing aid at the end of it and pressed it to the abdomen of the animal. He listened for a few seconds and then looked up and smiled.

"It's pregnant. I can hear the cubs moving inside."

"Tigers often stray when they become pregnant as the males keep chasing them to mate again," remarked Prof. Bhaduri

"Dada, that's good news, but we need to hurry, as the drug will soon be losing its effect," said Sumon.

Meanwhile, a group of villagers came in, carrying axes and other weapons. One of them came charging towards the cage, but Brother Lobo caught him with a scissor kick on his heels, and he fell to the ground. The Brother helped the man get up and massaged his back. Slowly, he seemed to come to his senses.

"Sorry dada, I did not mean to do this. The tiger is not at fault. It is a harmless animal. Come with me and I shall show you why."

Prof. Bhaduri, Brother Lobo, and the forest department workers all sat down with the few estranged villagers and made them see sense. Sumon, however, had another very important responsibility to complete. He had to relocate the tigress into the wild and that had to be done as quickly as possible.

He instructed that the ropes be cut. Rahul took this opportunity to feel its paws and its nails sticking his hand through the bars of the cage. Its paw was bigger than a full-grown human head and one could feel the power it wielded just by touching it.

Eventually, it was time to leave the island. The cage was transferred to the bhotbhoti. It took around twenty men to do that. The entire village wanted to watch, but they were kept away and the youngsters had to hold a rope to keep them at bay as too many people around would have unnerved the animal. Sumon did not want to take any chances. In about fifteen minutes the bhotbhoti set sail down the emerald river. The cage was set at the stern of the boat. The gate of the cage facing the river was left open to help the tigress leap out into the water

The bhotbhoti meandered through the mangroves, swam into the main channel, and picked up speed. The villagers from the banks were waving and smiling. Deep inside they were happy that none of them were injured and the animal was being set free into the wild.

The bhotbhoti was moved down the main river when Sumon looked at the tiger inside the cage. The big cat was waking up slowly and stretching its muscles, wondering where it was, and the forest officers were monitoring this recovery process. The growls started again and Sumon asked the man at the engine room to stop the boat.

"Dada, stop the boat here … turn off the engines and let it flow with the current as the noise of the engine agitates the animal. It is low tide now, the water is subsiding, and we cannot go into the smaller channels as we might get stuck in the silt. This is a good enough place to set the animal free."

He put a finger to his lips to maintain silence. The friends gathered together behind the cage to get a last glimpse of the animal. It paused looking out into the river in front of her, then it glanced behind towards the friends at the back of the cage

Myth has it that the Royal Bengal tiger has hypnotic powers and for Imran it was certainly the most bewildering experience. In that fraction of a minute he seemed to grasp the divine mystery inside the tiger, to penetrate its essence, as it were, with the result that the whole scene had a transcendental effect on him. He could hardly move; such was the overpowering effect the supreme carnivore had on him.

Then came the dramatic moment. It moved ahead towards the mouth of the cage, stood for a second before it took a grandiose leap and dived into the river.

Keya was ready with her camera and she took a series of pictures of the animal being set free and a few of the images she captured was of the animal in the air before it touched the waters. It splashed into the water and swam swiftly towards the mud banks throwing one cursory glance back towards the boat.

"Look, the tigress is looking back at us. It is acknowledging us, like the dolphins," said Imran dreamily.

"We shall never know," said Hazel. "But now it is free to roam the islands again."

The friends sat on the floor of the bhotbhoti experiencing a superb feeling of achievement inside. They had successfully set a Royal Bengal tiger free, and it was on her way back to where it belonged. The feeling was similar to the churning they had felt in their bellies when Don's song at the Raidighi market had led one and all to resonate "Vande Mataram".

35 Goodbye

On their way back to Marshall School, the youngsters fell despondent. Their stay on the islands had been a dream and they had become an intrinsic part of the tides. Now it was time to leave. Word had come from Mumbai that they needed to go back immediately as their college results were to be out in a few days. Hazel had to return to London too. That they would have to eventually return to Mumbai was a forgone conclusion, but it had not bothered them so much until now as they were so deeply enmeshed in the whirlwind of activities that had left them overwhelmed.

All their dormant dreams had taken flight—they had actually initiated a process in microfinancing which was just another textbook lesson till the other day; the beginning of the insurance policy for the honey collectors was a light at the end of the tunnel for so many impoverished villagers; finally, establishing the Marshall School was the brightest feather in their cap.

From Don they had learnt "to dive within, to soar beyond". All these achievements in such short a time had shaken them out of their self-imposed slumber of city life, where the body and the mind merely floated on a log of convenience. Here in the pristine islands of rural India they had experienced the pulse of life like never before. The thought of going back was immensely depressing.

"Why are you going back? Why can't you stay here?" Bhor shuttled around from one to the other asking them the same question.

"Please take care of her, else she will drive them crazy."

Brother Lobo carried her on her shoulders and placed her on ABC boudi's lap.

Prof. Bhaduri, however, had to leave immediately as there was an urgent matter to attend in Mumbai and he took the next steamer out of the island.

"Remember, I am expecting you all tomorrow, and don't start any other expedition. All your tickets are booked." He warned them lovingly!

Prof. Bhaduri's boat left for Raidighi in the evening and for the friends, this was their last night at Marshall School.

The villagers had got news that the guests would be leaving, so they came visiting with little gifts from their side. Lobo bhai's football-team players thought that their coach was also leaving, and so they began to shed tears in anticipation. Women who had come to say goodbye could not hold back theirs either. The maudlin excesses made the youngsters extremely uncomfortable. Then there were all the honey collectors and the fisherwomen for whom the insurance policy had been a boon. They collected on the grounds and decided to spend the night at the estate. They had cornered Brother Lobo in the garden and shed copious tears.

"Lobo bhai ... these youngsters have done magic for us." A villager wept as he spoke.

"Didi, God sent you here. What the politicians could not do in years, you did in weeks. Why don't you stay back here? We can serve you for our entire lives."

Brother Lobo signalled Jasho and she spoke to the woman and pulled Keya away.

"Didi, ... they have their own lives in the city. They will surely come back, but now they need to leave."

In the middle of the wailing and weeping, Don started a song with his khomok, a percusson instrument, which lent the surroundings a divine ambience. The sudden onset of music charged the youngsters as well. They sat down on the grass with their instruments.

Rahul had scribbled a few lines since he had set foot on these islands, and took this opportunity to put them to tune. They lit a bonfire to create a celebratory ambience and drew everyone around it.

Rahul strummed a few chords, Keya joined in with her flute and they started jamming. Soon, they were harmonising beautifully, with Jassi setting the rhythm on his congo.

Rahul sang as if it was his last song. His song summarised their experiences in tide country. It was about the revelation that they had been led to, and about the tiger within them that they were discovering.

A fiery spirit at last unleashed
The tiger within has awakened
To be caged no more, to leap and soar
To dream and dare, and know no fear
Blaze new trails, and despair quell
The tiger within has awakened
A fiery spirit at last unleashed
Within you and me
Come behold!

This trip had been so much more than a holiday for the friends. It had been a churning process which put them on a roller-coaster ride, discovering overwhelming emotions within them. In this pristine island Bhor gave them the gift of innocent joy; Brother

Lobo instilled confidence; Shikari da became a model of triumph of the human spirit; Jasho's fiery spirit and wisdom stood for the achievements of an ordinary village woman; ABC boudi reinforced the power of love; Kinu, Sushil da, Don, and everyone else together contributed to raise the level of consciousness of the youngsters to the level that transformed them beyond their imagination.

The villagers were dancing around the fire to the music. These were not choreographed movements set to tune. They were a random expression of *joie de vivre* by throwing around limbs by satisfied, lean, hungry, impoverished, villagers with wounded lives, who had been granted a fresh lease of hope by unknown youngsters from a distant land. They danced without a care in the world.

Lobo bhai also did a jig around the fire, with Bhor on his shoulders, and everybody hooted and screamed with joy. He soon got tired and went to a corner to grab a drink of water when his wife, ABC boudi, encountered him.

"Lobo, our honeymoon is over, and now it's time to work. We have given these villagers some hope in their lives. The challenges will be steeper, and we have to consolidate our efforts, so that whatever has been started does not go to waste," she spoke in a slow, strong, deliberate manner

"Listen lady, let me enjoy the moment. But yes, what you say is absolutely correct, and I would like to set the ball rolling by doing something, for which I shall need your help."

"Whatever you do in life involves me, you know that. Go ahead, tell me." They were speaking in English for a change, and Bhor, who was sitting around, could not understand anything. She kept looking from one face to the other.

"I would like to adopt this little girl, and I need your permission."

ABC boudi paused and walked a few paces away, deep in thought. Then she turned around and embraced her husband.

They both held on to each other for a few minutes, and Bhor came and wriggled in, between the two.

Far way, around the fire, the friends were still singing the title song of their lives. They looked at the three of them in an embrace and acknowledged that miracles still happened.

That night, the friends slept peacefully without the slightest care in the world. Imran even forgot to snore, which was clearly noticed by one and all.

It was about six in the morning when everybody got up from sleep. Packed and ready, they headed for the jetty humming the tune of the song that they had composed. At the edge of the water there was an army of young and old villagers assembled to see them off. The Gram Sarpanch or Mukhiya was at the head, waiting to thank the friends on behalf of the people, for all their efforts.

It was also the day of the elections. Chants of, "Shikari da jitbe, Shikari da jitbe … Shikari da will win." rang out in chorus. Deep within their hearts, the villagers had already voted. Together, they sang the song that they had composed, and finally the bhotbhoti set off for Raidighi.

Don rowed alongside the bhotbhoti on his small boat.

"When shall we meet again?" Hazel was leaning out of the bhotbhoti, trying to catch Don's attention. She had developed a special affection for the baul singer.

"Think of me, and I shall be there. As for now, listen to this."

Saying this he broke into another special baul song, professing love for the humanity, and sailed away from the bhotbhoti, towards the deeper end of the river, in his own little boat.

At 1:00 pm that afternoon, a plane took off from Kolkata airport and climbed into the clouds towards Mumbai. It was a special plane, with special cargo on board.

Roughly at around 1:15 pm, Don was still rowing on his small boat in the middle of a small creek, deep within the pristine islands of the Sunderbans. He stopped rowing and looked closely at his ektara. He crept below the overhead branches of the mangroves and took his small boat deep into the floating vegetation. Here he unscrewed the gourd resonator of his musical instrument and upturned the bottom dome. The words "Amaar Desh" (My country) was cut apart in two. First, a five-hundred-rupee note fell out. It was the note Hazel had given him in the bus. He had cherished it as a memento. A satellite phone also fell out in his palm. Don went to its phone book memory and dialled for BOSS.

As a young science graduate, in Kolkata, Aditya Mondol had been musically inclined and had engaged with the bauls—the wandering musical minstrels of Bengal. Then, one day he got handpicked by an organisation called "Save My Country", which mobilized young people—burgeoning promising idealistic young souls, from all over the nation, towards establishing a utopian state.

Thousands of kilometres away, in Mumbai, Prof. Bhaduri was conducting a seminar for the Alcoholics Anonymous when his phone rang.

"Excuse me, I need to take this call," he said and went to a corner behind the pillar and spoke in whispers.

"I told you never to call on this number, unless very urgent."

Don answered in impeccable English. "Boss, this is urgent. Mission accomplished. Five tigers have been set free. Jai Hind."

"Jai Hind." Prof. Bhaduri smiled, switched off his phone and went back to address the alcoholics.

Yes, he would be waiting for the tigers. He thrust his hand into his trouser pocket to keep back his mobile and felt the cool touch of metal. He brought out his car keys and looked at his keyring—the miniature ektara.

He had already planned Don's next mission.

Acknowledgements

My colleague, Madhukar Kotian comes to my mind as I sit to write my acknowledgements. It is he who planted the thoughts of writing in my head, for the first time. But it was easier said than done. As I sat mulling over the idea, I realised I neither had the time to write, nor a subject captivating enough to inspire me.

The inspiration came quite suddenly one day, as I sat talking to Shibam Kar Chowdhury, my brother-in-law. Posted in the Sunderbans as a forest ranger, his many stories and experiences from his boat, made me sit up and got me thinking. I felt the urge to write a book on the tiger. But I was not thinking of the tiger in the jungle. The "tiger" within is what I wanted to explore.

The Sunderbans opened a whole new world for me. It is impossible to thank everyone I met while I researched for my book on the islands, for nearly two years. I must start by thanking the mangroves and the river dolphins, and one very special gentleman, Dilip Kumar Halder, from the Digambarpur Angikar, without whom I could not have got started.

I thank my stars thereafter, for getting an opportunity to meet such lofty souls as Sachindranath Kayal, Gopal, Mohan, and the honey collectors—Aslam Javed, Muskfikur, and Ganesh—the real faces behind the characters in this book. Impoverished, but not poor, they radiated an energy that I have attempted to capture here. I thank them for their time and affection, and also the unforgettable rice and fish they cooked and fed me during our numerous boat rides, while scouting for hives and dolphins. I shall remain forever grateful to the family of villagers I lived with during my prolonged stays—homes where cellars did not have rice, and toilets did not have doors; people with hearts larger than their hopes and views ahead of their times. This book gained a lot from my conversation with all of them.

Special thanks to Boudi Shibani Baur on whom Jasho, one of the central characters in this plot, has been crafted. From her mango pickles to her mashed potatoes, their lingering taste added a special flavour to this book. I shall, also never forget the mystifying Madhushudhan—a little mad, a lot drunk, and an avid footballer, he was sheer magic. The characters of Kinu, Brother Lobo, and a few others were inspired by him.

I thank my friend Anuj Alia; my graphic designer Barun Roy; film-maker Marlon Rodrigues; my sand-artist Kaushik Banerjee, and other innumerable friends who gave many valuable ideas at the design stage.

Deep thanks to Tigmanshu Dhulia, Shantanu Moitra, Boria Majumdar, music director Rana Majumdar, actor Irfan Khan, and the rest, for their constant encouragement.

Thanks also to my office colleagues, Shankar Pleni, Mangesh Muchalambe, Rajesh Pakhare, Rajendra Belgaonkar, Hirleyn David, and Dhananjay Kunder, for giving me a patient ear while I talked endlessly about my book.

I thank my literary agent Urmila Dasgupta from Purple Folio who selected my manuscript and made it publication worthy. Thanks to my niece, the academically brilliant and wannabe writer Sohini Bagchi, for proofreading my manuscript.

I am deeply indebted to my publishers Bikash and Tultul Niyogi, and especially my editor Jayalakshmi Sengupta, for reposing their trust in me and pushing me to fine-tune my work.

I owe this book to my wife Japasree Mukherjee, my biggest critic and strongest supporter, who I cannot thank enough. For the two years I roamed the islands, she held fort and patiently nurtured my every attempt to put my thoughts to words.

I deeply thank my father, Santosh Mukheree, the original Tiger, and my mother Dipali Mukherjee who made me what I am today.

Last, but not the least, I thank you my dear readers, for believing in me and reading this book.